G
9/07

ls
son Pub.

9/07

JUST BETWEEN FRIENDS

Books by Sandra Steffen

THE COTTAGE

DAY BY DAY

217 BEULAH STREET

COME SUMMER

JUST BETWEEN FRIENDS

JUST BETWEEN FRIENDS

SANDRA STEFFEN

ZEBRA BOOKS
KENSINGTON PUBLISHING CORP.

ZEBRA BOOKS are published by

Kensington Publishing Corp.
850 Third Avenue
New York, NY 10022

ISBN 0-7394-5072-7

For Janet Sinke, a gifted story-teller, accepting, sensitive, funny, and one of the busiest people I know. And just think, I get to call her "friend."

We cannot direct the wind, but we can adjust the sails.
—Bertha Calloway

CHAPTER 1

Brooke Valentine's eyes opened before her alarm went off, just as they had every morning this past year. She moved to get up. Instead of finding the edge of the bed, she encountered a warm, solid obstacle, namely, her husband, Colin, who was lean and athletic and had the physique of Adonis, but was a barricade just the same.

"Out of bed is that way," he mumbled, ninety-nine percent asleep.

She lay back down groggily, trying to get her bearings. This new bed was going to be the death of her. She never could seem to find her way out of it. The problem wasn't really the lovely antique four-poster with a thick mattress and luxurious Egyptian cotton sheets. She couldn't even blame it on exhaustion, although she had been incredibly tired lately. The problem was that she was sleeping on the wrong side of the bed. An entire year and she still wasn't accustomed to the change.

An entire year.

Their move to one of Philadelphia's most picturesque and historic neighborhoods a year ago had been a symbol of their new beginning. Society Hill was a magnificent area. Sophie loved her school. Colin loved the prestige of living in a historic town house. And Brooke loved her husband and daughter to be happy.

Colin sighed in his sleep, and yearning welled up inside her. If only she could stay right here and forget about the rest of the world and all the outside forces that pulled at them. Sophie could sleep in while she and Colin *didn't* sleep, like they'd done so many years ago. Later, they could make up excuses not to go into the office, and she would fix an enormous breakfast for the three of them and never once worry about the calories. They would all lounge in their bathrobes, and she wouldn't even think about donning her smart, pencil slim gray skirt and jacket and the gray-blue silk blouse, the one that matched her eyes, the one she'd bought specifically for today's meeting.

Today's meeting.

Her eyes were wide open now. Still, it was a shame she couldn't stay in bed, for her husband was an incredibly fit and exciting man. She'd known it the first time she'd laid eyes on him fifteen years ago at college. Brooke's roommates had warned that she would never be able to keep him. She'd kept him. But there had been a price.

That was behind her, and behind them.

The clock-radio came on. Listening to the quiet music, she wondered what time Colin had finally gotten in. Poor man worked as hard as she did. Leaving him to get another half hour of much-needed sleep, she swung her legs—left this time—over her *new* side of the bed. Rising with as little jostling as possible, she pressed the radio's OFF button, her hand going to the book on her nightstand. *One Hundred and Ten Ways to Sex Up Your Marriage.* Tonight, she would suggest they try number seventeen again.

She had it all planned. The bottle of chardonnay was already chilling. And since Sophie was spending the night at a friend's, Brooke and Colin would have the house and the evening to themselves. They had much to celebrate, for they'd spent their first year in their new home, their marriage was solid once again, Sophie was flourishing, and Brooke's career in advertising was on the rise. Malcolm Klein was making an important announcement at today's board meeting. Brooke's colleagues agreed that all her hard work was sure to be rewarded. She smiled tiredly in anticipation, for she *had* worked hard, giving one hundred percent to every aspect of her life.

A glance at her watch told her she'd started her day a few seconds behind schedule. She made up for it by bypassing the window where she usually took a minute to greet the dawn. By habit, she drew her nightgown over her head upon entering the large master bathroom. Naked, she stepped on the scales. Next stop, the shower. Thirty minutes later she was clothed, made-up, scented, and ready for the daily juggling act of marriage, motherhood and career.

The lights were on in the kitchen when she got there. Twelve-year-old Sophie glanced up from the window seat where she was petting the family cat.

"Morning, Shortstuff. You, too, Fluffy."

"I'm the second tallest girl in my class. You have to stop calling me Shortstuff." Her daughter rose on gazelle legs— God, she was beautiful—and Fluffy skulked off, skirting Brooke entirely, gray tail straight in the air.

They'd had the cat a year, and she still hadn't warmed up to Brooke. No matter what Brooke tried, she couldn't seem to win the feline over.

"What would you like for breakfast, Sophe?"

"Blueberry pancakes with real maple syrup and hash-browns and do we have any more glazed doughnuts?"

Brooke opened the airtight container and handed the doughnuts over. "Are you sure you don't have a hollow leg?"

"I have a high metabolism."

Sophia Nicole Valentine had her father's metabolism and her mother's eyes. She'd most likely gotten her self-confidence from Colin, too, but her quirky personality was all her own, and had been apparent when she was still in the highchair.

Wearing an old-fashioned apron, a cherished artifact from her teen years when she'd dreamed of becoming a world-renowned chef, Brooke took down the skillet, turned on the stove, reached into the cabinet for a bowl, and cracked an egg with one hand. There was a rhythm to cooking, a timing of movements and a blend of scents and sounds.

Sophie was an early riser, too. She sat in the pale yellow sunshine which slanted through the windows, prattling on about any number of things. Today she complained about her best friend's annoying little brother.

"I used to wish for a baby brother or sister, but now Makayla wishes she was an only child."

"Toby's seven, Sophe. He'll outgrow pretending he's Spider-Man." Brooke flipped the pancakes then stirred the hash-browns, now perfectly golden on one side. "What are you and Makayla going to do today?"

"Get our tongues pierced, pick out a tattoo, hitch a ride out to the race track, talk to our bookie. You know, the usual."

Yes, Sophie had her mother's bone structure and her father's brains, and as they used to say, *the poolboy's sense of humor.* She and Colin didn't refer to the joke anymore. Not because it wasn't funny, per se, but because Brooke had discovered firsthand that there was nothing funny about infidelity.

Sophie sputtered. "You know today's Thursday, and—"

"Every Thursday Mrs. Prescott takes you and Makayla riding."

"—takes Makayla and me riding."

Mother and daughter spoke at the same time. They smiled the same way.

Sophie continued to talk while her breakfast was being prepared. And laugh. And gesture and giggle. And Brooke thought, was it any wonder this was her favorite time of the day?

Arranging everything on the plate, she stood on the opposite side of the counter, watching her daughter take her first bite. Sophe's eyes rolled back in her head. Born dramatic, everything the girl felt showed on her face. Brooke took a bite of her dry whole wheat toast and wondered what she'd done to deserve this child.

Colin entered the kitchen just as she was cutting a banana in half. "Good morning, ladies."

"Hey, Daddy."

He kissed Sophie's cheek and handed her a napkin, then waited to see that she used it before continuing on his way to the coffeemaker. The cat appeared, winding around his ankles, purring. Brooke stared at the creature, and then turned her attention to Colin. He wore a dark Italian suit and crisp white shirt. His eyes were deep-set, his hair the color of rich coffee. If Adonis had turned gray, Brooke had no doubt he would have done so as Colin was, with a slight brush of white at the temples. His cheekbones were as prominent as his lineage, his jaw angular and symmetrical. Few men on the planet were as handsome.

He laced his coffee with cream, took a satisfying sip, then placed the cup on the counter near her dry toast. "Are you dieting?"

Nothing got past Colin Valentine.

Two stinking pounds, she thought as she sliced her allotted half-banana. "I probably had too much salt yesterday."

Colin moved directly behind her, his hands gliding to her hips covered by the new pencil-slim skirt. "The scales don't lie. But you sure feel good to me."

It was a compliment. She knew it was a compliment, and yet it burned like a slap. Something she couldn't name seared the back of her eyes.

"You smell good, too."

He nuzzled her neck, and she relaxed. "You know I'm ticklish in that spot."

"I know another spot where you're ticklish." His voice was deep and quiet, loud enough for her ears alone, and sent those first, delicious flutters of desire swirling low in her belly.

From across the island, Sophie polished off the last of her

pancakes and went to work on the hash-browns. "I'm trying to eat over here."

Colin winked, Sophie grinned, and in that moment, everything felt right with Brooke's world. She poured batter into the skillet while Colin settled himself at the table and shook out the *Wall Street Journal*. He called himself a glorified number-cruncher, but the truth was, at thirty-nine years of age, he was a brilliant problem solver with a long list of credentials, including an MBA from Columbia. He had a reputation for getting results, and was sought after by major corporations both in the city and across the country.

He'd been extremely affectionate these past few weeks. Probably because he knew that although she'd forgiven him, the indiscretion still weighed on her mind sometimes, and on her heart, especially at this time of year, for it had been early summer when she'd discovered his affair. He'd tried so hard to make it up to her these past two years. It had taken months before she'd been able to make love with him without crying afterwards, and a full year before she'd stopped wondering if he was comparing her to his former lover. Counseling had helped her deal with the hurt. She'd forgiven him. Not that she would ever forget. She'd discovered that forgiveness didn't miraculously wash down from the sky. It was a conscious decision, requiring strength and tenacity on her part, and patience on his.

When it came right down to it, he'd won her over all over again. No other man had ever made her feel the way Colin made her feel. She loved him. Deep inside she'd always known her life would have been simpler if it wasn't true.

Sophie ran upstairs to get her riding clothes. Alone in the kitchen with Colin, Brooke removed her apron and carried the plate to him. He thanked her, squeezing her hand.

"You know those ticklish spots you mentioned?" she said. "I was thinking I'd dab them with the new Château Latour before our celebration tonight."

A look crossed his face so quickly she wondered if she'd imagined it.

"Is something wrong?" she asked.

He turned his attention to his coffee, his hand steady as he stirred cream into his second cup. "McCowan invited me to accompany him and the new vice president to dinner. I'll let him know I can't make it."

Brooke smiled as she stacked the dishes in the sink for Portia, the housekeeper who came for two hours each morning. Leaving Colin to his breakfast and his paper, Brooke brushed her teeth in the half-bathroom. She was checking her appearance one last time when Sophie raced into the kitchen carting a bulky nylon duffel bag that held everything she would need for her overnight stay at her friend's.

"Are you moving out?" Colin asked.

"No silly. I'm going to Makayla's. Bye, Daddy." She kissed his cheek.

Brooke reached for her own leather bag. "I'll see you tonight, Colin. Wish me luck."

He rose to his feet, smoothing a hand along his tie, his blue eyes giving her a thorough once-over. "We make our own luck, Brooke."

Why on earth did the statement leave her feeling empty? She started for the door Sophie had left open.

"Brooke?"

She glanced over her shoulder. He'd picked up the cat and was stroking its sleek fur. She understood the cat's rapture.

"You look beautiful, and if it wouldn't smear your lipstick and make you late, I'd prove it to you. I'll be tied up in meetings all day, but I should be home by seven. We can begin the celebration then. Don't uncork the wine until I get here. I'm going to enjoy watching you apply it to those ticklish spots almost as much as I'll enjoy sampling it."

Brooke's knees went weak. She wouldn't have cared if her lipstick smeared and she wouldn't have minded being a few minutes late. Pride and experience kept her from saying it.

He put down the cat, folded his newspaper and carried his

plate to the sink. She walked out the door, her makeup impeccable, her schedule intact.

Brooke's cellphone began to ring just as she was entering the lobby of the building that housed Wilson Advertising Agency. The drive downtown had been harrowing. The founders who'd dubbed the city Philadelphia, which means the City of Brotherly Love obviously never endured a typical morning commute.

This life in Philadelphia was a far cry from her life in Alcott, New Hampshire, where she'd grown up. She and her sister, Eve, had been born late in life to strait-laced parents. They'd had a quiet childhood, but not an unhappy one. Back then, it had seemed as if the long, lazy summer days would go on forever. She'd had caring parents, a loving younger sister, and two best friends who'd understood her better than anybody else in the world. Until Colin, that is. She couldn't remember the last time she'd talked to Sara or Claudia. The Three Potters, they'd called themselves. Sometimes she got so busy she forgot how much she missed them. It occurred to her that she missed Colin, too, which was strange considering she lived with him, slept with him, shared her life with him. She was in a weird mood today, no doubt about it.

She reached into her bag for the ringing phone as she was rounding the landing at the top of the first flight of stairs. Placing the small device to her ear, she said, "What did you forget, Sophe?"

"Close but no cigar."

"Eve! I was just thinking about you." Brooke paused for a moment at the top of the second flight of stairs, damning those blasted two pounds!

"Really?" Eve asked. "Listen, I know you're busy." Her sister knew her well. "I have good news. I'm getting married."

"You mean Jack McCall finally—"

Eve laughed, and Brooke could picture her in her mind,

five-foot-eleven, and most of that legs, hair down to her waist, eyes the color of pewter.

"Not Jack," Eve said. "His brother, Carter."

Brooke entered the suite of offices on the third floor where she worked. "You mean you? And bad-boy Carter McCall? Are you kidding? Are you crazy?"

"Crazy in love. You know how that is."

In her reflection in the window, Brooke's smile lost its brilliance. Placing her heavy bag on her desk, she lowered into her chair. "When? How? My, you've been busy."

"You don't know the half of it. He asked me two weeks ago, and I hardly know where to begin, Brooke. Tommy's cancer is back, but he's doing better again."

"Oh, Eve, that precious child. Leukemia, isn't it? And you've really been engaged for two weeks?"

"It came about suddenly. I'm so happy I wanted to wrap it around me, around us, just us for a few weeks, savor it, relish it."

Brooke had misgivings about Eve's news. She voiced a few as gently as she knew how. Eve sounded very sure of herself, secure in her decision, and very sincere in her feelings for Carter McCall.

They talked until Mr. Klein opened his office door, his signal that he was ready to begin the meeting. "Eve, I have to go. Congratulations, sweetie. As long as Carter really loves you, and you really love him, I'm happy for you."

"We do, Brooke. Neither of us had any idea love could feel this way."

"All right, then. I'll call you later."

She replaced the phone. Rising, she smoothed her skirt into place, rehearsed her acceptance speech in the back of her mind, and followed her coworkers into the conference room.

"Brooke. No one can believe this."

"Yeah. It's so unfair."

"We all know the economy has been horrible. It's inspired us to work even harder. None of us dreamed it would come to this."

"It's a shock, all right." Brooke didn't look up from the box she was filling with personal items from her desk. If she did, she knew she would lose the battle of restraint and cry. She felt it coming, the welling up, the hot throat, the tight, aching chest. Pain was trying to get in. But she didn't let it. She couldn't. Not yet.

She hadn't gotten a promotion. She'd gotten . . .

She couldn't even form the word in her mind. It hadn't been easy for Malcolm Klein to do. She was certain his remorse had been sincere, for the president of Wilson Advertising possessed an honor she'd always respected.

"Money is tight," Malcolm had said.

Evidently the agency was hurting. Consumers weren't buying, and only a handful of companies could afford to pay top dollar for advertising these days, and those wanted talking ducks or mud wrestling. This morning Malcolm had announced that he'd hoped the agency could ride this out until the days of tasteful advertisements returned. Evidently, that wasn't the case. The bottom line was money. It was nothing personal. It had been a corporate decision.

It felt personal to Brooke. Intellectually, she knew it had to do with seniority. She'd left the Pratt Agency a year ago, shortly before she and Colin had moved, because this commute was much shorter, and she and Colin had agreed that it would be better if she were home more with her family.

She wasn't the only one to get the ax. Doogan, the still-wet-behind-the-ears college graduate in design, and Polly from accounting, were both filling boxes, too. Others wondered if they would be next.

With nothing more to say, the two colleagues hovering around Brooke's desk shuffled away to their own cubicles. Brooke picked up the last item on her desk. Colin didn't like clutter, so she'd brought the framed photograph of The Three Potters taken the summer after high school graduation here.

She stared at the smiling faces in the photograph, then tucked the memento into her bag along with her pink slip and severance check. Biting her lip, she cast a look at all her coworkers—make that her *former* coworkers. She nodded a quick goodbye, hefted the cardboard box into her arms, then followed Doogan out the door.

"This sucks," he said at the elevator.

Brooke nodded.

"I've got bills, man."

In the lobby, Brooke said, "Well, good luck."

"You, too."

What was it that Colin had said that morning? *We make our own luck.*

Tears stung her eyes. The thought of Colin kept them from falling. She dreaded telling him about this.

In the parking lot, she fumbled for her keys, only to drop them, nearly dropping everything. By the time she deposited the carton on the backseat and managed to unlock her door and get behind the wheel, her hands were shaking.

She wanted . . .

What? A friend to talk to? A shoulder to cry on?

She wanted Colin to hold her. She wanted that so much she ached.

Gripping the steering wheel with both hands, she watched for traffic and kept her mind blank. She wasn't surprised when she found herself near the office building where Colin worked.

Parking was always a problem downtown. Today she didn't mind, for looking for a parking space gave her a focus. She found a spot three blocks from Colin's building. Calmer now, she began to walk, noticing for the first time what a beautiful day it was. The weather, at least, was lovely. It was a sunny, breezy eighty-two degrees. Perfect July weather. She would find another job. Of course she would! Meanwhile, she had her health, her family, and sunshine.

She was going to have to rethink the private celebration she'd planned for tonight. She felt vulnerable and disappointed. She needed Colin to hold her, and make her feel cherished and safe. The counselor she'd seen had told her she had to learn to ask for what she needed. She was working on that.

She waited with the hordes of other pedestrians for the WALK sign to light up at the intersection. Keeping pace with everyone else, she breathed in the scents of ginger and orange and teriyaki wafting on the breeze from the outdoor café at the end of the next block. It was eleven-thirty and she was starving. Perhaps Colin would have time for an early lunch. Perhaps, now that she was between jobs, she could meet him for lunch often. That sounded lovely, actually. She was thirty-six-years old, and she couldn't remember the last time she'd had an extended vacation.

She would get through this. Hadn't she worked through worse things?

Her steps quickened and her spirits lifted somewhat. It didn't take long to catch up with a group of tourists from the Midwest. Since she now had all the time in the world, Brooke slowed to a stroll and breathed deeply again.

She was close enough to see the patrons enjoying lunch at the small umbrella tables in the little courtyard up ahead. A mix of tourists and business people, most appeared to be enjoying the food and fresh air. A blond woman in a stunning red suit caught Brooke's eye. She could have been Marilyn Monroe reincarnated, complete with full lips and plenty of cleavage. She was with a dark-haired man in a dark suit. The man looked good from behind, but it was the way the woman moved, sinuous and seductive, that captured Brooke's attention.

The Midwesterners stopped in front of Brooke to admire something in a window. Brooke stopped, too, intrigued for reasons she couldn't name. Perhaps it was the way the blond woman's fingernails flashed bright red as she slid one inside the man's cuff. Perhaps it was the way the man reached toward her, indulging her, exciting her, luring her to lean across that small table and kiss him in front of God and everyone.

The kiss went on and on. When it finally ended, the woman smiled breathlessly. Giving him an extended view of her breasts, which were straining the buttons of her bright red jacket, she reached over and wiped her lipstick from his lips with her thumb. He said something that made her smile broaden, then handed her his napkin. There was something familiar about the way he did that.

Just then the waiter appeared. The lovers turned their heads and looked up, smiling. And Brooke got her first glimpse of the man's profile.

The tourists moved on. Brooke was frozen in place.

Colin.

The man was Colin.

She darted to the cover of a nearby store, then stood, hiding, as if she had done something wrong. What she'd done was witness her husband kissing another woman. Her husband, who hadn't kissed her goodbye for fear of smearing her lipstick, had just kissed another woman senseless in broad daylight. He certainly hadn't been concerned about *her* lipstick.

The realization burned Brooke's eyes, her throat, her chest. She turned, stumbling. Righting herself, she fled back the way she'd come.

He'd promised, *promised* it would never happen again.

Today was the anniversary of the day they'd started over. A year ago they'd recommitted to each other, turning over a new leaf, embracing the future instead of the past.

There would be no celebration tonight.

Damn you, Colin Valentine.

CHAPTER 2

The house was quiet, immaculate, and scented with the lemon cleaner Portia was so fond of. It was giving Brooke a headache.

The heels of her shoes echoed as she walked through the beautifully furnished, uncluttered rooms in the refurbished old town house where she'd lived for the past year. She could have turned on a radio or the television to cover the emptiness. It seemed more fitting this way.

She changed into loose-fitting chinos and a white tank top, then stared at her reflection for a long time. Her chin-length brown hair was dull, her face pale, her eyes blank.

People said she possessed a timeless beauty. She didn't look beautiful today. She looked lifeless. It wasn't that she looked sickly, exactly. She looked faded somehow. Where was her spunk, her flair, her spirit?

In her mind she saw the image of Colin kissing that other woman. Brooke wanted to curl up into a ball and sleep for a year.

Why wasn't she spitting mad?

Time passed slowly, but it did pass. It had been hours since she'd lost her job and witnessed Colin partaking of his little tête-à-tête. She still hadn't cried. The need to piled into her chest, making it difficult to breathe. She'd never wept easily or well. She wished she could get it out, and get it over with. Dry-eyed and silent, she wandered through the quiet, meticulous house she and Colin had purchased as a symbol of their new beginning.

It had all been a lie.

The house was Federal in style. It had three stories and high ceilings, the original fireplaces and lovely architecture. Other than Sophie's room, which was a disaster much of the time, the kitchen was the only room that bore Brooke's personality. Perhaps that was why she felt less lonely there. It was no surprise it was where she whiled away the remaining hours before Colin's footsteps sounded on the back stairs.

Keeping her back to the door, Brooke heard him sniff appreciatively. "Something smells delicious. Since when do you have time to cook on Thursdays?"

She glanced up as he approached. Before she could answer, he handed her a stunning bouquet of yellow roses. There must have been two dozen, at least. She gasped. She couldn't help it. They were that spectacular.

"The most beautiful flowers in the world for the most beautiful woman in the universe." He sampled a stuffed mushroom straight from the pan, grinned his Adonis smile, and said, "And you can cook, too."

If Brooke didn't know better, she would have believed his devotion was real. She watched his face and changing expressions, wondering how a man could go from kissing his mistress to handing flowers and compliments to his wife without a trace of guilt in evidence anywhere.

"It's quiet without Sophie, isn't it?"

Brooke nodded. Colin may have been a cheating sack of shit of a husband, but he was a good father. He'd been at Brooke's side through obstetrician's appointments, twenty-seven hours of labor, and Sophie's birth. He'd changed diapers and had taken his turn getting up in the middle of the night. She'd loved listening to the sound of his voice as he'd talked philosophy with their precious baby. They'd chosen day-care together, and hand-selected their daughter's preschool. As Sophie grew, had they grown apart? Was that what happened? Or had he cheated even then? Brooke had wanted another child. At first Colin hadn't been ready, and later he always seemed to have a reason why the timing wasn't right. She couldn't remember the last time she'd brought it up.

"How long have you been home?" he asked.

"Since shortly after the meeting this morning." She took a lead crystal vase from a glass-fronted cabinet. Why was she doing this? Why didn't she just throw the bouquet in the trash and get it over with?

He shrugged out of his suit coat, loosened his tie and rolled up his shirt sleeves. Nature had bestowed on him a fabulous physique. He helped keep it that way by playing tennis. Fast and savagely focused, he had a fierce competitor's spirit. Brooke enjoyed tennis, but lacked Colin's killer instinct. She'd learned early on that she was better off getting her exercise at the gym where she could set her own pace.

"Aren't you going to tell me your good news?" he asked.

"I'm afraid not." Her voice sounded weak in her own ears.

"What do you mean?"

"There is no good news, Colin." The understatement of all time. She carried the flowers to the counter and began arranging them in the vase one stem at a time.

"You didn't get the promotion?" he asked.

"There was no promotion." It still wasn't easy to say it out loud. "Wilson Advertising is downsizing. That's why I'm home."

Colin hung his jacket over a chair then stared at her. "You mean Klein let you go?"

His voice was incredulous. She didn't think he was faking that, but how would a person tell?

"Is he crazy? He would have to be to let you get away."

Suddenly he was on her side of the kitchen island, taking her into his arms. "Oh, baby, I'm so sorry. It's his loss. You worked so hard, too."

Brooke felt sick from the struggle within her. Surely, Colin felt her shudder, but since there was no way he could have known the cause, he undoubtedly assumed her reaction was a result of her disappointment over losing her job.

He nuzzled her neck and massaged her back. "Everything is going to be all right. Maybe Pratt would take you back. If not, the city is filled with opportunities. You'll find another agency, a better one that appreciates your creativity and ethics."

Ethics. Oh, that was a good one.

"In the meantime, it's summer, and it'll be good for Sophie if you're home. It'll be good for me, too, if it means you'll be preparing meals like this on a regular basis. You'll have to increase your workouts at the gym, but you'll have time for it, right?"

His insinuations and belittling innuendoes were delivered so smoothly and effortlessly and efficiently it was difficult to refute them. Somewhere along the way, Brooke had lost the energy to try.

"Are you hungry?" she asked.

"Yes, but there's no need to rush. We have all night." He ran a hand up her bare arm. "I've been looking forward to tonight, haven't you?"

Bending slightly, he kissed the side of her neck. It wasn't easy to keep from recoiling. Easing away gently, she said, "Why don't you pour the wine?"

He took the bottle from the refrigerator, expertly popped the cork, and poured. He held both glasses for a moment, and she knew he wanted her to stop stirring the wild rice long enough to take the glass so he could propose a toast. Brooke would never be able to pull that off, so she continued to busy herself with last-minute meal preparation.

Only mildly deterred, he placed her glass on the counter,

and swirled his dark wine. He took a sip, then stood leaning against the counter, ankles crossed, perfectly at ease, as if nothing out-of-the-ordinary had happened today. But then, it hadn't been out-of-the-ordinary for him, had it?

He drank his wine and talked, telling her about a meeting he'd attended that afternoon and the heads that had rolled. He spoke of new office politics, the increasing problems with gangs in England, and the growing tensions with a business his company was taking over in Europe. He was extremely eloquent, knowledgeable, well-read and interesting.

Her mind wandered.

Was the woman in red a colleague, a client, or just someone he'd happened to meet? Brooke had searched for clues in the pockets of every suit he'd worn this past month. Finding no evidence there, she'd gone through the drawers in the desk in his home office, being careful to leave everything as she'd found it. The last thing she'd checked was his private e-mail account.

Her stomach roiled. Placing a hand over her flat stomach, she swayed slightly. She feared she was going to be sick.

"You're hungry, sweetheart."

It was all Brooke could do to keep from blurting that she'd been hungry for years. She wore a size six. What good had it done her?

"What can I do to help?" he asked.

She took two plates from the warmer and expertly arranged their glazed chicken, smoked Gouda-spinach stuffing and wild rice. After adding steamed vegetables and a garnish of mustard greens, she handed the plates to him, indicating that he carry them to the table.

Her stomach rumbled again. "I didn't feel up to eating today. How about you? What did you have for lunch?"

She hadn't even choked on the question.

Normally, Colin didn't appreciate her curiosity—her unhealthy preoccupation with food, he called it. Either it didn't bother him today, or he chose to humor her. Guilt had to be good for something.

He said, "I was so busy I hardly came up for air all day."

She didn't like the image that popped into her mind. "You don't normally skip lunch."

"Don't worry. I grabbed take-out and ate at my desk."

Liar.

Reaching for her wineglass gave her a place to look and something to do with her hands. She swirled the rich, dark liquid, sampling it.

He did the same, saying, "I can understand why Australian vineyards are gaining notoriety. This is very good, isn't it?"

She made an agreeable sound in the back of her throat.

"You're awfully quiet, Brooke. It's been a difficult day for you."

She stared into her wine. Taking a deep breath, she forged ahead to the inevitable. "It has been a long day. I have a lot on my mind. I was in your neighborhood today."

She felt the swift flicker of his gaze. "You should have stopped in."

"I thought it best not to bother you."

"I'm never too busy for you, Brooke."

Oh, but he was good at this.

"You had your hands pretty full." She looked him in the face in time to see something glimmer far back in his eyes. Reaching out, she smoothed her thumb over his upper lip the way she'd seen the blonde do hours earlier. "She missed a little."

"A little what?" How could he sound so innocent?

Brooke didn't have it in her to further the drama. "I saw you, Colin."

"I have no idea what you're talking about."

"Have you ever considered taking up acting?"

"I don't appreciate your insinuation."

"I don't appreciate you sticking your tongue down some other woman's throat in broad daylight, either."

"I won't even address how crass that sounded, but then you've always had a streak of that in you, haven't you?"

She stared at him, unflinching. "I saw you."

Since his strategy wasn't working, he changed tactics. "It wasn't what you think. Deirdre is terribly forward and flirtatious. And that's what you saw, her being forward. It's completely one-sided."

"You're saying it's meaningless, is that it?"

He wore a pained expression. "Of course it's meaningless."

"It's just sex, is that it?"

"I didn't say it involves sex."

"You didn't admit it, you mean."

"Believe me, Brooke. Please. I wouldn't risk losing you a second time."

Once upon a time, she would have believed him. That was how pathetic she used to be.

"Are you trying to tell me you're not having an affair, Colin?"

He looked her in the eye. "Of course, sweetheart, of course that's what I'm telling you."

Once upon a time she would have believed that, too.

"Then you'd swear on a stack of Bibles?"

He looked into her eyes again, pleading. "I'll swear on anything and everything. I'll do whatever it takes to prove it to you."

He moved as if to take her into his arms. She held up a hand, halting him. Paper crinkled as she drew something from her pocket. She unfolded a single sheet of paper containing letters he and *Deirdre* had exchanged through e-mail. Very slowly, she handed it to Colin.

He scanned the damning evidence. "How did you get my password?"

She tipped her wineglass up, polishing off the entire glass. The liquid heated a trail to her stomach.

"How dare you invade my privacy."

"How dare I?" Brooke shook with emotion. Tears welled up in her eyes, a delayed reaction if there ever was one. "The two of you practically sucked each other's lips off in broad daylight, and yet you wouldn't so much as kiss me goodbye this morning lest you might smear my lipstick."

"Maybe you should try opening your mouth when you kiss."

One minute the crème brûlée was on the counter. The next it was on Colin.

Brooke didn't know who was more surprised, but she knew who was more angry. Fury glittered in Colin's eyes.

Slowly, the creamy mixture slid down the side of his face, dripping down his chest. Brooke followed the trail of a dollop until it landed on the top of his new Ferragamo loafer.

His voice shook with anger as he said, "You've sunk to a new low."

Tears coursed down her face. "I was just thinking the same thing about you. Now get out."

"What?"

Did he have crème brûlée in his ears? Probably. He had it everywhere else. "What part of that didn't you understand?"

Dripping as he was with dessert, he was hardly dressed to go out. Brooke was crying a river now. Her eyes were burning. Her nose was running. Her chest was heaving. "G-g-get out. I-I-I don't w-w-want to look at you."

Just then the back door opened and Sophie called, "Mom, Daddy, I'm back. Makayla's little brother got the chicken pox so their mom brought me home."

Colin and Brooke turned in unison toward their daughter's voice.

"You should see poor Toby. He's—" Sophie stopped in her tracks in the kitchen doorway, her tennis shoes squeaking on the hardwood floor. Eyes round, her gaze went from her mother to her father and back again.

The day just kept getting worse.

"What are you two doing?" She dropped her duffel bag at her feet.

Brooke couldn't even imagine how this must look to a

twelve-year-old. Dinner was served, Brooke was crying uncontrollably and Colin was wearing dessert.

Colin came to his senses first. "Your mother and I are discussing a problem, Sophia. It's personal. Please go to your room."

Looking like a frightened waif suddenly, the child darted across the room and did as her father said.

Back in control, Colin unfolded the linen napkin and began cleaning his face. "She'll probably need therapy for that one. I hope you're proud of yourself."

Brooke turned her back on him, thinking he was a fine one to talk about pride. She sniffled loudly. Uncaring that it was uncouth, she dried her face and blew her nose on a kitchen towel.

"Just go, Colin."

"You don't really expect me to leave. That can't be what you want. Is it?"

"What I want has nothing to do with today."

"What are you going to do?" Clearly, he wasn't in control as much as he'd wanted her to believe.

Her gaze went to the old framed photograph of The Three Potters she'd unpacked earlier. Until that moment, she'd had no idea what she was going to do next, let alone what she wanted. Sniffling again, she said, "I'm going to talk to Sophie, and then I'm going to call Eve and tell her that Sophe and I are coming to visit."

"You can't do that, Brooke."

"I can't take our daughter to visit her aunt?"

"You can't take her away from me."

Brooke took a shuddering breath. "Give me a little credit, Colin. I'm a fool, but not that big a one. I'm not going to turn her against you. Not because you don't deserve it, but because that would hurt Sophie. She loves you. Give me a few minutes with her. And then come on in and reassure her that this has nothing to do with her. Tell her you love her and always will."

"We can't work on our marriage if you're in Alcott."

We? Oh, that was priceless. There was no we.

She looked at the vase full of yellow roses, and then she looked at Colin. He wasn't an Adonis. He was just a man in a soiled white shirt and a loosened tie and guilty blue eyes.

A lump came out of nowhere, lodging in her throat. Swallowing it, she said, "I'm not going to Alcott to work on our marriage. I'm going to Alcott to decide what to do about this farce *we* call a marriage."

And maybe, just maybe she would discover how she'd become this hungry, lonely, invisible, dispensable woman.

Sophie was sitting in the middle of her bed, petting Fluffy when Brooke knocked and entered. Her daughter looked up, her gray-blue eyes round, her expression one of interest and amazement. "Did you really dump that white goo on Daddy's head?"

Brooke closed the door behind her and picked her way across the floor that was littered with shoes and clothes and wrappers. When she'd made the crème brûlée, she'd done so because it had sounded good to her. Now that she thought about it, the way it had ended up had been even more satisfying. She sighed. "I didn't plan to do that, and I'm not proud of it, but yes, I did dump it on your father's head."

Sophie stared at her mother in astonishment. "Wow, he must have done something really bad."

"That is between your father and me." Brooke lowered herself to the bed within touching distance of her child.

The gray tabby cat stopped purring and eyed her suspiciously.

"I want to talk to you about something, Sophe."

Sophie quit petting the cat and said, "Is Daddy screwing somebody again? Is that it?"

Brooke could not believe the things twelve-year-olds knew these days. "Your father's sex life is none of your business."

Sophie was quiet for a moment, digesting that, as if something in this household that wasn't her business was a new concept. Looking across at her mother, she said, "Is his sex life *your* business?"

"Oh, yes. It's definitely my business."

"What are you going to do about it?"

The cat rose, stretched, and arched her back. Giving Brooke a wide berth, the feline skulked off the bed, disappearing under it.

"That cat doesn't like me."

"You named her Fluffy. What do you expect?" Sophie flopped onto her back and asked, "Mom? Have I ever had the chicken pox?"

Like a typical adolescent, Sophe's world revolved around herself. It made life simple. Fleetingly, Brooke wished there was a way for parents to keep their children's lives so simple. Through no fault of her own, Sophie's life had just gotten far more complicated. Brooke didn't know how to protect her from this.

"You had the most horrible case of chicken pox when you were three. We'd opted not to have you vaccinated because it was relatively new and we were concerned about possible side effects. So you caught the virus. Itch? Oh my goodness. It's a miracle you aren't scarred. But at least I don't have to worry that you'll come down with it when we're in Alcott."

Sophie turned her head. "We're going to Alcott?"

Brooke nodded.

"Is Daddy coming?"

"No."

"So we're going, like, for the weekend?"

"A little longer than that."

"How much longer?"

"For a few weeks, at least. Maybe for the remainder of the summer."

Sophie sprang to a sitting position. "We can't! What about your job?"

"It seems I'm between jobs as of today."

"But I can't leave Makayla. Or Toby."

Just this morning Sophie had complained about Makayla's little brother. But Brooke let that pass. "Aunt Eve is getting married. You should have heard how happy she sounded on the phone. I'll have to call her back to get the details, and to let her know we're coming."

"Do I have to go?"

Brooke would have appreciated a little enthusiasm. "Yes, Sophe, you do. We'll leave in the morning."

"What about my riding lessons?"

"Believe it or not, there are horses in New Hampshire."

"But Mom, how can you fix things with Daddy if we're in New Hampshire?"

Sometimes Sophie was her father's daughter through and through.

Brooke made no reply.

And Sophie said, "Won't Daddy be lonely without us?"

Brooke commended herself for refraining from saying what she was thinking. Laying her hand on Sophie's knee, she said, "Your father can take care of himself. Besides, we're going to Alcott, New Hampshire. Not the North Pole."

Sophie gave her mother a look that expressed quite clearly that as far as she was concerned, Alcott might as well have been the North Pole.

Brooke said, "Your father can visit, and you can call him every day if you want to, and he can call you. You don't have to like the fact that we're leaving Philadelphia, but I expect you to keep an open mind regarding our visit to the seacoast. Who knows? You might even have fun."

Sophie stared at her hands in her lap.

Just then a knock sounded on the door. Without looking up, she called, "Come in, Daddy."

Colin entered. He'd changed his shirt and washed his face, but his hair still looked sticky. Brooke could hardly believe she'd done that.

Rising to her feet, she nodded at Sophie. Head held high, she looked Colin in the eye for a moment, then left the room, closing the door behind her.

Out in the hallway, she sagged against the wall. She released the breath she'd been holding, then went to call her sister.

Sophie cried when she said goodbye to her father, big, fat wet tears trailing down her cheeks. Colin's eyes were wet, too.

He was going to miss them. And all Brooke could think was, why on earth hadn't he thought of that before he'd started his latest affair? How many others had there been?

She'd left the roses on the counter in the kitchen, and tossed the sex guide book into the trash. She'd cleaned up the sticky kitchen floor, but hadn't cooked breakfast this morning. No one was hungry. Not even the cat.

Sophie sniffled as Brooke started the car. Colin stood, alone and forlorn in the alley behind the beautifully restored town house in one of the quaintest and most historic neighborhoods in Philadelphia. Brooke remembered clearly the day they'd signed the papers. A few weeks later they'd moved in. Colin had carried her over the threshold. And later, after Sophie was asleep, they'd made love. Number twenty-two.

Even on such a special occasion they'd needed the manual. She bet Deirdre didn't go by the book.

Sophie waved her hand forlornly out the window. Colin lifted his hand and did the same. Brooke kept both hands on the wheel.

He'd tried to talk her out of leaving, following her from room to room, relentless in his pursuit. He was sorry, he'd said. Maybe he was. He swore he loved her and only her. She'd heard it all before. And it was like she'd told him last night. He had strange ways of showing his love.

He'd had nothing to say to that.

He was hurting. Brooke had seen it in his eyes before

she'd backed from the driveway. He had the most amazing blue eyes. They were the first thing she'd noticed about him when they'd met at Columbia. They were the first part of him she'd fallen in love with. And they would be the last thing she got over. The thought made her sad.

Sniffling, Sophie said, "You should have tried number eighty-three."

"Number eighty-three what?" Brooke asked.

"In your book."

Understanding dawned. "My bedroom is off limits to you, young lady." Besides, Brooke hadn't even read that far.

Was that the problem? Was she boring? Did she not kiss well, as Colin had insinuated? Is that why he strayed? Was the fault with her? Or with him?

And what difference did it make? How on earth would Brooke ever trust him again?

Questions. She had so many questions.

And for the biggest question of all: What was she going to do now?

When she'd been young, the answer had been simple. Back when she'd been one-third of The Three Potters, working at the pizza place with Claudia and Sara every Friday night, she'd known exactly what she would become. Perhaps part of that, most of that, had been the blind arrogance and self-confidence of youth. Was there any of that girl left in Brooke today?

Brooke Nelson Valentine was a thirty-six-year-old, unemployed woman with straight brown hair and a closet full of clothes she had to starve herself in order to wear. She had an unfaithful husband, a beautiful, smart and perhaps spoiled daughter who was huddled in the passenger seat, arms folded, her chin stubbornly down, and a cat that evidently didn't like its name meowing from the backseat.

"This isn't the end of the world," she said to anyone who was listening, including herself. "Everything is going to be all right. You'll see."

Fluffy hissed.

Sophie sulked.

Brooke drove.

Just another day in paradise. But as they left the city behind, she was certain of one thing.

It felt good to be going home.

CHAPTER 3

There were roughly two-hundred-fifty miles between Brooke's home in Philadelphia and the seacoast town of Alcott, New Hampshire. The drive would have been accomplished in a relatively short amount of time if Boston and New York hadn't been in the way. Getting around them took patience and nerves of steel. Thankfully, Fluffy gave up yowling an hour into the ride. Sophie had far more stamina. Brooke's every attempt at conversation was met with a clipped "yes," "no," or Sophe's apparent favorite, "I guess." After several of those, Brooke honored the girl's apparent need to sulk.

Sophe and Fluffy both slept through the final two hours of the journey, so that Brooke was the only one who saw the grasses in the salt marshes swaying in the wind, the fleeting glimpses of the sparkling blue ocean, the clumsy flight of a gangly blue heron. She hadn't expected the rush of emotion as she read the hand-made signs for fresh seafood. Straight ahead was the white steeple on the old Stone Church on the outskirts of town, and the village limits sign.

Alcott, New Hampshire, population three thousand.

It had seemed so big when Brooke was growing up, small

when she came home from college. Now it was neither. And both.

"Wake up, Sophe. We're here." Brooke rolled down her window, inhaling the scent of the ocean and the wind and the sky. "Smell that?"

Sophie looked around. Blinking owlishly, she wrinkled her nose as if she'd gotten a whiff of something offensive.

Eve must have been watching for them. She threw open the door and raced down the porch steps the moment the car came to a stop in the driveway. Wearing aquamarine Capris and a matching sleeveless shirt, she looked like a tall, cool drink of water rushing toward them. Her long hair blew in the breeze, and her smile was alive with affection as she opened the car door.

"I thought you'd never get here!"

The next thing Brooke knew she was being drawn out of the car and into her younger sister's embrace. Brooke's throat closed up and tears flooded her eyes.

"Don't cry," Eve whispered in her ear. "Unless you want Carter's first impression of you after all these years to be of a woman with a red nose, puffy eyes and splotchy skin."

Not only did Brooke not cry. She laughed. "I rue the day you grew taller than me."

"Atta girl." Next, Eve ran around to the other side of the car. "My goodness, Sophie, you're beautiful! What have you done with my little girl and who is this svelte creature? How was the ride?"

"Getting around New York was a bitch."

Eve's eyebrows raised, but she laughed. "It always is."

And then Sophie was being drawn from the car and hugged, too, and twirled and fawned over. Not even Sophie could keep up the grumpy front beneath all that enthusiasm.

"Oh my goodness, you brought Fluffy. Is she pregnant?"

"No, just fat."

"What does she like to eat?"

"She's okay with cat food but adores tuna."

"We'll have to get some. Let me look at those jeans. Is

that what kids are wearing in Philadelphia? And your hair! It's almost as long as mine. When did you get your ears pierced? Did it hurt? Oh my gosh, tell me that's all that's pierced."

It did Brooke's heart good to see the bloom on her daughter's cheeks and to hear the lilt in her voice as she answered question after question. But Eve wasn't finished. She drew Brooke into the circle, catching her up in her exuberance, too.

Carter McCall sauntered outside, standing back, out of the way of the effusive females. His hair was brushed straight back from his forehead and hung a few inches above his shoulders. He wore faded jeans, a white T-shirt and no shoes, and stood, feet apart, hands on hips, head tilted slightly, so that the sun caught on the diamond stud in one ear.

"*You're* Aunt Eve's fiancé?"

Carter gave Sophie the first smile. Holding out his hand, he said, "I'm Carter McCall. And just between you and me, I still can't believe she said 'yes.' You must be Sophie. Come on. I'll help you drag in all your gear."

Sophie reached for the cat carrier and Carter loaded up with bags. On their way by, Brooke heard Sophie say, "Does everybody in Alcott go barefoot?"

He hefted the cases higher into his arms before replying. "When we're not fixing to sail off the edge of the flat, flat world, you mean?"

Sophie's eyes went as round as her mouth. And Brooke thought that perhaps her daughter had met her match. At the very least, she doubted Sophie would underestimate Carter again.

Eve happened to be barefoot, too. And was that whisker burn on her cheek and neck? Suddenly Brooke knew why her sister looked so radiant, so relaxed and glowing. She and Sophie had been here for five minutes. Already Brooke felt in the way, and was second-guessing her decision to come here. Where else could they have gone?

Glancing over her shoulder to make sure the coast was

clear, Eve said, "This is as good a time as any to tell me what Colin's done now."

Brooke took the case Eve handed her. "The question should be *who* he's doing, not what."

"Oh, no."

"Her name is Deirdre, and she has a body like Marilyn Monroe and lips like Angelina Jolie."

Leading the way toward the house, Eve said, "I doubt it matters what she looks like. If Colin's interested in her, she most likely possesses that rare and endearing talent of being able to suck a golf ball through a garden hose."

Brooke was too stunned to speak for a moment. "Eve, for heaven's sake!"

Eve made a face. "It's true. But I understand your surprise. I think I'm finally coming out of my shell. It's about time, isn't it?"

"It's lovely, I'm sure," Brooke said. And then, because it was second nature, she added, "But I thought you liked Colin."

Eve opened her front door. "I used to like him just fine, but then I'm not the one he cheated on. What does he have to say for himself?"

"He says he's sorry, and he says he loves me, and he says he wants me—needs me to forgive him."

"Can you?"

Not *will* she. *Can* she? Eve understood her well.

"I don't think so. Not this time. It's going to break Sophie's heart."

They met Carter and Sophie coming down the narrow staircase as they were going up. When everything had been brought inside and deposited in the minimally furnished spare bedroom, Eve said, "We'll be in the kitchen, which, by the way, Brooke, I'm turning over to you while you're here."

With that, the lovebirds disappeared.

Sophie eyed the small room with its sloped ceiling, one window and twin beds. "We really have to share a room?"

Opening the top drawer of the little dresser near the door,

Brooke said, "I haven't shared a room like this since Eve and I were children. I'm rather looking forward to it."

Sophie shrugged, a gesture she'd picked up from somewhere and Colin hadn't been able to break. Getting down on her knees, she peered under the bed. "Think Fluffy will ever come out from under there?"

"She'll venture out when she's ready." More concerned about Sophie's adjustment, Brooke fished her cellphone out of her purse and handed it over. "Why don't you call your father and let him know we arrived safely. Perhaps you'd like to call Makayla, too."

"Would I ever!" Sophie's face sobered. "Mom? I don't mean to be a pain."

Brooke hugged her daughter. "I love you, Sophe. I'll be downstairs."

Finger poised above the final digit of her own home phone number, Sophie said, "Want me to tell Daddy anything for you?"

Brooke looked back at her child. "Tell him we both got here in one piece."

Sophie sighed. And Brooke left her to her phone calls.

Carter and Eve were laughing when she entered the kitchen. She paused just inside the doorway.

Noticing, Eve said, "Tell me you aren't waiting for an invitation."

"Sophie's calling Colin. I think I'll just read a magazine for a while in the living room."

Carter and Eve exchanged a private look. Brooke noticed he'd fastened his hair in a ponytail and was no longer barefoot. He looked more like the other McCalls as he sauntered toward her. The McCalls were good, hard-working, honorable people.

"If you want to read a magazine," Carter said, "go for it. But don't worry about Eve and me finding time to be alone. Where there's a will there's a way. I never met your husband, but he's a fool. I'm going to the barn while there's still some natural light left in that sky. It's good to see you again,

Brooke." He looked at Eve last, slanted her a smile warm enough to melt a glacier, then ambled on outside.

Brooke watched him through the window. "Bad-boy Carter McCall is in love. There is no doubt about that."

Eve joined her at the window. "I don't think Carter was ever bad. He was a rule-breaker, a risk-taker. People assumed that meant he was wild."

Carter donned a helmet, kick-started a big, heavy-looking motorcycle, then looked back toward the window, as if he'd known Eve would be watching. He chugged out of the driveway, leaving her with a smile.

Colin Valentine III had been well-groomed, well-bred, well-educated and well-behaved. He'd followed the rules straight up the ladder of success. He'd never once looked back at Brooke the way Carter had looked at Eve. And Brooke knew she'd missed out on something precious.

"Did Carter say he's going to the barn?"

"It used to be a barn," Eve said. "Now it's a studio where he turns steel and iron and copper and sometimes tin into works of art."

"Carter's an artist?"

"He calls himself an artisan. It was Liza who actually convinced him to part with his work. You wouldn't believe how much some people are willing to pay for one-of-a-kind gates, sculptures, tables, fireplace screens, and trellises."

"Who's Liza?"

They stood arm-to-arm, Eve, three inches taller, and so, so beautiful, especially when she smiled. "Liza and Laurel Cassidy were identical twin sisters."

Were? Brooke remembered hearing about the mysterious Laurel Cassidy when the redhead had breezed into town six years ago. Eve had been beside herself when Laurel and Jack McCall had fallen in love at first sight. Laurel left town suddenly less than a year later, taking Jack's heart with her, and leaving behind their newborn son, Tommy.

Propping the window open, Eve said, "Laurel didn't just up and leave town, as we all thought. She had a brain tumor and died in surgery at a medical center in Boston. We all assumed she was having migraines. Even Jack had no idea she was dying. It's a long story, but he didn't know Laurel had a sister out west, either, and Liza didn't know Laurel had a son. It seems Liza had started having dreams about a little boy with red hair. I guess they freaked her out pretty bad. When the dreams stopped suddenly, she came to Alcott looking for answers. Months before Liza showed up, Carter came roaring into town on his Harley. He'd been bouncing around from place to place, and had just found out about Tommy's leukemia. His arrival coincided with Tommy's remission. Carter was just arrogant enough to think he might have had something to do with it, and just superstitious enough, and terrified enough to stay."

Brooke must have been wearing her dismay, because Eve grinned sheepishly and pulled out a chair. "You've been gone a long time. Sit down and I'll fill you in on everything that's been happening in our little metropolis a mile from the sea."

An hour later Brooke had learned that Tommy McCall was responding well to his new round of chemotherapy. His father and Liza had married quietly a week ago. And not only was Eve, who'd pined after Jack for twenty years, happy for them, she *liked* her future sister-in-law. The middle McCall brother had performed the private wedding ceremony. Brooke couldn't quite picture the Brian McCall she remembered as a preacher. Apparently he was engaged, too, to a woman named Natalie.

"Wait until you meet her," Eve said. "She's an attorney. High-heeled shoes, fishnet stockings, and a potty mouth like you wouldn't believe. Natalie was the one who insisted I make a play for Jack, and open his eyes once and for all. It all backfired, and I ended up opening Carter's eyes, instead. All those years I'd been waiting for Jack who was all wrong for me. And suddenly there was Carter, so, so right."

The warm July breeze billowed through the curtains at the window. Beyond the glass, the sun was starting its slow glide toward the west. Brooke heard birdsong outside, and the occasional thud of Sophie's footsteps and soft voice overhead. She could tell from the pitch and the giggling that the person on the other end wasn't Colin.

"I'm doing the right thing, aren't I, Eve?"

Her sister looked at her. "Have you ever *not* done the right thing?"

It gave Brooke pause.

Eve said, "It was a rhetorical question. You'll do what's best. You always do."

"I'm not even sure what that is."

"You've come to the right place to figure it out. And while you're here, you can help me plan my wedding. Six weeks! What on earth was I thinking when I set the date for the end of August? *This August.*"

"You tell me."

A dreamy warmth passed through Eve's eyes. "I was thinking, oh man oh man oh man, I love this man! And the sex, Brooke, I never knew it could be this way." Eve blushed.

And Brooke knew her sister didn't need a guide book.

"I'm thirty-five years old," Eve said. "I've waited so long for this and I just don't see any reason to wait any longer."

Brooke reached across the small table and squeezed Eve's hand. "We can plan a wedding in six weeks. No problem."

Eve let out a sigh as tall as she was. "I am so glad you're here."

"Tell me something I don't already know."

Eve's eyes took on a fiendish gleam. "Okay, you asked for it." Rubbing her hands together, she launched into the long and varied tales of the more newsworthy and notable happenings of the people in and around Alcott. By the time she ran out of material, the tea she'd brewed during the telling was half gone, as were the store-bought, artificially flavored cookies she'd found in her cupboard.

"That about covers it, I think. Oh, Miss Rose and Miss Addie are still growing their flowers, but Rose is slowing down. I worry about her. It's working out beautifully for them all now that Sara and Seth have moved into the aunts' garden apartment."

"Sara? Do you mean Sara Walsh?"

"Formerly Walsh. You remember when she married Roy Kemper."

Of course Brooke remembered. She'd attended the wedding.

"Something must be in the air," Eve said, "because Sara finally gave Roy the boot, too. Jack, Brian and Carter had a hand in that. You can catch up with Sara tomorrow at the Saturday baseball game. Her son, Seth is the star pitcher."

"What did the McCall brothers have to do with Sara leaving Roy?"

"You knew Roy beat her, didn't you?" Eve asked.

"I know there used to be rumors."

"Yeah, well, those rumors escalated into visible bruises a few years ago. And if poor Sara didn't have enough to deal with, last month somebody started vandalizing the street lights on the town square. Jack figured teenagers were responsible. More likely there was only one teen responsible, one boy with an accurate aim and a strong pitching arm."

"Alcott High's star pitcher?" Brooke whispered. "You mean Sara's son, Seth?"

Eve shrugged. "Nobody has come right out and said he did it. In a hundred years, I don't believe he would ever be cruel. If he *did* do it, he did so to force Sara into leaving Roy. At least that's what I think. Maybe Sara will tell you the rest."

Poor Sara, Brooke thought.

One thing she'd noticed about coming home. There was always somebody with problems bigger than her own.

Sara Kemper sat where she always sat to watch Seth's baseball game, toward the center of the old wooden bleachers, in the second row from the bottom. People sat around her, parents and friends of the players, mostly. No one sat with her.

That had been her doing a long time ago.

It was a hard behavior to break. Her counselor told her she needed to take one step at a time.

She'd finally left Roy three weeks ago. That had been the first step. The most important step. She woke up every night in a cold sweat, terrified that she would find herself back in bed with Roy. Gradually, she would make out the shape of the window in her tiny bedroom in the aunts' garden apartment, and her terror would subside. Leaving Roy hadn't been a dream. It was real. She'd done it. It had taken her years to work up the courage. She figured it could take the rest of her life to work out everything else.

Maybe now she would have a life. Maybe Seth would, too. That was what truly mattered. If Seth was okay, it would be enough.

Right now, Seth's life was baseball.

He stood on the pitcher's mound. It was the top of the fifth. The sun was blinding, the air humid, the people in the stands quiet. Sara was the quietest of all.

Roy was here.

Inside, she implored her son to ignore him. *You can do it. Pretend he isn't here.*

Roy stood at the fence, a looming, brooding presence.

Sara sat stone still. Inside, she screamed at Roy.

Your boy has been playing baseball since he was eight. You never once came to a game. He was doing so well before you arrived. Leave. We don't need you. And we don't want you.

From the corner of her eye she saw Roy look her way from time to time. She never looked at him. She wouldn't give him the satisfaction.

She knew why he'd come. He was here to make her suffer. The only way to do that anymore was through Seth.

Precious, strong, amazing Seth.

The boy bent down, picked up some dirt. Straightening, he sifted it between his fingers, gauging which way the wind blew.

That's it, Sara thought. *It's just you and the baseball and that boy with the bat.*

She'd always been amazed at the strength and agility and sheer determination in her son. Although he'd been taller than her for three years, it still surprised her at times. At fifteen, he was as blond as she was, but his face was changing. Soon he would look like a grown man. In the ways that mattered, he already was.

He stepped to the center of the pitcher's mound, did something with the brim of his cap, pulled at his shirt sleeve, planted his cleats. He stared straight ahead. Concentrated. When he finally moved, it was to twist, winding up like a coil.

Sara held her breath.

The ball left his hand like a rocket. And missed the strike zone by a foot.

The spectators groaned as the third batter in a row walked to first. The bases were loaded. And the fans were getting fidgety.

"That's okay, Seth," one of his classmates yelled. "You'll get the next one."

Sara saw the coach motion to a player who'd been sitting on the bench. After listening intently to the coach's instructions, the boy nodded, then ran onto the field and took Seth's place.

Her boy's humiliation was nearly complete.

It was all she could do not to cry. The game continued. Sara just wanted it to be over.

She'd never hated Roy Kemper more than at that moment.

If she'd left him sooner, this would be behind them. She should have done it sooner. She should have left him after he hit her that first time.

Some of the later instances blurred in her mind, but she remembered those first incidents as clearly as if they'd been etched with a sharp blade and then burned into her memory like a brand in old westerns. The first time, Seth had just turned seven. She'd had a birthday party for him that day. Roy had worked at the factory over in Manchester then. By the time he got home, the little boys had been picked up and she had most of the mess cleaned up. Seth was spending the night with a friend because she and Roy were going to her ten-year high school reunion that evening.

She remembered being surprised Roy had wanted to go with her. Surprised and pleased. Instead of mingling, he'd sat at a table and drank. He was quiet during the drive home from the VFW hall.

Roy was quiet a lot.

Happy and light-hearted from the festivities, she'd helped him from the car and into the house. As soon as she closed the door, he'd sneered. "My wife, the slut."

Sara had had a marvelous time, but she hadn't so much as danced with anyone. She certainly hadn't flirted. She'd spoken mostly to women. Which was what she was telling Roy when his arm shot out, striking her with the back of his hand.

The force sent her stumbling backwards, and caused Roy to lose his balance and fall to the floor. She stared at him, her mouth gaping, her cheek on fire. He mumbled something derogatory and offensive then passed out.

In shock, she went crying to her mother.

Looking back, Sara realized that was where she'd gone wrong. Her mother adored Roy and always had. According to Agnes Walsh, Roy Kemper was perfect. If anything was wrong, it was Sara's fault.

Sara returned home, wounded in more ways than one.

The next morning Roy didn't remember anything about the incident. At least that was what he said.

Sara never forgot it.

The next time it happened, Seth was ten. Again, it was just a slap. Just. As if that made it less offensive, less brutal, less wrong. Roy passed out, but the next morning she told him if it ever happened again, she would leave. She'd meant it.

Maybe he believed her. Maybe he didn't. It was two-and-a-half years before he erupted again. It happened after her mother broke her hip and had to go to a nursing home. Sara knew it was very honorable of Roy to foot the bill, especially since he had to work so much overtime in order to do it. Sara delivered newspapers and did other odd jobs to help make ends meet. She wanted to get a full-time job, but he wouldn't hear of it. Money wasn't the only thing that was tight. Roy was on edge, and Sara could feel trouble brewing.

One Saturday night, Roy insisted he'd seen her flirting with an usher at church the previous week. At the time, she'd thought it was odd that he'd waited until Saturday to say anything. When he hit her that time, he used his fist instead of his open hand. The black eye kept her home Sunday morning. By then, Sara had no one to run to. Bills mounted. It seemed Seth outgrew his shoes every other month. Roy said it was a full-time job to keep one boy fed.

Sara stayed. Perhaps it was fear. Perhaps it was hopelessness. Surely it was dependency.

As long as she tiptoed softly enough, spoke quietly enough, kept to herself completely, things were okay. For a while. But then something would happen, and Roy would become distant, and then he would accuse her of flirting with the mailman or the teenage bagger at the A&P. A few months ago he swore she was having an affair with Sheriff McCall.

Inevitably, he would hit her. He always waited until Seth was gone or in bed. But Seth knew. To this day, that shamed Sara more than anything.

She'd never feared for her life like so many battered women. He'd never let it go quite that far. She didn't know how Roy restrained himself or why. She'd convinced herself that that made her less battered. As long as Roy didn't lay a hand on Seth, she told herself, they could still be a family.

Roy's rage didn't make sense. When he'd first started paying attention to her, he'd seemed like the answer to her prayers. She'd been jilted by her high school sweetheart the previous winter, and her two best friends were about to go off to college. She'd dreamed of becoming a concert pianist, but there was no money for advanced music lessons or higher education. Autumn was looming, and it would be just Sara and her bitter, fault-finding mother again.

And then one day a tall, good-looking boy from Rye stopped by the pizzeria where she worked. His name was Roy Kemper, and he seemed like a white knight in a fairy tale. Bringing him home to meet her mother was the first thing Sara had done right since nineteen seventy-nine. Or at least that was what she'd jokingly told Claudia and Brooke.

Claudia and Brooke and Sara. They'd dubbed themselves The Three Potters in tenth grade pottery class. And for the next three years, they'd been inseparable. Oh, those were the days.

"Strike three!"

All around Sara fans cheered. Her vision cleared in time to see a batter on the other team walk forlornly back to the dugout. Another player stepped up to the plate. The new pitcher sifted dirt between his fingers the way Seth had done. The spectators yelled their encouragement as the pitcher, a ninth grader named Billy, lobbed a ball toward home plate. The batter reached for it and hit a pop-up fly into left field. Fans cheered as the fielder caught it easily. With his new-found confidence, Billy struck out the next batter, too. And the inning was over.

Now, Seth's humiliation was complete.

Still refusing to look at Roy, Sara escaped to her thoughts again.

She'd been thinking about The Three Potters a lot lately. Just this morning she'd learned that Brooke and her daughter were in town for a visit. Claudia hadn't been home in years. The last Sara knew, the other two Potters were as successful as she always knew they would be. Brooke had married some rich man whose ancestors traced back to the Mayflower. And Claudia made hats.

Sara wore one of them today.

She plucked it from her head and turned it over in her hand. She'd found it in a bottom drawer three weeks ago when she'd packed up hers and Seth's things. It was a pristine white billed cap devoid of all ornamentation but for a single row of embroidery encircling the band. Inside was a tiny tag. Hats by Claudia. As Sara put the cap back on, she thought of all the wide-brimmed, bruise-hiding hats she'd left on the pegs near her old back door.

She'd been hiding more than bruises. It had taken her son to make her see what she'd become. Her precious, talented, defiant, sad-eyed son.

It wasn't easy not to cry for him today.

"Scoot over."

The voice came from behind, and took Sara back. "Brooke!" Sara made room beside her. "Just this morning I heard you were in town."

After she was settled, Brooke looked at Sara, and Sara looked at Brooke.

Brooke spoke first. "The rumor mill is rusty, because I've been here since yesterday. Roy's looking pretty smug. We'll make believe he isn't here."

"So you've heard."

Brooke's smile was small but heartfelt. "I said the rumor mill is rusty. It isn't broken." After a few more moments of awkwardness between the former best friends, she pointed to the far end of the bleachers. "That's my daughter, Sophie, sitting over there by herself, sulking. She'll be thirteen in August."

Sara digested the information. Pointing in the other direction, she said, "That's my son, Seth, sitting on the bench, sulking. He was fifteen in June."

Two mothers looked at one another. The years fell away, and two friends smiled.

Brooke's lips quivered. "Please," she whispered, "don't say anything that will make me cry or I'll hold you directly responsible for my puffy eyes and red nose."

Brooke never had liked the way she cried, Sara thought. "Don't make me cry, either," she whispered. "I'd sooner die than give Roy the satisfaction."

They both took deep breaths. Shaking her head, Brooke whispered, "Boy, we sure can pick 'em, can't we?"

Sara studied the other woman's profile. Brooke was thinner than she remembered, and her hair was shorter, but the classic beauty was just as apparent. Miss Addie had said Brooke was visiting. She hadn't mentioned problems. Sara knew better than anyone that that didn't mean they didn't exist.

"Do you ever hear from Claudia?"

Brooke shrugged. "A card at Christmas."

"Same here. What do you think she would say if she were here?" Sara asked.

Brooke cocked one eyebrow. "She'd probably suggest we tie Colin and Roy to a leaky rowboat and wait for the tide to come in."

The people around Sara looked at each other when she laughed. It was a new sound.

"It's probably a good thing Claudia never married," Sara said.

That struck them both silly.

By the time they stopped laughing, the game was over. But the renewed friendship had just begun.

CHAPTER 4

The kitchen in Eve's little house didn't have enough counter space. Or measuring cups. Or mixing bowls.

It hadn't kept Brooke from improvising.

She'd prepared a big breakfast for Sophie hours ago. Although complaining about boredom, Sophie had talked, more like her old self, before retreating back to the spare room to write in her journal. An elementary schoolteacher who had summers off, Eve preferred cold cereal for breakfast. The last Brooke knew, her sister was compiling her wedding guest list at her home computer in the living room.

It was Wednesday, and Brooke had a lot on her mind. She thought best when she was busy. Consequently, every inch on every flat surface was covered with the fruits of her labors. The best evidence was in the mouth-watering aromas wafting through the house.

Carter was the first person to follow his nose to the source. As he so often did, he sauntered into the kitchen, opened the refrigerator, and stood there as if he needed the cool air to wake up. Not that he woke up here. Brooke wasn't sure where he slept, but she appreciated his and Eve's efforts to set a good example for Sophie. That didn't mean Brooke hadn't noticed fresh whisker burn on Eve's cheek on a regu-

lar basis. Evidently, Brooke wasn't the only one good at improvising.

"Would you like me to fix you something for breakfast?"
she asked.

He looked at the clock, scratched his chest through his
faded T-shirt, and finally got out of the refrigerator. "No,
thanks."

He snitched a lemon tart and popped it, whole, into his
mouth. Moaning in ecstasy, he said, "You are a wizard."

Carter McCall had grown up in a house full of men. Jack
had been a grade behind Brooke in school, Brian a grade behind that, and Carter a few grades behind him. Somebody
had made certain they all knew which fork to use. Carter
said "please" and "thank you" when it suited him. It just didn't
always suit him. Brooke found that aspect of his persona
very interesting.

"Have you got me figured out yet?" he asked.

He did that a lot, broaching a subject very close to what
she was thinking. "I'm not very adept at figuring people out,
men especially. My husband is a prime example."

"He's a prime example of an asshole."

"You haven't met Colin." There she went again, defend-
ing him.

"I don't have to meet him." Carter leaned against the
counter, crossed his ankles, and ate another lemon tart. "A
man screws around on a woman, especially a woman like
you, he's an asshole."

She looked across the small kitchen at her future brother-
in-law. It was nice having people in her corner, but it didn't
change what was wrong with her life or her marriage. She'd
watched Carter this past week, paying close attention to the
way he treated Eve. He truly seemed to be sincere in his ac-
tions and feelings.

"I appreciate the vote of confidence, Carter, but I read
somewhere that if someone betrays you once, it's his fault. If
he betrays you twice, it's your fault."

"Whose fault is it that he's an asshole? Men are easy to

categorize," Carter said. "Unlike you women, who are complicated."

Brooke removed the first batch of espresso fudge cookies from the oven. "Tell me about these categories all men supposedly fall into."

"You already know about the asshole category, having been married to one for—how many years, thirteen?"

"Fourteen."

She appreciated the fact that he didn't gloat.

"The assholes are by and large the worst. Then there are the dumbasses, the smartasses, the sorryasses, and last but not least, the wiseasses."

She'd never heard anyone use that particular word so often in one sentence, and smiled in spite of herself. "Which category would you say you fall into?"

He tucked his thumbs into his pockets and rocked back on his heels. "I'm a wiseass, of course. Sometimes the boundaries overlap, but for the most part, one of the asses pegs us all pretty accurately."

Brooke was grinning openly now. "You've certainly cleared that up. Tell me this. Why do we women bother with you?"

"Because we're irresistible." There was a long pause. "This is the part of the conversation where you get to say what you're thinking."

She slid the second cookie sheet into the oven. "But isn't the art of conversation not only saying the right thing at the right time, but leaving unsaid the wrong things at the most tempting moments?"

"What fun is that?"

She blinked.

"If it ain't fun, it ain't art."

"Isn't," she said automatically.

"Now you're getting the hang of it."

She stared at him. "Does anybody get the last word with you?"

He shrugged, and it reminded her of Sophie. "Eve has her ways, but that's something I'd be more apt to share with the guys at the pool hall than her sister. Never let it be said that a McCall doesn't know his etiquette."

Brooke closed her eyes and shook her head. Eve wasn't going to have a dull moment with this one.

Fluffy padded into the room, going straight to her dish. Finding it empty, she stood with obvious disdain until Brooke shook out the last of the dry cat food. "Nice kitty."

Ignoring Brooke *and* the cat food, Fluffy walked stiff-legged to Carter and rubbed her head on his ankle. Carter leaned down to pet her. Of course she let *him*.

"How can a cat I rescued from the animal shelter on the very day time was running out hate me?"

"You try too hard."

She looked at Carter, and then at the cat purring beneath the slow, smooth motion of his hand. "Seriously?"

He nodded. "If you want a cat to like you, ignore her. Let her come to you. Works like a charm every time."

"I'll take it under advisement."

"Glad I could help."

"Men!" She muttered into the sink.

Carter chuckled on his way into the next room. "I warned you I'm a wiseass."

He was gone before she realized that he'd had the last word.

The cookies were done when Eve joined Brooke in the kitchen. "Wow." Eve looked around. "I don't know how you do it."

Brooke squirted dish soap into the sink. Turning on the water, she said, "Baking isn't difficult, but it is messy."

Eve helped herself to the last cup of coffee in the pot. "Speaking of messes, how did your phone call to Colin go this morning?"

"Not so good."

"That explains the baking marathon. What did he say?"

Scrubbing a pan with unnecessary force, Brooke said,

"He's deeply saddened that I've run away from *our* problems. Apparently, he mistook me for a woman who had more depth and strength of character."

Eve started to open her mouth.

Brooke held up a hand. "Before you call me a wimp, you should know that I told him his speech would have had more oomph if I hadn't heard a woman's voice in the background when he first picked up the phone."

"You said 'oomph'?"

"It was the best I could do on the spot."

"There was a woman in your house?"

"He insisted it was the television, but that wasn't Katie Couric's voice."

"Oh, Brooke, no. He never deserved you." Eve motioned to the newspaper lying open to the classifieds. "Are you looking for a job?"

"Not exactly."

Coffee in hand, Eve walked to her table where she read the ad Brooke had circled. "You're interested in renting a house for the rest of the summer?"

"I think it would be better for Sophie if we had our own place. You're not angry?"

Eve wore her long straight hair pulled back on the sides and secured with two red clips that matched her simple knit dress. The color made her face look pale and her gray eyes like liquid pewter. "Angry that you're staying in Alcott for the summer? Are you kidding?" She moved the newspaper aside and reached for an espresso fudge cookie. "You know you're welcome to stay with me as long as you'd like, but I'll honor whatever you choose to do. Carter's on his way to his studio, and I have to run, too. The Pilgrim Women's Society is meeting in five minutes and I'm acting secretary."

"Wait." Brooke arranged a selection of cookies and tarts on a large plate and hurriedly covered it with plastic wrap. "Take these with you. We'll be ill if we try to eat all this by ourselves."

Eve winked. "Expect compliments from everyone."

Brooke wasn't thinking about compliments when Sophie's footsteps sounded near the doorway a few minutes later. She was thinking about that voice she'd heard in the background in her own kitchen back home. Had someone been there with Colin? Should she have stayed and faced this?

She'd been devastated when she'd discovered Colin's affair two years ago, and had mourned as if something precious had died. She tried to categorize what she felt this time. Throughout the process of stirring up lemon tarts and three kinds of cookies, she'd come to the conclusion that she felt sad, disappointed, disillusioned and *stupid*. And underlying it all, she felt strangely unsettled. She was thankful it was summer, for it gave her time before Sophie had to return to school.

"Smells good in here." By now Sophie knew her way around Eve's kitchen, evidenced by her economy of motion as she made herself a peanut butter and jelly sandwich. "I talked to Makayla again. Guess what?" Sophe moved her tongue across her lips in the same direction she moved her knife across the bread. "The Prescotts are going to Europe for three whole weeks as soon as Toby's over the chicken pox."

"That's nice, honey."

"They're so lucky." She added the top to her sandwich, then stood near the stove to take her first bite. Looking at the stack of baking tins and utensils waiting to be washed, she said, "I bet you miss having a dishwasher, huh?"

Brooke rinsed a handful of measuring spoons. "I suppose."

"And there's no warming oven, either."

"Aunt Eve isn't much of a gadget girl," Brooke agreed.

"Guess not," Sophie said amicably. "Our kitchen back home has the best gadgets. I bet you miss it, huh?"

It didn't take a rocket scientist to understand what her daughter was doing. Brooke washed another cookie sheet.

"Hey, Fluffy." The girl lowered gracefully to the floor near the door. Sitting cross-legged, she petted the cat with one hand and held her sandwich with the other. "And there's not much room for Fluffy's litter box here, is there? I don't know how many times I've seen somebody trip over her food dish."

"It is crowded here. I want to talk to you about that."

"You do?"

Brooke nodded. "We don't want to wear out our welcome, do we?"

Sophie shook her head dramatically.

"Feel like taking a walk in a few minutes?"

"A walk?"

Brooke nodded. "It's a beautiful summer day."

"But shouldn't we be packing?"

"First we have to take a look at the summerhouse."

"What summerhouse?" Sophie jumped up as if bracing for a fight.

"The one up on Captain's Row. I circled the ad." Brooke gestured to the local newspaper open on the table. "It's reasonably priced, and vacant. I'm concerned about its condition, but it won't hurt to take a look at it."

"You don't expect me to stay in this bumfuck town, do you?"

Brooke spun around. Hands dripping, she stared at her child.

Maybe the cat gave Brooke the cold shoulder because she tried too hard. And maybe Colin cheated because she'd somehow enabled him to do it. But Sophie was on the brink of her teen years, and Brooke knew that how she handled this situation would affect them both for a long time. "You want to raise your voice, you go right ahead, let the pressure off. Vent if you have to. But that is not acceptable language. I will not tolerate it. And I hope you don't, either."

Sophie took a sudden interest in the toe of her shoe.

"I understand how difficult this is for you, Sophe. I know you miss your friends and your room and your father. And maybe you would rather be going to Europe, but that doesn't give you the right to be disrespectful to me and to use language far beneath your sensibilities, and mine."

Eyes downcast, Sophie mumbled, "Sorry."

Tears burned the back of Brooke's throat. Sophie was hurting, and Brooke's first impulse was to rush to her child and hug her, the way she always had. Brooke would have felt better. But this wasn't a mosquito bite or skinned knee or hurt feelings, and a hug wouldn't fix it. "It's difficult, what you're going through."

"It stinks."

"Yes, it does. Things have happened, through no fault of your own, and you have no control over them. You're angry with me? I don't believe it's warranted, but at least the emotion is honest. And honesty is our purest and most precious resource. Honesty is renewable. Words are not. Once uttered, we own them. They can't be taken back. Do you want to own the word 'bumfuck'?"

Sometime during the lecture, Sophie had raised her head and looked at her mother. She wore a chambray shirt and shorts with embroidery around the hem. The color matched her sad eyes. "I guess not."

"Think about it. I don't want you guessing here. I want you sure."

The girl sighed. "I'm sure. I don't want to own that word. Makayla says it to her mom. Now Toby says it, too. Guess their mom shouldn't stand for it, huh?"

Brooke dropped the towel on the counter. She didn't believe Priscilla Prescott was doing her children a favor by allowing disrespect, but Brooke had her own situation to deal with, her own family, and all the problems it entailed. "Now are you ready for that walk?"

"May I have a glass of milk first?"

"Yes you may."

"And one of those cookies?"

"Of course."

"I love you Mom."

"And I love you." Now, she hugged her child.

Soon she was closing Eve's back door and pocketing the

key. Feeling that they might just be okay yet, Brooke walked into the late morning sunshine with her daughter.

Mackenzie Elliot steepled his fingers beneath his chin, nodding at one of the five women who'd driven up together from Boston for today's group therapy session. All were wealthy and ranged in age from mid-thirties to mid-forty. They'd been meeting as a group for nearly four years. Even Mac's unexpected and temporary move from Boston to Alcott hadn't deterred their wish to continue.

Most of his patients were women. A psychiatrist specializing in family and group counseling, Mac was good with women. They loved him, and the truth was, women and all their nuances and layers and hidden agendas fascinated him. Take Nadine, who sat near the credenza across the room. She'd lost her daughter four years ago, and only recently had begun to lose the haunted, tortured look in her eyes. Next to her was Rita, who at forty-five looked thirty-five, compliments of Botox and her most recent Parisian peel. She tolerated her husband's infidelities in return for spending his money as she pleased. Meredith, the graying woman sitting beside Rita, hated her father and most other men including her ex-husband, but trusted Mac implicitly. By the end of the third session, he'd been fairly certain she was a lesbian. She knew he knew, which was one of the reasons she trusted him. After a few private sessions, she'd told him her reasons for remaining in the closet. He honored her silence. To Rita's left was Tess, who used to talk at great length about the abortion her parents had forced her to have when she was sixteen. She and Nadine had become very close these past four years. Married the second time around, seemingly happily, Tess had two healthy children, and often spoke of parenting issues these days. That left Georgeanne, who seemed to have no unusual skeletons in her closet, no nightmares, phobias or obsessions. She was delightfully funny and supportive of the other four. Besides boredom, her biggest problem was her penchant for trying to squeeze Mac's ass whenever the situation presented itself. He always made sure there were at least two people between him and Georgeanne.

A year ago he'd expressed his belief that this group no longer needed him, telling them in all honesty that he'd felt as if he was taking their money for nothing. All five had arrived at the next session with enough issues and tales of woe to last into the next decade. On the way out the door that day, Rita had smiled at him and said, "Are you ready to cry uncle? Because this is good for us. Your insights are incredibly valuable to us. It's our choice to spend a hundred dollars to talk to our friends for an hour. Last week Stanley spent more than that on flowers for his latest mistress."

So, Mac let them pay him. Recently, Meredith had begun to talk about her sexual preference, and Georgeanne finally opened up about her own hidden past. Mac did what he could to help them help themselves. And if, when the session ended, he felt less fulfilled than when he met with the small group of battered women in the church basement over near Manchester, so be it.

Deep inside this monstrosity of a house at 211 High Street, the phone rang. His answering machine discreetly answered. In another room on the main floor, his father was yelling for something cool to drink. Mac had taken him something cool to drink five minutes ago. His father enjoyed yelling almost as much as he enjoyed making Mac's life a living hell. Mac needed an assistant to answer the phone and a nurse to help with his father. The agency was sending over candidates for both positions this afternoon.

Three out of the last four nurses hadn't lasted a day. Mac didn't blame them. He wouldn't put up with his old man either if he had a choice.

His old man. Mac didn't have one clear memory of a time when his father had seemed young to him. Not that Archibald Elliot had taken an active role in raising Mac. Mac had been a year old when his parents divorced. From then on, his mother had made certain he and his father knew each other's whereabouts, but their paths had seldom crossed. The arrangement had suited them both.

Until, out of the blue, Mac had been called to his estranged father's deathbed nearly a month ago. Mac had told his associate in Boston that he'd be back in a week. He should have known the ornery old codger would be too stubborn to die. He'd been too stubborn to come back to Boston with Mac, too. So here Mac was in Alcott, New Hampshire, caring for his eighty-four-year-old father who disapproved of everything Mac said and did, listening with half an ear to Rita Delaney talk about the tummy tuck she planned to have next while Tess tried to talk her out of it.

"Damn it all to hell, Mac!" his father yelled. "Are you going to let me die of thirst in here?"

Rita stopped talking and looked at the clock. "I believe our hour is up."

Actually, it had been up ten minutes ago.

Mac rose easily to his feet. The women were in the process of sashaying en masse to the foyer when a knock sounded on his front door. His patients opened it and rushed past him.

"Bye, doctor!"

"See you next month, Meredith. You, too, Rita."

"I look forward to it."

A slender woman and a girl stepped aside to miss the stampede. He didn't see a car, which accounted for the sheen of perspiration on their faces.

On her way past Mac, Tess said, "Nobody would fault you for putting the old bastard in a nursing home and leaving him there."

Nadine agreed. "Better yet, the attic."

Mac smiled. Where was Georgeanne? He sidestepped her wandering hand in the nick of time. While five pairs of feet clattered toward Rita's Mercedes and five mouths ran at once about where to go for lunch, Mac turned his attention to the pair waiting on his stoop.

"Are you a doctor?" the girl asked.

"A psychiatrist." He sized them up. Pre-teen and mid-thirties, similar hair and eye color. The daughter had an air of curiosity about her, the mother an air of caution. Both carried themselves regally, the girl on coltish legs, the woman in a pair of beige chinos and Prada loafers if he wasn't mistaken.

And Mac was rarely mistaken.

"I'm here about the ad."

He had no idea why a woman would bring her daughter to a job interview, but he was desperate enough to overlook it. "I asked the temp service not to send any candidates until after lunch, but as long as you're here, please come in."

The mother and daughter looked at one another. "The temp service?" the woman asked.

"You're not here to apply for a temporary nursing or clerical position?"

She shook her head. "We're here about the ad regarding a house to rent."

"Ah." He'd put that ad in the paper three weeks ago at his father's insistence. It hadn't garnered a single response, and he'd forgotten about it.

"You called it a summerhouse," the girl said. "Mom says you couldn't possibly be from around here."

The woman's eyes widened, and Mac knew she would have nudged her daughter if she could have done so discreetly. He studied the woman's face, feature by feature. She had nice eyes, good skin, delicate bone structure. Her mouth was a little too wide for the rest of her face, but her lips were full enough to be interesting.

The daughter looked a lot like her, and Mac smiled at her. "I would love to hear your mother's reasoning."

Like most females on the planet, the girl responded to his easy manner and slow grin. "It's because of the way your ad was worded. Mom says people in Alcott don't call these places summerhouses."

The woman said, "Although the street signs say High

Street, people here have always referred to this as Captain's Row."

She had a cultured voice he liked. And a wedding ring and four-karat rock on her left hand.

"And why do they call it that?" he asked.

The daughter said, "Because this is the only place in Alcott with a view of the ocean, so rich old sea captains built their big houses in a row up here before the turn of the last century."

The woman stepped forward. "And that ends today's little history lesson. I'm Brooke Valentine, and this is my daughter, Sophie."

"Mackenzie Elliot." He shook both their hands, Brooke's last. Her fingers were long, her grip firm. For an instant, her glance sharpened. The handshake was over before he'd pinned down the reason.

"Damn it all to hell Mac, are you in there?"

Great. His father.

"Do you have a ghost?" Sophie asked.

"I should be so lucky. Please excuse me. If you'd like to wait, I'll only be a moment."

He left them in the foyer and strode toward the large living room that now contained a hospital bed and other medical paraphernalia. From the doorway he saw victory on his father's face.

"Maybe now that those women are done playing grab-ass with you, you'll get your bony butt over here and get me something to drink!"

Behind him, Sophie said, "We weren't playing grab-ass with him. Do you think the doctor has a bony butt?"

Mac thought about that ring on the mother's left hand, and knew better than to be disappointed because he didn't hear Brooke Valentine's reply.

Sophie's question had caused Brooke to look, briefly, but she made no reply. Many women noticed shoulders, others hair or smiles. And there were those who noticed rear ends. Brooke noticed eyes.

Eyes first.

All the rest followed, but eyes she remembered. Mackenzie Elliot's eyes were green and steady and intelligent. Something in the pit of her stomach reminded her that she hadn't come here to look at him. She'd come to look at the house, and that was where she turned her attention.

Captain's Row followed a curved rim on the northern edge of town. She hadn't been up here since she was in her teens. By then, many of the old captain's houses had either been converted into apartments or abandoned. This one was intact. The ceilings were high, the floors and trim original, the light fixtures antiquated but seemingly in working order. It was big and breezy, shadowy and secluded. Brooke could imagine the house in its day when it was new and gleaming and opulent.

She couldn't imagine living here for the rest of the summer.

Sophie's outburst in Eve's kitchen had driven home her daughter's need to know that her mother was steady and stable. Brooke vowed to pay close attention to her instincts and intuition, and her intuition was telling her that she and Sophie would be happier some place cozier and closer to Eve.

She'd seen enough. She wondered how long they would have to wait for Dr. Elliot's return. She could hear more swearing coming from a room toward the back of the house. Despite the verbal abuse, Mackenzie Elliot's voice remained calm.

The other man's didn't. "Get your lily-livered hands off me. I can do this myself."

"Dad, you're going to fall."

"Then I'll fall. Now get the hell out of my way."

"What do you think is going on?" Sophie whispered.

"I don't know."

Surely, it was curiosity that drew Brooke and Sophie deeper into the house toward those voices. They moved furtively, the way Fluffy did when her better judgment was being overrun by pure nosiness.

"You know I'm not going to do that, Dad, so just knock it off and let me help."

A series of expletives rent the air with enough ferocity to make Sophie giggle. The sound drew both men's attention.

Brooke and Sophie had stopped just inside a room that appeared to be a living room but now also contained a hospital bed and wheelchair and adult walker. A stooped, bone-thin old man was perched on the edge of the bed, hands gripping the metal side rails. There was a broken drinking glass lying in a shallow puddle on the floor. Beyond him was a window showing a large expanse of lawn, and then sky and ocean. Sea birds glided on invisible currents of air, and sunlight glinted on water far in the distance. The old man didn't seem interested in the view. He coughed and sputtered and swore, determined to do without his son's help.

"Are you all right?" Brooke asked.

Faded green eyes turned in her direction. "Do I goddamn look all right? I dropped the glass and need another and my no-good-no-account son doesn't give a crap."

"Maybe you should try asking nicely," Sophie said.

He looked at Sophie, and in a raspy voice, said, "I call a spade a spade."

"A minute ago you called him an f-ing idiot."

"Sophie!" Brooke said.

"Well, he did." She moved closer to the bed. "Except he didn't say f-ing. He used the real word. You know, mister, honesty is a renewable resource. Words aren't. Once you say something, you can't take it back. You own it. You want to own everything you just said?"

Of all times for Sophie to have been paying attention. "What my daughter means—"

"She talked in my good ear. I heard her. Put it pretty well, too." He was shaking, but he'd stopped swearing and coughing. "I'm dying. If I want to grouse a little, I figure I'm entitled."

Sophie said, "If you're dying, why aren't you in the hospital?"

Brooke was surprised when the old man answered politely. "Hospitals are for sick people."

"Then you're faking it?"

Brooke turned to the old man. "Please excuse my daughter, Mr., er, Elliot is it?"

"Why? She pass gas?"

"You'd know it if I did."

Brooke was horrified. It didn't lessen when the old man cracked a smile. She turned to the son for help. He appeared to be studying the situation, his pose typical for a man in his field, one arm folded across his ribs, forming a shelf on which his elbow was propped, his chin resting lightly on his loose fist.

His hair was five shades of brown, his eyebrows straight and thick, his skin tan. There were lines beside his eyes, from laughing or squinting in the sun, she didn't know. He transferred his gaze to her, seemingly as puzzled by the conversation between his father and her daughter as she was. She took the nearly imperceptible shake of his head as a silent request to wait and see.

The old man's grip had loosened on the stainless steel bed rails, and he no longer seemed intent upon getting up, unaided or otherwise. "It's about time I met somebody who doesn't pussyfoot around me. My name's Archibald Elliot. My friends call me Archie. I'm sick, but mostly I'm just old. There's only one way over that. In the meantime, you wouldn't think it would be too much to ask my no-good son to bring me something cool to drink."

"Maybe he thinks if he waits long enough, you'll die of thirst."

Brooke took Sophie's hand and drew her out of the man's reach.

"Smart girl you've got there," Archibald Elliot said. "My bark's worse than my bite. Truth is, I couldn't hurt her if I wanted to, and I sure as hell don't want to."

He winked at Sophie.

Something unspoken passed between them, and she grinned at him. "May I use your restroom, please?"

"Sophie," Brooke admonished. "We'll be going home soon."

"When you've gotta go, you've gotta go. Isn't that right, young lady?" Archie pointed with a shaking hand. "Down that hall. Second door on the right."

The instant Sophie left, Brooke became aware of the silence. Attempting to fill it, she gestured to the tall windows. "That's a magnificent view you have there."

The old man leaned back on his pillows, sullen again.

Brooke glanced at the son. He smiled easily, and she knew what had caused those lines beside his eyes.

"I take it you and your daughter are from Alcott?" he asked.

"I grew up here, but Sophie and I are just visiting."

He gave her one of those swift but thorough glances only a man could pull off. His gaze didn't linger in any one place longer than was considered polite, and yet something came over her, settling deeper, slowly tugging on her insides. She couldn't think of anything else to say. His gaze locked on hers, and it occurred to her that he was having trouble coming up with a topic, too.

It was a relief when Sophie returned, a glass of water in her hand. Being careful not to step in the puddle on the floor, she shook the old man's shoulder gently. "Mr. Elliot?"

He opened his eyes, blinked, and wet his dry lips. "Finally, somebody around here who listens." Taking the glass in both hands to help with the shaking, he drank the water down. Wiping his mouth on the back of one liver-spotted hand, he handed the glass back to her, empty. "You got a job young lady?"

Brooke said, "Sophie is too young to have a job."

"How old are ya?"

"I'll be thirteen next month."

"When I was thirteen, I worked from sunup to sundown. Kids are spoiled today. Parents wonder why our society's going down the tubes."

"Dad, maybe you should show our guests all your father-of-the-year awards."

The old man's face turned red. The son's jaw was set. Looking from one to the other, Brooke waited for the explosion.

Through the roaring silence came Sophie's quavering voice. "What would I have to do? If I worked for you, I mean."

"Sophie," Brooke said.

"Dad," Mackenzie said.

"What?" Sophie and Archie said at once.

"I'm looking for someone with medical training," Mackenzie said.

"It's my money that'll be paying her."

"Only because you refuse to accept any monetary help from me."

"Damn right I refuse. I don't need your money. Got plenty of my own. Plenty." Archie caught Sophie's eye. "You one of those spoiled little girls whose biggest worry is getting in the right club?"

"Mr. Elliot," Brooke said more loudly than she'd intended. "Whether my daughter is spoiled or not is not your concern."

Sophie said, "I didn't think I was spoiled, but lately I've been acting it. I'm pretty strong and sort of smart. You want to pay me to do stuff?"

"Might."

"What kind of stuff?"

"Sophie, I don't think—"

Sophie persisted. "You don't wear old-people diapers, do you?"

Brooke was more than horrified.

The old man's face was so lined and his eyes so faded it was difficult to tell whether he was preparing to swear or laugh. In the end, he simply said, "My plumbing still works most of the time, but that's about all." He was tiring. His breathing was labored and his eyes were drooping. "There are a couple of letters I'd like to write, things I want to put in order. Maybe you could help me with that. My eyes aren't worth a damn anymore. Maybe you could read to me. Do you play chess?"

"Yes, but not well."

"Then you need to practice. I'll let your mother and Mac work out the details. Might as well put that fancy education of his to good use." He slumped deeper into his pillows.

"We should be going," Brooke said firmly.

Sophie turned watery eyes to her mother. "I want to do this. He doesn't even have to pay me. We can just talk and stuff."

"We'll discuss it at home."

"We're not going home, remember? Not for weeks and weeks. You want me to make friends here. I just made one. Archie likes me. But this is another one of those things I don't have any control over, isn't it?"

"Sophe, he needs a nurse."

"I know, but he wants me, too. I'll bet he knows a lot of stories, and we could play games." The girl released a loud breath. Handing the empty glass to the doctor, she said, "It was nice to meet you, Dr. Elliot." She looked at the old man. "You, too, Archie."

Archie grunted a reply.

Raising her gaze and her chin, Sophie turned to her mother. "I'd like to go back to Aunt Eve's now."

The doctor said, "Do you want to see the summerhouse?"

She shook her head. "It doesn't matter what I want." Looking at her mother, she said, "May I go, please?"

Brooke handed her daughter the key. When Sophie was out of sight, Brooke said, "I am so in trouble."

Mackenzie Elliot grinned, sending that peculiar feeling to

the pit of her stomach again. After saying goodbye to Archie, Brooke followed the son from the room. In the hall, she whispered, "It's not funny, Dr. Elliot."

"Laughter is good medicine. I counsel mothers and daughters, husbands and wives, sisters and friends, and occasionally enemies. You've probably noticed the one area in which I sadly lack any kind of insight is the relationship between my own father and me. It looks as if you and your daughter are doing okay. And call me Mac. Would you like to take a quick look at the house next door? My father owns them both, but that's the one that's vacant."

"I've decided I should be looking for something smaller and closer to my sister."

He fell into step beside her in the wide central hallway. "Your daughter gets on well with my father. God knows she must be gifted. I need a nurse to help with his care, but perhaps Sophie would like to sit with him for an hour or two a few days a week. It might help pass the time, and perhaps she would feel as if she has a little control over her life this summer."

He looked at her with his green eyes that saw God only knew what. More than she wanted him to see, that was a given. It made her wonder about him, and when a woman was wondering about a man, she was thinking about him. Something told her he did that on purpose. It was part of the persona, part of his charm. He was confident, intelligent and well-spoken, something she was certain he knew very well. And used very well.

She came to her senses. "Sophie is already going through a difficult time."

"Because you and her father are separated?"

Brooke didn't want to talk about that, not now, not with him. "Forgive me for being blunt, but I'm concerned that the first person Sophie has befriended in Alcott is so ill. It'll hurt her if she becomes attached to him."

"Maybe it will hurt her more if she doesn't."

She had nothing to say to that.

Mac settled his hands on his hips. "It's been my experience that situations like these often work themselves out."

His self-confidence was off-putting. Again, it made her wonder about him. Oh, he was good.

"Look, I don't know you and you don't know me. Maybe I'm crazy and don't need to say this. I'll say it anyway. Smooth talk and beguiling grins might work on those women who nearly ran me over when I first arrived, but I've already been exposed and therefore am immune."

"Why do I get the feeling I've been insulted?"

He didn't look insulted. He looked as if he was enjoying this a great deal.

"Good day, Dr. Elliot."

He opened the front door for her. Making certain not to touch him, she walked outside.

"Brooke?"

She glanced over her shoulder.

"If you want to take a look at the summerhouse, it's open. Feel free to go through it by yourself. It would certainly be convenient to Sophie's work."

"You're very funny."

"Do you really think so?"

"You're doing it again," she said. "Trying to charm me, which is just a glorified word for flirting."

He stared into her eyes longer than she considered polite. "If I'm doing anything," he said quietly, "I'm flirting back."

The door closed, and Brooke was left standing on the stoop in the sunshine, the scent of the ocean in the air, and one thought in her head.

Carter McCall wasn't the only wiseass in town.

CHAPTER 5

Sophie was sitting on Eve's porch floor, the cat on her lap, her legs dangling over the side, looking utterly forlorn when Brooke returned from Captain's Row.

Choosing a spot on the top step nearby, Brooke faced the street, quiet at midday. "I'm doing my best, Sophe. I'm figuring this out one day at a time. This is where I grew up, and it feels good to be here right now. I need this time to think, but even more I need you to be okay. Will you be utterly miserable if we stay here for the rest of the summer?"

Sophie remained quiet for so long Brooke began to wonder if she would answer the question. Finally, she said, "Utterly?" She stroked the gray tabby's back. "Maybe not utterly."

That was one of the things she loved about her daughter. Sophie always managed to find her sense of humor.

"You're still really mad at Daddy, aren't you?"

Brooke smoothed a wrinkle from her wrinkle-free chinos. Was it any wonder advertising jobs were a dime a dozen? Joe Public was tired of being duped. Brooke knew the feeling. "This would be easier to deal with if all I felt was anger."

"What did he do?"

Somebody started a lawnmower two yards down, and Bruce and Doreen Briggs waved as they walked their dog on the sidewalk across the street. "I couldn't have asked for a man who loves his daughter more than your father loves you."

"Doesn't he love you? Is that what you think?"

What Brooke thought was that Colin didn't love her the way she wanted and deserved to be loved. She was trying very hard not to be one of those bitter women who encouraged her child to choose sides. It always ended up hurting the child, and that was the last thing Brooke wanted to do. "I think he loves me in his own way."

"But he still screws around on you."

Brooke swiveled so fast her hair flew into her face. "Who told you he was having an affair?"

"I figured it out." She sighed loudly. "Daddy likes me to use the proper words. Okay, I surmised. You wouldn't have dumped crème brûlée on his head unless it was very bad. Are you and Daddy going to get a divorce?"

Brooke had been expecting the question. "I'm not sure." But she didn't see any other way around this.

"I don't want you to."

"I know, Sophe." Brooke covered her daughter's hand with her own.

Sighing again, Sophie said, "I'd like to box Daddy's ears."

Honestly, Brooke never knew what was going to come out of the girl's mouth. Although if truth be told, it wasn't Colin's ears that Brooke would box.

"You want me to pretend that staying here is an adventure? Is that what you want me to do, Mom?"

Brooke knew better than to let her guard down. Measuring her child with an appraising look, she said, "Define adventure."

"I've never had a grandfather. Having one would be an adventure. I could pretend Archie's my grandpa while we're here."

A pretend grandpa who was dying. Sophie was well aware of that fact, and she wasn't giving up. Perhaps Mac was right, and it wouldn't hurt her if she got to know his father. "I want to do some checking. For all we know, the man could be on the FBI's Most Wanted list."

"And if he isn't, I can visit him?"

Brooke nodded.

Sophie sighed again. "I'll try to stop complaining."

"Atta girl." Mother and daughter watched as two children rode by on bicycles eating pizza.

"That looks good."

"It is lunchtime," Brooke said. "Are you hungry?"

"Am I ever! Know what sounds really good?"

"Better than pizza?" Brooke asked.

"A cheeseburger and greasy French fries."

Brooke stood. Reaching a hand to help Sophie up, she said, "Let's put Fluffy inside. I know a place that used to make half-pound cheeseburgers and the greasiest French fries in the world."

Brooke didn't recognize the woman sitting on the bench outside Cooper's Café on the village town square, but there was something familiar about each of the four red-haired girls sitting with her.

"All the tables inside are full," the woman said.

"We have to wait 'til somebody comes out before we can go in," the girl sitting closest to her added dejectedly.

The woman had a faint southern accent and brown eyes. All four of the girls' eyes were blue. "I'm Brooke Valentine. And this is Sophie. We're visiting my sister for the rest of the summer."

"Ginger Callaway." She patted the knee of the girl on her right. "This is Rachel. She's fifteen."

"Get away from me. Mom, Reba's leg is touching my leg."

"Next to her is thirteen-year-old Rebecca."

"Nuh-uh. Renee's leg is touching mine."

"Is not."

"Is so."

"And those two angels are Reba and Renee."

"You two are such babies," the girl Ginger had just introduced as Rebecca admonished.

"Well, you're a brat."

"Yeah."

"You think of *yeah* all by yourself?"

"Mom, Rebecca's ridiculing me."

The oldest daughter turned to her mother. With a martyred expression only a girl with three younger siblings could manage, she said, "Now do you see why I didn't want to come? We can't take them anywhere."

Ginger glanced up at Brooke. "This is why guppies eat their young. Excuse me for a moment." She turned on her offspring. "Thank y'all for making such a wonderful first impression. Remind me to pick up some notebook paper on the way home so I can start circulating a petition for year-round school. In the meantime, keep this up and you'll be mucking out stalls instead of riding horses when we get home."

The girls didn't look terribly worried, hurt or repentant, probably because they'd heard it all before.

"You have horses?" Sophie asked.

The second to the youngest girl piped up. "Mine's a paint named Polly." Adorable, the child looked to be about ten, and wore cowboy boots with her shorts.

Her younger sister said, "Mine's Polly's mother, Bunny."

"Bunny was born on Easter," Rebecca sneaked in. "I'm thirteen, so I get to ride a gelding. He's a Morgan named Big Fella."

"Part Morgan," either Reba or Renee—Brooke still wasn't sure which was which—corrected.

"Well he looks *all*-Morgan. So there."

Conversation bounced from one end of the bench to the other. In her element, Sophie said, "My friend Makayla has three Appaloosas."

"She has three horses of her own?"

"Well, her family does."

"We have six horses."

"Plus all the ones we board."

"When Mama was little she had an Albino."

"Had blue eyes like Daddy's. He was the hardest horse to ride in all of Kentucky."

Ginger winked at Brooke and mouthed, "Don't ask."

"In all the South!" the little girl qualified.

"That, too," Rebecca said. "You ever ride an Albino?"

Sophie shook her head dizzily.

"Me, neither. Yet."

Some of the cars going by had loud radios and old mufflers. Rather than waiting for them to pass, the girls simply talked louder. Reading Brooke's look of dismay, Ginger said, "In this family conversation is a contest. The first person to take a breath is declared the listener. My darlings haven't breathed since school let out. Looks like our girls have hit it off."

"Yes, it—"

"Care to join us for lunch?"

Brooke discovered it was easier to simply nod. When everyone started talking at once again, she found herself nodding a great deal.

In seemingly no time at all, the lunch crowd thinned out and the Valentine and Callaway entourage went inside. Ginger put all the girls at a large table in the corner. "No swearing, no talking with your mouth full and no arguing. Reba, I'm leaving you and Renee in charge. That all right with you, Sophie?"

"It isn't all right with me!" Rebecca said. "They're only eight and ten!"

Rebecca would have continued to complain if her mother hadn't sent her a quelling look. The youngest Callaways handed out the menus and spread out the cutlery. They were so busy being in charge they had no time to argue. Brooke considered taking notes.

As if it was the most natural thing in the world, Ginger

led the way to the opposite side of the room. "I thought we'd sit over here, unless you don't care if we don't get a word in edgewise."

Brooke grinned and pulled out her chair. She hadn't been inside Cooper's Cafe in years. The décor was still early fish shanty. The same twelve Formica-topped tables were surrounded by the same painted chairs. The curtains were fashioned from real fishnets, and the specials were listed on a chalkboard in a seashell frame above the counter where three diners sat on bar stools fashioned out of driftwood. The only thing brand new was the sketch of a mural on one wall.

"There's a new artist in town," Ginger said. "There'll be a lighthouse in the distance when Liza's done. Pete wants to commission her to do something on one of our barns."

Settling in, Brooke said, "Pete Callaway was three grades ahead of me in school. Six-foot-three, two-ten, all-star running back."

Ginger said, "Goes two-thirty now. Played football and pulled straight A's at Kentucky State. Met him there my sophomore year. He was going to be a historian and I was going to be a large animal vet. I got pregnant the first time he looked at me. As you can see, he looked at me a lot. After Renee was born, I told him that unless he had his heart set on trying again for a boy, he had two options. The least favorable of them involved having his eyes poked out."

Brooke couldn't imagine saying such a thing to Colin, but she grinned anyway, and asked, "How's his eyesight?"

"Twenty-twenty." Studying the plastic-coated menu, Ginger said, "I just love a man who knows what's good for him."

The girls may have acquired their eye color from their father, but their love of talking had filtered down from their mother's side. Brooke was glad Sophie had been hungry for greasy French fries. She was glad they'd come to Cooper's today. More than anything, she was glad she'd come to Alcott this summer.

"Pete teaches history and coaches varsity football in

Portsmouth. In our spare time we raise girls and horses on a farm that's been in his family for two hundred years. And I only threaten to make a gelding out of him on days that end in Y."

Brooke laughed.

On the other side of the room, Sophie stopped listening to the Callaway sisters for a moment, and listened instead to something she hadn't heard in a long time. It was her mom. And it was the sound of happiness.

The breeze was hot, the town still sleepy this early on a Friday morning. With the exception of one dog-walker, Mac had the sidewalk to himself. He paid little attention to his surroundings, focusing instead on keeping his gait even and his breathing steady.

A loud crash had awakened him at four A.M. He'd bolted upright in bed, pulled on sweats and dashed down the stairs toward his father's makeshift bedroom. The stubborn fool lay on the floor, one arm clutching his chest, the rest of him tangled in the walker he insisted upon using instead of a wheelchair.

The new nurse came running at the same time that Mac reached for the phone. He didn't care if doctors didn't make house calls anymore. With the obscene amount of money his father was paying Giles Grayson to insure that his living will be honored to the letter, the doctor could damn well afford to make an exception.

The physician arrived within minutes, clothes wrinkled, what little hair he had left sticking straight up. By then Archie was breathing easier.

After an examination, Dr. Grayson quietly said, "I believe he's suffered another mild heart attack. He's resting comfortably and his color is improving."

In other words, today most likely wouldn't be *the* day.

The doctor planned to stick around for a while. Greta had

put on a pot of coffee. And Mac dug his Nikes out of his closet.

He hit the pavement running and didn't stop until he came to the end of Breakwater Road. The incident had scared the hell out of him and he didn't know who to curse, the stubborn old man who'd sired him or the most manipulative woman on the planet.

His mother.

Hands on his thighs, Mac breathed deeply and scowled at the ocean. This had been all her idea. The last thing he'd wanted to do was hover at his father's death bed. He'd told his mother that in no uncertain terms when she'd called him nearly a month ago.

She'd said, "It's not something anybody enjoys, but it needs to be done. No one should die alone, not even your father."

"If it's so important to you," he'd said, "you go."

"Your father hasn't been my responsibility since I had the good sense to divorce him thirty-eight years ago. He's *your* father. You're all he has."

Yvonne Mackenzie Elliot had raised him, and she knew how to get her way. She'd gotten it into her head that Mac needed to make peace with his father, whom he barely knew, before it was too late. The one thing Mac and Archie agreed on was that it was already too late. Yet here he was, making absolutely no headway in the peace department, while the end loomed ever nearer for his father.

"Fate will prevail, darling," his mother had said the last time she'd called.

Fate, hell. It was his mother's wishes that would prevail.

Mac turned away from the ocean and headed back the way he'd come. He wasn't a firm believer in fate, but the truth was, if High Street hadn't dead-ended at a bluff thirty feet above Harbor Road, he wouldn't have had to take the long way back. He wouldn't have found himself at the corner of Marsh and Maple at eight-fifteen on this Friday morning. And he would have missed seeing Brooke Valentine running toward him.

Even from this distance, he knew it was her. Her light brown hair swung loose, not quite touching her shoulders. Her legs were long, her body lean but well-proportioned. She had a steady gait and good form, burning up a lot of sidewalk for a woman who moved so gracefully. He half-wished he was behind her where he would have gotten the full effect.

She wore navy running shorts, a white tank, and from the looks of things, a thin wisp of a bra. On second thought, he liked the view from here just fine.

He had a hell of a time looking away.

A warning sounded in his brain. She was married. Obviously there was trouble in paradise, but her wedding ring was still solidly on her left hand. And Mac didn't get involved with married women.

He wasn't getting involved. He was just looking. And she looked damned good.

"I thought you walked like a runner." She stopped a dozen feet away. "You know what I mean."

Actually, he did know what she meant. And it was a compliment. "Running is good for mind, body and soul," he said. "You must be seasoned, too. You're not even winded."

"I've only gone three blocks."

Such honesty. He was tempted to smile for the first time since his feet hit the floor at four A.M.

"I'm glad I ran into you," she said.

He liked the sound of that far more than a man who was just looking should.

"I was going to stop over later to tell you that if your father would still like Sophie to visit him, I've decided to let her."

"I'll tell him," Mac said. She would have run a background check for her daughter's protection. Mothers today had to think of everything.

She gestured to the house on the corner. "Do you see that

quaint cottage? We called it Stone Cottage when I was a child."

He looked at the aptly named house.

"The Baileys lived here when I was growing up. They moved years ago," she said. "I wonder who owns it now. That looks like a sign nearly hidden in those wild roses."

They strode closer to take a look.

Arriving half a step ahead of him, she reached carefully into the thorny bushes. "The place is for rent, but the sign has been out in the elements so long I can only make out part of the phone number." She looked at the stone house and surrounding lot. The weedy lawn had gone to seed and the small yard was surrounded by large cedars, birch and beech trees, tangled chokeberry bushes and more wild roses.

"Sophie would love this place." Her excitement was apparent in the way she slipped around to the side and looked through a low window. "It's furnished, too."

Mac joined her at the window. They both peered in, hands cupped beside their eyes like field glasses.

"It would take some cleaning up," she said, thinking out loud. "But the advertising agency where I worked downsized me right out of a job, and since suddenly I can't stand the sight of my husband, it isn't as if I have anything more pressing to do." She reached in front of him and tried the door knob. "It's locked."

"I assume the reason you can't stand the sight of your husband isn't because he grew a second nose."

"His face is as handsome as ever. The blonde he's seeing appeared quite taken with it." She looked sideways at him. "Which is more information than you asked for. Speaking of information, I had no idea your father won a Pulitzer Prize in the fifties. Rose and Addie Lawson couldn't stop talking about him when I mentioned his name. It seems they knew some of the same people when they were all young. They said he was an orphan, and has donated nearly three million dollars to orphanages throughout the course of his life."

Mac grasped the door knob. "My old man, the humanitarian." The feeble lock gave way the first time he slammed his shoulder into the solid oak door.

"Mac, what are you doing?"

The door swung in on squeaky hinges. "The lock appears to be faulty."

"It does now."

"As long as it's open we might as well take a look."

"We'd be breaking and entering," she said.

"Are you planning to damage anything?"

"Of course not, but—"

"Neither am I." He walked in, still rubbing his shoulder.

Brooke stared at Mac's back. There was something different about him this morning. He moved easily enough. Just under six feet tall, he had a runner's physique, wide at the shoulders, narrow at the hips, but there was an edge about him that hadn't been apparent yesterday. She didn't think it was anger, although Archie Elliot was not an easy man to deal with.

"How's your father today?" she asked, holding her position in the doorway.

"He was asleep when I left. The new nurse and his doctor were regrouping." He felt for the beeper clipped to the pocket of his running shorts.

"The doctor was there?" she asked quietly.

She sensed more than saw his nod.

"Trouble?" Even though he only shrugged, she thought she was getting closer to the root of his agitation. "It must be difficult, watching your father's health decline."

"Everything's difficult when it comes to my father."

Mac Elliot asked a lot of questions but kept his own replies short, leaving a great deal unsaid. In this instance, that was even more telling.

She stayed in the doorway, and he stood near an old six-burner gas stove, his white running shoes and socks in stark contrast to his tan legs and dark clothing. "You don't want to, but you love him."

"Is that your professional opinion, Mrs. Valentine?"

It seemed she'd gotten a little close to a nerve. "It's my honest opinion. Sometimes, there's just no accounting for taste, is there? I'm a prime example."

He opened a door she assumed led to a basement. Closing it, he opened another.

"What's in there?" she asked.

"See for yourself." It was a dare if she'd ever heard one.

She cast a furtive glance behind her. "If I wind up in jail, Sophie's going to have a fit."

But she went in. And it felt forbidden and dangerous and completely out-of-character. And fun.

Being careful not to upset anything, she looked around. Everything, from the table and four mismatched chairs to the chipped white cabinets and scarred linoleum floors would need a good scrubbing. She discovered two small bedrooms on the first floor, and a living room that contained a sofa, two overstuffed chairs, a scarred desk, and some discarded junk.

"Is that why you're in Alcott?" Mac asked from the kitchen where he'd remained. "Because you discovered your husband's affair?"

"The first time I stayed and toughed it out, but yes, this time I needed a place to go. Maybe it was fate that my sister called to tell me she's getting married next month."

"Do you believe in fate?"

It was a strange question, but he was a psychiatrist, and they were known for asking strange questions. "Don't you?" she asked.

"Fate is what my scheming, wheedling, will-bending mother calls my sojourn here."

"Ah, motherhood. Sophie and I have declared a temporary truce." Brooke opened the old oven door and peered inside.

"How is Sophie doing?" he asked.

"Better, I think. It helps that she's made new friends. Four sisters, actually. I guess you can never have too many friends. It had to be fate that they have horses. Sophe's mucking out stalls as we speak. She doesn't like to pick up things in her room back home, and yet she offered to help with the dirtiest and smelliest job on the farm. Of course they welcomed the help. With open arms. And open mouths. You wouldn't believe the chattering. They all talk at once. Nonstop."

"I have a therapy group like that."

She chuckled. "If this range works, it would be a chef's dream."

"Do you like to cook?"

"That's what I wanted to be when I was growing up. Instead, I became an out-of-work advertising wizard. What about you? Did you always dream of becoming a psychiatrist?"

"I had my heart set on becoming a fireman."

"You're good at busting in doors. Why didn't you?"

"My father approved of it."

She stopped fiddling with the old stove and turned around. Mac stood three feet away, the light from the room's only window falling across his shoulders, leaving his face in shadow. It was amazing how, despite that, she could see his eyes so clearly. He looked back at her, and the room seemed closer suddenly, and airless.

"Um," she whispered. A sheen of perspiration formed on her skin, gathering in the little hollow at the base of her neck.

His left eyebrow rose a fraction.

"It would help if you would say something."

"What would you like me to say?" he asked.

"Whatever you want." She managed to take a step back. "My future brother-in-law calls it the art of conversation. Remind me sometime to tell you about Carter's five classifications of men."

"I'm listening."

He was a good listener, a rarity in men, if you asked her. But they were far too alone, and she was far too aware of that fact. "You're quiet this morning," she said. "You could tell me why."

"There is no companion as companionable as silence."

"As solitude," she said. "There is no companion as companionable as solitude. Thoreau wrote that."

"I stand corrected."

He stood, feet planted, jaw squared, his eyes searching her face. He looked at her for so long she thought he might . . .

What, move closer? Touch her?

The moment passed, and instead of easing toward her, he moved away, all the way out the door. Brooke hadn't realized she'd been holding her breath until she released it and drew another. Alone in the dusty kitchen, she took a moment to reorient herself, then followed the course he took outside.

It was already eighty degrees in the sun, and promised to get hotter, but at least out here there was a breeze. She wished she'd remembered her sunglasses.

"Are you going to look into renting this house?" he asked.

"I think so." She glanced sideways at him as she closed the door.

"I'd have the locks changed if I were you."

"You would, would you?" she asked.

"Anybody could break in." One corner of his mouth lifted slightly.

Everything was back to normal now that they were out in the fresh air. They were both breathing easier, and she could think coherently. "Anybody already did."

"I won't tell if you won't, Brooke."

There he went again, and there went the pit of her stomach. "I think you may have gotten the wrong impression about me."

"My impression is that your husband and my father have placed us in situations over which we have little control. It's only natural that we empathize with each other."

She hadn't considered that, but it made sense.

"Unfortunately," he added, "this attraction has nothing to do with empathy."

She placed a hand on either side of her face. "You're not helping!"

"I'm just making a friendly observation."

"You call that friendly?"

"I believe you're the one who said you can't have too many friends. You'll have to deal with the attraction from your end, and I'll deal with it on mine, because I don't trifle with married women."

"Did you say trifle?"

He cast her a smile he'd probably perfected on dozens of women over the years. "I read *Pride and Prejudice* the summer I turned seventeen."

Brooke considered herself to be fairly intelligent, but she had trouble making sense out of that explanation. "You read *Pride and Prejudice* during summer vacation, without being forced?"

"I was trying to piss off my father."

Ah. "Did it?"

"It worked like a charm. But it backfired, because some of the language stuck."

"Seventeen is an impressionable age." She found herself smiling.

They stared at each other again.

"You're serious, aren't you?" she asked.

He nodded. "Very serious. Bring Sophie by anytime to visit my father."

They both fell silent.

"It was good talking to you, Mac. I mean that." Before those green eyes pinned her in place again, she said, "I guess I'll be seeing you. I'll bring Sophie by soon."

Mac was the first to resume his run. He hadn't gone far when something bigger than he was caused him to stop and turn around. Brooke was heading in the opposite direction. Light on her feet, she was a graceful runner.

He'd been right. She looked good coming *and* going.

He walked the rest of the way to Captain's Row.

CHAPTER 6

Brooke stared at the cellphone ringing on the table in her newly rented cottage. It was five o'clock on Friday, and according to the caller ID, the call was coming from Colin's office. She never knew whether it would be Colin himself, or his assistant putting him through.

"Do you want me to answer that?" Sara asked quietly.

"I'm being ridiculous. I've got it, thanks." Brooke placed the phone to her ear. "Yes?"

"Hello, Brooke."

Colin was making his own phone calls these days, her first and only thought.

"Are you there?" he asked.

"I'm here, Colin."

"How are you?"

"I'm okay." She was very aware of the dead silence. There had been a lot of dead air between them these past two years.

"Sophie says you've rented a house for the remainder of the summer. Is that true?"

She released a quiet breath and looked around at the quaint cottage she and Sara were cleaning top to bottom. "It's true."

"Why?" The question cut to the chase. He was good at that.

Brooke took a deep breath before replying. "You know why."

Eve hadn't known who owned Stone Cottage, but she'd known whom to ask. They'd paid Addie and Rose Lawson a visit. After that, it had taken a few phone calls to reach the owners, a retired couple who had lived here briefly before moving to Manchester to be closer to their son and his family. They'd been happy to drive down and show it to her and Sophie this afternoon.

"You're staying in Alcott for the remainder of the summer no matter what I do or say? Do you want me to beg? Is that what you want?"

"I don't want you to beg."

Sara looked from Brooke to the floor she'd been scrubbing. She got off her knees. Pushing her pale blond hair behind her ears, she quietly left the room.

Brooke went to the screen door and stood in the slight breeze. A car drove by slowly, and children ran through a sprinkler in the yard across the street. Somebody on the block had started a charcoal grill. "Eve is getting married next month. I'm staying to help with the plans."

"You're keeping Sophie away from me as punishment and you know it."

She felt a headache coming on. "I'm doing no such thing." Truthfully, she couldn't think of a punishment that would cancel out his infidelity.

"She's my daughter, too, Brooke."

"Would you like to drive up to get Sophie this weekend, perhaps take her back to Philadelphia and spend next week with her? Is that what you want?"

"You know I can't take a week off on such short notice."

Which meant he expected her to bring Sophie to him, and be responsible for her care. Brooke was doing that here.

"I have to work," he said. "Or have you forgotten that we have a mortgage?"

She hadn't forgotten anything, least of all how good he was at trying to make her feel inept. So far she and Sophie were living on her severance pay. She and Colin had a sizable savings account and other investments, and were far from destitute.

"What do you want, Colin?"

"Come home, Brooke. Please. The house is empty without you. Our bed is empty. My life is empty." His voice cracked. "I love you."

She thought of Deirdre. "You have a strange way of showing your love."

"I'm sorry. I don't know what I was thinking, but I ended it when you left. You're the only woman I love."

His apology made her sad. "As I said, I'm going to stay here until after Eve and Carter's wedding. If you'd like to make arrangements to take some time off to spend with Sophie, I know she would enjoy it. I'll leave the decision and details up to you."

"Is Sophie there?"

"She walked up the hill to visit a friend." Brooke had gone along, and they'd both met Archie's new nurse, a woman who had violet eyes and a steady smile. When Brooke left, Sophie had been accusing her pretend grandfather of cheating at checkers. Mac hadn't been home. It was just as well, for it gave Brooke time to put their earlier encounter into perspective.

"Sophie will be back in an hour. I'll have her call you then."

The rest of the conversation dealt with the details Brooke usually saw to. Many of their bills were paid electronically. She could manage them from here with her laptop, but Colin would need to put the garbage out on Monday morning. Portia was accustomed to being paid on the fifteenth, and the date was approaching. They'd been invited to a dinner party tomorrow evening. Unless he wanted to go without her, he needed to call the Hanovers and either tell them the truth or make up an excuse.

Brooke heard Colin scribbling notes. "Is there anything else?"

She was quiet for a moment. "I think that covers everything."

"Everything?" His voice dropped in volume. "Do you miss me at all?"

This time she didn't care that he heard her sigh. "I can't begin to name everything I feel, Colin."

He sighed, too. "I was vulnerable, Brooke. Can you understand that?"

She made no reply.

"I want you back. I'll do anything if you'll just give me another chance."

That was what he'd said two years ago.

Two years. Did he have any idea what it felt like to be cheated on, lied to, to try so hard to believe his promises, only to discover it had all been for nothing? Could he even fathom how much work, how much energy it required, day in and day out, to forgive? And for what? To wind up right back where they'd started? All because he'd been *vulnerable*? What was vulnerable about crawling into bed with somebody else? It was cruel. It was selfish. Colin wasn't a man who lacked self-confidence. He didn't need to have an affair to get attention. Which meant he did it because he wanted to, and because he could. He'd given her his *word*. His word was no longer worth very much to Brooke.

There was nothing she could do to keep her lower lip from quivering. And she knew it was time to end the conversation. "I'll call you if I think of something I left out. Otherwise, I'll probably talk to you next week."

She hung up without saying goodbye, then stood, staring at the phone in her hand. A sound behind her drew her around.

Sara waited in the doorway, her eyes blue and big in her narrow face. She'd always been shy. This reticence was different. Sometimes, it seemed to require effort for Sara to meet Brooke's eyes.

"Think it'll ever get easier?" she asked.

"God, I hope so." Brooke set the phone down. Donning rubber gloves, she began scrubbing the kitchen cabinets. "Men."

"Yeah," Sara agreed.

"Billions of them in the world, and I married one who can't keep his pants zipped and you married one who beat you. Could we have been any more stupid or unlucky?"

Sara dipped the scrub brush into the bucket and went to work on the floor. "Would you have married Colin if you knew then what you know now?"

"Do you mean if there were do-overs in life? Good question. Would you have married Roy?"

Sara stopped scrubbing the floor with such vehemence, and quietly said, "I wouldn't have Seth otherwise."

Brooke had been back for a week, and during that time she'd often wondered how Sara could have stayed with a man who beat her. Bit by bit, she was discovering that whatever Sara's reasons for staying were, they had to do with desperation, not weakness. And desperation and weakness were two very different things.

"And I wouldn't have Sophie." Brooke returned to the cabinets. She and Sara had grown apart over the years, and yet their lives had paralleled in many ways. Their most common thread was also their most precious. Their children. "Sophie weighed six pounds, eleven ounces. She was born crying. I'm not kidding. The doctor didn't have to spank her."

Sara said, "Seth weighed eight-and-a-half pounds. Most of it was in his head. It was as bald and round as a cantaloupe. He was almost four before the rest of his body caught up with it." She smiled behind her hand. "I've never told anyone that."

Brooke and Colin had told everyone about Sophie, all their family and friends and colleagues. And Sara had told no one. The reality and enormity of Sara's isolation brought tears to Brooke's eyes.

"I don't want your pity." Sara was looking at the floor she was scrubbing.

Brooke pulled herself together. "Good, because pity takes energy, and these days I don't have any energy to waste."

The friends stared at one another. Sara was the first to smile. "Tell me more about your daughter."

Returning to her scrubbing, Brooke said, "Oh, honey, you asked for it. When Sophie was a year-and-a-half old, one of the mothers in her play group bragged that her daughter, who happened to be two months younger, already loved classical music and could pick *Goodnight Moon* out of a hundred books on the shelf."

"Could Sophie?" Sara asked.

Brooke made a face. "Prior to her third birthday, Sophie's love of books involved ripping the pages out of them. That's not to say she wasn't brilliant. When she was sixteen months old, she could do a dead-on impersonation of a police siren."

"My, she was gifted."

Brooke laughed. "I told you. What about Seth? Did he walk and talk early?"

"He walked at ten months, but Seth was a quiet baby. He's still quiet. He was a year-and-a-half old before he said his first real word."

She smiled shyly again, and Brooke was struck by her fragile beauty. "What did he say?"

"I was always pointing out objects and people. Mommy. Daddy. Bye-bye. Baby. Puppy. Night-night. One day he picked up one of Roy's homemade iron anchors and heaved it through the picture window. It weighed almost as much as Seth did. While the glass was shattering, he very clearly and calmly said *ball*."

"A star pitcher even then."

Sara smiled. "I hadn't thought of it that way, but you might be right." A faraway look came into her eyes and her smile drained away. "All Seth has ever wanted to do is play professional baseball. I pray Roy doesn't come to the game tomorrow."

"What time should I pick you up?"

Sara's lips quivered. Ducking her head, she quietly said, "The game starts at two."

"I'll pick you up ten minutes to."

"Ten before two," Sara said, scrubbing again. "I'll be ready."

"It's going to be hot out on that ballfield today." Sara stirred milk and powdered cheese into the tender macaroni.

Screwing the lid back on the jar of generic peanut butter, Seth said, "Coach makes sure we get plenty to drink when we come in from the playing field."

They were preparing an early lunch. He sliced the sandwiches and placed them on a plate while she transferred the macaroni and cheese to a serving bowl. They could have done without the extra dishes, but mealtimes were for families, and she and Seth were a family.

They sat at the little table in the garden apartment where they'd been living for a month, and bowed their heads for grace. This was the third day in a row they'd had peanut butter sandwiches and boxed macaroni and cheese. Seth didn't complain. He never complained. It wasn't normal for a fifteen-year-old boy. But Seth wasn't like most boys his age.

She watched him, pleased that he ate with such gusto. Roy loved to eat like that. Seth had inherited his father's height, too, but thank God, not his temper.

Surely, all mothers believed their children were beautiful. Seth had a poet's mouth and the beginnings of a strong chin. Older than his years, he was the pride of her life.

Just looking at him brought tears to her eyes. Before he caught her staring, she reached for a sandwich and said, "How many lawns did you get done this morning?"

"Three. I hope it rains soon so everybody's grass keeps growing."

More ambitious than a teenager ought to have to be, he'd been mowing lawns since school let out. Sara knew he worried about their finances, but she wouldn't let him give any of his earnings to her. Instead, every week they paid a visit to Sheriff McCall, turning in as much money as they could scrape together. Nobody said it went toward paying for the street lights that "somebody" had broken. Only a handful of people knew Seth had been responsible for the damage. Those same people were discovering just how responsible he was, for he was paying back every dime of damage he'd caused.

He could have gone to jail.

And it would have been her fault.

She hadn't been strong enough to do what she should have done years ago. She used to tell herself that as long as Roy didn't lay a hand on Seth, everything would be all right. She'd made excuses in her mind.

Roy beat her, but not that often.

He hit her, but he'd never broken any bones.

Roy was a good provider, but sometimes he couldn't control his temper.

But. But. But.

Risking his own future, Seth had taken matters into his own hands. He'd forced her to see that Roy's beatings weren't hurting her alone.

Seth had nearly lost his chance for a baseball scholarship. The very idea that he might have ended up in a juvenile center or county jail still jolted her awake in the dead of night. Reverend McCall was counseling Seth. Sara attended a group therapy session at the church near Manchester once a week, and met privately with Dr. Elliot, too. She was making progress, but she had a long way to go.

She got up early every morning and delivered newspapers. In return for helping the aunts care for their garden and home, she and Seth had a roof over their heads. They weren't going hungry, and Seth was smiling more. She would do whatever was best for him. Dr. Elliot said it was imperative that she do what was best for herself, too.

She wasn't sure what was best for her. Yet. This for starters. This peace.

"Are you going to eat that sandwich, Mom?"

She glanced at the one in her hand. "Go ahead. I'm having trouble finishing the one I've started."

He reached for the last half on the platter. "I think I can get the Havlicks' lawn mowed before warm-up practice. What are you going to do?"

She wet her lips and swallowed. "I'm going to visit Grandma Walsh at the nursing home."

The sandwich disintegrated in Seth's fist. Forcibly loosening his grip, he met her eyes nervously, then clamped his poet's mouth shut, as if holding a raw emotion inside. The raw emotion was fear. And it very nearly broke her heart.

"It's time I told your grandmother I've left your father."

"She isn't going to like it."

He was right about that. Sara's mother hadn't liked anything she'd done in years.

"I'll go with you," Seth said.

Tears blurred Sara's vision. He didn't trust that she was strong enough to do what had to be done. She'd gone so many years without giving him any reason to trust in her strength.

No more.

Giving her head what she hoped was a firm shake, she said, "You need to pay off your debt. And I need to do this alone."

"She'll cry. And then she'll make you go back." Instead of rising, his voice cracked.

It cut off Sara's breath.

Counseling was helping her see how Roy had robbed her of herself. In turn, that had robbed Seth of security. She couldn't let him rob either of them of another single second of their lives. All the women in her support group had different stories, different circumstances. But their fear was the same. She knew the statistics. She knew that many battered women went back to their husbands. These men represented security and safety. Sara longed for it herself. Mac was trying to make them see that it was a contorted image of safety and a false security.

What was safe about living in constant fear? Where was the security when she was crouching in pain and begging Roy to stop?

Dr. Elliot didn't mince words. He knew the truth was hard to hear sometimes. He made sure they heard it often.

They began each session with a declaration. *I will not allow the fear of tomorrow rob me of the joy of today.*

She said it to herself right now.

She had so far to go, and every step felt like a baby step. Dr. Elliot had said the future was a culmination of a thousand baby steps taken one at a time.

Sara took a deep breath and looked her son in the eye. "I talked to Dr. Elliot about this, son. I've already given you my word, but I'll say it again. I'm not going back to your father. Not today. Not tomorrow. Not ever."

Part of her wanted to. Part of her was desperate to. But she wouldn't. One month down, the rest of her life to go.

"Now finish your sandwich and then go over to the Havlicks. Brooke is picking me up at a few minutes before two. I'll see you then."

She carried their dishes to the sink, then walked on rubbery legs into her tiny bedroom to change her clothes.

Sara's palms were sweaty as she pulled her rusty van into a parking space at the convalescent home on the outskirts of Manchester. She dried her hands on her cotton slacks and straightened her windblown hair before starting across the parking lot.

Her legs felt wobbly as she walked through the long corridor to her mother's semi-private room. Knees shaking, she paused in the doorway. The woman who shared the room slept around the clock. Her mother lay in bed, too, eyes closed. Some of the residents grew plants in their rooms and made pomanders and knitted sweaters and slippers and socks. This room was shadowy and smelled like sour milk and old breath. When her mother first came here, Sara had torn the room apart, cleaning every corner. The sour scent remained. It didn't come from the room, but from the very pores of the residents themselves. Her mother complained about everything else, but never seemed to notice the smell.

Agnes Walsh was a large woman who rarely smiled. Deep grooves cut lines beside her mouth and crisscrossed her ruddy face. Many people shrank with age. Sara's mother loomed, as large as ever.

"Hi, Mama."

Agnes turned her head and opened her eyes.

Sara saw the lighting of those watery eyes as her mother looked past Sara, to the hall. And she saw the lighting fade when Agnes realized Sara had come without Roy.

Sara sank unsteadily to the chair beside her mother's bed. Agnes had raised Sara by herself after her husband died. Sara didn't remember her father, but she used to look at photographs and imagine. Like her, he'd been fair and slight. Surely, he'd been kind and gentle, too. Like her.

"How are you feeling today, Mama?"

Agnes cleared her throat noisily. "The nurses in this place are horrid. If I've told you once I've told you a hundred times."

More like a thousand times, Sara thought.

At seventy-five, her mother was one of the younger residents at the County Manor. She was also one of the meanest. The nurses and aides weren't as patient with her as they were with the sweeter residents, but they weren't cruel.

"And the food. I wouldn't feed it to a dog." Her voice was raspy and grating. "When are you and Roy going to bring me home? Is Roy working? Such a wonderful provider. You're lucky, Sara. So much luckier than I ever was."

Sara looked at her clasped hands. Try as she might, she couldn't bring herself to say what she'd come here to say.

Her heart raced and her mouth went dry. She fumbled for something, anything, to say. "The weatherman says today is going to be the hottest day so far this summer."

"Weathermen, smeathermen. What do they know?"

"Are you practicing walking with your walker?" Sara asked.

"I'd like to see that idiot doctor use that thing."

Meaning she hadn't.

"You can't leave this place until you can walk, Mama."

"Roy is strong. He can lift me. And I can get a wheel-chair."

"Roy isn't going to be lifting you."

Her mother opened her mouth, only to clamp it shut. She turned shrewd eyes to Sara, who was rubbing the slight indentation her wedding band had left on her bare hand. "Why aren't you wearing your wedding ring?"

Meekly, Sara hid her hand.

"You complain to me when Roy gets mad. What do you expect?"

"I don't expect anything from you, Mama."

"Oh, here we go again. Here comes the guilt trip. You've always been whiny. It's no wonder Roy gets fed up with you. You'd better march right back home and put that ring on before he sees, if you know what's good for you."

Sara stared at the woman who was supposed to love her above all else. Innate sadness welled up in her chest. She wasn't completely sure what was good for her, but she knew she wasn't going to get it from her mother or her husband. Dr. Elliot said it was going to have to come from inside herself. It was in there. She just had to find it.

"I won't be complaining to you about Roy anymore, Mama."

"Well, Hallelujah. It's about—"

"I left him."

Her mother's mouth opened. "You lie."

"I'm not lying. I left him a month ago."

"You'll go back."

"I won't."

"You have to go back." Her mother's voice rose, part panic, part rage.

Sara's heart beat so fast she was afraid it showed. Trying to breathe deeply, she shook her head and wouldn't let herself cower. "I can't. I've promised Seth and I've promised myself."

"Seth? You spoil him! You always have! What about me? How could you do this to me?"

"Roy beat me. And you know it. You've always known it. At first it didn't happen often, but these past three years I've lived in constant fear and dread." Her voice quavered. "That's no way for your daughter and grandson to exist."

"He takes good care of you and Seth." He'd taken good care of Agnes.

Dr. Elliot had said it was highly likely that Roy had taken care of Sara's mother because it had given him leverage over Sara. He'd used Agnes's dependency on him to control Sara, to insure that she stayed where she *belonged*.

"You've always been a selfish girl. I don't know where I went wrong. Without Roy, I'll rot in this place."

"Practice using your walker, Mama."

Her mother started to cry.

Sara cried, too, all the way down the corridor and all the way home.

Sara felt drained when Brooke arrived at a few minutes before two. Surely, she looked awful. She'd had only enough time to splash her face with cool water and grab Claudia's hat.

Brooke had to know that she'd been crying. Sensing that Sara didn't have the strength to explain right now, Brooke carried on a one-sided conversation about the wedding shower she was planning for Eve.

It continued through the drive to the baseball diamond. It didn't let up until Sara took her usual place in the old wooden bleachers. Brooke sat next to her. Without a cloud in the sky, the sun was merciless. Brooke donned a pair of sunglasses. Sara pulled the bill of her cap lower. People behind them were passing around sunscreen. The stands were nearly full.

And Roy was here again.

He stood at the fence, a looming, brooding presence. Beyond him, Seth was warming up his pitching arm behind home plate. Evidently he'd been keeping an eye out for her. The moment he saw her, he walked to the fence a good distance from his father and looked at Sara, asking a silent question.

She nodded, all that was necessary to let him know she'd kept her promise to him. He tugged at his baseball cap, and although he didn't smile, she knew he wanted to.

The game started in earnest. Today, Seth struck out the first batter, and then the second.

Like last week, Sara felt Roy looking at her from time to time. She couldn't bring herself to meet his gaze. Instead, she watched her boy, listened to the fans, basked in the heat of the sun.

Tears coursed down her face as the last batter walked forlornly back to his team. The crowd went wild.

Seth had pitched a no-hitter. A perfect game.

His teammates rushed him and hoisted him onto their shoulders, parading him around the field. The spectators jumped up and danced and cheered.

Sara remained seated. Steadfast beside her, Brooke linked their arms.

"A thousand baby steps," Sara whispered, and her tears dried in the onrushing breeze.

CHAPTER 7

There was a party going on at the Valentines'.

Balloons bobbed from red ribbons and cars lined the drive-way and street. Mac parked near the corner between a Harley and a white car with several dents and one green fender. Sophie hadn't mentioned a party when she'd visited Archie earlier. Drumming his fingers on the steering wheel, he considered returning later. But he had the housewarming gift with him, and he'd promised Greta the evening off, and he would feel better if Brooke had this before nightfall. Deciding he would deliver the gift, then leave, he started up the cracked sidewalk, package in hand.

Music and laughter carried from the backyard. A little girl of about ten was sneaking around the corner, a Super Soaker aimed and ready. A slightly younger girl hid near the stoop. Braving the bumblebee buzzing around her head, she crouched low and placed a finger to her lips.

Mac winked at the child in hiding, and addressed the dogged pursuer who was sneaking up on the nearest shrub. "Is Brooke Valentine home?"

"Uh-huh." She doused the unsuspecting chokeberry bush. Seemingly satisfied that her sister wasn't hiding there, she said, "That present for Seth?"

"Seth?" Mac asked.

Next, she released a stream of water on an innocent rose bush. "Seth Kemper pitched a no-hitter today. That's who the party's for. You see a girl with red hair around here?"

"You have red hair."

Dismissing him as useless, she inched closer to the stoop. Mac decided it would be in his best interest to take himself out of the line of fire, or water, as the case may be, and knocked on the screen door.

Sara Kemper came to the door. "Dr. Elliot."

"Hello, Sara. Is Brooke here?"

"It's been a little crazy around here since Seth's game, but yes, Brooke is here somewhere." Balancing a large tray on one hand, she opened the door.

"How are you, Sara?"

She didn't answer immediately. That was all right. Mac was accustomed to waiting.

His patience paid off when she finally said, "I told my mother I left Roy."

He waited for her to look at him. "How does it feel?"

She bit her lip and took a shuddering breath. "I feel like a bad child. And relieved. And like always, scared."

"Very understandable reactions. Did Roy come to your son's game today?"

She nodded. "But Seth didn't let it affect him. He's never played so well. And it's just like you said. He's starting to trust me to do what's best for us. And I just can't thank you enough." She halted suddenly, looking everywhere but at him.

"Don't stop on my account."

She took a quick, sharp breath, but at least he had her attention. He saw in her eyes that she wasn't accustomed to banter. Smiling kindly, he said, "I never interrupt when I'm being flattered."

Sara's grin transformed her entire face. It was Mac's first glimpse of how she would have been before her husband started beating her. He would have enjoyed ten minutes alone in a dark alley with Roy Kemper. But this was Sara's fight, not his. Counseling was ninety-five percent listening, five percent suggestion, and zero percent punching some wife-beater's face to a pulp, no matter how much personal satisfaction it would bring.

"Brooke was in the kitchen a few minutes ago," Sara said. "Let's see if she still is."

Mac followed as far as the doorway. Although Brooke wasn't there, several other people were. The place had been cleaned since he and Brooke had looked at it. Windows were open and the floor shone. Sophie and yet another red-haired girl giggled at the table as they arranged what appeared to be tiny frosted cakes bearing letters of the alphabet.

A woman who'd been stirring a pitcher of something yellow leaned over them and read the message they'd assembled. "'Rachel has the hots'—Girls, I do declare. Put those little cakes back the way they were, do you hear me? And make sure you spell congratulations correctly." Next, she turned to a tall man who'd entered the room from the other door. "And you, you overgrown lummox. You're supposed to be helping. Put that Super Soaker down and make yourself useful."

The man Mac assumed was her husband and the likely father of the red-haired girls put down the squirt gun, but instead of taking the pitcher of lemonade she was shoving at him, he swooped down and kissed her on the neck.

"That isn't going to get you off the hook, buster."

He kneaded her shoulders.

Her head lolled forward. "That, on the other hand, will get you anything."

Just then the girl Mac had seen skulking around the side of the house earlier stamped in, planted her feet and glared all around.

"Mom," Sophie's friend said, "Reba's dripping on Brooke's clean floor."

"Reba, for goodness' sakes," her mother said.

"Don't blame me," the girl sputtered. "Blame him!"

The woman shook her head. "Honestly, Pete, how old are you?"

"Tattletale." He tossed the girl a kitchen towel. Grabbing the pitcher of lemonade and cups, he winked at Mac. "I don't believe we've met. I'm Pete Callaway."

Several pairs of eyes suddenly turned to him.

"Mac Elliot."

"Hey, Mac," Sophie said.

Still holding the heavy tray, Sara continued toward a door leading to the backyard. "I'll see if I can find Brooke."

Pete said, "This is my wife, Ginger, and two of our daughters, Reba and Rebecca. Come on out back. Thanks to the baseball team, we men aren't outnumbered out there."

"I'm not staying. If I could just leave this somewhere for Brooke . . ."

But Pete Callaway was already out the door Sara had just opened. And nobody else was listening. Behind Mac, an assortment of females giggled and groused and talked all at once. Mac decided to take his chances outside.

The grass was freshly cut and people huddled in groups wherever there was shade. One umbrella table held a spread of food that smelled delicious and reminded Mac how long it had been since lunch. Not far away three teenage boys were trying a little too hard to look cool in front of a girl their age. There was still no sign of Brooke, but a woman who looked a little like her sat at another table with a man and two white-haired old ladies wearing flowered dresses with matching crocheted collars.

"Do you know everybody, Mac?" Pete Callaway asked.

Mac shook his head.

"These two lovely ladies are Adeline and Rosalie Lawson," Pete said. "Miss Addie, Miss Rose, this is Mac Elliot."

Mac shook two frail hands.

"I do believe he has his father's eyes," one said to the other.

"Yes, that's absolutely right, sister."

Mac's gaze went from one old woman to the other. "Brooke mentioned that you knew my father."

"Rose and I met him years ago." Adeline poured lemonade for her and her sister. "Do you remember that day, Rose?"

"Remember!" Rose grumbled. "How could one forget? Archibald Elliot was loud and stubborn and, no offense young man, but he was very rude."

Adeline leaned ahead. "Rose swooned."

"I did no such thing."

"You most certainly did!" Adeline smiled sweetly at Mac. "Sister and I met your father at a cotillion. He arrived with cousin Theresa."

"Who?" Rose asked.

"Theresa. She wasn't actually our cousin, of course, having been related to Uncle Robert's second wife, Aunt Sonia."

"Sonia was Uncle Robert's third wife. Ursula was his second wife."

"Ah, yes, Ursula. She thought she was the belle of the ball. No one could stand her. Not even Uncle Robert, which is why he divorced her, as I recall."

Addie and Rose Lawson picked up their glasses and sipped their lemonade as if completely unaware that they'd derailed the conversation. Fascinating creatures, women.

Pete caught Mac's attention. "And this is Eve Nelson."

"You're Sophie's aunt," Mac said.

Eve smiled.

"And," Pete said, "the guy with the earring and the attitude sitting next to Eve is Bad-boy Carter McCall."

Carter shook Mac's hand. "It's just Carter. Eve's the only one who calls me Bad-boy, and she's earned the privilege, if you know what I mean."

Mac suspected that people always knew what Carter McCall meant.

Eve said, "Brooke tells me Sophie has befriended your father, Dr. Elliot."

While Mac was nodding, Pete said, "You're a doctor?"

"A psychiatrist."

Mopping his brow with a paper napkin, the tall brute of a man said, "In that case maybe you can talk some sense into Carter before it's too late. Tell him marriage is a three-ring circus. Engagement ring. Wedding ring. Suffer-ing." He lunged forward and spun around, sending lemonade sloshing in the pitcher. "Damn that's cold!" There was a large wet spot on the back of his shirt, and thanks to his quick spin, a matching one on the front.

"Gotcha!" The girl who'd dripped on the kitchen floor lowered her Super Soaker.

"What did you fill that with?" Pete grumbled. "Ice water?"

"It's your Super Soaker. You tell me." She darted away, cowboy boots clopping.

Pete raced after her in hot pursuit. Everyone at the small table watched until the duo disappeared around the side of the house.

"He doesn't look like he's suffering to me," Carter said.

Mac had been thinking the same thing.

"Hey, everybody." Sophie sidled up to the table. "Mom says I'm supposed to ask Miss Addie and Miss Rose if I can get their plates for them. And then Mom says everybody else had better eat if you ever want her to fix another meal for you as long as you live."

"Nelson women are bossy!" Carter said.

Eve nudged her fiancé, but Sophie smiled. "Mac, who's the present for?"

"It's a housewarming gift for you and your mother."

"Mom! Look what Mac brought us!"

And there was Brooke, heading his way in sandals, a summer skirt and a gauzy sleeveless blouse. Every muscle in his body tensed.

He'd done his dissertation on physiological impulses and the human reaction to natural chemical substances, most specifically, pheromones, the chemical substances released by animals to attract the opposite sex. There was evidence of pheromones in human beings, but scientists hadn't yet proven that the substance affected human behavior. On this particular evening in mid-July, Mac was trying valiantly to keep the proof to himself.

"Can I open it?" Sophie's voice came from far away.

Feeling the gift being tugged from his hand, Mac turned his attention to Brooke's daughter. All around him, sound resumed. Paper tore, voices carried, mosquitoes buzzed, people laughed.

Sophie held up the open box. "Doorknobs? You bought us doorknobs? Why did you buy us doorknobs?"

Brooke's hands went to her daughter's shoulders. "I think they come with locks, Sophe. This old house could use new locks. Thank you very much."

Mac didn't expect anyone else to catch the private joke, but surely he wasn't the only person who heard the low croon of Brooke's voice. If she was wearing perfume, he couldn't smell it. Even her makeup was subtle. He couldn't take his eyes off her. "Sophie didn't tell me you were planning a party."

"She didn't know."

He thought her smile looked tired.

"Until a few hours ago," she said, "I didn't even know. Have you eaten?"

"I can't stay." His gaze was riveted on her face.

"There's plenty."

"Thanks, but I have to get back to my father."

"How is your father, Dr. Elliot?" Addie Lawson's feeble voice jolted Mac back to the plane where the rest of the world existed.

Looking at the woman who had spoken, he said, "He's about the same."

"Give him our best."

"I will. It was nice meeting all of you." He spoke to everyone and looked at Brooke last. With a curt nod, he left.

* * *

"Mac?" Brooke caught up with him on the front lawn.

He stopped in the dappled shade of a dying birch tree and faced her. Tension radiated from him. Seth and his friends had arrived tonight wearing cutoff sweats with drawstrings or baggy shorts with oversized pockets. Pete and Carter had shown up in faded jeans. Mac wore gray chinos and a white shirt, the sleeves rolled up, his only concession to casualness.

They both turned their heads at the sound of a vehicle driving slowly by. The man behind the wheel had a stocky build and dark hair. Instead of waving, he glowered all the way by.

"I haven't seen Roy Kemper in years."

"That was Sara's husband?"

Brooke caught herself peering uneasily at the brake lights in the distance. "Yes. He showed up at Seth's ballgames two weeks in a row."

"Do you know if he's shown up anywhere else?"

"No, but I'll ask her." Brooke shivered at the thought of that man using his fists on her friend. After Roy's taillights disappeared down the street, Brooke turned her attention back to Mac. "What's bothering you?"

"Who says anything is bothering me?"

"Sophie said your father wasn't very talkative when she visited today."

A muscle worked in his cheek, her only indication that he'd heard her. Okay, he didn't want to talk about his father. She respected that.

"Did you and your father argue?"

He folded his arms in that universal way men do, clearly indicating that wild horses couldn't drag it out of him. And men claimed women were stubborn.

The shade brought some relief from the heat. Unfortunately, the gnats swarming in front of Brooke's face preferred it, too. Waving them away, she studied Mac. It occurred to her that he was a man of almosts. He was almost tall. Almost blond. Almost handsome. There was something about him that turned heads. He had an air of refinement and class, and yet there was a vein of the uncivilized in him. Mackenzie Elliot was one of those men who walked right up to the line and peered over, almost but not quite stepping across the boundaries.

Somewhere Reba Callaway screeched. Brooke said, "All the Callaways have screams that can shatter glass. Discovering four girls in one family has been a treasure trove for Sophie. She hasn't stopped talking about them."

"It sounds as though she's adjusting well to her temporary stay in Alcott. What about you?" he asked. "How are you adjusting?"

In all honesty, Brooke was feeling a little lost. But she hadn't followed Mac away from her guests to talk about herself. "My friend Claudia claims you can learn a great deal about a man by two things."

"I've heard this one. It has something to do with tangled Christmas tree lights and a rainy day. Or is it lost luggage and the flu?"

She cast him a look she usually reserved for Sophie. "As I was saying. You can learn a great deal about a man by the shoes in his closet and the car he drives. You don't buy your shoes off the rack at Wal-Mart, and I don't see a Mercedes, Porsche, or a Corvette, which happens to be Colin's favorite. Your car of choice would be boxy, not small. Quick but not too quick. And it wouldn't be red." She motioned toward a silver Volvo parked in front of Carter's Harley. "There. I believe that one's yours."

They fell into step together, shoulders close but not quite touching, their shadows floating across the grass far ahead of them. "A convertible. Nice touch. Hard lines, rich interior. We bid on the advertising account, but lost it by that much."

He looked sideways at her. "You're very sagacious."

"Sagacious." She tried the word out. "It sounds better than saying I'm a shrewd old bat."

Mac shook his head. There was something very appealing about Brooke Valentine. It wreaked havoc with his breathing, dulled his thoughts, and sharpened his senses. "Know what I think, Brooke?"

"It just so happens that's what I came out here with you to find out."

"I think this is the only car here with a Massachusetts license plate."

She laughed. "You're on to me, but I'm on to you, too."

"Are you saying you have me all figured out?" he asked.

"All? Hardly, but I do have a few things about you figured out."

Her eyes sparkled. She was enjoying this. That in itself was dangerous. And tempting. Desire reared again, and it had nothing to do with pheromones.

"I think I know what the problem is," she said.

"You do?"

"It's not really a problem."

Maybe not for her. "I'm listening."

She backed up, giving him room to open his door. "It's good to acknowledge something like this," she said. "And even better to bring it out into the open."

He slid into the driver's seat and shut the door before replying. "What exactly did we just bring out into the open?"

"Why, your—" She paused, looking closely at him.

"Yes?"

"There's no reason to be embarrassed or ashamed."

Clearly, they weren't talking about the same thing. Men were proud, lofty, downright boastful about these *things*, but rarely embarrassed and never ashamed.

"Really, Mac. There's nothing wrong with being shy. I think it's sweet."

Now that was a brand new word for it.

He looked at her.

She looked at him. "You seem surprised."

She was getting warmer. Hell.

He took his time formulating a reply. In the end, he forewent all his tried and true, even his wittiest rejoinders and simply said, "As part of your housewarming package, I hired a local locksmith to install those new locks."

"That wasn't necessary, but thank you." She studied him unhurriedly. "You're doing it again."

"What am I doing?"

"You're trying to change the subject. More proof that I'm right about your shyness. It's why you answer questions with questions. You're more comfortable talking about other people's problems than your own."

"I'm shy." Mac started his car.

"There, see?" Her diamond flashed in the sun. "Now you can admit it."

He glanced at her left hand, and drove away, leaving it at that.

"I think that's everything." Eve covered the bowl of left-over potato salad with plastic wrap then handed it to Brooke. "Come to Dusty's Tavern with us."

Brooke put the dish in the refrigerator along with the other leftovers, not that there was much. The boys on the baseball team had devoured nearly everything in sight. "Thanks, Eve, but I'm dead on my feet."

Eve washed her hands and reached for a towel. "I wish Sophie hadn't gone home with the Callaways."

"I'll be fine."

"What will you do?"

Brooke watched Eve's reflection in the darkened window over the sink. "Sleep comes to mind."

"Brooke."

"Eve, I appreciate your concern. I'll get through this. Don't we Nelson women get through everything?"

Eve sighed. "I'd like to tell Colin what I think of him."

"I wouldn't mind being present for that."

The sisters shared a smile.

Brooke said, "I've been thinking about the menu for your

wedding supper. Why don't you and Carter come over after church tomorrow? I thought I'd make up hors d'oeuvres for you to sample."

"What kind of hors d'oeuvres?"

Brooke nudged her tall, svelte younger sister who'd always been able to eat whatever she pleased. "I'll start with asparagus sandwiches on crustless soft bread, goat cheese with basil and mushrooms, and peeled tomatoes in balsamic marinade and bits of garlic. And then for the entree I would suggest lemon chicken or beef tips with portobello mushrooms."

Eve got a dreamy look in her eyes. "It's going to be lovely, isn't it?" Her expression became serious again. "Are you sure you won't come to Dusty's with us?"

Brooke squeezed Eve's hand and nodded.

The party for Seth had gone well. The baseball team had stuck around to help take care of the tables and chairs. A locksmith arrived while Sara and Eve were helping Brooke put the food away. Brooke had no idea how much the company charged to install new locks at eleven-thirty on a Saturday night, but the man made short work of it while Carter collected soda cans and trash. Any minute now Eve was going to stop hovering and let Carter drag her away, and Brooke was going to be alone.

It happened exactly that way.

Within minutes, headlights flickered on the living room wall. A moment later the rumble of Carter's Harley faded in the distance. Brooke turned on the radio and wandered from room to room.

Now that it was cleaned and aired, Stone Cottage really was a charming little house. The furnishings were more of the garage sale variety, but comfortable and functional enough to suit her present needs. The bouquet of daisies, asters, foxglove and roses the aunts had brought from their garden sat in a pitcher on the scarred pine table in the kitchen. Faded curtains billowed on the late-night breeze. Insects fluttered and buzzed against the screens, and the floors creaked in places.

She'd been running on pure adrenaline for two weeks. As midnight approached, the adrenaline seeped out of her. Arms folded, she clasped a hand on either side of her waist, and stared blindly out the living room window.

She was lonely.

She had difficult decisions to make. She'd known it the moment she'd caught Colin kissing Deirdre. Sooner or later she was going to have to go back to Philadelphia and face the music. What then? More loneliness. She'd better get used to it.

She yawned. She was tired, and everything always looked worse when she was tired. Before she got completely maudlin, she prepared for bed. Donning her knee-skimming white nightgown, she turned off the radio and all the lights except the milk-glass lamp in her new bedroom. Not surprisingly, Sophie had requested the room with the wagon wheel head-board and a plaid horse blanket at the foot of the bed. The only other bedroom was done entirely in white: Painted white floors and a white iron bed and white flowered wallpaper and mismatched white dressers.

Brooke automatically sat on the right side of the bed. For some reason, she turned around, staring at the other side. She was up on all fours and over before she'd analyzed why. In the early years of her marriage, the only thing she and Colin argued about was which side of the bed they slept on. Both insisted they could only sleep on the left. Last year Colin had finally worn her down. She'd been waking up on the wrong side of the bed ever since. Tonight, she burrowed in on the left side.

The percale sheets she'd bought in Kittery that morning were far less luxuriant than the Egyptian cotton sheets on her bed in Philadelphia. She'd washed them in the washer she'd discovered in the basement. Since there was no dryer, she'd hung them outside to dry. She'd left the towels in the sun too long and they'd dried stiff. The sheets fared better, and smelled like deep summer.

Yawning, she plumped her pillows. A plaintive meow carried through the quiet house. Next, footsteps padded across the hall. Evidently Fluffy was finally venturing out from underneath Sophie's bed.

The cat paused in Brooke's doorway. A stare-down ensued.

"You know where your litter box is."

Fluffy didn't so much as blink.

"And I just filled your water bowl with fresh water."

Still more staring.

"If you want to eat, you'll have to snack on your dry food."

Mention of food elicited a slight change in attitude.

"Sophie's spending the night at the Callaways. So it looks like it's just you and me. Carter says I try too hard. He's probably right. So. Where does that leave us?"

Fluffy made one of her cat sounds, part meow, part question.

And Brooke said, "Don't worry. She'll be back in the morning."

"Reeeooow."

"Everybody knows meow begins with an M." She kept her voice gentle, but she'd meant what she'd said. She was done begging.

"Reeeooow."

Brooke hugged her knees. "Don't tell me you miss Colin."

Fluffy sat down on the braided rug and swished her tail.

Brooke sighed. "He has the touch, doesn't he? Unfortunately, too many of us females are familiar with it. Maybe that doesn't bother you. But it bothers me. He says he loves me. Maybe he does love me in his own way. Maybe that's as much as he can love anybody. It's not enough for me. I'm not going to take him back."

There. She'd said it out loud. The sky hadn't fallen. The

earth hadn't opened. The only physical confirmation was the emptiness in the pit of her stomach. And that was hardly new.

"You're the first one I've told. I need to see a lawyer. I'll have to tell Colin and Sophie. It's going to break her heart. How can I do that? Damn Colin anyway."

Fluffy looked over her shoulder toward Sophie's room. Brooke fully expected her to flounce out the door, tail straight in the air. Instead, the cat padded closer and jumped on the bed, landing on all fours.

Another stare-down ensued. Brooke waited to see what the cat would do.

"Reow."

"I know the feeling." She offered the cat the back of her hand. Fluffy sniffed it, then butted it with her head. "All right already." Brooke laughed. "I'll pet you."

The gray tabby made herself comfortable at Brooke's waist. Easing onto her side, Brooke brought her knees up, curling closer, gently stroking the cat's back. "This isn't such a bad house, is it? Who needs Egyptian cotton sheets? Do you know what else?"

Fluffy purred.

"From now on, I'm sleeping on the left side of the bed."

The purring grew louder.

"Which doesn't mean a thing to you, because you sleep wherever you please." She sighed. There was no sense looking back. From now on, she would look forward.

A breeze billowed the gauzy curtains. The air smelled like the ocean and felt blessedly cool after the day's heat.

Her eyes closed and her thoughts slowed. This wasn't the end of the world. Oh, her marriage was over and she didn't have a job, but she wouldn't live a joyless life. She had a beautiful daughter and a soft bed and family and friends. She had her past to draw from and the future ahead of her. For now, she had peace.

She was almost asleep when her cellphone rang on the night stand. Fluffy opened one eye.

Brooke groaned. "Who could that be?" The caller ID listed the number as unknown.

She placed the phone to her ear and tentatively said, "Hello?"

"Did I wake you?"

"Mac. No. Almost."

Fluffy commenced purring.

And Brooke said, "I was afraid you were one of those heavy breathers who makes obscene phone calls in the middle of the night."

"I can if you want me to."

"No thanks." But she smiled.

"What are you doing?"

"Petting the cat." She reached over and switched off the milk-glass lamp. She could see the half-moon out her window, but all the houses in her view were dark. "What are you doing?"

"Let's just say I don't have a cat."

She smiled again. "If you start breathing heavy I'm hanging up."

His chuckle was deep and resonant and worked like a balm in the pit of her stomach.

"Where are you?" she asked.

"I'm in bed. If you ask me what I'm wearing, you're going to hear that heavy breathing you mentioned."

This time she laughed. It disrupted Fluffy, who stood stiffly then moved to the foot of the bed where she curled into a ball and promptly went back to sleep. Brooke stayed where she was, curled on her side in the dark, her eyes on the moon, the phone against one ear.

"There's not much to do in Alcott, is there?" he asked.

"That's part of its charm. Alcott didn't even have sidewalks to roll up when I was a child." She smiled at the memory. "It was so boring back then. Looking back, it seems so idyllic."

"You had a happy childhood."

"I did. I had a warm bed and my younger sister and parents who loved me and friends and dreams. Oh, I thought my parents were too old-fashioned and strict and I thought Alcott was too small and I thought I was going to conquer the world, or at least feed most of it."

"From the looks of the spread at the party tonight, I'd say you're feeding a good share of Alcott."

She hadn't thought of it that way. "Sara helped a lot. She's always been that way. Even back in high school, she was the nurturer, I was the achiever, and Claudia was the free spirit. We worked at the pizza place every Friday night and planned our futures." Brooke hadn't planned to marry a man who cheated, and Sara hadn't planned to marry one who bruised her.

"Brooke, are you there?"

"Sorry. I was thinking about something."

"Care to talk about it?" he asked.

"I'd rather talk about you."

"Trust me, you don't."

"Where did you grow up?"

He was quiet, making her wonder if he would answer.

"I can guess if you want me to. But it could be a long night."

Finally, he said, "I was born in upstate New York but grew up in Seattle after my mother divorced my father."

"How did your parents meet?"

"My mother moved to New York City to become a model. She ended up working at Saks. Evidently, Archie was in town on a book promotion. It was raining. He needed an umbrella. They met. She got pregnant. And he married her."

"With a few more details, that would sound very romantic."

"You don't really want to hear this, Brooke."

"You're wrong. Any idea why the marriage didn't last?"

"It lasted. For a year and a half."

"What happened?" she asked.

"My father was never a one-woman man."

Apparently there were a lot of men like that. The line was quiet on his end. She wondered what he was thinking.

"Talking about yourself isn't so difficult, is it?" she said.

"You're easy to talk to."

"You mean boring."

"Don't put words in my mouth. You have a calming effect on me. Well, on most of me."

When she laughed this time, he joined in. They talked about the weather and politics and books they'd read and the hole in the ozone. She told him about Fluffy and he told her about the dog he'd had when he was a boy. Most of Brooke's friends were women. Her father had loved her, but had left most of the parenting to her mother. Brooke liked men, but even Colin, who was always well-spoken and well-mannered— even when he was having an affair—often seemed to be of another species. Men had deep voices and Adam's apples and whiskers and a fascination with the television remote. Mackenzie Elliot most likely shared many of those traits, which made the fact that she was so comfortable talking to him all the more surprising.

"You meant what you said yesterday, didn't you?" she asked quietly.

Silence.

"Are you asleep, Mac?"

"I'm listening. I always mean what I say, but why don't you refresh my memory."

"You said you don't trifle with married women."

"That's right. I don't."

"Then why did you call?"

Mac started, bumping his elbow on the massive head-board of the king-size bed he'd had delivered when it became apparent that his stay in Alcott was going to be an extended one. "Oh. I guess I got a little side-tracked. I called to ask if the locksmith installed the new locks."

"Yes, he did. Again, thank you. Now, back to your mother."

Mac settled deeper into his pillows and stared out the

window. He'd chosen this third-floor bedroom because of the view. Tonight all he could see was the black sky and a spattering of stars. Maybe it was the dark. Or maybe it had to do with the way he and Brooke were both stranded in Alcott between lives. Whatever the reason, it didn't feel strange to talk to her about personal matters. And she certainly asked her share of personal questions.

"What about my mother?"

"Did she remarry?"

"Why would she do that when she's always had me to coerce and manipulate?"

"I hate to be the one to tell you this, but I heard affection in your voice just now. You love your mother and have a love-hate relationship with your father."

"Put that way, I should be a textbook case of arrested development."

"Who says you're not?"

His chuckle was a low rumble through the dark bedroom in the big old house on Captain's Row. When she yawned noisily, he said, "We should both get some sleep."

"I'm glad you called, Mac."

"May I ask why?"

"I'd fall asleep before I ever explained this properly. Suffice to say that I really needed a friend tonight. Goodnight."

She hung up before he'd answered. It was as if she'd known he hadn't planned to.

Mac lay in the drowsy warmth of his bed, covered to the waist with a sheet, lost in thought. How had he put it yesterday? Due to circumstances beyond their control, he and Brooke were both stranded here temporarily. They had a mutual understanding, and thus a unique friendship had begun.

He had to wonder if he was playing with fire.

CHAPTER 8

"There's Greta," Sophie said.

Brooke parked the car and peered through the gray drizzle at the woman trying to stay dry beneath the drooping blue and white awning. Greta Cavanaugh claimed she was only forty-five. Brooke would have guessed fifty, and that was being kind. She had linebacker shoulders and light brown eyes, a toe ring and at least one tattoo. She was wonderful with Archie and Sophie, too.

"Hey, Greta," Sophie called, being careful to stay under the umbrella her mother was holding over their heads. "I thought you were quitting."

The heavyset woman took another draw on her cigarette before snuffing it out beneath her sandal. "I've been quitting for twenty years." Noticing that their hands were full, she opened the door and held it.

"How is Archie today?" Brooke asked on her way in.

Greta grimaced. "I think the aliens forgot to remove the probe."

Brooke entered Mac's house smiling.

It didn't sound as though there was any smiling going on inside 211 High Street. Archie was yelling and coughing and sputtering. "Get that putrid poor excuse for food away from me. Are you trying to poison me?"

"I'm not poisoning you and you know it. Come on, Dad. You have to eat."

"Stop treating me like a goddamned two-year-old."

"Then stop acting like a goddamned two-year-old."

Brooke and Sophie hurriedly arranged the hot food on a plate then stacked everything on an old tray. Slipping two daisies into a makeshift vase, Brooke added it to the tray as Sophie entered the living room.

"Try the soup at least," Mac said.

"You try the soup!" Mac's back was to them, but Archie knew darned well Brooke and Sophie were there. It didn't keep him from grumbling. "How the hell can anybody burn canned soup?" He coughed. When he spoke again, his voice was weaker. "I would have thought a mama's boy like you would have learned how to cook."

"Hey, Archie. Hi, Mac." Sophie walked carefully so as not to spill anything. "Mom and I brought you a surprise."

"What is it?" Archie groused.

Brooke eased around to the far side of the bed. Lifting away whatever Mac had been serving, she made room for the new tray. "Seasoned rice and beef tips with—"

She glanced at Mac. His hair stood in rows as if his fingers had recently raked through it. His cheeks and jaw bore the shadow of a five o'clock beard.

"Portobello mushrooms, and—" The entire house grew silent. "Steamed asparagus and—" The air darkened. He'd done it all with one long, steady look.

Asparagus and what?

She looked out the window. Thunder rumbled in the distance. Rain pelted the wavy glass and formed a gray curtain between here and the ocean.

Mac hadn't darkened the sky. The storm had.

She'd heard of people whose brains got foggy when the barometer fell, but it didn't usually happen to her. "I prepared a few entrees as samples for my sister's upcoming wedding reception. I'll bring the glazed chicken tomorrow if you'd like."

Archie grunted something noncommittal, but at least he was showing some interest in the food on his plate. Mac left the room without a sound.

Brooke followed him into the kitchen. "Having fun?"

"The stubborn fool won't even try to eat my cooking."

She sniffed the air. "What is that aroma? Burnt something."

"Very funny. Okay, I burned the Hamburger Helper, but there's nothing wrong with the soup."

She sniffed the air again. "I mean it, Mac." She pointed to the smoke curling from around the oven door. "Something's on fire."

"Hell." Mac yanked open the oven door. Black smoke billowed out. The smoke alarm blared, one decibel shy of splitting their eardrums.

Brooke rummaged through cabinets for baking soda. He grabbed a fire extinguisher from the broom closet, opened the oven, and took aim. Smoke continued to billow. The alarm continued to blare. But the fire sputtered out.

Sophie raced into the room, her hands over her ears. "What's going on?"

Brooke spoke over her shoulder. "Something was burning in the oven, but Mac put it out."

Seeing that they had things under control, Sophie returned to the living room, sliding the heavy pocket door behind her. Mac opened the kitchen windows and Brooke turned on the exhaust fan over the stove. All the while, she fanned the smoke alarm with an empty pizza box. Finally, the horrendous blaring stopped.

Mac stood at the old stove, a kitchen towel thrown over one shoulder, the charred pan held in one oven-mittened hand. She joined him there, staring at what had started life as frozen Italian bread.

"Mac, I think your oven might be a little hot."

Mac had been in a battle of wills with his father all day. He hadn't intended to nearly burn the place down. He hadn't known Brooke and her daughter were going to bring food, and he sure as hell hadn't expected to be glad they had. Brooke's wry humor started a vibration deep inside him. One more thing he hadn't expected.

She bent over and smelled the soup, wrinkling her nose. "It probably tastes better than it smells, right?"

He nodded.

And she said, "Care to try it?"

The way he shook his head must have struck her funny, because she burst out laughing. Mac couldn't help himself. He threw back his head and laughed, too. He roared. She chortled. They wound up holding onto their stomachs, chests heaving, laughing so hard it hurt.

God, it felt good.

Trying to get themselves under control, they took deep breaths and made pained sounds. But then they looked at that charred bread and congealed soup and the guffaws and snorts started up again.

"Lord help me," she gasped, "I'm going to put out a rib."

Mac saw her with such clarity. She held one hand over her stomach and one over her heart. Her eyes were a startling blue in the early twilight, her teeth just crowded enough to keep her smile from looking like everyone else's. It would be easy to lift her face with two fingers placed gently beneath her chin.

He took an unsteady breath, and moved away.

Realizing he was still holding the charred pan, he tossed it, burnt bread and all, into the old cast iron sink. Brooke glanced at him, and he wondered if she knew how close he'd come to kissing her.

Her eyes brimmed with moisture from laughing. If she felt more, she hadn't analyzed it.

"You know, Mac, it's too bad Greta can't help out with the cooking."

"The Hamburger Helper was her idea."

Why that was hilarious, he didn't know, but they started to laugh all over again. It was how Sophie found them when she entered the kitchen, the tray in her hands. "What's so funny?"

Brooke said, "Nothing."

At the same time, Mac said, "Evidently everything." He took the tray from Sophie. "Is Archie finished?"

The girl shrugged. "He fell asleep."

Mac looked at the uneaten meal and instantly sobered. It wasn't just his cooking. Archie was losing his appetite. Dr. Grayson had said this would happen.

Brooke gathered the empty casserole dishes and bags and handed Sophie the umbrella. At the door, Brooke said, "I think I know why a boy who wanted to be a fireman became a psychiatrist instead."

Responding to the lingering traces of laughter in her voice, he said, "By all means enlighten me."

"You have the best of both worlds. You help people work through their problems *and* you put out fires."

He remembered her smile long after she'd gone.

Brooke drove slowly toward Stone Cottage. Sophie stared out the window. It wasn't like her daughter to be this quiet.

"Something on your mind, Sophe?"

"I was just thinking."

Tires splashed through puddles and Sophie continued to stare out the window.

"Mom, are there horses in heaven?"

Brooke didn't recall any mention of heavenly horses from the Bible stories she'd learned as a child. "I suppose it's possible."

"What about snakes?"

"If I remember correctly, the only snake was the serpent in the Garden of Eden."

"What about alligators."

"Alligators?"

"And spiders."

"There were scourges and famines and locusts, but those were on earth, not in heaven."

"What about bats and scorpions and sharks."

"What about them, Sophie?"

"There aren't any oceans in heaven, so there can't be sharks, right?"

"That makes sense to me."

"So I guess Archie will be okay there."

So that's what this was about. Brooke reached her hand to Sophie's long ponytail. Squeezing it gently, she said, "I think death is hardest on the people left behind. I'm pretty sure the souls in heaven love it there."

"So much that they wouldn't want to come back?"

Sophie asked the darnedest questions. Doing her best to put her daughter's mind at ease, Brooke said, "I read about a woman who died on the operating table and went to heaven. When the doctors started her heart again, she had to return to earth, and she wasn't happy about it."

"Why not?"

"She loved it there. Evidently, they don't call it heaven for nothing."

Sophie was quiet as she considered that. "Wait until Archie gets there and starts bossing all the angels and other souls around. They'll probably start a petition to get him sent back."

Brooke laughed. It seemed she'd been doing a lot of that today.

"Hello, Sara."

Sara froze in mid-step.

"How have you been?" Roy's voice came from someplace behind her, a deep baritone that carried over the rumble of an engine.

Her knees wobbled. Any second now, they were going to give out. "I'm fine," she said without looking at him.

"Your mother called me today. Why'd you go and tell her? Now she's all upset. Come on home, Sara."

The truck eased into her line of vision. She'd heard Roy bought a new truck. And she and Seth were eating peanut butter and macaroni and cheese. Sara closed her eyes. When she opened them, she focused on Stone Cottage, half a block away.

Seth was away for the week, and Sara had decided to walk to Brooke's house. It was Monday. Why wasn't Roy working?

She wasn't ready to face him, and Dr. Elliot had told her she didn't have to until she was ready. She repeated one of the affirmations he had the group say every week. *I am in charge of my own life. I am in charge of my own life. I am in charge of my life.*

At first her feet wouldn't move. But she forced one in front of the other.

"Sara, wait! Goddamn it, I just want to talk to you."

She started to run.

"Get back here. You're making a mistake! Do you hear me?"

She rushed headlong up Brooke's gravel driveway.

Behind her, Roy shouted, "You'll be sorry."

Her heart was jumping in her chest as she pounded on Brooke's door. Dear God, let her be home.

She pushed her way inside the instant it opened.

"What's wrong?" Brooke asked.

"Roy."

"Where is Roy?"

She couldn't bring herself to look behind her. "He followed me."

Brooke peered both ways. "No one's there, Sara. He's gone."

Finally, Sara looked, too. Finding the coast clear, she felt silly. She'd overreacted. She couldn't do anything right.

Brooke led her to the sofa and had her sit down. "Tell me what he did."

"He didn't do anything, really, except talk to me."

"What did he say?"

Worrying a wrinkle in her faded slacks, Sara whispered, "He said I'm making a mistake. And he told me I'll be sorry."

Brooke perched on the arm of the sofa. "Roy drove past this house Saturday night, too. He would have seen your van in the driveway. I have an appointment with an attorney in a few minutes. I think you should come with me."

"You're seeing an attorney?"

Brooke hesitated, then forced the words out of her mouth. "My marriage is over." Ducking down, she caught Sara's gaze. "So far I've only told you and the cat. I need legal advice. I think we both do."

Sara was shaking her head before Brooke finished speaking. "It took everything I saved from delivering papers to pay for Seth's baseball camp this week. I don't have any money left to pay for an attorney."

Finding her feet, Brooke pulled Sara up, too. "Then come along as moral support for me. Who knows, maybe Natalie Harper will give us a deal."

"What kind of deal?" Sara's eyes were blue and large and wary in her oval face.

"The kind of deal that was the rage last year in nearly every ad campaign. Buy one, get one free."

Sara's eyes were still large. It made her small smile all the more brave."

"What exactly did your husband say, Mrs. Kemper?"

Natalie Harper's law office was located in an old Victorian house around the corner from the village square. It contained suitable office furniture and the usual filing cabinets as well as the proper framed certificates on the wall. The walls themselves were the color of ripe plums and clashed with Natalie's orange and fuchsia skirt and blouse.

"Please. Call me Sara." Sara leaned forward, earnest and intense, fingers clasped in her lap. "Roy said he wanted to talk to me."

Brooke sat back, wondering if she should have looked farther for an attorney. Eve had recommended Natalie, who happened to be engaged to Carter's brother, Brian. Normally, Brooke trusted Eve's judgment, but now that she'd met the woman, she wasn't so sure.

Natalie glanced at Brooke shrewdly. Turning her attention back to Sara, the attorney said, "Is that all your husband said and did?"

"He said hello, then he told me to wait, then he swore, and then he told me to come home. He said I'm making a mistake. He said I'll be sorry."

"Were you afraid?"

Sara seemed to be trying to formulate her reply. "For a long time now, I've been afraid of my own shadow." She looked at her clasped hands and whispered, "I'm not very strong."

Natalie said, "That's what he wants you to think. You left him. That took guts."

Sara looked at Natalie. "I'm scared to death that Seth will go hungry. And sometimes I miss Roy."

"Do you miss being beaten?"

Brooke was all ready to intervene. Natalie stopped her with one shake of her head.

"Do you, Sara?" the shrewd attorney asked.

Sara stopped wringing her hands. "No."

"And?" Natalie prodded.

"And I'll never let him do that to me again. I won't go back to him."

"Who says you're not strong?" Natalie asked.

Brooke revised her earlier opinion. Natalie Harper may not have dressed like a typical attorney, but she knew what she was doing.

"Sara, your husband's statement that you'll be sorry could be construed as a threat. Given his history of abuse, and the fact that he's been seen driving past wherever you happen to be, we have grounds to file a restraining order. Sheriff McCall can help with that." She rummaged through a drawer.

In a small voice, Sara said, "I can't do that."

Brooke and Natalie both stared at Sara. "Why?" Natalie asked.

"I can't pay you right now."

Natalie waved that aside. "That house you and your son lived in all those years is half yours. And you're entitled to half of your husband's retirement, among other things. We'll let the man who beat you pay for this, in a roundabout way, of course. Believe me, it's the least he can do. I'll most likely have to go after it, but I don't mind. I consider it poetic justice. Besides, if I'd have wanted to be a rich lawyer, I would have slept with one of the senior partners in Boston when he wanted me to."

At Brooke and Sara's looks of dismay, Natalie released a deep breath and said, "I'm usually not quite this blunt." She pulled a face. "Okay, maybe I am. You may have heard I'm marrying Brian McCall."

"Is there a problem?" Sara asked quietly.

"Oh, there's a problem, all right. Marriage wasn't in my plans. Then in walked Brian McCall, a preacher, of all things. What can I say? I love the man, and love has a way of changing even the most carefully laid plans. The good reverend feels that we need to set a good example. He calls it practicing what he preaches, and since he advises the kids in his youth group not to have sex until they're married, well, you get the picture."

"Seth is in Brian's youth group."

"Then you know all about this. At first I thought it was sweet, but now it's driving us crazy. I guess you could say we're extremely . . ."

Brooke and Sara waited expectantly.

"Frustrated." Natalie winked. "But you didn't come here to talk about me." She looked at Sara. "Now here is what we're going to do." After Sara's options had been thoroughly discussed, the dark-haired attorney turned to Brooke. "Do you have a matter requiring legal advice?"

Brooke crossed her legs and straightened her watch. "Two weeks ago I saw my husband kissing another woman."

"Did he know you saw him?"

"I waited several hours and then I confronted him."

"Did he admit to an affair?" Natalie asked.

"Not until I produced some damning evidence. Then, he tried to make me believe his affair was all my fault."

"They usually do. What did you do?"

"I left him standing in the middle of our kitchen, crème brûlée running down the side of his face, dropping onto the top of his Ferragamo loafer."

"Nice touch." Natalie's mouth twitched. "Have you decided what you're going to do?"

"I'm going to get a divorce." It came out sounding flat and lifeless.

"Are you sure?" Natalie asked.

"This time, I'm sure."

Natalie absorbed that before asking, "Will he fight dirty?"

Brooke shook her head. "Colin will be angry, but he'll be fair."

"Are you sure?"

Brooke's stomach churned, but she nodded. "For the most part, yes. Telling him isn't going to be easy."

Natalie pushed a shock of curly black hair out of her face. "Sugar, somehow I think the crème brûlée spoke volumes, don't you? Now, this is what I suggest you do."

Brooke swirled the wine in the bottom of her glass. Across the narrow room, Sara poured herself another, a task that required concentration. "I think I'm getting a little drunk," she whispered.

They'd been a *little* drunk after the first bottle, and were on their way to getting sloshed. That hadn't been Brooke's intention when she'd uncorked a bottle of inexpensive wine and said, "To our marriages. May they rest in peace."

Somehow, with Sophie spending the night at Eve's and Seth spending the week at baseball camp, one toast had led to another. Sara lounged on the sofa and Brooke was sprawled in the overstuffed chair, one leg flung over the arm. Their cheeks were flushed, their clothes disheveled, their shoes somewhere. Looking out the window, Brooke wondered when night had fallen. She and Sara had talked about everything under the sun just as they had when they were kids. Sara told Brooke about the first time Roy hit her, and Brooke told Sara about the day she'd discovered Colin's affair two years ago. They discussed Sophie's love of horses and Seth's love for baseball, Eve's wedding and Natalie Harper's dilemma.

Sara said, "I remember when Reverend McCall told the youth group that he and Natalie were going to wait until they were married. I don't think he'd planned to, but Jeremy Baker asked point blank, and Brian couldn't lie. Before he knew it, it was all over town. Some of the parents were upset because he was talking about sex with their children. At church the following Sunday, a red-faced Brian tried to explain the importance of such discussions. You should have heard the cresh-cresh-crescendo."

"What crescendo?" Brooke had a little trouble with the pronunciation, too.

"Natalie plays the organ." Sara tipped up her glass. Smacking her lips, she said, "The one at church. I mean the one with pipes. Plural."

They cracked up.

When she was able to talk, Brooke said, "I don't know if it's me, if it's Alcott, or if something is in the air, but I haven't laughed so much in years."

"Neither have I." Sara drained the rest of her wine. "I'm doing the right thing."

"Yes."

"I really am doing the right thing."

"Yes," Brooke said again. "I'm proud of you. If Claudia were here, she'd be proud of you, too."

"Remember how Claudia used to make us laugh on Friday nights?" Sara asked.

Brooke smiled at the memory.

"Do you think she's happy, Brooke?"

"She's only a phone call away, right?" It took Brooke two tries to get out of her chair. She dialed information, gave the pertinent data, then let them connect her. "It's ringing."

"What are you going to say?" Sara asked.

"What do you want me to say?"

Sara sat up carefully. "Ask her if she's having any better luck with love than we are."

"Why don't I just ask her if she's getting any?"

They were both laughing when the ringing stopped on the other end.

Claudia Reynolds dragged her suitcases across the wide verandah, dropping everything as soon as she made it inside. Leaning against the door, she removed her hat, one of her earliest creations, and slipped out of her shoes.

Her big toe had been twitching for days, driving her crazy. Hopping on one foot, she rubbed the bothersome digit.

It was midnight, Charleston time. It had been midnight in Beijing eons ago. Mondays were never good days, but she really resented experiencing them twice. At least she was home.

Hat in hand, she stepped over her cases and moved away from the door. She'd purchased this house with its gleaming white pillars and three-story porches in Charleston's historic district five years ago. As usual, her timing had been perfect. There had been an explosion in the real estate market shortly thereafter. She'd been approached on more than one occasion to sell, and for a very tidy profit.

Her toe twitched again. Sliding it across the cool serpentine marble floor brought some relief. Julian must have come by earlier to turn down the air-conditioning when he'd instructed Marie to stock the cupboards. Julian thought of everything.

Limping slightly now, she followed the scent of gardenias into the library where her favorite blossoms floated in a bowl on her big mahogany desk. Next to the flowers was two weeks' worth of mail, stacked neatly, in order of importance. Beside it was the contract Julian was negotiating for the Lacroix line. All she had to do was sign on the dotted line and her profits would double. Again.

Her toe throbbed in earnest, in perfect tempo with the light flashing on her answering machine. Pushing her hair out of her face, she imagined a deep bath and her soft bed.

Flash, flash, flash.

She considered leaving it until morning. Who was she kidding? She never could leave anything until morning. She pressed the button and at the sound of the familiar voice, she was glad she did.

"Hi Claudia. It's me. Brooke. Valentine. Formerly Brooke Nelson. Remember me?"

Claudia smiled through twelve hours of jet lag. Perching on the corner of her desk, she listened intently. In the background, Sara Walsh said something Claudia couldn't quite make out. After that, there was giggling.

Brooke's voice came again. *"Claud, perhaps I should explain. You see, Natalie isn't having sex because she's marrying Brian McCall, the new preacher here in Alcott, and he feels it's important to set a good example. And Eve isn't because Sophie's spending the night, and Sara isn't because she left Roy, and I'm not because Colin's screwing Deirdre . . ."*

Claudia listened to the entire, garbled message, then played it a second time. Obviously, Brooke and Sara had dipped into the sauce. Much of the information didn't make perfect sense. Regardless, it was full of news. Brooke Nelson always did cram a lot into one little conversation, even when it was one-sided.

Leaving the denim and rhinestone hat on the desk, Claudia saved the message, turned out the lamp and headed for the sweeping staircase. She was thinking about Brooke and Sara and simpler times when she noticed the size eleven wingtip balancing precariously at the edge of the top step.

Well, well, well. What did she have here?

She discovered its mate around the corner. Next she came to two brown socks, lying a few feet apart.

It appeared she wasn't alone.

A little farther down the hall was a fine-gauge knit shirt that brought out the amber color of Julian's eyes. It was easy to picture him removing it, for she'd memorized it the last time she'd watched him take it off. She stepped over the pants last, the brushed leather belt she'd given Julian for Christmas two years ago still in the loops. Being careful not to disrupt the skimpy white briefs hanging on the doorknob, she entered her bedroom.

Julian Bartholomew was stretched out on her bed, propped on her pillows, wearing nothing but one of her hats and a knowing smile. The man had a lot of nerve, which was why she found him so damn appealing. The lights were dimmed, casting a golden glow across his bare chest and hairy legs. He was twenty-eight, seven years younger than she, too young by her standards. God, she couldn't tear her eyes away. "I thought you'd be on your way to Baton Rouge by now."

Julian eased a little deeper into the pillows and slowly bent one knee. "The Lacroix people will have to wait until I get there to start the negotiations."

That incredible British accent had captivated her the first time she'd heard it. And that attitude! She'd known she was in trouble the day she'd met him three years ago at a pub in Wales. The attraction had been so swift it was amazing they'd managed to wait until they reached her room. When she'd left the following morning, sleep-deprived but sated, she'd been convinced she'd gotten him out of her system. And then he'd shown up in Charleston two months later.

It seemed the man could do anything. He'd studied law, but hadn't taken the bar. He'd majored in business, but hadn't quite finished. He wasn't one to jump through conventional hoops, preferring to make his own way. He reminded her of someone. It was a few months before she'd realized who.

Her.

He'd hung around, and when she wasn't completely out of her mind with passion, she'd found she was able to discuss problems with him. On a whim, she'd hired him. He knew tricky contract clauses, tricky people. He had a brilliant business sense, and yet he always made board meetings look like poker games.

Julian had a poker face from way back.

Tonight, he watched her lazily. The semi-darkness deepened his eyes and accentuated every ridge, ripple and hollow from his head to his toes.

"What are you doing in my bed, Mr. Bartholomew?" Her breathing had deepened, too.

"It's my duty to anticipate your needs, Ms. Reynolds. How was the trip?"

She rubbed the back of her neck. "Long. And successful."

"Could you tone down the excitement?"

"I'm tired, all right?"

"Poor Claudia. Did you see the *Times*?"

She glanced at the bed stand where a newspaper was opened to a photo of the Queen Mother wearing one of her creations. "You Brits obviously love my hats." She gestured to the one he was wearing. It was the original prototype from which she'd designed the Queen Mother's.

Julian wasn't wearing it on his head.

"Don't you think it suits me?"

She felt herself starting to smile. "In all honesty I think it looks better on you than on the Queen Mother."

"Oh, Claudia, you are so wicked."

He made it sound like a compliment, but in truth there were thousands of women far more beautiful than she. She ran her hand over her face and raked it through her hair. She hadn't bothered with makeup. She'd been blessed with decent bone structure and good skin. Her eyebrows were dark, her lashes thick and long. Her hair was dark, too, and chin length. It had just enough wave to make it resist styling, and had been cut into long layers that framed her face and neck. She was considered pretty by some. Julian was prettier.

He hated it when she said it. She said it about once a week.

But she didn't say it tonight.

Noticing her rubbing her toe into the carpet, he patted the bed. "Come here. I'll take care of that toe, for you."

She could have taken a rain check, but a foot massage was just too much to resist. She sat on her bed. Behind her, the mattress shifted as Julian moved toward her. He smoothed her hair off her neck and massaged her nape then gently placed the hat on her head.

She was getting another mental picture, but just before Julian moved into her line of vision, he clapped twice, and the lights went out. He eased off the bed in the dark, his hands gliding along her calves, to her knees, up her thighs again, beneath her skirt. Finding the lace edge of her thigh-high nylon, he drew it down, over her knee, down her shin, and off her foot. It landed with a swish somewhere behind him. She groaned in anticipation as he took her ankle in his hand.

He massaged her arch, her heel, the ball of her foot and each of her toes, then slowly drew the sole of her foot down his chest, bringing it to rest, ever so gently, on his upper thigh. She moaned again as he repeated the process, with a few improvisations, on her other foot.

When he finished with her feet, he made his way up the rest of her body. By the time he reached her shoulders, the harsh, uneven rhythm of her breathing matched his. She flattened her hands on his chest, down his stomach, around to his back, kneading, molding, pleasuring. He kissed her everywhere, except on her mouth, drawing the anticipation out, and reeling her desire taut. Oh, those lips. He brushed them across her cheek, her chin, and the corner of her mouth. Still, she waited.

He touched her top lip with his tongue. When she groaned, he chuckled.

And she said, "Now who's wicked?"

Finally, he brought his mouth to hers. Claiming her lips,

he kissed her with a focus and a hunger that belied his outward calm and supposed patience. It sent the pit of her stomach into a wild swirl that was pure bliss, so much more enjoyable than the air turbulence on the long, boring flight.

She was glad she was home. And she was glad Julian was here. There was something startling about that. Like pinpricks on a comatose patient, it didn't completely penetrate her passion or desire.

He rolled her onto her back, covering her body with his. Easing her legs apart with his knee, he said, "Claudia?"

"Hmmm?"

"Who's Deirdre?"

It took her a full five seconds to realize he was referring to the woman Brooke had mentioned in her message on the answering machine. "I don't know, but whoever she is, it sounds as if she's the only one having sex these days."

She groaned again, and again.

"Well," she whispered, "Maybe not the only one."

CHAPTER 9

It was ten forty-five when Claudia entered her kitchen and poured her first cup of the best-smelling coffee in the world. She'd awakened in layers after sleeping deeply, compliments of Julian, her jet lag little more than a memory, also compliments of Julian. Her hair was still damp from her shower, her feet comfortable in a pair of sandals. Her silk T-shirt fit snugly, the hem stopping an inch short of the waistband of lightweight, baggy pants, held up by a loosely tied drawstring.

Marie had been here and gone, but her handiwork was apparent in the pitcher of fresh squeezed orange juice in the refrigerator, the small tray of fresh fruit on the counter and the blueberry pancakes in the warming drawer. Humming under her breath, Claudia took a sip of coffee, poured a glass of juice, and carried both to the library where the scent of jasmine was heavy on the cooled air. She stared at the blooms she hadn't taken the time to appreciate last night. Plucking a petal, she brought it to her nose and smiled.

The man truly thought of everything.

If a person ever figured out a way to market his foot massages, and everything that followed, jet lag would be a thing of the past. Claudia didn't dare mention it. Just her luck, it would be an overnight sensation, and another easy success.

Her toe twitched, blasted thing.

She'd taken her problem to a doctor ten years ago. Why they'd started out testing her head, she didn't know, but the specialists ruled out neurological disorders, such as brain tumors, epilepsy, and even scarier illnesses such as MS and ALS. Several doctors and a year later, a diagnosis had finally been made. It turned out her twitching toe was psychosomatic. In a sense, the first doctors were right. The problem was in her head after all. It was similar in nature to a facial tic, except her nerves manifested themselves in the form of a twitch in her big toe.

She could go months, even a year or more between bouts. And suddenly, *tic, tic, tic*, her toe twitched like a time bomb waiting to go off. Her shrink insisted she wasn't nuts. She was more of an eccentric.

Claudia touched a finger to the brim of the hat she'd worn home from China. Of course she was eccentric. She made hats. And in turn her hats were making her a fortune.

Tic.

Absently rubbing her toe, she listened to the message on her answering machine again. It was good to hear Brooke's voice, even if she was slightly inebriated. How long had it been since they'd seen one another? Five years, at least. Where did the time go?

She picked up the contract Julian had laid out for her, sticky notes placed strategically where he wanted her to read carefully. One of the biggest clothing chains in the United States wanted to buy a dozen of her designs and mass market her hats.

Tic.

She looked at the obscene amount they were offering. It would be easy money.

Tic. Tic.

Between sips of coffee, she reread the last paragraph. She

was staring at the amount, rubbing her toe in earnest when the back door opened. She glanced at her watch. Julian said he would be back at eleven. It was eleven-oh-one.

The familiar pad of footsteps stopped in the doorway. Looking up, straight into a pair of golden-brown eyes, she felt a ripple of excitement. Julian kept an apartment downtown. He always went there after they made love. Sometimes she thought it would be lovely to wake up with him. But she never invited him to stay. He never offered, and he certainly never asked.

He sauntered closer. He may have been dressed to the nines, but the man was an eleven all the way. Five-feet-eleven-inches tall, size eleven feet, eleven on a scale of one to ten.

She sipped her orange juice and smiled. "Sometimes I wonder why you're wasting your time on me."

A patch of late morning sunshine illuminated his young face, his slow smile of remembrance, and the flicker of something else far back in his eyes. *Tic.* She looked at him more closely. Whatever she'd almost seen was gone, or masked.

Tic. Tic.

"Something wrong with the contract, Claudia?" He pronounced it Claud-ya, and smiled with beautiful candor.

She'd seen him smile the same way at board meetings just before he called a bluff or rejected a six-figure proposal. What was that poker face of his hiding this morning?

She shook the contract, ruffling the paper. "They're offering a lot of money."

"Don't sign it. I can get you more."

She didn't need more, but she put it aside. Again, she studied Julian's eyes.

He came closer, took her orange juice from her, and drank half of it. "Don't think too hard, Claudia. We wouldn't want you to hurt yourself."

Now why on earth was he trying to get a rise out of her? *Tic. Tic.*

Because he wanted to call her attention elsewhere.

Tic. Tic. Tic.

She slipped out of her sandal and rubbed her toe on the leg of her desk. The question was, why?

"All right, Julian, I won't make a decision about mass market until you return from Baton Rouge."

"And where will you be this time?"

"What makes you think I won't be here?"

He stared directly at her. "Because I know you. You're thinking you'd like to chuck it all. Sell the house. Tear up that contract. Move to the beach somewhere. Build a hut, plant some vegetables, maybe get a dog or better yet, a parakeet and perhaps a macaw."

He was far too perceptive for someone so young.

"Yes, well, we both know that's not going to happen."

He smiled that all-knowing smile again, the one that made the back of her neck warm, among other things. "I can't stay, Claudia."

He knew. He always knew. And it was disconcerting as hell.

"I left my car running. They're expecting me in Baton Rouge, and I can keep them waiting only so long. I'll call you when I know more."

"All right," she said. "Good luck."

"When you're good, you don't need luck."

Tic. Tic. Tic. Tic.

He glanced at the flashing answering machine, and she swore he knew that, too. As soon as she'd put in an appearance at Hats headquarters, as soon as she'd checked on those talented people she employed to turn her designs into hats that were being sought by royalty and models and movie moguls and now commercial clothing makers, Claudia was going to take another trip. This time she wasn't going to the Orient, although Alcott, New Hampshire, seemed nearly as foreign. As soon as she could, Claudia was going home.

Staring at Julian as he left, part of her wanted to call him back. His footsteps grew faint. The outer door opened and then closed. Reaching down, she stuffed her blasted foot back into her sandal.

It was late when Brooke's phone rang Wednesday night. Sophie was asleep and all the lights were out at Stone Cottage. There wasn't so much as a hint of a breeze, but the moon was full, illuminating the bed stand and the corner of the bed where Fluffy slept.

She placed the phone to her ear. At first all she heard was music.

"Do you recognize this song?" Mac asked.

She listened intently, smiling in the dark. *"Moon Over Miami?"*

"You have a good ear for old songs."

"My parents were old, remember?" Her mother had been gone fifteen years, her dad twelve. She missed them so much she ached. She always missed them, but there was something about coming back to her hometown that made their absence feel more pronounced. She'd tried to explain it to Mac during one of his nightly calls. That was the night he'd tried to describe the relationship he'd had with his father while he'd been growing up.

These late night conversations had become a ritual. Sometimes they spoke for a few minutes, sometimes for an hour. She always hung up feeling understood.

"Although I love the music you're playing in the background, I can't talk long tonight, Mac. Sophie wants to get an early start."

"Are you going someplace?"

"We're leaving for Philadelphia first thing in the morning."

Mac tensed. It didn't help that the song had ended and the room was suddenly so quiet he could hear his own deeply drawn breath. After a series of clicks, another record was lowered on the old phonograph. He didn't bother to ask

Brooke to name the next tune. Keeping his voice neutral, he said, "Time to go home?"

"Sophie hasn't seen her father in three weeks."

It was difficult to read anything into that, and Mac would be damned if he would come out and ask. He'd been edgy ever since he'd been called to his father's deathbed. This tension had a different origin. He'd had trouble concentrating during the group therapy session earlier. More than once he'd had to ask one of the women to repeat a question or comment. As if that wasn't bad enough, Georgeanne had caught him completely off-guard, getting in a good squeeze before he jumped and swore under his breath.

"That's what I thought," he'd heard her say to Tess and Rita as they traipsed down the steps at the session's end. "He has a woman on his mind."

Mac stretched out on his back and scowled. Georgeanne didn't know the half of it. From the sounds of things, the woman on his mind was preparing to go home. For all he knew, she'd decided to work on her marriage.

He rubbed the bridge of his nose.

Brooke never talked about her marriage. And Mac never asked. He preferred not to think about what that signified.

"Does Sophie want to stop over and say goodbye to Archie?" he said.

"She told him today. Didn't Archie tell you?"

"He must have forgotten to mention it." At least Mac had a legitimate reason to scowl this time.

"We'll be gone for a few days," Brooke said.

Mac's grip on the phone relaxed and the fist that had wrapped around his windpipe loosened. "I was in a group therapy session when Sophie was here today," he said. "So I didn't get a chance to talk to her. Now that I think about it, she sounded extremely happy when she called goodbye through the closed door."

"She's excited about seeing her father. And she's thrilled because Eve asked her to be a junior bridesmaid."

Mac heard the pleasure in Brooke's voice as she launched into her favorite topic. "From the instant the doctor said, 'It's a girl,' I envisioned raising a child that was part ballerina, part rocket scientist. Just when I think I might be getting a glimpse of the ballerina, she throws me a curve. Today, it was in the form of a horse."

"If it's any consolation, girls who are interested in horses usually don't become interested in boys at a young age. What did she do?"

"She asked if she could ride a horse in the wedding."

"Is Eve having an outdoor wedding?"

"No, and I assured her that Reverend McCall wouldn't allow horses in church. She thinks he'll make an exception because the groom happens to be his brother."

Mac chuckled. "She seems to have it all worked out."

"She always does. But Mac, it bothers me that your father failed to tell you we were leaving. I don't understand why he treats you this way. I don't know how a man could fund your education, every last dime, and your trips to Europe, and yet fail to buy you anything for your birthday and Christmas when you were a child."

"I never understood it, either," Mac said, staring at the full moon. "In many ways my father has always been a generous man. When my mother's clothing store went out of business, he tried to pay off her debts. To this day, it's a bone of contention between them because she wouldn't let him. He's donated a lot of money to good causes. When he was young, he built a log cabin with his own two hands and then turned it over to a poor young couple in the area. He flew airplanes and wrote books. He was friends with Hemingway. Once, he led a lost safari out of the African jungle. The man could do anything."

"Anything except be a kind and caring father?"

He shrugged even though he was alone. "I'll get a little even in your absence."

"How?" she asked.

"He'll have to put up with my cooking."

"Now Mac, there's no reason to be cruel."

They both hung up smiling.

* * *

"Oh my gosh! This house is huge." Sophie pushed out of the car as if it had been three months since she'd been home instead of three weeks. She ran up the back steps, straight into her father's waiting arms.

Brooke followed more slowly. Colin stood in nearly the same place she'd seen him last. That day Sophie had been sullen and Brooke had been unsure. Colin had watched them drive away, alone and forlorn in the alley behind their beautifully restored town house in one of the quaintest and oldest neighborhoods in Philadelphia.

"Hello, Brooke." Colin had the most amazing blue eyes.

"Hello, Colin." She kept her distance, and although she smiled, it felt awkward.

"I'll get the cat," he said.

"We didn't bring her," Sophie said.

Colin regarded Brooke, and she found herself saying, "She doesn't like riding."

His glance sharpened. "Then you're going back?"

Sophie peered from one to the other. The adults exchanged a meaningful look before Brooke said, "Sophe, are you still hungry?"

"Am I ever!"

Colin smiled at their daughter. "You're in luck. Portia stocked the refrigerator with sandwich fixings this morning."

Sophie twirled on one foot and started for the back door.

"Wash your hands first." Brooke and Colin spoke at the same time. Brooke couldn't bring herself to smile.

Birds chirped, and far in the distance an airplane hummed. All was quiet closer to the ground. Brooke hadn't intended to let Colin know they were coming, and wouldn't have if they hadn't gotten a flat tire this side of Boston. They'd waited for a long time for the tow truck. Colin had called out of the blue while they were waiting. Sophie had talked to him, and told him about their problem. It hadn't taken him long to get results. It never did. He had one of those do-it-or-heads-will-roll telephone personas.

"Are you growing your hair out?" he asked.

"Not intentionally."

"You look good, Brooke."

"Don't, Colin."

"It's the truth."

Her gaze went to his. He sighed. She was the first to look away.

She picked up the overnight bag she'd brought with her from Alcott. He took it from her by the shoulder strap, and indicated that she should precede him into the house.

In the kitchen, Sophie was busy taking all the sandwich fixings from the refrigerator. "Do you two want one, too?" she asked.

"No," Brooke said. And then, "Thanks."

"I'll take one," Colin said.

Sophie built a thick sandwich for herself, and another one, without the pickles, for her father. Brooke poured herself a glass of mineral water and sipped it while they ate. Sophie did most of the talking. Despite that, she finished first. Dashing one way and then the other, she laughed. "I'll be right back."

"Where are you going?" Brooke asked.

"I want to check out my bedroom."

She was gone before Brooke could think of any legitimate reason to ask her to stay. The kitchen was quiet once again. Too quiet. Colin placed what remained of his sandwich on the counter. Evidently, he hadn't really been hungry, and had only eaten to keep Sophie company. This would be easier if he was a lousy father. Easier for her, but not for Sophie, and Sophie was the one who mattered most.

"I swear she's grown an inch since I saw her last," Colin said.

Brooke doubted that, but understood what he meant. He'd missed their child.

She glanced at the granite countertops and stainless steel appliances and six-burner commercial gas stove and oversized refrigerator. "The place is gleaming."

"Portia used a special cleaner to cut the stickiness."

She looked up and found him watching her. "I shouldn't have done that, Colin."

He shrugged. "I had it coming."

She swore his eyes were drinking her up. Before he got the wrong impression, she said, "I only came back because—"

He didn't let her finish. "Look, I don't want to make you uncomfortable. I'm just glad you're here. You're calling the shots. I guess we could say the ball is in your court. What would you like to do? Take a walk? Perhaps Sophie would like to go out for ice cream."

"That's a good idea."

He started to smile.

"It would be good for her if you spent some time with her."

His smile lost most of its brilliance. "All right, Brooke. I'll ask her."

"Ask me what?" Sophie stood there.

Brooke jumped.

Easing the awkward moment, Colin said, "Would you like to go out for ice cream?"

"Would I ever!" She sobered as she looked at her mother. "Are you coming?"

"Not this time," Colin said.

Sophie watched her parents closely but didn't say any more. Father and daughter left soon after. While they were gone, Brooke wandered from room to room, floor to floor, sinking her toes into the Aubusson carpet, gliding her hand over their beautiful antiques. She picked up the Ming vase, and thought about what she was going to say to Colin when he returned. She should have been spitting mad. Mostly, she felt sad.

He and Sophie were gone for more than an hour, returning with a movie Sophie had been wanting to rent. All three of them watched it, although Brooke couldn't have said what it was about five minutes after it ended. Yawning, Sophie hugged her father tight, kissed her mother then went to bed like a very obedient child.

"Remember how she used to fight bedtime?" Colin asked.

Brooke nodded but didn't encourage a trip down memory lane. Obviously, Sophie was on her best behavior tonight. So was Colin. He mentioned work, and some people they both knew. He asked after Eve and wondered how the wedding plans were coming. Brooke kept her answers short.

He kept his distance, as if uncertain exactly how to proceed. "I've been saving that Château Latour, 2000. Would you care for a glass?"

She thought about the last time she'd partaken and the headache she'd awakened with.

"Did I say something wrong?" he asked.

She held up both hands. "Not at all. It's just that—" She almost told him how she and Sara had gotten tipsy several nights ago.

"It's just what, Brooke?"

"I don't care for any wine right now. Colin, we need to talk."

"Not tonight, Brooke." His eyes darkened with an unreadable emotion. "Tomorrow if you must. But please, not tonight."

She wished he wouldn't have said please.

"It's late," he said. "You've had a long drive. Why don't you get some sleep?"

"This isn't going to go away."

A muscle worked in his cheek. "I understand that. Three weeks of loneliness makes a man understand a great deal."

She looked at the TV. The eleven o'clock news was over. There wasn't much else to do.

They went upstairs together. At the top, she turned right instead of left. She checked on Sophie, who was already sound asleep. Pulling the door closed, Brooke started toward the spare room.

"Brooke?"

She glanced at Colin over her shoulder and whispered, "I'll see you in the morning."

"You don't have to do this."

She swallowed. Was there an invitation in his blue eyes?

He said, "I can sleep in the spare room if you'd rather sleep in our bed."

She bit her lower lip. "I've been sleeping in a double bed in Alcott. You keep our room."

She felt his penetrating stare, and heard him sigh from ten feet away. They both looked at Sophie's closed door, then quietly entered their respective rooms.

She prepared for bed then crawled between the luxuriant sheets. She tossed and turned, and eventually found herself staring at the ceiling. She could hear Colin moving about the rest of the house. He couldn't sleep, either.

Was she doing the right thing?

The answer had seemed so clear in Alcott. Now that she was here, in their home, their precious daughter asleep in the room between them, nothing seemed clear. She'd been down this road before, and had experienced this uncertainty two years ago.

She wished she had someone to talk to. Turning her head, she looked at her cellphone resting on the antique chest next to the bed. She'd left it within reach, out of habit. Going up on one elbow, she picked it up. She stared at it for a long time before turning it off.

Sophie was the only one rested the following morning.

"Aren't you going to work today, Daddy?" she asked at the breakfast table.

He swallowed, and Brooke wondered what it cost him to refrain from mentioning that Sophie had smacked her lips. "I should, but I'm going to make a few phone calls and beg the day off."

Brooke sipped her coffee. "Are you working on something important?"

He shrugged. "I'm in the middle of some very big negotiations. It's helped pass the time."

"Could you tie up loose ends this morning?"

"Is that what you want me to do?"

They looked at each other over their coffee cups. "I thought I'd take Sophie shopping this morning," she said. "Maybe we could meet you for lunch afterwards. And talk."

Sophie looked from one to the other much the way she had last night.

Colin winked at their child. "Your mother worked hard preparing this breakfast. You're old enough to do the dishes." He turned to Brooke. "Why don't you walk me out to my car?"

Brooke patted her mouth with her napkin. While Sophie stacked their dishes, Brooke followed Colin out the door.

Outside, she hugged her arms close to her body and took a deep breath. "I think this is a good idea. We need to talk about what we're going to tell Sophie." To her dismay her voice shook slightly.

"Not yet, Brooke."

"We have to tell her."

"Tell her what? That you're divorcing me because I strayed? I can't bear the thought of her hating me."

"She won't hate you. She adores you. And besides, I haven't told her about Deirdre, and I don't plan to."

"Please, Brooke. Give me another chance."

She got lost for a moment in the depths of his eyes and in the history they shared and all that went with it. But then she thought about Deirdre. How many others had there been? And even worse, how many more would there be? Her heart raced as she shook her head. "I did that two years ago. I don't have any more chances in me. It's over, Colin."

"I refuse to believe that."

She stared at him, her mouth gaping. She thought about the legal advice Natalie Harper had given her. Brooke had followed much of it, recording account numbers and transferring money. The house was in both their names, one car in hers, the other in his. The checking account was joint, but their investments were divided down the middle in separate accounts under separate names. Financially, she was protected. She'd made sure of that two years ago. Emotionally, she wanted this over. "Believe what you want, but it's over, Colin. We need to get this handled."

"What's your hurry?"

She was speechless all over again.

He said, "If you won't reconsider for me, for us, do it for Sophie."

"That's low, Colin. I don't want there to be any delusions here. I don't want Sophie to harbor false hope. And I don't want you to, either."

He looked genuinely hurt. He released a deep breath. When he looked at her again, he was back in control. "Who's to say my hope is false? Marriages survive worse things than this. I take full responsibility."

That was a new one.

"I'm going to try to change your mind."

"It won't work," she said.

"If I can't, we'll tell Sophie together at summer's end."

"No good will be served by waiting until then."

"I love you, Brooke."

It was amazing how four such innocent words could bring tears to Brooke's eyes and a lump to her throat. He reached a hand to her face and touched her, then got in his car. He drove away without another word.

She stood in the morning sunshine, blank and shaken. Drawing herself up and reeling in her emotions, she finally went back inside.

Sophie was up to her elbows in suds. Leaving her daughter to her task, Brooke went to the stairs. Initially, she wasn't sure why she continued straight to the third floor. The door to Colin's home office was closed part way. Opening it, she went in. Going directly to his computer, she turned it on and lowered into his chair.

She typed in the pertinent information and pressed the

correct keys to gain access to Colin's personal e-mail account. Three weeks ago she'd done the same thing, with life-altering results.

Today, the computer told her the password was incorrect. She tried again, with the same results. A shiver passed over her from head to toe.

He'd changed the password.

Why, if he had nothing to hide?

Perhaps he'd ended the relationship with Deirdre. Then again, maybe he hadn't. Five minutes ago, he'd told her he loved her.

The words flashing on the screen might as well have been a tolling bell. PASSWORD DENIED.

She wondered when he'd changed it. Had he done it three weeks ago? Or yesterday right after he'd learned they were on their way?

No matter how much he claimed to love her, she didn't trust him. What good was love without trust?

"Are you and Daddy getting a divorce?"

Well. Sophie hadn't wasted any time asking that question. They hadn't even reached the outskirts of Philadelphia.

Brooke and Sophie had stayed another night. Colin had been kind, considerate, helpful and polite, no small feat for a man accustomed to using masterful persuasion to get what he wanted. However, he'd remained steadfast in his refusal to broach the topic of divorce. Obviously, Sophie hadn't been fooled.

Brooke tried to decide how best to answer. "Your father and I talked about it."

"I asked Daddy and he said he doesn't want a divorce."

Brooke glanced at her daughter in surprise. "He told you that?"

The girl nodded solemnly.

Damn you, Colin. "I don't think anybody ever really *wants* a divorce, Sophe."

"But you're going to get one anyway."

This was why Brooke had wanted to sit down as a family and have this conversation. Once again Colin had manipulated her. And she'd allowed it.

"I'm not going to lie to you, Sophie. Ever. This isn't something that's just come out of the blue. Your father and I have been having problems for a few years now. We've tried to shield you from them, but we moved to Society Hill because we were trying to make a fresh start."

"Really?"

Brooke nodded.

"Then you've, like, seen counselors and stuff?" Sophie sniffled.

Again, Brooke nodded.

"Have you talked to Mac about it?"

Mac. His name lingered around the edges of her mind. "No, honey, I haven't, but you can talk to him if you'd like. Or there are other counselors who specialize in helping children through times like these."

Big tears rolled down Sophie's face.

"And you can always, always talk to me." She could feel Sophie's eyes on her. And she rushed to reassure her. "Your father and I love you very much. So much we can't contain it all in our hearts. You are the most important person in both our lives. That is never going to change."

Sophie hiccupped. "Really?"

"Really."

"Promise?"

Brooke crossed her heart.

"Where will I live?"

In all her innocence, Sophie was most concerned with how this would affect her life. It was normal, and it was reassuring to Brooke. She was honest when she said she didn't know for certain where they would live. She insisted that Sophie would always have two parents who loved her, two parents who were proud of her, two parents who would do anything for her.

They talked for hours. Sophie dozed. When she woke up, they were pulling into Alcott.

Staring out the window at the familiar sights, Sophie said, "Am I supposed to tell people or what?"

"I'll leave that up to you to do whenever you're ready."

Sophie sighed. "I already told Archie."

"You told Archie your father and I are getting a divorce?"

"I told him about the crème brûlée."

Curious, Brooke said, "What did Archie say?"

"He told me that just because people get divorced doesn't always mean they don't love each other."

"Archie said that?"

Her daughter nodded. "And he told me it might be a good time to ask for a horse."

CHAPTER 10

The birds were busy today.

A few weeks ago Mac had put up a feeder and a birdbath in the little courtyard outside the window of his study. The potted flowers had been Greta's idea. The five women who met every Wednesday hadn't noticed, but Sara Kemper had mentioned it right away. She always chose the antique rocker closest to the window. She sat in her usual chair this afternoon. Instead of looking out the window, she spoke into her lap where her hands were clasped.

"He dislocated her shoulder and broke her wrist and cracked two of her ribs. Janet didn't come to support group last week, remember? It was because she went back to Roger."

Mac had been afraid Janet Phillips would go back to her bastard of a husband. It happened all too often with battered women. "Janet needs to rest, so she can heal and get better. If she's in the hospital, she's in good hands. She's safe."

"Is she?" Sara turned watery eyes to him. "For how long? Lily Smith called me this morning. Roger's in jail and Social Services took the kids. They put them in foster care."

Her voice broke and tears ran down her cheeks. Mac

steepled his fingers beneath his chin and waited for her to get herself under control enough to continue.

"Roger promised he wouldn't lay a hand on her if she came back." Her fingers shook. "He promised."

"They always promise. You know that."

"She shouldn't have gone back to him." Sara's voice was small.

"But she did. Maybe this time was the last."

"He beat her up bad. Why, doctor?"

Mac didn't know what to say. He'd spent years studying the human psyche, reading textbooks and true-life accounts of nearly every emotional problem and condition ever documented. He'd written papers, researched, attended lectures, listened and evaluated. And he didn't know what to say to Sara Kemper today.

Why had Janet Phillips gone back to the animal who abused her? Why did any woman? Maybe it was all she knew. Maybe in some perverse way she believed she deserved it. Most likely she loved him. Maybe for her, being with someone, even a man who caused her so much pain and suffering was better than being alone.

Or was Sara asking why men beat their wives in the first place? Analytically, the answer was diverse, but when everything was said and done, they did it because they could. It wasn't what Sara needed to hear this afternoon.

"And now she's lost her children." She wadded the tissue in her hand.

"It isn't necessarily permanent," Mac said. "The social worker warned Janet the last time. Those kids saw their father beating their mother. They heard her cries and saw her blood. Think about them, Sara. They need protection. If and when Janet can prove that she's capable of protecting them, her case will be reviewed and the situation reevaluated. It's possible she'll get them back."

"She shouldn't have gone back to him." Sara's voice was quiet again. "Men don't just change. No matter what they say."

Mac knew the statistics. He'd shared them repeatedly in group therapy and in individual counseling. With therapy and, in some cases, drugs that helped them deal with their rage, men *could* learn to reprogram their responses to anger. Most abusers never got that far because they refused to admit they needed help. Usually, if an abusive man couldn't convince, connive or coerce his wife into returning, he moved on to abuse someone else.

"I went to see an attorney," Sara said. "Brooke took me."

Mac held perfectly still. He hadn't talked to Brooke since Wednesday night. He'd wondered if she was back. Storing personal thoughts for now, he said, "What did your attorney say?"

"She talked about dowry and curtsy rights and how the house is half mine." Sara stared out the window. "It's quiet up here on Captain's Row. I'm not one of those people who loves the quiet. Most people don't know that."

"Why don't you like the quiet, Sara?"

She didn't answer immediately. When she did, he had to strain to hear. "It's lonely. I've spent too many days in the company of only silence and my own thoughts, asking why? Why did Roy hurt me? Why did he twist my arm and slap me across the face, bruise me and use his fists on me? Sometimes, in my dreams, I still see the look of hatred in his eyes. All I ever wanted was for him to love me."

"You deserve to be loved," Mac said.

She took a shuddering breath and it was as if she hadn't heard him. "And then there were all the other questions. If we left, how would Seth and I live? We had no money. What about my mother? Who would support her? But no matter what Roy says about how worthless I am and how I wouldn't have anything if it wasn't for him, I won't go back to him. I have my son, a roof over our heads and the possibility of a court order if Roy gets nasty. I don't want to be like Janet."

"Then don't be."

She looked down.

"Let me hear you say it, Sara."

At first he didn't think she was going to. But then, in a quavering voice, she whispered, "I won't be like Janet." She said it again, louder this time. "I won't be like her. I won't."

"I believe you."

She finally looked at him. Her hair was long and straight. It detracted from her delicate features. Although her eyes were watery, her gaze was steady. "You do believe me, don't you?"

He nodded. He thought she might smile as she glanced out the window at the birds on the feeder. Mac had always hoped Sara would reach inside herself and find the strength to stand on her own, but until today's session, he hadn't been sure. It was still possible that she would revert to her former patterns, but it became less likely every day. Sara Kemper had reached the bend in her road toward independence. It was a crucial point for the battered and abused. Sadly, many women in situations like Sara's succumbed to their insecurities, self-doubts and low self-esteem and returned to the very relationship that was at the root of it all.

"Lily called Tanya and Mary and me," she said. "She thinks we should go to the hospital to see Janet to give her moral support."

Sara and Lily and the others had met in his therapy group shortly after he'd come to Alcott. Lily Smith had made it out of a situation that had nearly killed her. Her soon-to-be ex-husband had beaten her the first time on their wedding night. She'd suffered the abuse for six years before she'd finally gotten out. Five feet tall and ninety-five pounds dripping wet, she'd become a strong advocate for the rights of battered women.

"Mary and Tanya can't come," Sara said. "I think they're afraid because they know it could be them next. It isn't easy to look in a mirror and see the future."

He saw her throat convulse on a swallow.

Sara whispered, "Janet needs to know she isn't alone."

"Then you're going?" Mac asked.

She nodded, and he knew she was stronger than she realized. He didn't know if she would ever learn to trust another man, but Sara Kemper was learning to trust herself. And he was proud of her.

When her hour was up, she stood. It was the same every week. Sara kept close track of the time. Her sessions never ran over.

Standing, too, Mac said, "Please tell Janet and Lily that I'll be here if they need to talk afterwards. That goes for you, too."

He took a deep breath. Something smelled wonderful. Brooke must have brought Archie's supper. That meant she'd returned from Philadelphia and was here in the old house on Captain's Row. A jolt went through him.

Brooke was back.

"Let me get this straight." Claudia Reynolds stood in Brooke and Sophie's way in the middle of the big old kitchen in Mac's father's house. "You left Philadelphia at seven-thirty this morning, drove two hundred and fifty miles, and then prepared a meal for an elderly man whom Mother Teresa here," she pointed to Sophie, "has befriended."

Brooke and Sophie shared a grin while continuing in their usual routine of arranging Archie's supper on a tray. Brooke had forgotten how funny life could be when Claudia was in it. She'd shown up unannounced at Brooke's front door half an hour ago. She'd had Brooke and Sophie in stitches in under five minutes. Claudia thought Sophie was beautiful and Sophie thought Claudia was *the best*. It so happened Brooke agreed with both of them.

The wind had wreaked havoc with Claudia's hair and her clothes were of the shabby chic variety. Both suited Claudia perfectly. She'd always been outrageously funny, even when she wasn't laughing on the inside. Brooke was still deciding if this was one of those times.

When everything was arranged, Sophie took the tray and carefully started toward the back of the big old house. Watching her go, Claudia said, "She's the image of you at that age."

"I'm taking that as a compliment no matter how it was intended."

Claudia's wink didn't give much away. She pointed to the meal Brooke had brought with her from Stone Cottage. "What did you conjure for the old miser anyway?" Her voice contained a hint of southern inflection that hadn't been apparent before she'd moved to Charleston.

Removing the lid from one dish, Brooke said, "Lobster and tangerine salad. For dessert I made lavender vacherins. The meringue melts in your mouth, and the raspberry coulis . . ." Her eyes closed automatically and her voice lowered. "Just a little on the tip of your tongue makes you lick your lips and beg for more."

"Are we still talking about food?" Claudia asked.

Brooke noticed that Claudia was massaging her big toe. "You always did have an X-rated mind."

"You're the only person I know who can make food sound almost as good as sex. Notice I said almost."

Brooke was in the middle of laughing when footsteps sounded near the doorway. Claudia yelled, "Sara!"

Sara rushed toward them. The three old friends converged in the center of the room, one smelling of tangerine and raspberry, one of an exotic perfume, and one of soap and water.

When they broke apart, Claudia said, "Looky what the cat dragged in, hmmm?"

Sara looked away.

Catching her eye, Brooke said, "Are you buying that southern lilt?"

Sara smiled, albeit shyly. "Any second now she's going to ask what's for *suppah*."

"I've lived in Charleston for seven years," Claudia grumbled. "I can't help it if I'm picking up the accent."

"It's good to see you," Sara said. "I knew that was your

voice, soft Rs or not. I was just telling Dr. Elliot that, wasn't I, doctor?"

Three sets of eyes turned to the man standing near the doorway. He smiled at everyone, and looked at Brooke last. His gaze was steady, his eyes clear and green. Her breath caught just below the hollow in her throat, and a sound only she could hear echoed deep inside her.

Luckily Sara had the presence of mind to make the introductions. "Claudia, this is Dr. Mackenzie Elliot. Doctor, Claudia Reynolds." She glanced at Claudia. "It is still Reynolds, isn't it?"

Claudia pulled a face. "Can you imagine me, married?"

Mac extended his hand. "It's nice to meet you."

"Likewise." She looked him up and down. And up. And down.

Mac was too busy looking at Brooke to notice. "I didn't know you were back."

"We haven't been back for long."

Her hair had fallen across one cheek. He would have liked to brush it away, and then, as long as he was touching her, he'd ease his fingers to her chin, and then slowly trail them down her neck. She had a beautiful neck. Slightly lower, her skin disappeared beneath the V-neck of her shirt. It wasn't easy to look elsewhere.

"How did it go?" he finally asked.

"It went well, all things considered." She breathed shallowly through parted lips. "How is Archie?"

He shrugged.

Claudia held her hand in front of her face, and then in front of Sara's. "Can you see this?"

"Yes, why?"

"Then we're not invisible."

Brooke didn't recall much of the twelve-mile drive to Portsmouth. She remembered leaving supper for Greta and Mac, and saying hello to Archie and goodbye to Sophie, who wanted to stay for a while and visit. Somehow The Three Potters wound up leaving Captain's Row together. It seemed to Brooke it had been Claudia's idea to drop Sara at the hospital in neighboring Portsmouth to visit a friend, although she couldn't say for sure because her last clear memory was saying goodbye to Mac.

She checked her forehead for a fever.

Claudia stared at her across the small outdoor table. The wind tousled her hair, and her eyes looked like brown velvet behind the light green lenses of her sunglasses. "Is it feed a cold and starve a fever, or vice versa?"

Squeezing lemon into her beverage, Brooke said, "Aren't you feeling well either?"

Claudia brushed a speck of imaginary lint from her leopard print trousers. "Or should I be searching for that other saying?"

"What are you talking about?"

Leaning forward, elbows on the iron table, Claudia said, "I believe the saying is *the way to a man's heart is through his stomach.*"

Brooke stared. Understanding dawned. It was possible her mouth had dropped open.

Claudia sipped her iced tea. Reaching for two sugar packets, she said, "Those confident, brooding, intellectual types are hard to resist."

"You've gotten the wrong impression."

"Then you don't have the hots for the good doctor?"

Brooke gasped. "I've never been unfaithful to Colin. Not once."

"I see."

"I mean that, Claudia. There's nothing going on between Mac and me."

"Do you prepare exquisite meals for anyone else in Alcott?"

"The food isn't for Mac. It's for Mac's father, who's dying."

"Who are you trying to convince?"

Brooke sat back, and then she sat forward. "What do you mean?"

Claudia shrugged. "I had the feeling you and Dr. Elliot couldn't take your eyes off each other. Believe me, I understand. It happened to me three years ago and I haven't been the same since."

"Mac and I are friends. We're both in Alcott temporarily, between lives, in a sense. He's here because his father is dying and I'm here, well, you know why I'm here. It's only natural that Mac and I empathize with one another. I love to cook, and this gives me an opportunity to do what I love. Things make sense when I cook, you know? And Mac burns water. I'm not kidding. He practically burned down his kitchen heating frozen rolls in the oven."

She clamped her mouth shut because she was doing it again. It did sound as if she was trying to convince herself.

After stirring sugar into her iced tea, Claudia said, "Okay, we've pretty much covered what isn't going on between you and Dr. Elliot. What's going on with Sara?"

Brooke told Claudia what she knew of Sara's situation. The ice had melted in their drinks by the time she finished.

Claudia said, "You're leaving an unfaithful man and Sara has left an abusive one." She reached down and rubbed her toe.

"Is something wrong with your foot, Claud?"

"Blasted thing. Can I ask you a personal question, Brooke?"

Eyeing her eccentric friend, Brooke nodded, albeit guardedly.

"Have you ever slept with a man who sucked your toes?"

Brooke choked on her tepid tea, then shook her head slowly.

"Are you sure?"

"I'm pretty sure I'd remember that. Colin and I kept a how-to manual beside the bed."

"Oh." And then, "Oh, that's too bad. I mean that."

Brooke threw a wadded up paper napkin at her.

Glancing in the direction of the hospital down the street, Claudia said, "I wonder what's going on in that hospital room."

"We can ask her when she returns. Meanwhile, we're not going anywhere until you tell me about Julian and your toes."

"Waiter!" Claudia snapped her fingers. "We're going to need more ice."

Sara tiptoed into the hospital room. The blinds were closed, the room shadowy. Lily was already there, holding Janet's hand. A few inches shorter than Sara and several years younger, Lily Smith had one of those faces that often got a second look, not because of its beauty, but because of its expressiveness. Today, her face was tight with strain.

Sara pulled up a chair. "Hello, Janet." It was difficult to look into Janet's blank stare, to see her bruised cheek, and cracked and swollen lip. Her arm was in a sling. The hopelessness, and sadness and the guilt were even more heartbreaking. "This isn't your fault," Sara whispered.

Janet averted her face and started to cry. She cried for her bruises and she cried for her pain and she cried for her children. Sara had missed Seth terribly while he'd been away at baseball camp. She couldn't imagine losing him to foster care. Janet Phillips was going to have to find a way to fight to get her children back. It was a daunting task for a woman with so little fight left in her. Sara relayed Dr. Elliot's offer to help and to listen. Sara and Lily both tried to convey hope and a positive attitude. They talked and they commiserated, trying to list Janet's options and outline a plan.

Staring blankly, Janet shook her head.

Lily said, "It's never too late to start over, Janet. In fact, today is the perfect day for it."

"Lily's right," Sara said. "None of us can change yesterday, but we all have control over what we do today and tomorrow."

Janet turned away. "I'm tired. I'd like to sleep now."

There was nothing more Lily and Sara could do. They were quiet as they rode the elevator down. They parted ways in the lobby. Sara was at the revolving door when she realized that no one was looking at her, at least not in an unusual way. Walking out into the sunshine, she thought, of course, they weren't. She didn't have bruises or a black eye or a swollen, cracked lip. She was just an average, normal woman, and it felt wonderful.

She hadn't gone far before she heard laughter in the distance. Her step quickened as she neared her old friends. "What's so funny, you two?"

Brooke and Claudia looked up at her. Still smiling, Brooke said, "Pull up a chair. You aren't going to believe it, but Claudia has found a man to kiss her feet."

"Why not just put it in the Portsmouth papers?" Claudia declared.

Sara gazed all around her. In centuries past, Portsmouth had been a bustling seaport town. Now it was a bustling tourist town, full of hills and history and strangers who paid little attention to three women sipping iced tea and telling stories and laughing out loud.

She could see the hospital from here. Sparing a thought for Janet, she offered up a silent prayer that the bruised and broken woman would know laughter again one day, too. Maybe friendship was the key to surviving this. Maybe friendship was the key to surviving everything.

"To The Three Potters!" Claudia held up her glass.

"Together again," Brooke said.

"At long last," Sara whispered.

All was quiet on Captain's Row as Brooke raised her fist to rap on Mac's front door. Night had fallen but the air hadn't yet cooled down. The local orchard growers and landscapers and avid gardeners were hoping for rain. It didn't feel rainy to Brooke. The weather was a strange thing to be thinking about as she waited for Mac to answer the door. The moment he did, even that thought fled her mind.

He wore dark pants, a white shirt, and no tie. It had been hours since he'd shaved. He hadn't turned a light on in the foyer. The semi-darkness made his shirt appear whiter and his eyes a deeper shade of green.

Her stomach heated. She hoped she wasn't blushing.

What was wrong with her?

"Is there a particular reason you're using the front door?" he asked. His shoulders were broad, his waist trim, his hands resting casually on his hips. Comparatively, she was a mass of jitters.

"As a matter of fact, there is." She decided just to say it and get it over with. "Claudia thinks there's something going on between us."

"The hat lady?"

"I assured her there isn't."

"Did she believe you?" he asked.

She hadn't expected the question. "Why do you ask?"

"No reason, except that she seemed very astute."

"There isn't anything going on between us, Mac."

"True."

She finally breathed.

"Still, it's possible she noticed that I'm profoundly attracted to you."

So much for breathing. "That's profoundly dangerous to a woman whose ego is smarting because her husband turned to another woman."

Staring into her eyes, he said, "Would you like to come in?"

She shook her head.

He studied her for several seconds before joining her outside. The instant the door was closed, she realized her mistake. The stone stoop was small, the houses on Captain's Row far too secluded, the summer night far too dark and quiet.

Being careful not to get too close to the edge, she put some distance between them and took a breath of air scented with the roses growing up the trellis beside the door. The barest hint of a breeze wafted over her, and she sighed.

He said, "Are you aware of where I am in a room, no matter who you're talking to or how many other people are present?"

"Oh my God." She clamped her mouth shut. Claudia used to say it was a good thing Brooke hadn't chosen a life of crime because she couldn't lie her way out of a hat box.

"That's what I thought," Mac said.

Turning slowly, she faced him. They'd mentioned an attraction before, but that had been different. Or at least it had seemed different to her, perhaps because it had seemed foreign to her. It didn't seem foreign now.

"Are *you* aware of where *I* am in a room?" she whispered, "No matter who you're talking to or how many other people are present?"

"Yes, I am."

She closed her eyes. "I'm sorry I asked."

"I've been profoundly attracted to you since the moment we met."

"Would you stop saying that?" She didn't care if it was gentlemanly of him to refrain from telling her she'd started this conversation. Hearing it did crazy things to her thoughts.

He caught her twisting her wedding ring on her finger. "Sophie told me you're getting a divorce."

She stopped fiddling with her rings and said, "I shouldn't be surprised she told you. She spoke to Archie about it, too. He told her that just because people get divorced doesn't mean they don't love each other."

"Are you trying to tell me you're still in love with your husband?"

"I don't know how I feel about Colin. I think Archie was talking about your mother."

"Really."

"You said she never remarried. Neither did he. Did you ever ask either of them why?"

"I've always gotten the feeling she likes her life exactly as it is."

She had to refrain from rolling her eyes. Men were so obtuse. Even when they were psychiatrists.

"Maybe she does," Brooke said. "Or maybe there's more to it than that. Maybe you should ask your father."

"I'd have better luck if I had Sophie ask for me."

Mac often made light of serious subjects. It put her in mind of the conversation she'd had with Carter a few weeks ago regarding his five classifications of men. She could only recall four, offhand.

Why she was standing in the dark thinking about that, she didn't know. She really, really, really wasn't well. "There's something I want to clear up, Mac."

"I'm listening."

"I'm afraid I've given you the wrong impression. You see, Claudia suggested that the way to a man's heart is through his stomach."

He chuckled. He actually chuckled. "I think your friend would agree that there are other ways to a man's heart."

Carter's fifth classification came to her out of the blue. Wiseass fit Mac to a T.

"I should be going," she said.

"Whatever you say."

"Goodnight, then," she said.

"Goodnight, Brooke."

Neither of them moved.

Finally she said, "What are we going to do about this?"

His sigh was a low croon, a slow sweep across her senses. "What do you want to do about it?"

"I want you to stop being a shrink and answer the question."

His eyebrows lifted as if he'd caught her statement in the middle of his forehead. "I haven't analyzed this. I haven't allowed myself to take it apart and study it too closely. All I know is that it feels dangerous and forbidden and intriguing and invigorating. I don't know what to do about it except resist."

"Of course," she said, relieved.

He looked at her, one eyebrow raised.

"You'll resist," she said. "I'll resist. We both will."

"All of us will."

Wiseass, definitely a wiseass.

He picked a rose from the trellis. He brought it close to his nose then slowly handed it to Brooke. "The lobster and tangerine salad was delicious, by the way. And that dessert. One taste, and I had to have more."

She swallowed. "Perhaps I should bring something a little less—"

"Sumptuous?"

If this hadn't been so serious, she would have boxed him on the arm. Brooke gave up and smiled. "Did your father eat any?"

"Very little."

Sighing, she started down the steps, the single rose in her hand. "I'd ask him, Mac. Before summer's end."

Mac heard the low drone of Greta's television as he passed her bedroom on his way to check on his father. It didn't drown out her snores. Somewhere a pipe rattled, which meant Archie was still up.

Ask him, Brooke had said. Before summer's end. She'd meant before it was too late.

Archie wasn't supposed to get out of bed unattended. He insisted upon using the walker, putting one foot in front of the other with a diligence that would have been admirable if it hadn't been fueled by pure stubbornness. It took him a long time to get to and from the bathroom. It would have been easier and faster if he accepted help. Sometimes he let Greta assist him, but he never let Mac.

He wore pajamas all the time now. Even with the elastic waist, it was amazing they stayed up. He was thin and stooped, his frame hollowed out, his eyes and skin yellow.

"You didn't eat much for supper," Mac said.

Grasping the hand rails, Archie lowered to the bed. He had to catch his breath before he could speak. "Wives and home cooking make a man soft."

With painstaking slowness, he eased backwards into bed. Mac had to stand idly by while the feeble old man who was his father got back under the covers.

"And *other* men's wives make a man s—" He was wracked with a coughing attack. When the spell was over, he closed his eyes.

Wondering if Archie somehow knew about his feelings for Brooke, Mac lowered into a nearby chair. "Other men's wives make a man what, Dad?"

Breathing heavily from the exertion, Archie shook his head.

"Were you going to say other men's wives make a man stupid?" Mac asked.

"Most men are that all by themselves."

"What then? What were you going to say?"

"Forget it."

"Is that why Mom left you? Because you had affairs with married women?"

Staring at the ceiling, Archie said, "The first time I saw her I knew I had to have her. Didn't take me long to get her on her back, either."

Sometimes Mac swore the man enjoyed being crude.

"She fell hard and fast. Your mother knew what I was like. She knew I had plans. Big plans. I told her all about them the day we met." He rasped when he breathed. "I took one look at her behind the counter at Saks, and it was like somebody hit me over the head with a scoop shovel. It didn't happen before I met her. And it hasn't happened since."

"You're saying all those other women meant nothing?" Mac asked.

Archie's mouth was set. And Mac realized that what Archie meant was that his mother had meant *everything*.

He'd loved her.

"Then why did you cheat, Dad?"

"I didn't. Not at first."

This was news to Mac. "When did you start?"

Archie shook his head.

And Mac thought there was a better question. "*Why* did you start?"

A change came over Archie's expression, a coldness and bitterness Mac had never understood. His voice was almost a whisper as he said, "Maybe that's the kind of man I am."

That was just it. Mac had never believed that. Something significant was staring him in the face.

"Now go on. Get out of here and let a dying man sleep."

Mac stared at his father's craggy features. Archie's eyes were closed, his gray lips pressed tightly shut. He was finished talking. Sitting back, Mac wondered what had happened between his mother and father. Because something had. Listening to his father's shallow, uneven breathing, he knew he didn't have long to uncover the truth.

Eventually, he wandered up to the third floor, then stood at the window staring out into the darkness. Until he'd come here, Mac had never known such silence and complete darkness. His associates in Boston probably thought he'd fallen off the face of the earth. They would still be awake if he called. He had no desire to talk to them.

His desires were tied up elsewhere.

Usually, he called Brooke this time of night. He thought of a dozen things to tell her. He went so far as to pick up his phone, only to replace it.

He remained at the window, thinking about what his father had said tonight. Archie had taken one look at Mac's mother, and he'd known exactly what he wanted. That, at least, Mac understood. It had happened to him. And it wasn't going to be easy to resist.

CHAPTER 11

Brooke locked her front door. Eve and Sophie were discussing a book they were both reading this summer. Sophe's points sounded more like complaints. All three of them paused when the local florist's van pulled up in front of Stone Cottage. Samantha Bell got out, a long, narrow white box in her hands. Eve's closest childhood friend, Samantha had married Jay Bell, the son of the local florists, and had taken to the flower industry as if she'd been born to it.

"Hello, Brooke. And you must be Sophie. Your Aunt Eve's told me so much about you."

"Are those flowers for me?" Sophie asked.

"I'm afraid these are for your mother, but tell me, do you get flowers often?" Samantha asked.

"Well, no."

Samantha handed the box to Brooke, her smile as straightforward as her approach to life. Brooke could see her daughter responding to both.

"Who are they from?" Sophie asked.

With a wink, Samantha said, "He said she would know."

Something unexpected and pleasant rose up inside Brooke. Removing the lid, she found the little card nestled in tissue paper.

All my love, Colin.

Staring at that card, she returned to reality with a sound-less thud.

"Brooke?"

"Hmm?" She found herself looking into Eve's gray eyes.

"Don't you want to put them in water?" her sister asked quietly.

Coming to her senses, Brooke said, "Of course. I'll be right back."

She filled a chipped glazed pitcher with water and placed them in it. The flowers were beautiful. Two dozen red roses always were. A few feet away, an old Coke bottle held the single pink bloom Mac had given her. As she watched, a petal dropped to the counter below. She should throw it away. She didn't know why she'd kept it.

Liar.

Turning her back on the flowers and on her conflicting emotions, she left the house. Samantha had gone and Sophie had climbed into the backseat of the family sedan.

Waiting for Brooke near the door, Eve said, "*Now* Colin's sending you flowers?"

Brooke nodded. She didn't tell Eve she'd thought the flowers were from Mac. She didn't tell her she was disap-pointed because they weren't, either.

Mac didn't call late at night any more. It was Tuesday, and she hadn't seen him since Saturday night. She had no business missing him, but her thoughts repeatedly filtered back to the conversations they'd had.

Sophie had walked up to Captain's Row earlier, only to return soon after because Archie had been sleeping. He slept more and more these days. Sunday they'd taken over a kettle of homemade chicken noodle soup and a bowl of Jell-O. Mac had been busy elsewhere, so Greta had helped them arrange everything on a tray.

Sniffing the steaming kettle approvingly, the heavy-set nurse had said, "This smells delicious."

"You sound surprised," Brooke said. "What were you expecting?"

"Mac said something about chopped liver. Personally, I think it would serve the old grouch right."

"Which one?" Sophie had asked.

She'd stared when Brooke and Greta had laughed.

Brooke had taken two entrees to Captain's Row yesterday. The first was more homemade soup, beef vegetable this time. The second was a surprise. It was the reason she'd thought the flowers might be from Mac. But they were from Colin, and she was going to have to call him and thank him.

She got in her car, fished her keys from the bottom of her purse, and drove Eve and Sophie to the bridal store for their final fittings. Eve and Carter's wedding was two-and-a-half weeks away. The invitations had gone out, and the final preparations were under way. Their engagement had come about suddenly. With only six weeks to plan the wedding, there hadn't been time to order gowns. Leave it to Eve to find the perfect dress on the rack at the local bridal store. Other than needing the hem let down, it fit her perfectly. Brooke and Sophie's dresses were simple and elegant. Sophie's had needed to be taken in. Today, she tried it on obediently, but didn't have much to say. It was unlike her to be this quiet.

She was listless as she petted Fluffy back at Stone Cottage later, too. She perked up a little when Rebecca Callaway called to invite her to spend the night, but the girl was quiet during the drive to the farm.

"Something on your mind, Sophe?" Brooke asked.

Sophie shrugged one shoulder.

"You didn't say much during the fitting this afternoon," Brooke said. "Don't you like the dress?"

"It's okay."

She'd loved it last week. "Aunt Eve was expecting you to try to convince her that you should ride Renee's horse down the aisle."

She perked up a little. "Do you think she might let me?"

"Well, no," Brooke said.

Sophie sighed. "It seems weird."

"What seems weird, honey?"

"Aunt Eve and Carter are getting married pretty soon. And you and Daddy are getting divorced."

"That does seem strange, doesn't it?"

"The roses didn't help even a little?"

Sophie looked at her mother, and Brooke saw such yearning in her daughter's eyes. How did a mother explain this without casting blame?

Pete Callaway waved from the fence he was mending along the road. Beyond him, two foals romped in the summer pasture. Last month one of the Callaways' favorite horses had gotten spooked during a thunderstorm. The gelding had cracked the top rail of the fence while scaling it just before being struck by a utility truck. As a result, the horse was blind in one eye and his leg was in a cast. He might walk, eventually, but the days the Callaway girls could ride him were over forever.

"Those flowers are beautiful, Sophie. They truly are. But flowers can't mend a marriage any more than they can mend Stomper. Do you understand?"

Sophie was silent for a moment, thinking. "You're saying if Daddy was a horse, he would be out in the pasture with old Stomper."

Brooke choked on thin air. Sputtering, she said, "That's not exactly what I'm trying to say, Sophie."

"Rebecca says if her dad ever so much as looked at another woman Ginger would send him to the factory where they make old horses into glue."

It was possible that Ginger had the right idea.

"I didn't know your parents still owned this place," Brooke said.

"*They* don't. My mother does." Claudia was poking through

an old trunk in the big old house on Maple Street where she'd grown up.

The Reynolds had gotten rich playing the stock market long before it turned sour. Being lucky ran in the family. Claudia didn't seem to think that was necessarily a good thing. They'd retired to the south of France shortly after Claudia graduated from high school, and divorced soon after.

"My mother is too attached to this place to sell it, so once a year she pays a cleaning service to rid it of spider webs and dust bunnies."

Brooke thought about that. Her own parents had preferred quiet and orderly lives, and Sara's mother had never liked Claudia. Sara's mother never liked anybody, actually, but that was beside the point. The girls had ended up here a lot. Tonight felt almost like old times.

"Getting back to Sophie," Claudia said. "And then what did you tell her?"

Brooke tugged at the zipper of the old prom dress she was trying on. "I told her it takes two to make a marriage work."

"Does that halo ever feel a little tight?"

Halo? Brooke turned in a circle, trying to see behind her. Sara reached over to help with the stuck zipper, and Brooke said, "Would you prefer I tell her her father's an asshole?"

"Now you're talking."

"Vindictiveness isn't a trait I care to pass on to my daughter. It isn't easy to refrain from saying nasty things about Colin. Do you think it would be better for her to hate her father?"

Brooke thought Claudia wanted to nod, but she couldn't do it. "You're right. There's plenty of time for her to hate him after she's grown up. Besides, in your case it did take two to make the marriage work. One to be the horse's ass, and one to forgive him for it."

The horse references just didn't stop.

Even Sara smiled at that one.

"What does Sophie say about what's happening between you and her father?" Claudia asked.

"She doesn't like it, but I think she's adjusting."

Claudia made an unbecoming sound. "You're kidding, right?"

Brooke said, "I've talked to her about it."

"And?"

"And she's sad at times, pensive others, but all in all, I think she's handling it well."

"No offense," Claudia said, "But I've met your kid, and she doesn't strike me as someone who would accept something like this without a fight."

Brooke looked at Sara. "Have you noticed the way people who've never had children always seemed so willing to give expert advice on the subject?" Brooke asked, tongue in cheek.

"Scoff if you want, but be ready for an explosion. It's what I did when I found out my father had moved in with someone a few years older than me."

"That was different," Brooke said. "And you were older. Sophie knows Colin loves her. Everything else is out of her control."

"All the more reason to be mad as hell."

Brooke was still thinking about that when Sara took a backward step. "What do you think?" she said shyly.

Brooke and Claudia looked at their blond friend.

Claudia snorted. "I think there ought to be a law against you two fitting into my old clothes from high school."

Brooke caught a glimpse of their reflection in the antique mirror across the room. The old cheerleading skirt and sweater Sara had put on was wrinkled and moth eaten. Besides being three inches too short, the prom dress Brooke was wearing was strapless. Her bra wasn't.

Eyeing Claudia, who'd donned an old football jersey, Brooke said, "Wasn't that Jason Zimmerman's number?"

"It sure was. He wore it the night he made that winning

touchdown in the last three seconds of the final playoff game. We were state champions that year."

"How did you end up with Jason's winning football jersey?"

Claudia answered without taking her eyes off the letter she was reading. "I gave him something. It was only fair he gave me something in return."

"You mean you and Jason?" Brooke asked.

At Claudia's nod, Sara said, "You're not kidding, are you?"

Claudia shrugged first, and then shook her head. "I never kid about sex."

"Was he your first?" Sara asked.

"I guess he was."

Brooke and Sara both gasped. "And you never told us?"

"There wasn't that much to tell. He was better at football, believe me. Listen to this." Claudia waved a crinkled sheet of paper.

Claudia, Claudia, I come to thee. On bent and humble and injured knee. Why, you ask? What do I seek? To ask for a kiss on your smooth cheek. I'll plant another on your lips so sweet. And then I'll sweep you off your feet.

"Who is it from?" Brooke asked.

Claudia scanned the paper. Turning it over, she shrugged. "It isn't signed."

And Brooke said, "Some boy wrote you love letters in rhyme? And you don't remember who?"

Claudia ducked her head. "A lot of boys wrote me letters. Half the time I didn't even read them." She dumped the box of letters out in the middle of the floor. "Here. Browse through them if you want. Maybe you'll recognize the poet's style."

Brooke caught Sara's eye. "I always wondered what she

was doing while I was practicing with the debate team and you were practicing the piano."

The truth was, Claudia had been in more clubs and organizations than either of them. Even skipping the fourth grade hadn't slowed her down. All three of them had graduated from high school near the top of their class. After graduation, life had taken them in different directions. Strange how, for now at least, they were back here where it had all started.

They'd been at Claudia's for more than an hour. Sara had talked about her life with Roy, and Brooke had relayed the crème brûlée incident as well as Colin's changed password. Sara and Claudia agreed that it was very suspicious.

"Tell us about Julian," Brooke said.

"There's not much to tell."

Again, Brooke and Sara exchanged a look, but it was Brooke who said, "The way there wasn't much to tell about how you wound up with Jason's football jersey? Where would one go to find a man who loves toes?"

"I met Julian in England." Claudia rolled her eyes. "You would not believe that Hugh Grant accent."

"How long have you been together?" Sara asked.

"We're not together."

"You broke up?" Sara asked.

"No." Claudia sat cross-legged on the floor. Wearing the oversized burgundy football jersey and a purple hat from her billed collection, she pointed to a page in their yearbook. "Look at these photographs. Brooke, you took the debate team to national three years in a row, and Sara, you played for all the musicals."

Brooke crawled closer on all fours, no easy feat in a strapless prom dress. "Forget the debate team. What do you mean you and Julian didn't break up?"

"Julian and I aren't a couple and never have been."

"Then how do you, how did he—" Sara couldn't help getting in on it, but she couldn't seem to bring herself to say it out loud, either.

"Are you telling us you found some guy on the street who does unspeakably delicious things to toes, among other things?" Brooke asked.

"Of course he wasn't just some guy off the street. Julian grew up in London on a cobblestone street called Astwood Mews. His parents still live there. I met them once. They're highly educated and extremely wealthy."

"How did they feel about their son seeing a woman from the States?" Sara asked.

Claudia shrugged. "They're so busy being upset with him, I doubt they give me a lot of thought."

"Why are they upset with Julian?" Brooke asked.

Again with the shrug. "He tends not to finish what he starts."

"Such as?" Brooke and Sara both prodded. It was like pulling teeth.

"He was the national billiards champion the year I met him, then dropped out of the competitors' circuit. He has most of a business degree and all of a law degree."

"He's a lawyer?"

"He never got around to taking the bar."

He sounded perfect for Claudia. "This man—" Brooke said.

"He's a boy, actually."

"How old is he?" Sara said, thinking of her Seth.

"He was twenty-five when I met him. I guess he's twenty-eight now."

"This younger *man*," Brooke said with quiet emphasis, "and you aren't a couple, and yet he makes passionate love to you? What does he do?"

Claudia put the letters she'd been reading down huffily, as if she couldn't concentrate with all these questions. "That's kind of personal, Brooke."

"For a living, silly. What does he do for a living?"

"Oh that. He's vice-president of Hats."

Brooke and Sara stared, mouths gaping.

"You sleep with your vice-president?" Sara finally asked quietly.

"He wasn't my vice-president when I met him, but really, Julian and I don't actually sleep when we're together."

Chucking the "Roses are red, violets are blue" love letter she'd been scanning, Brooke peered at Claudia and said, "What in sweet heaven are you doing in Alcott?"

"I wish I knew. When my toe starts twitching, it's time for a change."

"You came to Alcott because of your toe?" Sara asked.

Claudia leveled her gaze at the other two former Potters. "I suppose, and then there was that message on my answering machine from two slightly tipsy, dear old friends."

Brooke sat up, and then she sat back. She might have taken the debate team to the finals three years in a row, but how on earth could she argue with that kind of logic?

An hour later the love letters had been returned to the proper boxes and the yearbooks were stacked beside them. Her back against the sofa, Sara sat on the floor, reading old notes she'd passed to Claudia in Study Hall. "Claudia, you saved everything!"

"It's a curse."

Brooke was sprawled on the white sheet covering the chaise, and Claudia was stretched out on her side on pillows on the floor. It was eight o'clock in the evening and for once, none of them had any other place they had to be.

"It's quiet in Alcott," Claudia said.

She didn't get any arguments from Brooke or Sara.

Holding up a note, Sara said, "I wrote this to you the day after Joe Macelli kissed me the first time. It was after my piano recital. I received a standing ovation. And then he walked me home." Her voice took on a dreamy quality. "A perfect ending to a perfect evening."

"Whatever happened to him?" Claudia asked.

Sara shrugged. Joe Macelli had been her first love. He'd graduated a year ahead of her, and she'd pined after him, living for the days he would come home at Thanksgiving and Christmas. He ended it that first winter. She would never forget the day he told her. Until the first time Roy hit her, it had been the worst day of her life.

"Do you ever play the piano anymore, Sara?" Brooke asked quietly.

Sara looked at her hands, work-roughened and grass-stained. The closest she came to a piano these days was when she dusted the old upright in Miss Rose and Miss Addie's living room. Eyes downcast, she shook her head again. Some dreams simply died.

Claudia stretched. "If you had one wish, what would it be?"

After a moment Sara said, "I would like to be more brave."

"Such a serious wish, but whatever makes you happy. What would make you happy, Brooke?" Claudia asked.

Happy. The word hit Brooke hard. *Happy* birthday. *Happy* anniversary. Many *happy* returns. It was an overused word for an underrealized emotion. She'd been terribly *concerned* about Sophie's well-being, immensely *pleased* for Eve and Carter, and it was *wonderful* to see Claudia and Sara again. But was she happy? Oh, she'd been comfortable, fortunate in many ways, blessed even. How long had it been since she'd known true happiness?

She'd been in Alcott almost a month. It had taken until this week for her to feel completely unsettled. She was lonely. And the man she missed wasn't Colin. That most definitely did not make her *happy*.

What did she wish for? "I wish I knew what to do."

"About what?" Claudia asked.

"About this restless tossing and turning and yearning."

"If you figure it out, let me know," Claudia grumbled.

"What about you, Claudia?" Sara asked. "What would you wish for?"

"Hell if I know."

"Come on," Brooke said. "You must want something."

Claudia sat up, her brown eyes nearly black in the shadow of the bill of her hat. "There is one thing I want."

"What?" Brooke and Sara asked.

"I'd really like to get laid."

Brooke looked at Sara. And Sara looked at Brooke. Both gaped at Claudia.

Claudia winked. "Don't worry. There's still time to change your wishes."

The house was quiet. Until they all burst out laughing.

Gesturing to the three of them, Claudia said, "Just look at us. The cheerleader, the prom queen and the hat lady. What man in his right mind could resist us?"

"You're out of your mind, Brian!" Claudia said. "I'm surprised somebody didn't sue your . . . er . . ." She turned to Brooke. "Shoot. It's hard to say ass to a preacher, isn't it?"

It was the perfect opening for Carter to share his wisdom regarding his five classifications of men. Brooke sipped her wine, Claudia a beer. Sara hadn't been ready to join them, and had gone back to her garden apartment alone.

It wasn't exactly a rowdy bunch that had gathered at Dusty's Pub. All three McCall brothers were here, Jack with his wife, Liza, whom Brooke hadn't met until tonight, Brian and his fiancée, Natalie Harper, and Carter and Eve. The only other people present on this Tuesday night were two tables of regulars on the other side of the room, the woman who owned the place, the bartender, and a young fisherman holding up one end of the bar.

The McCall entourage was celebrating the results from the preliminary tests following Jack's little boy's latest round of chemotherapy. Tommy was doing better, and Jack and Liza were guardedly optimistic. Brooke didn't like to imagine what they were going through. But Tommy was improving, and they'd pushed three tables together near the pool table in the back of the room, insisting Brooke and Claudia join them. Brooke sat across from Eve, Claudia where she could keep an eye on the fisherman at the bar.

Dusty's Pub was on the village square between the pharmacy and Bell's Flower Shop. Brooke hadn't been inside the establishment in fifteen years. Not much had changed. The floor was still scuffed pine, the walls darkly paneled, the ceiling high and shadowy.

The group may not have been large, but they were boisterous. Brooke liked Jack's red-haired new wife, Liza, and despite Natalie and Brian's obvious differences, they seemed very committed to each other. Eve was going to be part of an interesting, close-knit family.

Brooke was thinking about that when she noticed the fisherman sauntering over to the jukebox. She wasn't the only one who noticed. Watching Claudia sashay over to help with the music selection, Brooke wondered if Claudia might get her wish tonight. She tried to recall if she'd ever known Claudia *not* to get something she wanted.

Claudia and her new friend spent the next twenty minutes talking by the jukebox, selecting one song after another. The longer they talked, the closer he leaned, until his hand rested on the small of her back and his lips were an inch from her ear. They looked pretty cozy by the time they joined the group at the table.

"Everybody," Claudia said. "This is Si Colter. Si, this is Brooke, Eve and Carter, Brian and Natalie, and Jack and Liza."

Si wasn't quite as young as he looked from behind. It turned out he wasn't a fisherman, either, but rather a crew member on a local whale watching boat.

"I remember you," Liza McCall said.

Jack agreed that they'd met on a whale watching excursion a few months earlier, which launched the topic of whales and the sea. The mood was jovial, the conversation interspersed with drollery and innuendo. Brooke joined in, enjoying the easy camaraderie.

Of course Claudia was the life of the party. Leaning across the table toward Brooke, she whispered, "If we play our cards right, we'll both get our wishes tonight."

"What do you mean?"

"Hey, Mac!" Claudia called. "Come on back."

Did she say Mac?

Brooke turned in her chair, and there he was, sauntering toward their table. She swallowed tightly.

There was nothing unusual about the cut of his hair or the angle of his chin. It wasn't surprising to see tanned skin at the end of July, and his blue cotton shirt and navy pants weren't much different from a thousand other men's clothes. She didn't feel buoyant when a thousand other men entered a room.

So this was happiness, this simple burgeoning joy.

Carter handled the introductions. Calling for another round of drinks, he said, "Have a seat, Mac."

The only empty chair was at the head of the table, at a right angle to Brooke and Eve. Mac took it, his knee brushing Brooke's. She eased hers out of the way, and continued to participate in the group conversation. Mac talked, too, but more often than not, she caught him looking at her as if he was as glad to see her as she was to see him.

She couldn't help it. She liked him, liked the way he looked, the way he talked, and the things he said. She even liked the way he resisted. It was so honorable and difficult and endearing.

Claudia challenged Carter to a game of pool, and Carter made the mistake of accepting. Being a McCall *and* a gentleman, he let her go first. Being a woman and no fool, she took him up on it, then strategically ran the table. Every time she put in another ball, more of the group wandered over to watch. Eventually, Brooke and Mac were the only two left at the table.

"Do you come here often?" she asked.

"I didn't expect to see you here," he said at the same time.

Both smiled.

"No," he said.

"It was Claudia's idea." Again, they spoke at the same time.

Silence.

This awkwardness between them was new.

"Do you play?" he asked.

"Pool? Not like Claudia. Do you?"

"I'm more of a chess man."

For reasons she didn't care to explore, she liked that, too. She told him about Eve's wedding plans and Sophie's upcoming birthday, and a few of Claudia's love letters. She didn't mention the flowers from Colin. He talked, too, telling her more about his father and his mother, where he went to school, his acquaintances from Boston, and Greta.

"I guess I shouldn't be surprised she liked the chopped liver."

"Greta ate the liver pâté?" Brooke asked.

He nodded.

And she laughed. "It was supposed to be a joke. I didn't think anyone actually ate chopped liver."

"She spread it on crackers and shared it with my father."

They smiled, and it felt intimate. Every so often she noticed that her knee was resting against his. Every so often she moved it. Each time it was more difficult to draw away.

In the background Claudia and the others were whooping it up. "Believe me, Carter, the fact that no one understands you doesn't make you an artist."

"Rack 'em up again, Hat Lady, and prepare to eat those words. This time, I'm going first."

Brooke and Mac paid little attention. They talked, and talked, knees sometimes touching beneath the table, gazes held above it.

The others returned en masse. Carter was grumbling and the others were laughing.

Claudia gasped. "Oh my God."

Everyone looked in the direction she was looking. A man had entered. A very attractive man.

"I don't know if he's a god," Natalie said, "but he's gorgeous enough to be one."

"If you like your men pretty, maybe." Si put a possessive arm around Claudia.

Staggering beneath the sudden weight, Claudia said, "Julian Bartholomew, what are you doing here?"

CHAPTER 12

"Did she say Julian Bartholomew?" Eve asked quietly.

"Yes, do you know him?" Liza McCall asked.

"No, but that's a lot of name."

"Something tells me he's a lot of man," Natalie said to her future sisters-in-law.

Claudia raised her eyes heavenward, for she'd heard it all before. Women got dreamy-eyed over Julian. Normally sane, intelligent, educated, women. Even the man-haters. She'd seen white-haired great-grandmas proposition him, college co-eds, teenagers, and middle-aged women who knew better, housewives, executives, hookers, women from literally all walks of life, and the occasional man. What could Claudia say? He was beautiful, Michelangelo's David, with one rather obvious exception.

"Excuse us," Jack McCall said.

"You do remember us, don't you?" Pastor Brian added.

"The men you're madly and hopelessly, not to mention *passionately* in love with?" Carter asked.

Liza, Eve, and Natalie linked their arms with their men's.

Brooke smiled encouragement at Claudia. "Are you okay?" she asked.

Good, steadfast Brooke. She, at least, recognized a troubling situation when she saw one.

"Who me?" Claudia quipped. "Aren't I always fine?"

The jukebox at Dusty's Pub didn't contain a single song that had been recorded after Dusty Anderson took over from her father in 1983. An old Abba tune was playing right now. It was unfortunate, because it had been playing the night Claudia had met Julian, too. He'd called her his dancing queen the first time they— She banished the memory. Still, coincidences like this were unnerving. Now, if only her accelerated heartbeat could be blamed on the music.

"Come on back. Julian, is it?"

If Carter McCall had been standing a little closer, Claudia would have stamped on his foot. She'd decided years ago that there was a conspiracy among men, and the smartest thing a woman could do was learn to work around it.

"I don't want to intrude." Julian looked pointedly from her to Si.

Oh, God, Si, the slightly intoxicated whale-watching crew member rubbing her back and hoping for the chance to explore other places. Claudia had forgotten all about him.

"Nonsense," Carter said. "The more the merrier."

The sharp, layered look she cast Carter was a complete waste of effort. He wasn't even looking. No one was. All eyes were trained on Julian. Even the regulars near the front of the room showed an interest in the dark-haired young man assessing everyone in one all-encompassing glance.

Si slid an arm around her waist. "Don' worry." He probably thought he was whispering. "If he gives you any trouble, I'll flatten him."

She wasn't worried, at least not about that. Julian wasn't a violent man. Even if he had been, Si wouldn't have been much help, two sheets to the wind, such as he was. She'd thought he had potential, too, at least in other areas. His appeal was waning fast.

Tic, tic, tic.

Great. Claudia's stinking toe started twitching. Gnashing her teeth, she tried to get out of Si's strong hold.

"Nobody's going to be flattening anybody," Sheriff Jack McCall said levelly.

That's right. Other people were here.

Julian glanced over his shoulder. "Bartender, be a good fellow and bring me a lager, would you?"

Julian wore faded blue jeans and a fine-gauge summer sweater that fit him like a glove. Only a Brit could get away with wearing that color and style. He was gorgeous, and most of the time he handled it well.

Si, on the other hand, wasn't handling Julian's arrival with much aplomb. Any second now the young sailor was going to start marking his territory.

Before things got uglier, Claudia looked at Julian. "You're supposed to be in Baton Rouge."

He took his time answering. "I finished early."

"And the deal?"

"Oh, that. I told them to shove their offer."

She perked up.

He said, "They upped it considerably just before I left. You were right. It's not even difficult any more. I brought the contracts."

"It was that urgent?"

He didn't have the decency to give a proper shrug.

"Then you followed me here?" she asked. He would have known she wouldn't appreciate that.

"Surely you know me better than that. I'm taking a little holiday. I am entitled now and then. Besides, call me curious."

"I'd call him anything he wanted if I were you, Claudia," Natalie Harper mumbled.

Again, it reminded Claudia that they weren't alone. It rankled almost as much as the fact that she needed reminding. Bother!

Brooke handled the introductions while Dusty, the owner, not the man tending bar, arrived with her tray and Julian's beer. He smiled, and poor Dusty could only stammer. Rolling her eyes and sputtering under her breath, Claudia whisked the long-neck bottle off the woman's tray and shoved it into Julian's waiting hand.

"Have a seat," Carter said.

"I appreciate the offer," he said.

His slight hesitation was a 'but' waiting to happen.

"But," he paused for emphasis—Julian always said it was all in the delivery—"I've been sitting for hours. I'm afraid my ass is still half-asleep." He patted it. Of course every man and woman in the place watched.

Oh, brother.

"If it's all the same to you, I think I'd like to move around a bit, maybe try my hand at a game of billiards."

"You play pool?" Carter asked.

"I'm terribly rusty."

"Rusty, huh?"

Since Carter was the one who'd invited Julian back here in the first place, Claudia didn't see any reason to rescue him from the sharks. The McCall party sauntered to the billiards table again. This time Brooke and Mac joined them.

Julian made a production out of choosing a cue stick. "Nice little town you have here."

"I guess," Carter said.

"This pub reminds me of taverns back home," Julian continued conversationally. "In English pubs, ale was ordered in pints and quarts. So, in old England, when customers got unruly, the bartender yelled at them to mind their pints and quarts and settle down. It's where we get the phrase 'mind your P's and Q's.'"

"No kidding. That's interesting." Carter was *so* in trouble.

"Just a little British trivia."

Carter appeared to be thinking about that. He probably had no idea that Julian was reeling him in.

Eventually, Carter said, "I'm a local artisan, and I think conversation is an art unto itself."

"Well put," Julian said. "Talk is cheap because supply exceeds demand."

"An optimist thinks this is the best possible world. And a pessimist is afraid that's true."

"In just two days, tomorrow will be yesterday."

"A day without sunshine is like night."

Claudia wanted to scream.

They were supposed to be playing pool. Instead they bounced idiopathic philosophies back and forth like Ping-Pong balls. The conspiracy among men was alive and well.

"Are you two going to play or are you going to talk?" Brian McCall grumbled.

Claudia could have kissed him.

Carter won the toss, lobbed the five into the side pocket on the break, and proceeded to put in three more balls before scratching. He wasn't bad. He wasn't bad at all.

Julian took his turn. And ran the table.

It wasn't pretty for Carter. "You call that rusty?" he asked, indignant at losing three times in one night.

Julian smiled kindly. "If I'd been in top form, I would have won the toss, too."

Not one to be outdone, Carter pushed his hair behind his ears and rocked back on his heels. "Conscience is what hurts when everything else feels good."

Julian settled his hands comfortably on his hips. "Even if you're on the right track, you'll get run over if you just sit there."

They were at it again. Claudia could not believe this.

Carter said, "The difference between stumbling blocks and stepping stones is—"

"How you use them." The dueling buffoons spoke at the same time and then had the audacity to grin about it.

How nice that they'd become bosom buddies.

"Oh, for crying out loud!" Claudia sputtered.

Julian looked all around. He looked at Claudia last. "I'll take that as my cue to leave."

"Where are you going?" she asked.

"Wherever I please. We agreed you're only the boss at the office."

"He works for you?" Natalie whispered.

"When he feels like it, evidently." Oh, but Claudia could be dour at times.

He said goodbye to everyone except her then sauntered toward the exit. Stopping at the jukebox, he deposited coins and pushed a button.

Every eye in the place was on him.

"Oh, my," Natalie said.

"Uh-hum," her fiancé grumbled.

Every woman except Claudia smiled.

Julian tossed the bartender a hundred dollar bill on his way by. "Another round for everyone."

Si nuzzled Claudia's neck just as Abba started singing again. She stiffened. Not *Fernando*. Any song but that.

Wrenching herself out of Si's grasp, she said, "You touch me again and I'll snap your arm off at the elbow and beat you over the head with it."

Evidently deciding that not even sex with a woman like Claudia was worth that much pain, he muttered something about minding his P's and Q's, then ambled to the bar where he lifted his free beer.

Brooke was just getting back from Claudia's when her phone rang in the bottom of her purse. She hadn't left the back light on, and had to fumble in the dark for her keys and phone.

She and Claudia had left the pub shortly after Julian had. Claudia had been very quiet.

"Any idea where Julian is staying?" Brooke had asked, helping Claudia remove the sheets from some of the furniture in her mother's house where Claudia was staying while in Alcott.

"No, but he'll make another grand entrance when he's ready."

"You don't sound unhappy about that, Claud."

"Yes, well." Claudia had tossed her hat onto a low table.

"Some mistakes are just too much fun to make only once."
She placed a hand to her forehead. "Oh, God, it's rubbed off
on me, too."

Claudia was a free spirit from way back. For a moment,
Brooke envied her that. If she'd been more of a free spirit,
she would have taken Mac up on his offer to drive her home.
It was what Claudia would have done. While she was at it,
she would have thrown caution and decorum to the wind and
seized the moment.

"Carpe diem." They'd been Claudia's parting words a few
minutes ago.

Enjoy the present. Seize the moment.

Unfortunately, Brooke wasn't a seize-the-moment kind of
girl. She'd enjoyed the evening with Mac tonight. She'd
missed him. She'd been careful not to admit it out loud just
as she'd been careful not to stand too close to him. They'd
learned that they could resist without completely avoiding
one another.

They were friends again. Granted, neither of them was
profoundly attracted to any of their other friends, but she and
Mac were keeping that to themselves. Just between friends.

The phone jangled again, bringing her to her senses. She
pushed the proper button in the dark, already smiling. "I
wondered if you would call."

"I thought you might call me."

Her smiled slipped. "Colin." She swallowed. "Hello."

"It's midnight."

Did that sound like an accusation, or was she imagining
things? Perhaps he was simply concerned.

"So it is." She entered Stone Cottage, flipping on lights as
she went.

"Didn't you get the flowers?"

Oh. Of course. The roses. "I meant to call earlier." And
what? Swallowing, she glanced at the vase of flowers. "Thank
you. They're very pretty."

She heard him release a pent-up breath. "I take it you're
just getting in?"

She felt guilty suddenly. "I've been out with friends."

"Plural?"

That was what he said. Brooke heard *male* or *female*?

She was lousy at this. How did he do it? "Claudia for one. You remember Claudia. She was in our wedding."

"At least you remember that you're married."

She bristled, because that *was* an accusation. "It seems to me you're the one who refused to discuss that when Sophie and I were there."

"When you were home, you mean." He took an audible breath and let it all out. "You're not making this easy. But that's okay. I deserve worse, so go ahead, have at it."

"Colin, this isn't something I'm going to get out of my system. I'm not trying to punish you. The days of public scourges are over and so is our—"

"Was Sophie with you when you were out tonight?" he asked.

The change of subject took her aback. "No. She's spending the night with the Callaways. She was going to call you. I'm surprised she didn't."

"Oh yes, the girls with the horses. She probably got busy. You know how she is when she's around horses." His voice lost its steely edge. "Her birthday's the week after next. Can you believe our little girl is going to be thirteen?"

"Actually, it's hard to fathom."

"I remember the first time I held her. We were happy then, weren't we?"

Brooke remembered, too, and yes, they had been happy then, but it didn't change the course the marriage was taking. She lowered into a wicker chair. "It's late, Colin. Again, the roses are lovely."

"Brooke, wait. I've been sitting here all alone in this big empty house missing you and Sophie so much I couldn't breathe. I want to see you."

"We were just there."

"I'd like to come for a visit."

"Here?"

"Yes," he said.

He hated Alcott. "When?"

"You're excitement is underwhelming. I suppose I deserve that, too. I was thinking it might be nice, that is, I was hoping to drive up the weekend before Sophie's birthday."

"That's next week."

"Yes, we determined that a few moments ago. She's my daughter, too. And I'd like to see her on her birthday. I'd like to see both of you."

Brooke's phone beeped in her ear, indicating that she had another call. Just in case it was Sophie, this time she looked at the caller ID. It was Mac.

She let it ring.

"I'm sure Sophie would love to see you on her birthday. You and I can discuss *everything* then."

"That would be a birthday she'll never forget."

"She's no dummy, Colin."

"If we must tell her, let's at least do it when the time is right."

"She already knows."

"What does she want for her birthday?"

He always did pick and choose what to ignore. Brooke sighed. "Actually, she wants a horse."

"We'll see what we can work out. I'll call again in a few days to let you know when I'll be arriving. Goodnight, sweetheart." He broke the connection. As usual, he'd gotten the last word.

She turned off the phone and stared at it. No matter what he said, there was nothing to work out. She'd never been more sure of anything in her life.

Mac recognized the woman running up ahead.

He knew that smooth, steady gait, the light brown hair, the way she held her shoulders back, her arms bent loosely at the elbows. Brooke turned onto Harbor Road a good eighth of a mile ahead of him. It was all the incentive he needed to run faster.

Harbor Road was a narrow gravel path with few houses and little traffic. Obviously a seasoned runner, Brooke glanced around often. When she noticed him, she stepped up her pace. She reached Breakwater Road a few steps ahead of him. Winded, she glanced at him, and he caught her smiling.

"Competitive, aren't we?" he said.

"It takes one to know one."

Taking a few seconds to catch their breath, they stared at the ocean. It was gray-blue today. Seabirds squawked at the water's edge. Waves broke noisily. The best beaches were south of Alcott. Much of the New Hampshire shoreline was rocky. Here at the end of Breakwater Road, a narrow strip of sand glistened white in the morning sunshine.

"When Eve and I were children, our parents brought us to this beach every summer. They didn't like crowds, so Hampton Beach was out of the question. Mother always insisted the water this far north was too cold for swimming."

Brooke smiled, staring at the sand, picturing her family as they'd been then. She could see Mac out of the corner of her eye. He stood catching his breath a few feet away, bent over slightly, hands on his thighs.

"Did you get in the water anyway?" he asked.

She couldn't help smiling. "Mother usually made the decisions where Eve and I were concerned, but in this instance Dad overruled her every year. Eve and I splashed and played and swam, insisting the water was warm. Ultimately, our lips turned blue and our toes got numb, and we would run into the sun-warmed beach towel Mom held for us. I haven't thought about that in years. Now that I'm here, it seems like yesterday."

Mac pointed to a sailboat on the horizon. "Have you ever been sailing?"

"I've always been more of a water's-edge kind of girl."

"The summer I was fourteen my father took me sailing

on a boat he'd built with his own two hands. I didn't often vacation with him, and I'd never been sailing, but I was a fast learner, especially around him. We were clipping right along off the Florida Keys when the wind picked up and a storm blew in. We nearly capsized the boat."

"Were you afraid?"

"I knew he would get us in."

He'd trusted his father. No matter what else was wrong between them, there was trust. No one knew better than Brooke how important that was.

On a whim, she bent over and untied her shoes.

"What are you doing?" he asked.

"It's been far too long since I waded in the ocean." Barefoot, she dashed to the water's edge.

"How is it?" he called.

"It's like bath water."

"You're a terrible liar!" But he removed his shoes and socks and followed her in. Bath water, hell. He kept an eye out for icebergs.

She pressed her toes into the sand and jumped a wave. Mac watched her, frothy water washing over his feet. There was something different about Brooke this morning. Her cheeks no longer looked like bruised hollows and her hips had lost their sharp edges. What he saw went deeper than that.

They both wore knit shorts. She wore a thick tank top and sturdy bra. He rather missed the flimsy one she'd worn the last time he'd seen her running. For the sake of *resisting*, he tried to think about something else.

"So what's the story between Claudia and Julian?" he asked.

"I don't know the whole story, but it has something to do with her toes." With a roll of her eyes, she said, "Don't ask."

"I wouldn't dream of it."

She laughed, the sound fitting so perfectly into his life. He'd tried calling her last night. He'd wondered why she didn't answer. If he'd been worried that he'd somehow mistaken the warmth in her eyes for interest, he wasn't worried now. She lit up every time she looked at him. His arousal settled low and deep and solid just as a spray of water hit him in the face. He started. And she darted away.

Chasing after her, he said, "So you're in the mood for a dangerous adventure?"

She shrieked when he caught her.

Turning her around to face him, his gaze homed in on her mouth. He left his hands on her upper arms, and very quietly said, "You're not an easy woman to resist."

"Thank you."

"What's going on, Brooke?"

"It's highly possible that I need my head examined."

"Who doesn't?"

The wind blew her hair across her cheek. "What would you tell me if I were your patient?"

"Are you trying to get free advice?"

She shook her head and smiled. She really was a terrible liar.

That smile did it, bringing his desire to life all over again. "I'd have to decline you as a patient."

"You'd reject me?" she asked.

"It would be unethical."

"This I've got to hear."

Even though her breathing had slowed, too, there was still a playfulness about her that was new. She liked him. It was obvious, and it was mutual. There was more to it than that, at least for him. He cared about her on several levels. He liked being with her, liked making her smile. He wanted to kiss her, and Mac hadn't wanted to kiss a woman simply because he cared about her feelings in years. Not that this was simple. Regardless, he wanted to kiss Brooke very much.

"Unethical in what way?" she asked.

"It would be unethical to treat a woman I want to take to bed."

Her blue-gray eyes showed surprise. "Well. I see." And

then, "Are you saying you don't normally want to take any of your patients to bed?" He'd barely shaken his head before she said, "I've always wondered about shrinks and, well, you know. Did you know you look like Archie when you hold your mouth that way?"

"What way?"

"As if you're going to bite through your cheek."

Damned if he didn't almost smile.

"You would be disappointed, Mac."

Mac had no idea what she was referring to. "In what way?" he asked.

"I'm not very good in bed."

He made a disparaging sound. Colin Valentine was the one who needed his head examined. "Bull."

He surprised her.

"You have sinful eyes. And women with sinful eyes are always good in bed."

"You've known a lot of women with sinful eyes, have you?"

"I was speaking hypothetically."

Brooke felt Mac's arms slide around her back, her body swaying closer, his breath hot on her forehead. "I have sinful eyes?"

"I said you did, didn't I?"

That moody edginess in his voice put her in mind of his father, again. Still, it was the nicest and most wicked thing a man had ever said to her. "You're wrong, Mac."

The set of his chin suggested a stubborn streak. Obviously, he wasn't accustomed to being told he was wrong.

She hid a smile. "I'm a good girl, and always have been. Good friend, good daughter, good sister, good dutiful wife, until recently at least, and I'm trying valiantly and desperately to be a good mother."

"There was a lot of information in that statement. It'll take me a while to analyze all of it. One thing is certain. You're all those things and more. You're a good woman and you have sinful eyes. Therein lies the truth and the contradiction."

His eyes, those moss green eyes, were half closed, his lips parted, his shirt ruffling in the wind. His voice had been low, cultured, relaxed and self-assured. It invited trust. His eyes invited something else entirely.

He didn't have to tip her face up. She raised it by herself. He lowered his, moving in for a kiss. All she had to do was let him. It was what she wanted; that connection was what she desired, yearned for. One more moment, one more breath, just one kiss . . .

"Colin's coming to Alcott."

They froze, their faces an inch apart, cold water lapping their ankles, sea birds squawking overhead. He was the first to open his eyes.

"When?" he asked.

"Next weekend, just in time for Sophie's birthday."

A wave broke, catching their bare legs in the spray. She shivered. He straightened.

"That's some mood breaker, isn't it?" But she didn't smile.

Raking a hand through his hair, he said, "Maybe now would be a good time to tell me about Colin."

Her gaze held his. And she swallowed. By unspoken agreement, they left the water and sat on a weedy spot on the beach while their feet dried.

She plucked a reed and glided it between two fingers. "Colin and I met in college and have been married for almost fourteen years. He's athletic, intelligent and driven. He's inflexible, but often kind and generous. He's had two affairs that I know of. He doesn't want to admit the marriage is over."

"You would be a hard woman to lose."

"Thank you for that."

Without going into unnecessary detail, she told him about the early years with Colin. Occasionally, Mac asked a question or two, but mostly he listened the way he always listened. Last night Carter had said that conversation was a lost art. Brooke thought that listening, really listening was even more rare.

When her feet had dried, she brushed off the fine beach sand. She put both socks on, and then her shoes, but noticed that Mac put on one sock and then one shoe before repeating the process with the other foot. When she'd first met Colin, she'd done it that way, too. When had she started doing it his way? On the tail of that thought came another: She didn't remember the last time she'd gotten on the scales. How long had she been suffocating from swallowing her dreams and succumbing to Colin's wishes?

"I made it so easy for him to mold me. That wasn't his fault. It was mine. Claudia visited us one time shortly after Sophie was born. After watching Colin with the baby, she told me I married a man just like my mother. At the time I thought she was crazy. Now I think she missed her calling. On second thought, Claudia doesn't miss anything. I've never quite figured out who Sophie's like. She has some of Colin's mannerisms, his intelligence, and some of mine as well. When she was four, we took her to Disneyland and she and Colin . . ."

Mac fell in love sitting in the sand while Brooke talked about her life with another man. He was a trained listener. He knew what a woman said, what she meant and often what she didn't say. Brooke was more resigned than sad, angrier with herself for being a fool than with Colin for being unfaithful, although she was still reeling about that. Mac believed her when she said the marriage was over, but the fact remained that Colin Valentine was coming to Alcott.

He bent one knee and reached for his shoelaces. He was still struggling with the realization that he loved her. Desire pooled low, and sitting so close to her wasn't helping.

"I have to pick Sophie up at ten, Mac."

"Give me a second to tie my shoe and I'll walk you back."

She jumped up. "I have a better idea."

So did he.

Brushing off the seat of her shorts, she took off ahead of him. "I'll race you."

That wasn't even close to what he'd been thinking. Hurriedly knotting his shoe, he yelled, "You realize you have an unfair advantage."

She answered over her shoulder. "Carpe diem."

He was thirty-nine years old, had a Ph.D. from Stanford, and had been a bona fide psychiatrist for over thirteen years. It was relatively simple to make an accurate self-diagnosis. He was an idiot. He was also in serious risk of emotional upheaval. The timing couldn't have been worse in either of their lives.

Brooke kicked up sand as she made her way to the road. He had a great view of her rear end from here. Men were visually stimulated. It was a proven fact. Mac had all the proof he needed.

Unfair disadvantage or not, he was off and running. The reason was textbook. He'd been a male longer than he'd been a bona fide Ph.D.

CHAPTER 13

Sara took a sip of hot tea. She didn't especially like hot tea, but for all her faults, Agnes Walsh had taught her only daughter to be polite. After carefully placing the dainty cup on its matching gilt-edge saucer, Sara hid her chapped hands in her lap.

Seth was back from baseball camp—oh, how she'd missed him. With the joy came reality. The peanut butter was almost gone. And she didn't have the money to replace it. She was trying not to worry. The air was still, the sky overcast, the garden a beautiful palette of palest blues and lavenders, whites, pinks and yellows, green foliage and red roses. How on earth was she going to feed him supper? Her stomach growled. Ignoring it, she turned her attention to the women around the outdoor table.

Brooke and Claudia had stopped by. To Addie and Rose Lawson, visitors were company, and company was treated like royalty, and royalty drank Earl Grey, preferably in the flower garden they so loved.

Sara wasn't accustomed to having friends drop in. She wasn't accustomed to constant conversation or to teas held in English-style gardens. Mostly, she wasn't accustomed to being treated like company, herself. She wished there was some way to repay the dear old ladies for their generosity and hospitality. At least they'd let her carry the tray containing the tiny tarts and cookies Brooke had made, as well as the teapot and all the other items a proper tea entailed.

Adeline and Rosalie Lawson were old-fashioned, cordial, and according to Claudia, a little kooky. Sara preferred to think of them as eccentric. They often bickered between themselves, usually wore dresses with lace collars, always used proper English, and never cussed. They loved their home, each other, memories, their tea and their traditions. Miss Addie always poured, and Miss Rose always sputtered at her for using too many sugar cubes.

Claudia's bangle bracelets jangled each time she took a sip of her tea. With her dark wavy hair, loose-fitting bronze colored dress and golden skin she was like a calico cat, spoiled, luxuriant and sensual. Brooke sat next to her looking upscale and pretty in linen pants and a sleeveless shirt with buttons shaped like daisies. Even the aunts, who were in their eighties and in declining health looked more vibrant than Sara in her faded homemade dress.

"It's so nice to see young people reading," Miss Addie said.

Brooke had brought Sophie and Rebecca Callaway along today. They sat on a bench in the farthest corner of the garden, books about horses open on their laps.

Claudia's bracelets jangled again. "If I were a betting woman I'd lay nine-to-one odds that the girls are only here to get a glimpse of Seth when he gets back from mowing lawns."

Sara and Brooke exchanged a look of surprise. "Oh, dear," Sara said.

Brooke agreed. "Sophie's not even thirteen."

"Isn't that when it all starts?" Swirling milk into her tea, Claudia said, "I'd already kissed a boy by then. It's never too early to have *the* talk. There are new diseases mutating as we speak."

"What sorts of diseases, dear?" Miss Addie asked.

Sara wondered if she looked as stricken as Brooke, but she was curious to see how Claudia explained this to these two innocent old women who'd never married.

Wincing, Claudia said, "Oh, um, you know, AIDS, and things."

"Is AIDS still a problem?" Miss Rose asked.

"You never hear about it any more," her sister added.

Claudia looked at Sara, Brooke, and then at the dear old women. Reaching for a sugar cube, she smiled brightly. "That's true. We don't hear about it. I imagine it all went tidily away. Ouch. I mean, would you pass the sugar, please?"

Brooke must have kicked her under the table. Sara handed Claudia the sugar bowl.

Taking it, Claudia said, "Pay no attention to me. I've been operating on half a brain ever since Julian showed up at Dusty's last night."

"Who's Julian?" Sara asked.

"Julian Bartholomew." They all looked at the old woman who'd spoken. Miss Addie smoothed her lace collar. "He's from Great Britain, and was once an international billiards champion. I understand he's quite nice looking, too." She smiled somewhat apologetically at Claudia. "I ran into Guenivere Sorrenson after the Pilgrim Women's meeting this morning. Her boy, Will, frequents Dusty's Pub."

"Guenivere's *boy* is pushing forty," Claudia said dourly. "Did she happen to mention where Julian is staying?"

Adeline shook her head. "Once she started talking about Brooke and Dr. Elliot she never got back to your young man, dear."

"He's not my young man!"

"What about Dr. Elliot and me?" Brooke whispered, glancing at the two girls sitting on the bench, pretending to read in the back corner of the garden.

"I don't think they heard," Sara said quietly.

"Don't worry," Miss Rose said sternly. "I assured Guenivere that you would be the last woman to do anything," her voice dropped, "Untowardly."

Sara didn't know what to make of Brooke's expression. Speaking for the first time, Sara said, "It seems I missed a lot because I came home instead of going to Dusty's."

"Now, aren't you sorry you chickened out?" Claudia asked, only to shake her head again. "I didn't mean it that way. Perhaps a bite of this raspberry tart will wash away the taste of my foot."

Sara stared at her clasped hands. It seemed each of the Potters was struggling with inner demons today. But Claudia was right. Sara had been too afraid to do something as normal as go to a local pub with her friends. "I am a coward. I've always been weak."

Miss Rose said, "You're no such thing! Oaks grow strong under contrary winds and diamonds are made under pressure."

"So true," her sister said. "We women are like teabags. Most of us don't know how strong we are until we're in hot water."

"Not them, too," Claudia muttered under her breath.

Sara paid little attention to the exchange, her thoughts turning to her empty cupboards and empty purse and her empty wish for courage. She had a boy to feed, to clothe, and to finish raising. What was she going to do?

"I believe it's starting to rain, sister."

Everyone looked heavenward. Clouds churned overhead and fine sprinkles fell to the ground.

Sara began gathering up teacups and saucers and the plate of cookies and tarts. "Why don't you two go in before you get wet?" she said to the aunts.

"We'll do that, dear. Thank you." The old ladies twined their arms and slowly made their way into their big Victorian house.

Giggling, Sophie and Rebecca rushed to hold the door then followed them inside. Without the chatter of the old and the young, the garden was quiet but for the patter of raindrops and the sighing of the waiting ground.

Sara handed the tray to Brooke, and the teapot to Claudia. "Go on ahead. I'll bring the rest."

Brooke took the tray, but didn't budge. "Is something bothering you, Sara?"

Sara blinked back tears. It hurt, kindness. Drawing herself up, she said, "My mother called this morning."

"Don't tell me. The old battle-ax tried to make you feel guilty," Claudia said.

It seemed Sara didn't have it in her to smile today. "Actually, she succeeded."

"You know she's the one who should feel guilty," Brooke said softly.

The sprinkles were getting closer together. There was no breeze, and the rain fell straight from the sky, the tiny droplets as warm as the air. "You two are going to get soaked if you stay out here much longer."

"We won't melt," Claudia said. "Brooke and I saw how deplorably your mother treated you all your life. I think it's rather fitting that she's stuck in a nursing home at her age. It just proves that what goes around comes around eventually."

Sara stared at her friends.

Claudia dropped her face into her hands. "Now I'm doing it."

Brooke said, "Are you sure you're all right, Sara?"

Sara nodded. But she wasn't sure. And she didn't know what to do about it. "Now go on in, please. I'll gather the rest myself. I'll talk to you again soon."

Brooke and Claudia carried their items inside. After saying goodbye to the aunts, they gathered the girls and left. Sophie and Rebecca ran ahead to the car. Pausing on the porch, Brooke said, "Something else is bothering Sara."

"I think so, too."

"What could it be?"

"I don't know, but I'm calling her later."

"What else are you going to do today?" Brooke asked.

"I thought I'd go to the nearest health and beauty counter and buy up everything I'll need for a luxuriant bubble bath, facial, manicure and pedicure. What are your plans?"

Sophie honked the horn. "I'm giving the girls and Mac a cooking lesson."

Claudia nodded thoughtfully. "You're cooking, and I'm lazing. If Sara was playing the piano, it would be just like old times."

They started down the steps, then began to run, rain falling on the sidewalk, on their shoes and shoulders, on Brooke's nose and on Claudia's wide-brimmed hat. They reached Brooke's car just as the rain got serious.

Sara whisked the linen cloth off the wrought iron table and gave it a good shake. Seth would come wheeling in any minute. It was only three o'clock, but he was bound to be hungry. She had one egg left and half a cup of flour. The milk had gone sour, the last apple bruised. What on earth could she prepare out of those ingredients?

"Hello, Sara."

She froze.

"Don't run away," Roy said. "Please. I just want to talk."

First her mother. And now Roy. She looked heavenward. *Why?* The sky was the same shade of gray as the old metal sink in the Aunts' kitchen, a fitting color on what was turning out to be an unpromising day.

"Won't you at least look at me, Sara?"

She turned around slowly. Clutching the tablecloth to her chest, she stared at Roy. He must have let himself in through the gate and now stood near the fence where the climbing roses were about to bloom again, not far from where Sophie and her friend had been sitting.

He smiled, and her heart turned over for a moment.

"See there?" he said. "You can see it for yourself, can't you? I'm not the same man I was a few months ago."

A voice whispered through her mind. *Men don't just change.* Dr. Elliot said it took years of therapy and often specially prescribed drugs to help a man learn to deal with and to control his rage.

She took a backward step.

"Goddamn it! I just want to talk."

"Like you wanted to talk all those times you hit me?"

It was the first time she'd talked back to him in years. He was as surprised as she.

"I said I'm sorry about that. That's all in the past now. You look good. Pretty as a picture."

It was raining in earnest now. And she knew how she looked. Faded and bedraggled and lost.

"What happened to your hands?" he asked.

Her fingers were stained from pulling weeds, her skin red and sore from scrubbing floors and walls, her fingernails cracked and broken. She forced herself not to hide them in the folds of the tablecloth. "I've been working hard."

"Come home, Sara. You miss me. I can see it in your eyes."

What he saw in her eyes was weakness and loneliness and perhaps even a little bit of desperation. "I have to get back to the Aunts."

"Those old crones."

"They've been very good to me." She'd almost said "and to Seth." Instinct, self-preservation and just plain experience made her think better of it.

He sneered. "Tell that to the blisters on your hands. No wife of mine has to be anybody's maid. My truck's parked right around the corner. I'll take you home."

Home.

She closed her eyes at the thought.

"Don't shut me out, Sara. Look at me."

She looked. His hair was getting wet, his shirt plastered to his shoulders. He was above average in height, stocky and strong. A long time ago she'd thought he was handsome with his thick, dark hair and brown eyes.

"Do you really want to talk?" she asked.

The smile on his face was one of victory. He started toward her.

She almost panicked. "Not here."

"Why not?"

"The Aunts are here." And any minute now Seth would be, too.

"Let's talk at home," he said. "You'd like that, wouldn't you?" His hand settled on his belt.

Her throat closed up.

"I know how much you love the place. You miss it, Sara. I know you do. You miss the curtains you sewed yourself, the rug you braided out of old sheets, the afghan you crocheted. All the things you made, they're all waiting for you."

Her stomach churned. She had loved making that house a home for her husband and son. "Not there."

"Where then?" His eyes narrowed suspiciously.

She was so hungry she felt faint. "Cooper's Café?"

He studied her through the warm, fine rain. "It's a little early for supper, but all right, if that's what you want. It sounds nice, sitting across from you over a hot meal. Let's go," he said.

"I need to change out of this wet dress." Thinking quick, she said, "I'll meet you there in, say, half an hour?" She started for the back door.

"I'm real glad you're finally coming to your senses, Sara. Real glad. You'll be glad, too. You'll see."

She slipped inside without comment, then stood shivering, dripping on the floor she'd washed that very morning. For some reason she found herself staring at the upright piano she dusted every week. She'd learned to play on one nearly like it. She'd spent her childhood practicing, losing herself in the notes and the music that had once been inside her. Roy had sold her mother's piano along with the house when he'd moved Agnes in with them, insisting the heavy old upright wouldn't fit in their home. By then, Sara had lost the music inside her anyway.

Closing her mind to what might have been, she carried the tablecloth into the laundry room, told Miss Rose and Miss Addie that she was going out for a little while, then dashed through the pouring rain to the garden apartment.

She looked at her watch. She had half an hour to dry her hair and change her clothes and stop shaking.

The scent of food assailed Sara the instant she set foot inside Cooper's Café exactly half an hour later. She was winded, but her hair was dry, her slacks and top fresh. Her jitters had moved inside.

Dixie, a heavyset woman who owned the restaurant with her husband, looked up from the chalkboard where she was writing the supper specials. "Be right with you, dearie."

"She's with me." Roy already had a table.

The place was almost empty. She could see the back of somebody's head at one of the booths. Otherwise, she and Roy were alone. She had to force herself to walk over to him. He didn't get up. He knew enough to eat with the proper fork, and he chewed with his mouth shut, but that was about as far as his manners went. For once, she was glad, for it allowed her to keep her distance as she slid into the chair opposite him.

"I'm glad you came," he said.

There was no sense trying to wet her dry lips. "Did you think I wouldn't?"

He looked at her long and hard. "Let's just say I wouldn't have been surprised."

She noticed he didn't say he wouldn't have blamed her. Her stomach rumbled. Embarrassed, she said, "Seth and I are almost out of food."

"There's plenty in the cupboards at home."

She would have said more, but Dixie arrived to take their orders. Taking the pencil she'd stuck in the curly gray hair above her ear, she said, "The catch of the day is flounder. The soup is clam chowder. The stuffed pork chops melt in your mouth."

Dixie looked from one to the other, and Sara wondered if the older woman knew about all the beatings. It wasn't easy not to hang her head in shame.

"Bring Sara the flounder and chowder. I want a steak. Medium. And when I say medium, I mean medium, not bloody, not dry as leather. Do you want bread, Sara?"

She nodded, pretty sure her face was red.

"And that coleslaw I had the other day," Roy said. "We'll see about dessert later."

Dixie trudged away as if her feet hurt. As soon as she was out of hearing distance, Sara forced her gaze back to Roy. She didn't know where to begin. She would have liked to start with Seth and what he needed. Roy never asked about Seth. Dr. Elliot had suggested she read a book that might help her understand. According to the experts in the book, she was the one Roy's ego needed. Evidently, men like Roy were sorely lacking in their own sense of self. They were like hollow, monolithic electrical vats. The women they beat were their energy sources, and these men went to desperate lengths to control the current, slowly draining it.

Roy had nearly succeeded.

"I need money for food, Roy."

He looked at her with unblinking brown eyes, then reached slowly into his pocket. She held her breath.

He brought out a red handkerchief and mopped his brow. "See there?" he said. "See how you keep at me after I've already told you how it is? I'm not going to lay a hand on you ever again. I'm not. But do you see why I did?"

Three months ago she would have nodded just to buy herself some time before the next beating. Something had taken hold inside her since then, and she couldn't bring herself to do it today. She stared at him, mute.

Dixie appeared with a small loaf of herb-rubbed homemade bread. Despite her nerves, Sara was starving. She took the knife and sliced off two pieces. Out of habit, she gave the first one to Roy. She took a bite of hers without bothering with butter. She barely chewed it before swallowing, then took another bite.

Roy watched her. "You're half-starved, aren't you?"

She almost believed he was concerned.

"There's beef in the freezer at home," he said. "Lots of it. And fish. And those vegetables you grew in our garden last year, and the blueberries you picked."

Was it possible he was offering her something?

She'd tried to get into the house while he was at work shortly after she'd left him. Her key didn't work. He'd had the locks changed.

He changed the subject, too, telling her about what a pain "Short Hal" still was, and about the promotion Roy had put in for at the plant. Sara finished her slice of bread and started on another.

"There's no need for you to be hungry ever again, Sara."

She looked at him.

"All you have to do is come home."

Dishes clattered, indicating that Dixie was coming with their meal. Huffing slightly, she placed the plates and cutlery in front of them, asked if she could get them anything else, then moved on to talk to whoever sat at the booth.

Sara's mouth watered as she looked at her food. "I didn't agree to meet you here to talk about coming home, Roy."

He stopped cutting his steak. "You think I don't know that? Like I said, I'm sorry for what I did. I got a little carried away that last time. It won't happen again. You forgive me for that and I'll forgive you for leaving."

He would forgive her? She stared at him, her stomach churning, her hands shaking.

"I phoned your mother just before I came today," he said.

Sara's blood rushed through her head, making it difficult to hear. "Why?" she asked.

"She said she hasn't heard from you in a while. What

kind of a daughter are you? I told her you were meeting me today. She was real happy to hear it's just a matter of time before we bring her home."

"You shouldn't have done that, Roy."

Something glittered far back in his eyes. Usually it stopped her in her tracks.

"I'm not coming home. I came here to tell you I'm getting a divorce."

He squeezed his beefy hands into fists. "What the hell are you talking about?"

"I've seen an attorney. We can do it civilly or we can let a judge decide who gets what."

"You bloodthirsty little tramp."

Hearing the commotion, Dixie looked up. "Everything okay?"

Swallowing hard, Sara said, "I'm afraid I can't eat this after all."

The other woman ambled closer. "Something wrong with it, dearie?"

"It's not that." Sara looked longingly at the steaming food. "It smells delicious. Would you box it up for me? I'd like to take it home for Seth."

"I'll be right back." Dixie took the plate away.

Roy lowered his voice. "You think I can't see what you're doing? You used me to get food. You're no better than a whore."

The man who'd been sitting at the booth got up. Sheriff McCall didn't come any closer, but he made sure Roy saw him.

"You called the goddamn sheriff?"

She took a shuddering breath. "Why would I when you promised you've changed?"

She didn't know why Jack McCall was here, but his presence gave her the courage to continue. Shaking slightly, she said, "I never deserved the beatings, Roy."

"I should have hit you harder."

She'd seen this look on his face, many, many times. Rage, loathing, greed. He was almost empty of everything else, and needed a fill-up.

Jack McCall must have seen it, too, for he came closer. Sara stopped him with a slight shake of her head.

"No, Roy," she said. "Nobody deserves to be bloodied and beaten. That's not something I can forgive. I'm not coming home."

"You have a boyfriend. That's what this is about, isn't it?"

She would have laughed if she could. "Do you really think any man would give me a second look?"

He calmed down slightly.

She said, "I once loved you a great deal, but every time you slapped me, jabbed me, bruised me, shoved me or kicked me, every time you bloodied my nose and pulled my hair, another piece of that love shriveled up and died. It's too late. It can never be resurrected."

"Bring out the violins! You egged me on, and you know it. You deserved everything you got and then some. You're nothing but a—" He looked all around him. Realizing there were witnesses, he lowered his voice, "Forget it. You just waited too long to come crawling back to me. You're damned right it's over. Look at you. You're nothing but white trash. You're scrawny, pale and ugly. Nobody in his right mind would ever want you. I sure as hell don't."

He shoved his chair back with so much force it hit the wall. The door stuck this time of year. He practically yanked it off the wall, then slammed it hard.

He was gone.

Sara hadn't realized she was standing until her knees refused to hold her. She sank to her chair. Still, her knees shook, but she'd done it. She'd faced Roy.

She feared she might throw up.

"Are you all right?" Jack McCall asked.

When she could force the words past her dry throat, she said, "How did you know?"

Just then Natalie Harper came out of the kitchen. "I

called him right after you left my office with that restraining order. I thought a little backup might be in order."

Half the time the new attorney in Alcott wore short skirts, fishnet stockings and high heels. Today she was dressed in coral slacks and a neon green and coral blouse. Sara had never been so relieved to see anyone in her life, proof that you couldn't judge a book by its cover, not that she'd ever been a good judge of character.

"I never got around to taking the restraining order out of my purse," she said.

"Do you think you'll need it?" the attorney asked.

Sara shook her head. "According to everything I've read, Roy will most likely go find himself some other woman to drain."

"Mind if I sit down?" Natalie asked.

Sara gestured to a chair. While Natalie took it, Sheriff McCall said, "I have to get back to the station. I'm having one of my deputies keep an eye on the Aunts' place for the next few days."

Sara nodded, but made no comment. It was over. She'd pulled the plug. Jack and Natalie exchanged a few words. Sara barely heard. He left, too. Dixie returned with the Styrofoam carton. Looking at it sadly, Sara said, "I can't take the food after all."

"Why not?"

"Roy didn't pay for it, and I don't have any money."

Natalie reached for her wallet. Dixie stopped her. "That isn't necessary."

Sara shook her head at both of them. "I can't accept charity."

"If you don't take the food, it's going in the trash. That seems like a waste, doesn't it?" Dixie said.

And Natalie added, "I guess it all comes down to foolish pride or providence."

The *foolish* part caught Sara between the eyes. Weighing waste against charity, pride against providence, she drew the container closer and said, "Thank you."

Natalie winked. "I knew you were smart."

Sara found that she could smile, too.

Dropping heavily to an adjacent chair, Dixie said, "You got a job, dearie?"

"I deliver newspapers part-time and I clean the Lawson sisters' house and tend their garden."

"Because I could use a part-time waitress," Dixie said as if Sara hadn't answered. "I know it's none of my business, but my first husband used to hit me, too. I finally got fed up and clobbered him back with a twelve-inch iron skillet. You remember those heavy black old monstrosities? Stopped him in his tracks, it did. Nowadays the police could have locked me up for that. I did a lot better the second time around. Married a man who can cook. A lot of people wouldn't know it by looking at him, but Coop's a keeper from way back."

Sara didn't know why that made her weepy.

The older woman pointed to her shoes. "They don't make soles thick enough for these poor feet. So what do you think? You interested?"

Sara had applied for a job here a month ago. Dixie hadn't been hiring then. Thinking about foolish pride over providence, she opted not to bring it up. "I haven't worked since high school."

Again, Dixie didn't seem to hear. "Can you start at eight tomorrow morning?"

Sara would have to get up earlier in order to deliver her newspapers, but she nodded.

"Be here half an hour early, and I'll take you through the paces." She took Roy's plate. "Give me a sec and I'll box up this meal, too."

When they were alone, Natalie Harper said, "In the future, I'd leave your lack of work experience off the résumé. I don't give free advice often. By the way, congratulations. You did it."

The bell jangled over the door.

Sara tensed.

Natalie and Dixie both looked at whoever had entered.

Natalie wasn't saying anything. Neither was Dixie. Sara tried to read their expressions, but couldn't. In her mind she heard one finger on the piano, duh-duh-duh-da.

Thinking the worst, that Roy had come back to hurt her, to get in one last taunt or slap or punch or to somehow get even, or worse, she turned in her chair and prepared to face the music.

CHAPTER 14

Sara braced for the worst.

Images flashed through her mind, headlines about predators who stalked and killed the women they'd beaten. Those cases were rare. She didn't think Roy fit that category. But she'd been wrong before.

Her eyes focused, and the terror left her.

It wasn't Roy coming back to hurt her.

It was her precious Seth. He stood, his back to the door, feet braced, as if he too expected the worst. His T-shirt was dirty, his jeans grass stained, his tennis shoes mud-spattered.

"The aunts said you were meeting Dad here."

His voice hadn't cracked like that since it had changed. It made her heart constrict. "Did you run all the way?"

He nodded, and she knew he'd come to save her. Fifteen-year-old boys should not have to save their mothers. She moved toward him.

"Your father's gone, Seth."

His shoulders slumped. Perhaps it was relief, or perhaps it was something as fundamental as the absence of terror.

It made her ache.

Seth had never been comfortable with open displays of affection. She wrapped her arms around her boy and hugged him anyway. He towered over her, smelling of rain and sweat and grass and something that was uniquely him.

"It's okay," she whispered. "It's over. All of it is over."

She felt him shudder. If she could go back in time to when he was a little boy, she would. She would protect him better, do everything better. But the wish was futile. They had today, and she'd just taken another step toward a full and peaceful future for both of them.

"I'm getting a divorce. I told him. The house will be sold, and we won't be broke anymore."

"And he didn't hit you?"

"He wanted to, but he knows he can't anymore."

Seth straightened, ready to be let go.

"Oh," she said, reluctant to release him. "And I have a job."

"What kind of job?" He drew away, and she let him.

"Your mother's going to be waiting tables here at Cooper's." Dixie was back with the second Styrofoam box.

"I start tomorrow." Catching him looking at the containers Dixie placed on a nearby table, Sara added, "It means we won't have to eat peanut butter every day."

"I don't mind peanut butter." He was watching her stack the dinners one on top of the other. "Sometimes. What's that?"

"Supper. Do you want the steak dinner or the fish?"

"You have steak?" He may have been fifteen years old, but he could have been eight again, hopping off the school bus, his shoelaces untied, his cowlick sticking straight up as he raced into the house, sniffing the air, asking what he smelled cooking for supper and calling "I'm home!" as if she wouldn't have known otherwise. Maybe men never outgrew their enjoyment of life's simple pleasures. She hoped this one didn't.

"Do you want to eat it here?" she asked.

He glanced shyly at Natalie and Dixie before turning back to his mom. "Let's go home."

Home.

It was no longer the house in the country where Roy now lived alone. Home was wherever she and Seth were safe.

They left the café. Although the rain had ended, there was no rainbow. She had something better. She had supper, another part-time job, and her pride.

"Now take a little in either hand," Brooke said. "Gently now."

"Is this gentle enough for you?" Mac asked.

"Pull them together. A little more." She leaned across him. "Now keep your finger there. Ah, that's perfect." By the time it occurred to her how provocative that sounded, it was too late.

"I love it when a chef talks dirty to me." Mac was smiling.

At least someone was enjoying her struggle to regain her composure.

"I had no idea learning to cook would be like this."

"Who's learning to cook?" she quipped.

Teaching Sophie and Rebecca and Mac the basics of cooking had been the plan. The kitchen at Stone Cottage *was* littered with vegetable peels and measuring cups and freshly chopped seasonings, and granted, the oven was preheating and the air smelled like grated lemon, fresh thyme and chives. The girls had retreated to Sophe's room before completing one task, each. Mac stood at the counter beside her, and no matter how often she moved away, somehow their hands always wound up touching, their arms brushing.

He whispered, "This might work better if you at least pretended to keep your mind on cooking."

"Me?"

His expression was a little too knowing, his eyes a little too smoldering, his mouth a little too enticing. He was right. Every time she looked at him she had to wrench herself away from her preoccupation with his face. Cooking should have been a safe pastime. Cooking with Mac brought to mind things that were forbidden.

It wasn't as if she'd chosen something exotic to teach him. She wouldn't dream of suggesting a supposed aphrodisiac, like clams or papaya and passion fruit. She'd toyed with the idea of trying something straightforward and everyday, like spaghetti, but she'd decided that preparing sauce made from sun-ripened tomatoes and onions sautéed in olive oil and fresh basil might be a little too earthy, even with Sophie's and Rebecca's presence. So near the seacoast, it had seemed only natural to attempt a simple fish dish called snapper en papillôte, a French term describing food baked inside a wrapping of parchment paper.

Mac had chopped the yellow summer squash while she washed the fish and Sophie and Rebecca cut the red peppers into thin slices. When they'd begged off grating the lemon rind, he'd taken over. He had good finger dexterity, and his eye-hand coordination was top-notch. Looking at him looking at her, she faced the fact that he wasn't any more interested in learning to cook than Sophie and Rebecca were.

"Would you like to have a seat over there and just watch?" she asked.

"Watching sounds interesting, but I rather like where I am."

There he went again, and there went her imagination. They'd talked this morning along the water's edge, and later during the jog back. They'd agreed they could spend time together doing innocent things like preparing a meal, thereby keeping their relationship platonic and tidy.

Maybe she shouldn't have attempted a French dish.

She'd always loved to cook. The very act of chopping and measuring and stirring and tasting was therapeutic and cathartic. She derived great satisfaction from cooking for people. Cooking *with* Mac was sensual. And messy. Getting messy didn't bother him. In fact, he seemed to enjoy that aspect of it. It put her in mind of other activities he might enjoy.

Thinking like this was dangerous, and resisting was trying her patience. When he snitched a slice of red pepper, she swatted his hand. "Must you sample everything?"

He looked at her mouth as if he wanted to sample her. Her impatience turned into a gentle mewling, a warm pining that wasn't in the recipe books.

She'd taken her rings off before starting. She always took them off when she cooked. Today, she didn't plan to put them back on. That didn't change the fact that she was still married. It didn't change the fact that Colin was coming to Alcott next week. God help her, it didn't change the fact that she wanted Mac to kiss her, either.

The rain had stopped hours ago, but the air still felt heavy. It would have been a glorious afternoon to spend in bed beneath the fan. Her pulse thrummed with everything she would have liked to do. Shaking her head, she moved away yet again.

"Did I miss the question?" he asked.

"Sophie and Rebecca are two rooms away."

"So they are."

Brooke didn't know what was wrong with her. It wasn't as if the conversation had been intimate. They'd talked about taxes and some of the problems organized religions were facing, and a documentary he'd watched about sand crabs. She liked listening to him, but even sand crabs sounded sensual when he spoke of them.

He placed his hand on the counter next to hers and quietly said, "It isn't easy to do the right thing."

He not only knew, he understood. It was intoxicating to be wanted, lusted after, and on a deeper level, appreciated for something so basic and inherent in who she was.

This time he recovered first, launching into what he called a sure mood buster: his childhood. She was laughing again in no time.

* * *

"Your mom sure likes to cook."

Sophie and Rebecca lay across her bed, Sophie on her stomach, Rebecca on her back, Fluffy looking from one to the other as if trying to decide whether to remain on the bed or retreat beneath it.

"She makes the best blueberry pancakes." Propped up on her elbows, Sophie brought the equestrian magazine closer to her face and reread a paragraph.

"She doesn't sound all that sad," Rebecca said.

Rebecca Callaway was about the most interesting girl Sophie knew. All the Callaways were smart. She liked Rebecca the best. For one thing, they were almost the same age. Besides, what Rebecca thought, she said, and what she said was hilarious a lot of the time.

Sophie didn't feel much like laughing right now. "What do you mean?"

Rebecca sat up and stretched. Sophe had seen the oldest Callaway sister move exactly that way. Rachel was fifteen, and had already had three boyfriends. Rebecca had been thirteen for four whole months, and turned all weird whenever she saw Seth Kemper. Sophie agreed he was cute and everything, but she didn't see what all the fuss was about. Of course she knew it had to do with growing up. She didn't really want to grow up, because growing up meant changing, and her life was already changing too much.

"I mean," Rebecca said with quiet emphasis. "She doesn't sound all that sad about getting a divorce."

"She's sad on the inside."

Just then her mom burst out laughing. Mac joined in, but his laugh was deeper.

Reaching for her cat, Sophie inched toward the door, Rebecca right behind her. They could see part of the kitchen from here. Sophie's mom was putting something in a pan and Mac was telling her a story or something.

"They like each other, don't they?" Rebecca whispered.

"They're friends."

"Did your mom laugh like that with your dad?"

"Not so much." Sophie thought about the time she came home from Makayla's and saw her mom crying and her dad wearing crème brûlée. Nobody was laughing then.

"Think he's still screwing around on her?"

Sophie's back straightened, a vertebra at a time. Now she wished she hadn't told Rebecca about that. "Of course not."

"How would you know?"

"My dad is very smart. He learned his lesson. He's just about the best-looking man on the planet, and he's very sophisticated."

"You ever see them kiss?" Rebecca asked.

"Who?"

"Your parents. Who else?"

Oh. No, she hadn't. "My dad is Main Line."

Fluffy didn't appreciate being petted so hard, and wanted to get down. For some reason, Sophie needed her cat's weight and warmth. She loosened her grip and tried coaxing Fluffy to relax by petting her softer.

"What does Main Line mean?" Rebecca asked.

Sophie rolled her eyes. "It means he has good lineage. All his relatives have always lived in old, elegant towns called Main Line towns."

"Sounds more like a railroad to me."

Of course it did! Main Line towns were west of what used to be the main line of the Pennsylvania Railroad. Anybody who was anybody knew that. Main Liners didn't send their kids to just any school and they didn't drive just any car and they didn't wear cowboy boots, ever. Exasperated, Sophie said, "Well maybe that's because you're a dumb hick living in this hick town, riding hick horses till the cows come home."

"Maybe you're a spoiled-rotten bratty snob."

"Am not."

"Then I'm not a dumb hick."

"Are so."

"Take that back."

"What's the matter?" Sophie taunted. "Can't you take the truth? At least my friend Makayla knows cowboy boots don't go with shorts."

Rebecca's face flushed and her mouth dropped open. A moment later, she rushed out into the kitchen and on outside.

The screen door was still banging when Sophie reached it.

"Something wrong with Rebecca?" her mom asked.

"There's plenty wrong with her. She's boy crazy and dumb and she has red hair."

"We don't choose the hair we're born with. Besides, she has pretty red hair. And she's not dumb, is she?" Brooke peered out the window. "Sophie, she's crying."

Sophie geared up to say the most unbecoming word she knew, but she saw that her mom was right. Rebecca *was* crying. Aw, hell.

Her mom reached for the box of tissues. "Why don't you take these out to her and talk things over."

"Because I don't want to." Sophie felt like crying, too, but she hated it when her mom told her what to do.

"I'll be right back." Her mom slipped through the door.

Finding herself alone in the kitchen with Dr. Mackenzie, Sophie wished she had taken the stinking tissues outside herself. Fluffy meowed to get down again. Sophie didn't see what choice she had except to let her. She bent down so the cat wouldn't hurt her paws landing.

"Did your friend do something to make you angry?" Mac asked. "Or vice versa?"

She rolled her eyes. Vice versa. What a lame phrase. "All she talks about is boys."

"Not horses?" he asked.

Sophie's shrug looked more like a hiccup.

Mac was quiet.

And Sophie found herself saying, "It's easy for Rebecca."

"What is?"

"Boys. Friends. Everything." She sniffed. Something smelled good. Something always smelled good in her mom's kitchen. "What else does she have to worry about?"

Mac leaned against the counter. Crossing his arms and his ankles, he made himself comfortable. He wasn't especially proficient in father-son relationships, most specifically his own, but he was good with women. He'd been raised by them. He liked them. And he liked to think he understood them. He didn't have as much experience with adolescent girls, but his track record gave him a level of confidence surpassed only by his desire to help.

Sophie's long brown hair was woven into some sort of loose braid that started at the top of her head. Fine tendrils had escaped, framing her narrow face. If the length of her legs was an accurate indication, she would be taller than her mother some day. She had a long way to go before she was grown up. Something was bothering her.

"Rebecca doesn't have much to worry about. What about you?" he asked. "Are you worried about something?"

She became engrossed in tracing a crack in the worn linoleum with her big toe.

"Your mom said your dad's coming to Alcott for your birthday."

She sighed. "They're getting a divorce." She pronounced it dee-vorce.

"Did Rebecca say something about that?"

"She thinks she knows everything because her parents still kiss. Gross."

"Are you mad at your parents?"

"No!" She said it a little too vehemently.

"But?"

"Everything's changing."

"And you're worried about that."

She shrugged again.

"Have your mom and dad always made sure you're safe, happy and cared for?" he asked.

"I guess."

"Do you think that will ever change?"

She seemed to be thinking about that. "I guess not."

"Do *you* think you're going to be okay?"

She took her time answering. "I guess." This time she said it begrudgingly.

"My mother and father got a divorce when I was a baby and I grew up pretty much unscathed. And my father was *Archie.*"

She finally looked at him. He let her stare, but couldn't help wondering at the cause.

"If you have something to say, you might as well say it." He used the tone of voice he reserved for therapy.

"I can't picture it."

He assumed she was referring to all the changes that were about to take place in her future: a different house, a different schedule, a different life. Since he'd found that it was best for a person to verbalize her feelings, he said, "What can't you picture, Sophie?"

"You," she said.

"Me?"

"As a baby. But I guess you were one back in the olden days."

He blinked. Twice. Well, then.

She looked out the window. "Mom's coming back in. I guess I should go out and tell Rebecca I'm sorry I called her dumb. And all the rest."

"That's a good idea."

She went outside, exchanging a few words with her mother as they passed. Brooke returned. Washing her hands at the sink, she said, "Rebecca wouldn't tell me what happened. Did you have any better luck with Sophie?"

"I think she's going to be okay."

"Whatever you said helped. Thank you, Mac."

"Sophie did it all by herself. I just listened. I don't often counsel adolescent girls. Now I know why."

"Why?"

"Never mind, but you wouldn't know where I might buy a good cane, would you?"

Brooke's laugh was a quiet sound, bringing Mac full circle. The steamy air had had its way with her fine, straight hair. Her shorts were wrinkled, and her top spattered with lemon juice. It wasn't a fragrance he usually associated with passion.

"It's going to be a long week."

She looked at him in surprise. "Is that what we're doing? Waiting until after Colin visits?"

"Honestly, Brooke, I don't know what I'm doing. I've never been in love before."

Brooke didn't know who was more stunned. "You love me?" she whispered.

The line of his mouth tightened a fraction at a time. He looked about as happy as a man who'd just been told he had a month to live.

He loved her.

She wasn't sure how she felt. Even if she were, she wasn't at liberty to say it. Still, he loved her, and being loved was a heady thing.

The girls were talking beneath the dappled shade of the birch tree in the front yard. She and Mac stood in the steamy kitchen looking at each other, *resisting*, and not enjoying it at all.

Something buzzed. At first she thought it was the oven timer. Whatever it was, it buzzed again like an intrusion out of the clear blue.

Reaching for the phone clipped to his belt, the man who rarely swore, swore under his breath. "Yes, Greta."

Mac's brow furrowed. Brooke didn't know what was wrong, but whatever it was, it was serious.

"When?"

He listened intently.

"How bad?"

He listened again.

"I'll be right there." He snapped the phone shut.

"Your father?" she asked.

He nodded.

"Is he—"

"Not yet. Dr. Grayson is on his way."

Placing a gentling hand on Mac's arm, Brooke said, "Do you want me to come with you?"

The muscles in his forearm tensed beneath her palm. "Under the circumstances, it would probably be best if you didn't."

She walked with him as far as the door, then stayed where she was until his car disappeared down the street. Hugging her arms close to her body, she turned and surveyed her kitchen.

And that ended Cooking 101.

CHAPTER 15

Claudia sat on the edge of the claw-footed bathtub, smoothing lotion on her hands, her arms, her shoulders, and slowly down every inch of the rest of her body. A warm breeze billowed the curtains, and the last of the water gurgled down the drain.

Her skin was pink, healthy and supple. The color went nicely with the polish on her toenails. She'd done her fingernails, too, but in a deeper shade of rose. Her dark hair was always naturally wavy. The humidity from her bath had left it a little wild. Just the look she was going for.

She padded into her old bedroom then stood in front of the closet where she'd arranged the clothes she'd brought with her from Charleston. She would have loved to go bra-less, but she was thirty-five and on the chesty side, so that just wasn't an option. She compensated by spending a small fortune on underwear. It was worth it, because the bra and panties she slipped on felt decadent. And the long, casual dress in muted shades of gold, brown and yellow would do nicely for what she had in mind.

The oatmeal scrub had left her face glowing. In keeping with her minimalist mood, she brushed on some bronzing powder, glided on long-lasting lip gloss, spritzed on Julian's favorite fragrance, fastened her wristwatch, and slipped into her ankle-strap sandals, sure thing shoes, she called them. Voilà!

She looked good. She should. She'd spent the past two hours pampering herself. It was exactly what she'd needed. Perhaps she wasn't the only one who could use a little pampering. Holding that thought, she rummaged through her case, then bent down and added an amber toe ring. The man on her mind loved toes, after all.

She wouldn't have been surprised if Julian had shown up here this afternoon. She wasn't surprised he hadn't, either. This was fun, this *not* knowing. Now that she'd had time to get used to the idea, she was glad he'd decided to *vacation* in Alcott. He had an uncanny ability to anticipate her needs. Just thinking about a few of those *needs* sent a low vibration all the way through her. She didn't know when he would turn up next, or where. But she was fairly certain it would be soon.

Right now she was hungry. Her smile in the mirror was that of the proverbial cat with a mouthful of canary feathers. The anticipation only enhanced the slow circling, advancing, and eventual seduction she had planned for her right-hand man.

Her mouth watered.

There wasn't a good Cajun restaurant near Alcott, and she wasn't in the mood for a bar hamburger. She would have enjoyed a good pizza, but the pizzeria had closed years ago, and the only other place that sold pizza was the convenience store out on the highway. They might as well call it gut-rot-by-the-slice-or-pan. Claudia was saving herself for another sort of adventure tonight. That left Cooper's Café. She wondered what today's catch of the day was. She smiled again. If things went well, she would be the catch of the day.

She drove her rental car to the town square, parked at the curb, and sauntered into the small café. It was much earlier than she normally had dinner. Evidently, it was even early for the regular supper crowd, for she had her pick of stations.

She chose a booth for its privacy and its view of the door, and had barely gotten comfortable when a shadow fell across the smooth, worn surface of the table.

She glanced up, straight into eyes the color of the Mediterranean on a cloudless day. "Hello, Julian."

"This booth is taken, Claudia." He pronounced it Claud-ya. He really did have a marvelous voice, deep enough to stir a woman's interest but not so deep it would ever become gravelly.

Other than the cutlery wrapped in a paper napkin, the table's surface was spotless, but if he said it was taken, she wouldn't argue. She was saving her strength.

"Would you like me to find another booth, or would you rather join me at this one?" she asked, the epitome of acquiescence.

He stared at her in that all-knowing, all-seeing, all-encompassing way he had. Slowly, he settled his lanky frame on the padded vinyl bench across from her.

For the first time, she noticed the leather briefcase under his arm. "I thought you were on vacation."

He looked at her through half-closed lids. "Call me a working fool."

She leaned forward and lowered her voice. "Now Julian, you and I both know you're no fool."

Claudia thoroughly enjoyed watching warmth spread across his features. She would have made her move then and there if Dixie Cooper hadn't trudged over and interrupted. "I thought you'd left!"

"Without paying for the tea?"

Claudia would have sworn to God the woman was about to twitter like a schoolgirl. Smoothing a hand over her apron, the older woman said, "I wouldn't have cleaned off your table if I'd known you were returning."

So this *was* his table.

"I appreciate a clean establishment, Dixie."

You'd have thought he'd told her he *appreciated* her hips. Accustomed to such reactions, Claudia said, "Would you bring me a southern iced tea when you get a minute?" She smiled nicely. "And perhaps a menu?"

"Of course, dearie." The gray-haired woman ambled away to the kitchen as if her feet hurt.

Julian reached into the case and rummaged around inside. Claudia didn't mind being ignored, for it presented her with the perfect opportunity to watch him. He liked to be watched.

She knew a great deal about him. He liked old-fashioned, barbershop shaves, the Knicks, *the Queen Mother*, museums, tea (the aunts would adore him), bourbon and the rain. His bed stand always held at least one book he never finished. She'd asked him about it once, and he'd said, "I like to keep a book on hand that will make me look good if I die in the middle of it."

For all his beauty, youth and incredibly virile appeal, sometimes Julian Bartholomew was, well, a little strange. Perhaps that was why they got along so well.

Her toe tingled just enough to remind her it was there.

"What kind of work did you bring along?" she asked.

"The contracts for the Baton Rouge deal. This afternoon I lost track of time dabbling with a few ideas I have for Hats."

She was always curious about his "dabblings." They didn't lean toward design, but rather along distribution and marketing strategies and ploys. Often they were just as creative as the hats themselves. Claudia was certainly intrigued. By the time he'd finished telling her about his latest advertising brain child, their meals were finished, and their plates had been removed. Both sat forward, elbows on the table, their coffees cold between them.

"Julian, this is brilliant."

He patted his mouth with his paper napkin.

"I mean it." Her gaze strayed to his hands. He really had amazing hands. She'd often been mesmerized watching his hands on her.

Now, where was she? Ah. Advertising and marketing strategies. She looked at him as she had countless times in the past. Julian Bartholomew was one of those men who never appeared to be busy, and yet he accomplished more than a committee, hell, more than a platoon of men. He was an asset to Hats.

Now, about after-hours.

"I know what you're thinking," he said.

"You know I'm thinking you have a poet's mouth?" she asked quietly.

"You probably say that to all your vice-presidents." But his smile spoke of conquest.

Conquest was good.

She slid her foot out of her sandal and glided her toe up his calf, gently pressing the ball of her foot onto his lap. He closed his eyes for a moment, a rapturous look crossing his face.

"Uh, uh, uh." He very gently but firmly removed her foot from his lap. Instead of releasing it, he massaged her arch and said, "There'll be none of that."

"None of what?" she asked, her eyes practically rolling back in her head.

"I believe they called it hanky-panky in the movies."

In forty-year-old movies, maybe. She'd heard what he said, such as it was. She also saw where he was looking. Talk about saying one thing and meaning another. She smiled. Two could play this game. "What, pray tell, are you talking about?"

"No lovemaking."

She noticed he didn't smile. "You mean sex?"

"No."

What a relief.

"I mean no sex."

He was serious.

"Are you all right?" she asked.

He made no reply.

Reaching across the table, she patted his hand. "They make a pill for everything these days, Julian. It's nothing to be ashamed of."

He took a sip from his water glass, moved his hips slightly in his seat, then drummed his fingertips on the table. "I don't need a pill. I'm taking a vacation. From Hats. And from that."

"A vacation."

Someone yelled for a refill. Cutlery jangled. When had the café filled up?

Julian inclined his dark head. "Don't get me wrong." He smiled. "You can look."

She already was looking. "Oh, I can, can I?"

"But you can't touch." He released her foot.

"What the hell are you talking about?" Her voice rose an octave and her foot hit the floor.

Every diner in the place turned to stare at them. Nonplused, Julian smiled all around.

Dixie arrived just as Julian was fishing some bills from his pocket. "Keep the change, Dixie dear," he said.

It was an obscene amount of money for the mediocre service and bland food. No wonder the old hen twittered.

He slid from the booth, touched two fingers to his lips, and extended his fingertips toward Claudia. Reaching for his briefcase, he walked out the back door. Conversation resumed throughout the restaurant. And Claudia's toe twitched in earnest.

She sipped her lukewarm coffee, thinking. *Look but don't touch?*

She would just see about that.

The sun was setting.

Mac hadn't moved since the last time Dr. Grayson had listened to his father's heartbeat an hour ago. A knot the size of his fist had formed between his shoulder blades. Pain kept him from dozing. Or perhaps dread did that.

Scant rays of sunlight had crept through the wavy glass in the front door, gradually stretching into the foyer, inching all the way into this room. His father's breathing had grown slower and slower, until Mac expected every breath to be the last.

He could hear Dr. Grayson and Greta speaking in hushed tones in the dining room. Brooke had brought over the snapper en papillôte a few hours ago. Mac hadn't left his father's side, but he'd heard her voice, and had smelled the food long after she'd gone. He hadn't eaten any of it. Perhaps later.

Archie took another breath.

Mac held perfectly still in the chair beside the bed. His father was eighty-four years old. His heart was weak, and he was tired. A lesser man would have given up and died. Archie struggled to open his eyes. When he finally had them open, his gaze darted about the room before settling on Mac.

"Oh, it's you."

What had Mac expected? Joy? Gratitude? An apology for yesterday, for the day before that, or for the Christmas he'd been twelve, the day he'd turned eighteen? *I'm proud of you, son*? A feeble smile would have been nice. Mac knew better than to expect it, and yet he was disappointed. He'd grown adept at accepting it. That didn't mean he wouldn't have changed it if he could.

Archie had been dying for two months. Soon it would be over.

"Are you comfortable, Dad?"

"What difference does it make?"

The man had been an ornery son of a bitch most of Mac's life. It seemed he was going to be consistent to the end.

"Is there anyone you'd like me to call?"

This time Archie answered with his eyes shut. "When it's all over, call your mother." His breathing was labored, his voice raspy and weaker than a whisper.

"You have my word, Dad."

Even close to death, Archie's lip curled snidely.

The sheet was folded beneath his arms, his dry, bony hands resting limply at his sides. His chest rose and fell slowly and shallowly.

Mac said, "We can do this any way you want. I can stay. Or I can leave. The choice is yours."

"Now you sound like her."

Mac wouldn't have been surprised if Archie had told him to get the hell out of his room. He'd been prepared for *that*. This was a twist he hadn't anticipated.

"Who do I sound like?"

Of course, Archie didn't reply.

Mac ran through a list of possibilities in his mind, finally settling on the only person it could be. "I sound like my mother?"

He assumed the raspy grunt meant "yes."

"Mom says I remind her of you."

Mac's father didn't look any happier about that than Mac was.

"You love her. You've always loved her." Mac spoke quietly, reverently.

"Quick, get the violins."

"Get them yourself." Mac had surprised the old goat. "You could do anything you put your mind to. You could have stayed true to Mom. If you had, she wouldn't have left you."

"A fat lot you know."

Mac waited.

And Archie rasped. "The choice was hers. Not mine."

He'd said it before. Mac didn't understand it any better this time. Rather than upset his father at this late stage, Mac let it go. "I know we haven't had a normal father-son relationship, but I appreciate all the things you taught me."

"Shut the hell up."

That was a long way from "I'm proud of you, son."

"I never wanted to be a father."

A lot of men didn't want to be fathers, but they adjusted. Again, Mac kept the observation to himself.

Archie said, "Don't get all maudlin. It wasn't personal."

It was personal to Mac.

"She knew," Archie whispered. "And living with me would have been hell. So I made it easy for her."

"What did you make easy for her?" And then, "You made *leaving you* easy for her?"

Understanding dawned, and with it enlightenment.

"You had affairs so she would have a *reason* to leave you."

The rest fell into place.

"That's what you meant when you said she made her choice. You weren't talking about the divorce. You didn't want a child. Any child. And yet I came along. And she chose *me*, over you. Would you have been happier if she'd given me up for adoption?"

"Not adoption." It was the equivalent of a yell. And it cost him.

Mac was on his feet. "All these years you've wished she would have aborted me. What a dad! You can go to hell for all I care!"

"She." Archie wheezed. "Made." He rasped. "Her choice."

It required every last breath he had.

Every last one.

The sun dipped below the horizon, taking the last rays of light with it. Archie's eyes didn't twitch. His chest didn't rise. And never would again. Mac continued staring into his father's face, even though he knew.

Archibald Elliot had died.

"Did I wake you?"

Brooke grasped the phone. "Mac." It was past midnight. "No. I was lying here with the cat, wondering." Worrying. "Is he?"

"Yes."

Brooke closed her eyes for a moment. It struck her how the smallest words were always the strongest, the hardest to say and the most difficult to get over.

She swung her feet off the bed, jostling the cat. She wanted to go to Mac. Sit with him. Be with him. Pass the time with him. She made it as far as the doorway to Sophie's room. She was sound asleep, arms akimbo, mouth open slightly. Although her daughter was nearly thirteen, Brooke didn't feel comfortable leaving her alone in the middle of the night.

"Is anybody there with you?" she asked.

"I'm all right."

That wasn't what she'd asked.

He said, "Giles Grayson and the coroner just left. My mother's catching the red-eye from Seattle. Greta is getting some sleep."

His voice sounded heavy with exhaustion.

"I'll call Claudia. If I can't reach her, I'll try Eve. I'm sure she won't mind coming over to stay with Sophie. When you hear a knock on your door, it'll be me."

"That isn't necessary, Brooke."

"What are friends for?"

Archie Elliot was laid to rest the following morning at ten o'clock. There had been no viewing. No wake. No flowers or music or eulogy. He'd been a well-known man, a pioneer of sorts, an award-winning writer and gifted storyteller, an entrepreneur, and an adventurer who'd hobnobbed with diplomats and stars.

Per his final wishes, only a handful of people had gathered on the tiny hillside cemetery a few miles outside Alcott. Mac stood with his mother. Archie's doctor and former nurse stood to one side, heads bowed, Brooke and Sophie near Reverend McCall. No one shed a tear. It was exactly as the man who'd seemed larger than life had wanted it.

The weather was windy and a little bit wild. It wouldn't have surprised anyone if Archie had had a hand in that, too.

Brian McCall said a short prayer, then invited anyone who so wished to say something meaningful or fitting. Mac declined. Brooke certainly had nothing to add. Greta and Dr. Grayson passed, too.

Looking uncharacteristically shy, Sophie stepped forward. Without letting go of her mother's hand, she said, "Archie was a jerk sometimes, like my dad. I loved him anyway."

There was a collective gasp, and then a hush all around. Certainly, no one could, in good conscience, refute it.

Finally, Yvonne Elliot laughed. "Well put!"

At seventy-two, Yvonne Taylor Mackenzie Elliot had a slender build and classic features. Her silver-gray hair had most likely been enhanced, her clothes stylish right down to her shoes. She was the epitome of understated elegance. Her laugh was something else entirely. Brooke responded to it, and so did Sophie. It put everyone present at ease.

Greta gave Mac a hug, shook Yvonne's hand, winked at Brooke and thanked the reverend. She gave Sophie a high five before ambling toward her old Malibu and her next job. Giles Grayson said goodbye next.

Brian exchanged a few words with everyone. Grasping his tattered prayer book loosely in his right hand, he left, too. That left Brooke and Sophie and Mac and his mother.

Brooke had been worried that Sophie would have a difficult time letting go of the old man she'd befriended. Surprisingly, she hadn't wanted to go to Captain's Row with Brooke to deliver supper last night, saying that she and Archie had already said their goodbyes. Brooke didn't know what Archie had told her, but it seemed to have prepared Sophie. Although she'd cried when Brooke broke the news this morning, her daughter seemed to be handling the old man's death well, accepting it as she'd accepted him. Wasn't that the kind of relationship she and Archie had had right from the start?

Mac had borne the brunt of the past two months and especially the past twenty-four hours. He looked tired, his green eyes hooded. He'd been quiet when she'd arrived last night. She'd made a pot of coffee. Neither of them took more than a token sip. He didn't tell her how he was feeling.

Instead, he talked about his father's final wishes, the weather, a ship he'd spotted on the ocean earlier. He didn't have to talk about anything deeper. It was enough that she was there. Shortly after three A.M., she'd left him with strict instructions to get some rest.

Sophie and Claudia had been sound asleep back at Stone Cottage. Rather than wake Claudia, who was sprawled across the bed, Brooke had curled up on the sofa and had fallen asleep immediately.

Mac didn't look as if he'd gotten any sleep at all. It put her in mind of the first time she'd seen him. That day he'd mistaken her for someone the temp service had sent over. She'd thought his gaze had been deliberate then. Now it was even more so.

She'd never attended a funeral quite like Archie's. The casket was a plain pine box made by a friend of his years ago. The fact that he had several million dollars and yet chose to be buried so simply said a great deal about him. The short service had been blunt, and completely lacked pretense or tradition, much like the man they were burying.

Now that it was over, awkwardness set in. Brooke could feel Yvonne Elliot's eyes on her. She was curious about this woman who had loved Archie Elliot, heart and soul, up close and from far away, all these years.

This was the woman who had raised Mac.

"Can we go now, Mom?" Sophie asked.

Brooke dropped an arm across Sophie's narrow shoulders. "Of course."

"Bye, Mac," Sophie said.

"Goodbye, Sophe."

"Bye, Mrs. Elliot."

While Yvonne was returning Sophie's parting courtesy, Brooke looked at Mac. The wind fluttered his tie, blowing his hair straight off his forehead. Brooke's wide-brimmed hat had been Claudia's idea. Before the wind whisked it off her head, she removed it herself, and held Mac's gaze. Something unspoken passed from his eyes to hers. She offered him a small smile. For the first time all morning, his tight expression relaxed.

"Ready, Mom?" Sophie asked.

"Yes." Brooke replied without breaking eye contact with Mac. Rather than exchanging any of the usual parting words, she nodded again, turned around, and left it at that.

CHAPTER 16

"It's finally happened." Yvonne Elliot unclipped her pearl earrings as she walked through the kitchen in Archie's old house on Captain's Row. "I was beginning to think it never would."

"We've known he was dying for two months."

She doubted Mac was being intentionally dense, although, in his defense, they *had* just come from the cemetery. Placing the simple earrings on the windowsill over the kitchen sink, she turned to her son and said, "I wasn't referring to your father."

Mac's sigh had a lot in common with the heaving of the ocean. "You're bursting with something, Mom. You might as well say it and get it over with."

The first time she'd seen this particular look on her boy's face, he'd been two years old. It had reminded her of Archie then. Some things didn't change.

"Why, I'm talking about you and Brooke Valentine, of course."

Mac folded his arms.

"There's no need to scowl, darling."

Of course, that only made him scowl more.

"The bigger they are, the harder they fall. Brooke is

pretty, smart, well-spoken and well-mannered. Greta says she's a marvelous cook. Remember how you refused to learn to cook when you were a boy? She sounds perfect for you."

"Maybe she'll introduce you to her husband sometime."

Yvonne's eyebrows rose slightly, but in the end she shrugged. "No one ever said love was uncomplicated. No one knows that better than I."

She would have liked to relieve Mac of everything that was bothering him, but there was only so much a mother could do. It was one of the less pleasant realities in life. She'd reared a smart and charming boy who was audaciously stubborn at times. He'd become a smart and charming and caring man who was audaciously stubborn at times. It was hard to believe he was thirty-nine. Wasn't she thirty-nine?

"Have I told you I've enjoyed being your mother?"

"Once or twice. A month."

At least the scowl was gone from his finely sculpted face. "It was an honor, all of it. Your grandmother used to complain that I spoiled you. Perhaps I did in some areas, but not where it counted."

The coffeemaker hissed and steamed and gurgled. The windows were open; there really was a marvelous breeze up here. No wonder Archie had been so taken with this area. Archie was gone. She'd been saying it to herself since Mac had called her last night. It would take some getting used to.

"Let's take our coffee and a plate of those cookies Brooke made out to the patio, shall we?"

He agreed, although if he'd had his way, he probably would have gone for a long run. There would be time for that later. First, there were some things she needed to tell him.

As she poured the coffee and arranged everything on a tray, she couldn't help noticing the items that belonged to Brooke Valentine and her daughter. Casserole dishes sat on the counter. The soda Sophie liked was in the refrigerator, and a paperback novel Brooke had lent Mac was on the hall table.

He carried the tray, which he placed on the table between

two comfortable lawn chairs, then waited for her to be seated before he did so, too. He'd always been a gentleman.

She nibbled a cookie. And moaned. "This is heavenly. Honey-date something. Have you tried one?"

"I've *tried* several. They're very good. Somehow, I don't think you came out here to talk about cookies."

"You always were astute. And I've always tried to be open with you, haven't I?"

Settling back more comfortably in his cushioned rattan chair, Mac shrugged. "You've been open with me about everything except my father."

"That's because I made a promise to him years ago. I'll get to that in a minute. All the girls were after you in high school."

"A handful of girls were after me in high school."

"I never minded sharing you. It was good for a young man to play the field. I wasn't concerned when you settled into your career, seemingly in no hurry to get married. All I've ever wanted was for you to be happy. You would agree that I've been supportive, wouldn't you?"

He made a sound in the back of his throat. "Supportive, understanding, cunning, manipulative. You name it."

She laughed. And he almost did, too.

Mac yawned. Had he ever been so tired? The air in the shade beneath the hundred-year-old oak trees was a comfortable seventy-eight degrees. The feeder birds were quiet this time of the day, but farther away, ocean birds squawked noisily. Watching them, he thought about all the hints his mother used to drop about grandchildren. And then, six or seven years ago she'd shown up on his doorstep out of the blue. She'd looked at him in a kindly manner and sighed deeply. "It's all right, dear. It's taken me a while, but I finally figured it out. And I just want you to know that I accept it completely."

"Accept what, Mother?" he'd asked blankly.

"Your sexual preference," she'd whispered.

He'd gaped at her. "My sexual—"

"There's nothing to be embarrassed about, especially in this day and age."

All these years later, Mac still lifted his eyes heavenward when he thought of it. None of his friends or associates had problems like these. He'd decided to let her think whatever she pleased. But when she'd tried to fix him up with the son of her accountant, he'd finally set her straight.

He stared at his mother today, noticing the lines beside her eyes and the spunk in them. Despite her meddling, she had been a good mother.

She popped the last of her cookie into her mouth. "What is it, dear? What are you thinking? Don't worry. You can tell me."

"I used to wonder why I couldn't have normal parents."

"Instead you got Archie and me." She sipped her coffee. "I've done everything I know to encourage and teach you, to set you free and let you know I'm always here if you need me. And yet you still never found the right woman. I decided it was all your father's fault. What wasn't? The old goat withheld his acceptance from you. I suppose that's what's eating at you."

Mac watched a tanker ride the glistening horizon. "When I was twenty I wrote down everything I wanted to tell him. I'd planned to turn it into a screenplay. There would be three acts, and each one would have been delivered at a deafening decibel. Yet I never so much as raised my voice to him." His voice sounded flat in his own ears. "Until thirty seconds before he took his last breath."

"You two argued?" she asked.

The tanker lumbered, changing course. "I told him to go to hell. He had the last word when he up and died."

"All the better."

Mac looked at his mother. Once, just once, he would like her to react the way he expected.

"The only thing your father loved more than winning a good argument was winning a bad one."

He thought about that. "The only thing he loved was you."

She looked at him, and whether her eyes showed spunk or not, they weren't young eyes. When she'd met Archie, she'd been a thirty-two-year-old aspiring model. By then, she'd been neither naive nor innocent. She'd known what she was doing. Sure, there had been men in her life before the divorce and after, but she hadn't married any of them. She'd married Archie. Less than two years later, she'd divorced him.

"He said you made your choice."

"He told you about that?" she asked.

The tanker disappeared over the horizon. The ocean looked big and empty without it. "Archie was referring to me. You chose me. And he resented me for it with his dying breath."

His mother made a sweeping gesture with her hand. "It wasn't a matter of choice for me, darling. I loved your father, but I couldn't have lived with myself or him if I'd have done what he thought he'd wanted. You see, I harbored a fantasy that he would grow to love you once he got to know you."

"That never happened."

"But of course it did. It was the only thing that truly terrified him. He tried not to, but he loved you. How could he help himself? And for your information, a woman doesn't need to choose between a man who loves her and the child they created out of that love. You know as well as I do that the heart is a fascinating organ. It's barely as large as a fist and yet it has the capacity to love a hundred people, each one in a different way. Archie wanted to believe he only loved me, but I knew better. And so did he."

"But . . ." Mac said.

"But things happened to him in his childhood. There was never anything wrong with you. It was him. He was a wonderful, exciting man. Things were done to him during that crucial time when behaviors and concepts are formed, when he was too young to protect himself from life. A piece of him was shaped by the unspeakable and grotesque. He survived, amazingly intact for the most part."

Mac had wondered but he hadn't known. "He did it by closing himself off," he said. Textbooks were filled with such cases.

Yvonne nodded. "He remained that way until he met me."

"He said he knew the moment he saw you."

She nodded. "I knew, too."

"You knew you loved him?"

"That, but I sensed the unrest in him. I was his balm. He couldn't share me with anyone, not even his own child. I discovered that later. He rose above nearly everything, but there was a part of him that remained damaged from what he saw and experienced when he was a small child. When we discovered I was pregnant, he shared some of those memories with me. He never told anyone else, and I promised I wouldn't, either. But I cried. Sometimes I still do. He did many wonderful things with his life, but I still wish things could have been different for him and for you." Now she stared out at the ocean, too.

Mac watched her, intrigued. "He told me the choice was yours."

"If only it were that simple. Don't you see? There was no choice for me. I never stopped loving him. It was that kind of love. He came to realize what I'd discovered in the beginning. I couldn't repair what had been done to him, and neither could he."

Mac said, "So he could do anything, anything but that."

Her eyes were at once sage and sad. "At your college graduation, I asked him if he had any regrets. Do you know what he said?"

Mac wasn't sure he wanted to know.

His mother said, "He looked at me long and hard, and then he found you with his gaze, and he shook his head and said, 'No, Yvonne, no regrets.' You see? He wasn't sorry you were born. Quite the contrary, actually."

"Even though he knew that you would have stayed with him if not for me?" Mac asked.

"Would I have? Having you, raising you has been the best thing I've ever done, my purpose for living. That's not to say it hasn't been great fun needling you."

"Glad I'm so entertaining."

She'd given him a great deal. Psychiatrists had long believed that every person was a product of his or her childhood. Mac agreed. In a sense, his mother had dedicated her life to seeing that he was safe, secure, educated and relatively content. Perversely, his father had had a hand in that. Had Archie loved Mac? Probably. Had he been proud of him? It was hard to say. Mac had hoped to reach some sort of understanding with his father these past two months. Professionals called it closure. Mac didn't care for the term, for it seemed inadequate and limiting. For lack of a better word, he'd gotten closure, he supposed, just not in the manner he'd hoped.

A colleague of his in Boston had a plaque on his desk. *Tell me what you need and I'll tell you how to get along without it.* Mac had learned at a young age how to live without what he'd needed from his father.

"I don't believe he was sorry you were born, darling."

Mac still wasn't so sure about that.

His mother said, "Because of you, part of him lives on." She rose to her feet and patted his shoulder. "I think I'll go in and lie down. The flight last night was long."

"Yes, get some rest." Mac followed her inside, then went in search of his running shoes.

By Sara's second day as a waitress, it was apparent that Cooper's Café didn't see a lot of business on weekdays between lunch and supper. Coop was fixing the walk-in refrigerator in the kitchen and Dixie had put her feet up and was watching her favorite soap in the back room. As soon as Sara finished replacing all the tops on the salt shakers she'd just filled, she could go home.

It was a surprise when the door opened, a pleasant surprise, for Brooke bustled in and Claudia followed, taking her own sweet time. Both had shopping bags in their hands.

Hurrying toward them, Sara said, "You have your choice of tables and booths."

"We didn't come to eat," Claudia said.

"We came to say hi," Brooke amended.

"We've been shopping."

Sara recognized the store logo on their shopping bags. Sharla's Dress Shanty was an exclusive clothing boutique across the village square. People came from the surrounding towns of southern Maine and even northern Boston to shop there. It was trendy and pricey, and Sara hadn't been inside it in years. "What did you buy?" she asked shyly.

Claudia said, "Brooke bought a dress that flows over her like water. You'll see it tonight at the rehearsal supper. Mine's for the wedding tomorrow, and it's crimson, otherwise known as passion red." She held up a sleeveless silk sheath with a V neck in the front and back. "What do you think of this one?"

The color put Sara in mind of the aunts' blush-tipped roses just before they opened. "It's beautiful. I don't believe I've ever seen you wear pink."

"It isn't my usual color." Claudia placed the dress in Sara's hands. "It's yours."

The dress felt rich and was as light as a feather. "What do you mean?"

"I bought it for you."

Sara pushed it back to her. "You shouldn't have done that, Claudia."

"Sure I should have."

"I can't accept it."

"Why the hell not?"

Back and forth the dress went.

"I have enough clothes."

"Enough is a relative term. Women have enough socks. We can even have too many socks, but we never have too many clothes."

"I can't accept charity."

"It cost less than most of my hats," Claudia said.

"That's not the point."

"It was on sale. And you just said it's beautiful."

That wasn't the point, either. Sara glanced at Brooke, who only shrugged. Folding her arms at her ribs, Sara shook her head firmly at Claudia.

"You mean it." Claudia looked incredulous.

Sara nodded.

Not a very good loser, Claudia grumbled, "I swear nobody appreciates a thing I do around here."

"I appreciate your friendship."

"You have a funny way of showing it."

Brooke said, "She's been edgy with everyone." She mouthed the word "Julian."

"You've seen Julian?" Sara couldn't help asking.

"Stubborn man!" The pink dress fluttered as Claudia gestured effusively. "I discovered where he's staying, where he's eating, even where he goes for his evening cognac."

Sara glanced at Brooke, who shook her head almost imperceptibly. Sara took the silent advice and didn't ask how Claudia had gone about discovering all those things. "Then you've talked to him?" she asked instead.

"Yes, and he's always extremely happy to see me, if you know what I mean."

Sara and Brooke looked at each other, eyebrows raised.

"But he staves off my every advance with the same line: *Uh-uh-uh. Look but don't touch.* I flew back to Hats headquarters, only to discover that he'd been there the day before. When I arrived back in New Hampshire, he was already here. It's disconcerting. I invited him to be my guest at Eve's wedding, and he accepted without reservation. Let's see him hold me at arm's length on the dance floor."

Claudia tried one last time to leave the dress with Sara. Once again Sara shook her head firmly. Amazingly enough, Claudia stopped persisting. Walking with her friends to the door, Sara thought of all the times she'd succumbed to other people's wills these past ten years. This was a summer of firsts. She'd stood up to her mother, to Roy, and even to Claudia, who really did mean well.

She returned the salt and pepper shakers to every table, removed her apron, said goodbye to Coop and Dixie, then started toward home. The first thing she did when she reached the sidewalk was remove the rubber band from her hair. Shaking her hair until it fell into place around her face, she immediately felt more like her old self.

She'd gotten up at four-thirty to deliver newspapers, and then had put in seven hours on her feet at the café. Surprisingly, she wasn't exhausted. Actually, there was still a little spring left in her step. She counted her blessings. Seth was happy. Sara had her health, good friends, a paycheck coming at the end of the week and thirty dollars in tip money in her pocket in the meantime. She felt rich beyond belief, and couldn't think of anything in the world she needed. Certainly, she didn't need the flowers in the window of the florist shop, or the furniture strategically arranged in the big old store that encompassed three storefronts on East Street. She admired the dresses in the window of Sharla's Dress Shanty, smiling to herself because seeing them reminded her of Claudia.

Sara's own reflection in the window made her gasp. She looked like a waif with her fine, straight hair hanging so close to her face. She'd worn it this way for years. Trying not to think about the bruises, scratches and slap marks the plain hairstyle had hidden, she glanced over as a woman with coiffed gray hair walked out of the beauty shop next door. It was where Sara's mother had taken her for haircuts when she'd been a girl. She slid her hand into her pocket. Tip money crinkled in her fingers. Her mind still on the past, she strode to the beauty shop window. The eyes of the waif staring back at her from her own reflection steadied. Sara opened the door and went in.

"Come in!"

Mac recognized Brooke's and Sophie's voices, but couldn't be certain of the third. He entered Brooke's kitchen quietly. Even so, three pairs of eyes turned to him.

"Hey, Dr. Elliot," Rebecca Callaway called. "Sophie's teaching me to play chess."

Evidently, the girls had made up.

Brooke was stirring something on the stove. It smelled wonderful. She looked wonderful. It was three o'clock on Friday. He hadn't seen her since the funeral three days ago. She wore baggy chinos and a black tank top. If she'd applied makeup, it was subtle. Her hair had grown since the first time he'd seen her. Now it brushed the delicate ridge of her collarbone. A single charm hung from a gold chain around her neck. She wore small hoop earrings, her watch, and no other jewelry, not even her wedding ring.

"What are you cooking?" His voice had gone noticeably deeper.

"This is the raspberry glaze for the cheese cakes for Eve and Carter's rehearsal dinner this evening." She cast a furtive glance at the chess players at the table, and Mac knew she was holding back. She was resisting, her smile so tentative it made him want to reach out and touch her, to hold her hand and watch her smile grow.

"She's been cooking for two days," Rebecca said. "It's our job to sample everything."

That explained the trays of hors d'oeuvres and sweets and confections on every available flat surface. The girls continued to study the board. Reaching across the table, Rebecca moved her game piece. "Check. I can do that, right?"

Sophie nodded, and Rebecca looked very pleased with herself, until her opponent moved hers and said, "Checkmate."

Sophie sat hunched over the table, her chin in her hand.

"For someone who just won, you look less than thrilled," Mac said.

"My birthday's in three days. Mom says I can't have a horse this year, but maybe next year." Leaving her chin propped in her hand, she said, "Are you going someplace, Mac?"

Not much got past this girl.

Mac reached into the breast pocket of his dark suit coat and drew out a letter. "I've just come from the reading of my father's will. Your mother might have to rethink your birthday gift for next year."

"What do you mean?" Brooke asked, turning off the burner.

He handed her the letter. While she was shaking it open, Sophie and Rebecca crowded closer.

"What does it say?" Sophie asked.

"Archie mentioned you in his will, Sophie," Brooke said, scanning the legalese.

"Did he leave me his checkers set?"

Standing back, apart from the rest, Mac said, "No, but you can have it if you want it."

"Horses, Sophe," Brooke said, staring at the letter. "Archie left you two horses."

"Let me see that." Sophie grabbed the letter. Heads bent close, the girls read it together.

"Holy crap!" Rebecca said. "Sorry." The red-haired girl ducked her head. "He left you a two-year-old Appaloosa from his horse ranch in Kentucky and a Paint that's mostly blind and too old to ride. That's weird."

"I can read. I didn't know he had a horse ranch in Kentucky. And it's not weird. Archie said life should always be fifty percent pleasure and fifty percent responsibility. Even-Steven. He's giving me one horse to enjoy and one to take care of."

"You have horses, Sophie!"

The girls danced around the cluttered kitchen.

"I can't believe it."

"It's what you've always wanted."

"And it's just in time for my birthday."

"We have to tell somebody."

"Mom, can we go to Amanda's?"

Brooke looked across the kitchen at her daughter. A few months ago, Sophie would have wanted to call Makayla in Philadelphia. Amanda Baker lived two blocks away from Stone Cottage and was in Rebecca's class at school. "Be home in half an hour," Brooke called.

When they were gone, she and Mac stared at each other for several seconds. She had a hundred things to do to get ready for Eve's rehearsal supper tonight. Sophie's birthday was on Monday. Tomorrow was the wedding. Colin was due to arrive just in time for the ceremony.

"You have a nice smile."

Surely, surprise showed on her face. "Was I smiling?"

"No. But if I don't *say* something, I'm going to *do* something, and talking is safer."

Now she smiled, and it was as if that had been his intention.

"Don't worry about the horses' care," he said. "Archie included enough money in a trust fund for that."

"Your father was not an easy man to understand." That was what she said with words. She tried to tell him so much more with her eyes. "What about you?" she asked quietly. "Did Archie remember you in his will, too?"

"He left me the sailboat."

"The same sailboat he used to teach you to sail?"

He nodded.

"Then it must have held meaning for your father, too."

"As you said, he wasn't an easy man to understand."

Brooke watched Mac closely. He was quieter than he'd been a week ago. He was grieving. His dark suit gave him an air of culture and refinement, and yet there was a vein of the uncivilized in him. Claudia had come right out and asked about him earlier.

So are you sleeping with him?
Sleeping with him. They hadn't even kissed.

It occurred to Brooke that neither of them was talking again. She understood what it meant when a man looked at a woman the way Mac was looking at her. And she understood what could happen when a woman understood what it meant. Claudia thought they should just kiss and get it over with. Brooke knew Mac wanted her. But this wasn't simply a case of feeling wanted. There was nothing simple about any of it. He hadn't brought up the subject of love since his father's death four days ago, and neither had she. But his declaration was in the back of both their minds.

Carpe diem, she'd said last week. Seize the day. It sounded good, but she couldn't seize the moment with Colin's arrival hanging over her head.

"What will you do now?" she asked, her gaze on his eyes.

He was looking at her mouth.

"I should probably be going."

Had he moved closer?

"That would probably be best."

Or had she?

There was a scuttle of footsteps on the back porch. The chatter of young voices carried through the screen. Brooke backed up slightly. "Wasn't Amanda home?" she called before Sophie was through the screen door.

"We never got to Amanda's."

"Look who's here, Mrs. Valentine!"

Brooke looked.

"It's Daddy," Sophie said, as if Brooke wouldn't recognize the man who followed the girls inside.

CHAPTER 17

"Hello, Brooke." Colin insinuated himself between her and the ancient stove and kissed her cheek.

"Colin." She felt the blood drain out of her face. "I wasn't expecting you until tomorrow."

"I thought I'd surprise you." He glanced at Mac.

Her cooking marathon had overheated the kitchen. Suddenly, it felt airless, too. No one moved, and Brooke couldn't think of a thing to do or say. Extremely perceptive, Sophie had grown serious, quietly taking everything in.

Oblivious to the ragged undercurrents, Rebecca said, "Tell your dad about your horses, Sophie."

"What horses?" Colin's question was directed at Sophie, but his gaze went from Brooke to Mac and back again.

"You tell him, Rebecca," Sophie said quietly.

Born into a family of talkers, Rebecca was happy to keep the conversation flowing. "Dr. Elliot just brought over a letter that says his father left Sophie two horses in his will. By the way, my name's Rebecca Callaway and I know all about your ancestors being from Main Line towns."

He indulged the charismatic child with one of his winning smiles. "It's nice to meet you, Rebecca. I'm Colin Valentine." He cast a pointed look at Brooke.

She'd almost forgotten how easily he could make her feel inadequate. "Colin Valentine," she said quietly, "Dr. Mackenzie Elliot."

Another tense silence ensued.

Mac made his living watching people's body language and subtle changes of expressions. He certainly had no trouble reading Colin Valentine's measure of him. Tall and athletic looking, the man had a withering stare. He appeared to be intelligent, and evidently was well-mannered enough to extend his hand toward Mac.

Before the brief handshake was over, Mac re-evaluated. That wasn't courtesy. It was castigation.

Colin disliked Mac on sight.

It was mutual.

Talk about blaring silences. Even Rebecca was beginning to notice. This time, Sophie came to the rescue. Wrapping her arms around her father's waist, she pressed her cheek to his chest. "I'm so glad you're here. Two horses, Daddy. Can you believe it?"

"I'd believe anything right about now, Shortstuff."

Mac took that as his cue to leave. "If I don't see you on Monday, happy birthday, Sophie. Goodbye, Rebecca." He looked at Brooke last, and left without having said a word to Colin Valentine.

"A lot has happened since our last session, Dr. Elliot." Sara glanced at Mac shyly from her usual place in the wooden rocker near the window. "I don't know if Brooke or Sophie told you, but I'm a waitress at Cooper's Café on the town square."

Mention of Brooke had Mac sitting up a little straighter. Meeting Colin Valentine had left a bad taste in his mouth. Worse, the image of the three Valentines together had lodged itself in his mind. It required effort not to scowl. "No, I didn't know that. Congratulations."

He'd hardly recognized Sara when she'd knocked on his door for her weekly counseling session nearly an hour ago. Her hair had been shorn close to her head, showcasing her delicate bone structure, narrow nose and large eyes. She'd blushed when he'd called her a blond Halle Berry, but he knew she was pleased.

When she'd first started counseling three months ago, it was all she could do to meet his eyes. She might always be shy, but she'd come a long way from that frightened woman. She was fidgety today. For the third time in as many minutes, her fingers went to her short hair.

"What made you decide to cut it?" he asked.

Her gaze swung to his. "I don't need long hair anymore."

Again, it wasn't easy to wait for her to continue. There hadn't been enough time to go for a long run after returning from Stone Cottage. Consequently, patience came at a higher price today.

"Have you always worn your hair long?" he asked.

"I wore it short in high school, but not this short. I played the piano, and it was either wear my hair up or keep it short."

Mac looked more closely at Sara. "You play the piano?"

"I used to."

She looked down again, and he felt on the verge of understanding something important about her. "When did you stop?"

He could see that she didn't want to answer.

"A long time ago?" he prodded.

"It wasn't like I just stopped overnight. It was a gradual process."

Mac pictured the music draining out of her over the course of time. "Were you good?" he asked.

Again, it took her a while to answer. "I received a standing ovation more than once."

"That must have been very gratifying."

"I didn't play for the applause." She spoke into her lap.

"Why did you play?" he asked.

She shrugged.

He tried a different tack. "You took lessons when you were a child?"

"Not from famous musicians or anything like that. My father died when I was very young, and there wasn't any money for extras. Once I started school, Fridays were my favorite days because we had music class on Friday afternoons. I loved the sound of the piano. I could play by ear, and used to sneak into the building at recess and practice on the upright in the music room. I tried to play softly so no one would hear, but one day the janitor caught me. I had to go to the principal's office. I couldn't utter a word for the sobbing. Instead of punishing me, Mrs. Ferguson gave me my first piano lesson. I was a fast learner. I had an ear for music, but it was more than that."

"You felt the music."

"Yes." It was almost as if she hadn't expected him to understand. "Do you play?"

Sara Kemper didn't often ask questions. The fact that she was interested enough in this topic to keep up her end of the conversation said a great deal about how important it was to her.

Propping his right ankle on his opposite knee, he said, "My mother was a menace. If I wanted to race my dirt bike, I had to play a musical instrument."

Sara grinned. "Your mother sounds smart to me."

Once again Mac got a glimpse of how Sara had probably been before she became a victim. "You women always stick together."

He caught her looking at the piano across the room. It seemed to require a conscious effort to force her gaze away.

"I don't know what I would do without my friends. Men are different. I don't mean you don't care, I just mean—"

"I know what you mean. Men have needs, too, but yes, we are different from women."

He could tell she was relieved that he hadn't taken offense. Mac hated the man who'd made her fear something as innocent as voicing her opinion.

"I heard your father died. I'm sorry for your loss."

"Thank you, Sara."

She looked around the room and slowly stood. Her hour was up. He never saw her glance at her watch, and yet she always knew.

"Will you be returning to Boston soon?" she asked.

Now there was a question. He'd done everything he'd come to Alcott to do. And then some. A brown-haired woman flashed through his mind. "I'm making some important decisions regarding my future."

He wondered what Archie would have done.

"Those are the hardest decisions, aren't they?" She was looking at the piano again.

"Yes, they are. I have a few opportunities simmering on the back burner. I've found a counselor to carry on my work with your group. I think you'll like her."

"I wasn't worrying about me. I was thinking about Brooke."

That made two of them.

The phone rang in another part of the house. Mac usually let the answering machine get his calls. Following a hunch, he said, "I need to take that. I won't be long. If you'll wait a moment, I'll give you Dr. Gregory's card before you leave."

He hurried away to his office to answer an important call from a telemarketer selling magazine subscriptions in a heavy Middle-Eastern accent.

Sara had been coming to this house on Captain's Row once every week all summer. Apparently Dr. Elliot was making plans to leave Alcott. She wondered where this associate of his, this Dr. Gregory, would want to meet. Chances were it wouldn't be in a home setting like this one.

She looked around the room. Everything was old: the

bookshelves, the rocking chair, the brocade sofas, the mahogany desk and ladderback chair. And the piano.

She'd tried not to notice the piano.

Spinning around, she ran her hands through what was left of her hair. What had she done? It would grow back. Of course it would grow back.

She strode to the window and looked out. Joe Macelli used to bring her up to Captain's Row to see the ocean. Not that a person could see the ocean at night. She'd known that as well as Joe had, but asking her to look at the ocean sounded better than asking her if she wanted to make out. He'd wanted to do more than make out, but she hadn't been ready, and he'd been gentlemanly enough not to press her for more.

A year later, after Joe had broken it off and moved away, Roy had pressed her plenty. If she could do one thing over, she wouldn't have saved her virginity for Roy. She doubted it would have changed the outcome. Joe still would have gone away to college. And she still would have married Roy. She'd loved Roy then. But it was Joe Macelli's name that was still an ache in the very center of her. She wondered where he was now, and if he ever thought about her. Probably not. Why would he?

She tried to concentrate on the view. Everything was big and blue. Big blue sky, big blue ocean. Even the sailboat skimming across the water in the distance had a blue sail. People traveled thousands of miles to fill their souls with what she was seeing.

It didn't fill her soul. It never had.

She must have turned, because she found herself staring at the piano across the room. It was big and boxy and bare, its wood darkened with age. She crept closer much as she had when she'd sneaked into the music room during recess all those years ago. Lifting the lid soundlessly, she gasped, for there were the keys, dusty and yellowed with age. She traced the chipped edge of middle C, then pressed it with one chapped finger.

She snatched her hand away as if she'd been burned, only to reach out again, this time with all her fingers extended. She ran up and down the scales. The piano was out of tune. It sounded wonderful.

She looked around nervously, wondering how much longer Dr. Elliot was going to be. Biting her lower lip, she pulled out the bench and sat down. Heart racing, she placed her hands on the keys again, and closed her eyes.

In the next room, Mac hung up the phone and leaned back in the cracked leather chair. He didn't know what he was going to do with a life-supply of mechanic's magazines. He wasn't a putterer, or particularly mechanically inclined. He didn't even change his own oil.

The nearly unrecognizable notes of *The Flight of the Bumblebee* carried through the big old house on Captain's Row. Sara Kemper was rediscovering the music that was within her.

Mac had needed that today.

"I just hope I don't trip on my hem and fall on my face." Sophie held her bridesmaid's gown to her and swished her hips to and fro.

"You're more graceful than a gazelle," Colin said. "Of course you won't trip."

Sophie giggled a little too loudly. "Oh, Daddy, I'm so glad you surprised us."

In the kitchen, Brooke covered the leftover stuffed mushrooms with plastic wrap. She wasn't nearly as enthusiastic about the surprise, and Sophie's forced enthusiasm grated on her nerves. Earlier, Sophe had cornered her at the punch bowl, saying, "For my birthday present, I want Daddy to stay here with us instead of going to a hotel."

Brooke had seen the ploy for what it was: A child's last desperate effort to hold her parents together. Brooke's first impulse had been to say "no." She'd considered pointing out the fact that there were only two bedrooms at Stone Cottage. But Sophie knew that. Kids today knew a great deal.

Sighing, Brooke had said, "Your father is welcome to stay here."

Sophie had beamed.

"But that isn't your birthday gift."

"What do you mean?"

Guests were milling about, and Brooke didn't have the time or the privacy to explain that she understood that this was a difficult situation. She also believed that it wouldn't help anyone if she allowed Sophie to manipulate her, Colin, or their situation. So, Brooke had said, "Your dad is welcome to stay here because he's your father and always will be. I have a surprise in mind for your birthday."

"What?" This excitement had been more genuine.

"Your birthday isn't until Monday. You're going to have to wait until then." She'd glanced across the crowded dining room and found Colin looking at her.

It happened again.

"It's late, Sophe," he said. "And you have a big day ahead of you tomorrow."

The girl looked wistfully from her mother to her father, but she kissed them both. Her voice small, she said goodnight, then went obediently to bed.

Brooke returned to her task, and Colin paced. Stopping abruptly in the middle of the room, he said, "God, I've missed her."

She was struck by how handsome and tired he looked. "She's missed you, too, Colin. If you give her a few minutes to get ready for bed, I'm sure she'd love it if you'd tuck her in."

"You don't think she's too old for that?"

"Girls never outgrow their daddies."

He smiled tiredly, and Brooke remembered what she'd seen in him all those years ago. She returned to her tasks, and after giving Sophie a few minutes, he knocked on her door and went in. He stayed in her room for a long time. Brooke finished cleaning up in the kitchen. Turning out the lights and locking the doors, she tiptoed past her daughter's doorway, pausing out of sight. Colin was telling Sophie about a book he'd read. One of the things she'd always admired about him was his voracious thirst for the written word. He was passionate about so many things.

Lost in thought, Brooke continued on into her room where she removed her necklace, earrings, watch and bracelet. She was taking a blanket off the bed when a floorboard creaked near the doorway. Colin filled the space, watching her.

"Is Sophie asleep?" she asked.

He nodded. "I think I bored her."

"I doubt that."

"Thank you."

She didn't know what to say.

"You've changed, Brooke."

"In what way?" She shook the blanket then folded it in half.

"You didn't let her railroad you earlier, for one thing. You look beautiful tonight, by the way."

Fluffy appeared in the doorway. Looking around as if to make sure all the guests were finally gone, she rubbed her head on Colin's shin, then padded to Brooke and wound around her ankles.

"And I see you've made friends with the cat."

Brooke smiled for the first time since Eve had squeezed her hand when she and Carter left. "I took Carter's advice."

"Carter gave you advice regarding the cat?"

She nodded. "He said I tried too hard." It was advice that pertained to more than the cat.

"I see. You know, once I got past his long hair and earring, I realized Carter's a decent man."

"He and Eve are very happy."

"I'm glad."

Brooke believed him.

Following his surprise arrival and hostile handshake with Mac, Colin had been on his best behavior. He'd joked with Carter, and hugged and complimented Eve. He'd gotten on

well with the other members of the wedding party, and he
doted on Sophie, who basked in all the attention. The biggest
shock of the evening had been Sara. When Brooke had exclaimed over her new hairstyle, Sara had pulled at the short
wisps that comprised all that was left of her hair and whispered, "Honestly, I don't know what I was thinking. I feel exposed."

Brooke had looked at Colin. Finding him watching her,
she'd known the feeling.

He'd been watching her all evening, and was again, his
eyes blue against the tan of his skin, his gaze intense.

She turned her attention back to her task.

"Is there anything I can help you with?" he asked, entering the room.

"The sofa makes into a bed."

"Don't, Brooke." He stopped directly behind her, his
hands going to her upper arms.

Don't what? she thought as he turned her to face him.

The lamp was behind him, his pupils dilated in the semi-
darkness, so that only a narrow ring of blue encircled them.
He breathed between parted lips. She couldn't breathe at all.

He was going to kiss her.

How many times had she longed for him to look at her
the way he was looking at her right now? How many times
had she wanted him to kiss her, just kiss her, long and
thoughtful, hungry and deep?

He bent closer, his hands warm on her shoulders, his features blurring before her eyes. His lips were a hair's-breadth
from hers when she averted her face.

A muscle worked in his cheek. She finally breathed.

Straightening stiffly, he released her without comment,
took a pillow from the bed, and reached for the blanket she'd
gathered and then dropped. He left the room before she realized he'd said goodnight. She hadn't answered.

Closing her door, she turned back to her bed only to discover that he'd automatically taken the pillow from *her* side.
Their bid for the same side of the bed had been a bone of

contention early in their marriage. Perhaps they'd been doomed from the start.

The sofa in the living room creaked as the apparatus was yanked from its hiding place. It was nearing midnight, and tomorrow was Eve's wedding day. Brooke and Sophie were helping decorate the hall in the morning. And they had appointments for their hair, nails and makeup in the afternoon. It was unlikely there would be time for her and Colin to talk.

As soon as she donned her nightgown and climbed into bed, Fluffy took her usual place near Brooke's waist. She stroked the cat's soft fur for a long time. A slight breeze stirred the curtain at the window. Fluffy purred contentedly. Brooke envied the cat that.

Colin had nearly kissed her tonight.

He wasn't the man she wanted to kiss. And she was pretty sure he knew it.

CHAPTER 18

"Eve, if you wiggle your foot any faster you're going to be airborne." Bonnie Stevens, owner and operator of Bonnie's Clip & Curl, handed Eve a frothy, fruity blender drink along with strict instructions to try to relax.

Eve turned beseeching gray eyes to Brooke.

For weeks, Eve had been the epitome of serenity and calm. She'd lovingly planned her wedding, designed her own invitations, found the perfect gown, made the centerpieces and organized every detail from the music, to the ceremony, to the reception. Today was the big day, and she was about to fall apart.

Brooke eased the glass from Eve's amazingly strong grasp lest she shatter the glass. Taking a sip through the straw, Brooke handed it back to Bonnie. Next, she drew Eve to her feet.

"Sophie," she called, "Aunt Eve and I are going to run over to Bell's to pick up the flowers. We'll be back in ten minutes."

"Okay," Sophie yelled over the whir of the blow-dryer.

"You know exactly how she wants it, right?" Brooke asked Bonnie's only employee.

Emily, the young stylist with streaked blond hair and

four-inch heels, waved the picture from Sophie's teen magazine. "It's going to look great!"

Emily had fashioned Brooke's hair on top of her head. Bonnie had styled Eve's into a mass of curls that cascaded down her back. Sophie's would be some of both.

Outside, Brooke said, "Everything's going to be fine, Eve."

"Why didn't we elope? Carter wanted to."

"Because a long white gown, caring guests, flickering candlelight, blessed vows, and the man you love waiting for you in the front of the church has always been your dream, and your dream is about to come true."

Eve shook her head and took a deep breath. "I don't know what's wrong with me."

"You've just planned an entire wedding in two months. You're entitled to a few last-minute jitters."

The sisters cut across the corner, making a beeline for the flower shop. "Did you go through this on your wedding day?" Eve asked.

Brooke had a vague recollection of her wedding. It had been big and formal. Very big. And very formal. Her mother had been gone by then, and Colin and his mother had definite ideas about how things should be. Once, Brooke had joked that all she'd had to do was show up. They hadn't seen the humor. A sea of people she'd never seen before or after had been present that day. Much of it was a blur now.

"No," she said, looking up into her sister's worried eyes. "I was very calm."

"Maybe my little nervous breakdown is a good sign."

Brooke nudged Eve. "Once a bratty little sister, always a bratty little sister."

At least Eve smiled.

Brooke hadn't gotten much sleep last night, and was running on pure adrenaline. Colin hadn't slept well, either. Although he hadn't complained, he'd been pensive at breakfast. He was going to have his say, of that she was certain. Brooke's only sister was getting married in less than three hours. They still had makeup to do, flowers to pick up, and pictures, the cake, the caterers to let in.

"Did I tell you I can't find the guest book? I hope the cake is moist. What if I trip walking down the aisle?"

"The guest book is in my car. Of course the cake will be moist. And Saxon McCall could clear a path through a tornado without flinching. He'll have you to the front of the church without incident."

They reached the flower shop as the door opened. Mac came out as Eve was going in.

"Don't ever have a big wedding," Eve said shrilly. "It'll ruin your life."

She disappeared inside, leaving Brooke and Mac alone at the door. They looked at each other. And smiled.

He had a nice smile, unpracticed, unhurried. His shirt was open at the neck, the color a close match to his eyes. He reminded her of a nearly finished sculpture. That hint of what was left undone or unsaid, the promise of what lay just beneath the surface was very appealing.

"Pre-wedding jitters?" he asked quietly.

"What?"

"Your sister?"

Oh. She nodded.

"You look beautiful, Brooke."

Gesturing to her simple cotton shirt, drawstring shorts and running shoes, she said, "I wouldn't have thought this hairstyle went with this outfit."

"Are you questioning my judgment or my sincerity?" He folded his arms at his chest and cocked his head slightly, a wise-guy all the way.

She laughed. She always seemed to laugh when with him.

A full minute elapsed. Last night Colin had told her she was beautiful. He might have meant it. She hadn't felt like breaking into song.

A car with a noisy muffler drove past, drawing them out of their stupor. Mac stepped back, holding the door.

She entered the flower shop humming under her breath.

* * *

The sun was nearly blinding when Sophie, Brooke and Eve walked out of the beauty salon, makeup, hair and nails professionally done. Three doors down, three men and a little boy walked out of the barber shop, the sun glinting off four bald heads.

"Is that Carter?" Brooke asked.

"Uncle Carter?"

"Oh, my God," Eve said.

The men walked, four abreast, the women, three. As if by some cosmic force, all of them stopped a dozen feet apart.

"Look at us, Aunt Eve," little Tommy McCall said.

Eve was looking.

"Uh-oh," Jack McCall said.

"The moment of truth," Brian McCall muttered.

"Eve, I can explain," Carter said.

Eve looked at each of the McCalls, as bald as cue balls, every one. "Your beautiful hair," she said to her fiancé.

"Mine fell out," Tommy exclaimed. "So they shaved theirs."

The child had lost his hair to chemotherapy. Recently, the doctors had deemed him back in remission. He tired easily, but right now, he was beaming.

She looked at Carter.

"How mad are you?" he asked, his tiny diamond earring glinting nearly as brightly as his head.

"Mad?" Eve started toward the McCalls.

"What's Aunt Eve going to do?" Sophie asked her mother.

"I don't know."

Almost as tall as they were, Eve appeared to be planning to plant a great big kiss on each mouth, in turn. First Brian.

"Well, hello," the reverend said.

Then Carter. "Hi sweetheart," he crooned.

Then Jack, whom she'd had a crush on most of her life. BC, she called that phase. Before Carter. "Hey, Eve," Jack said.

She kissed Tommy last. He wrinkled up his nose, but he giggled. Picking him up, she hugged him.

"You." Carter took Tommy from her and set the child on his feet. "Quit hogging my woman."

Assuming his best bad-attitude stance, feet apart, hips forward, chin cocked at a haughty angle, he said, "Come here. I want some more of that." He drew Eve into his arms and kissed her long and deep right there on the town square not far from where he'd kissed her the first time two-and-a-half months ago when all of this had started.

Behind them, Brian nudged Jack. "I hope Natalie is that kind of mad. What do you think Liza will say?"

"Liza already knows."

"Married wuss." Brian said, "Does anybody else feel a draft?"

"Draft, hell, we're going to get sunburned."

"Hey, Tommy, do you have any more hats?"

"Lots."

Eve and Carter drew apart, winded.

"Didn't I tell you she'd like it?" Carter said.

"Listen to him."

"Like he wasn't scared shitless."

He stared into Eve's eyes. "Ignore them."

Taking a shuddering breath, Eve ran her hands over Carter's pale head. "Any man who would do this for his nephew, especially a man who prided himself on his in-your-face long hair, on his wedding day, mind you, is an incredible man, indeed."

"You want incredible, wait until tonight."

Sophie nudged her mother. "I thought it was bad luck for the bride and groom to see each other before the ceremony."

"I believe this is the exception, Sophe."

Eve smiled serenely. Turning, she stepped between Sophie and Brooke, linked her arms with theirs, and started toward the car, as regal as a queen. It was official. Her pre-wedding jitters were a thing of the past.

* * *

Colin was waiting for Brooke and Sophie back at Stone Cottage.

"Hey, Daddy!"

"If you two don't look pretty." Continuing to tie his tie, he looked at Brooke. "Do you have a minute?"

A knot formed in Brooke's stomach. "We have to be at the church in half an hour for pictures. And we're not dressed."

"It will only take a minute."

"Colin."

"Come here, Sophe."

As she had so often these past twenty-four hours, Sophie watched them both closely. "What, Daddy?"

"I know your birthday isn't until Monday, but I can't wait another second." He handed her an envelope.

Brooke had a bad feeling about this.

Opening the envelope, she removed three airline tickets. "What are these for?"

Brooke watched the man she'd been married to for fourteen years ease into a winning smile. "They're plane tickets to Seattle," he said.

Sophie screeched. "Seattle, Washington?"

"The one and only. Home of the Space Needle and the Pacific Northwest. We can hop on another plane and fly down to Hollywood, maybe keep our eyes open for some movie stars."

Sophie's eyes were huge. "But there are three tickets."

"Colin."

He ignored Brooke's penetrating stare. "One for each of us."

"Colin," Brooke said again.

"When?" Sophe asked.

"We leave first thing Monday morning."

"That's my birthday!" Sophie didn't know where to turn first. She started toward her father, then toward Brooke. Eyes glowing, she said, "Mom, is this the surprise you were talking about?"

Oh, it was a surprise, all right. "No, Sophe, it wasn't. Colin," Brooke said again.

"You're between jobs, sweetheart." He smiled encouragingly.

She wasn't fooled.

"A family vacation will do us good."

Only an experienced listener would pick up the critical tone in his voice. "This isn't a decision you can make without consulting me, Colin."

"I've missed you. I've missed both of you." He implored them both. "Don't say anything yet. Think about it."

"Mom," Sophie said. "Daddy wants us to be a family."

He couldn't do this. Brooke wanted to scream.

Colin stepped forward. "Your mother's right, Shortstuff. I probably shouldn't have brought this up when there wasn't enough time to discuss it properly." He took the plane tickets from his daughter's hand and slipped them back into the envelope. "You both have to get dressed. We'll talk about it more later."

No dummy, Sophie kept her feet rooted to the floor. She wasn't going to leave the room until she was certain her mother had, too.

Brooke tried to think. She touched her temple, and then her hair. The wedding. She glanced at the clock on the stove. "The photographer will be waiting for us." She looked at Sophie and glared at Colin. "Yes, we'll definitely discuss it later."

Mother and daughter walked together through the living room, to the short hall. At her doorway, Sophie said, "Don't say no, Mom. Please."

Brooke didn't say anything, at least not out loud.

Damn, she looked good.

It wasn't like Claudia to be ready early. Her dress hadn't needed ironing and her hair had cooperated. She was good at applying makeup. And her jewelry was just right. She had good taste. She couldn't help it.

The dress was two filmy layers of deep crimson. Although not low, the neckline was cut wide from the shoulders, the fabric just loose enough so that it gaped a little, drawing the eye, and setting the tone for possibilities. It was nipped in at the waist and slightly flared at the hips, not loose, not tight, just right. It had a flirty hem that caressed her calves when she moved. Her sandals were strappy and made her feel tall. She hadn't bothered with hose. All the better for later.

She fanned herself with one hand.

Looking at her watch, she wished it was already later. Julian wouldn't arrive for at least forty minutes.

She left her bedroom and meandered down the winding staircase. Her sketch pad and pencils were on the Duncan Phyfe dining room table. Flipping the pad open to a sketch she'd been working on a week ago, she picked up the pencil and made a few minor adjustments.

Under her hand, her vision changed. Soon, there was a curve here, a dip there, flowing sweeping lines in between. The lines became more fluid, her movements a fervor. She flipped the page over, and started fresh. The room was quiet but for the scratch and scrape of her pencil, both tools and a means to channel the passion that had always been inside her. She flipped the page again, and again, and again.

Eventually, the fervor ebbed and her hand stilled. Flushed, she surfaced slowly, and smiled at Julian. Vaguely she remembered him entering the room. He'd shaken his head in that way he had that meant don't stop.

She felt the sketch pad being lifted from her lap, the pencil being eased from her grasp. Cool, deft fingers massaged her cramped hand. Blinking, she looked up at Julian. "You should have stopped me."

"I'll never stop you." His voice was deep. "You know I love to watch you create."

Her toe tingled.

He'd gotten his hair cut, a strange thing to be thinking, but then, she was strange sometimes. She always liked to run her fingers through his hair when the ends were crisp and freshly cut.

"Did I hear church bells earlier?" she asked.

"An hour ago."

An hour. She'd been drawing for a long time. "We missed Eve and Carter's wedding."

"I doubt they missed us." He carried the sketch pad across the room.

She rather enjoyed watching him walk away. She rather enjoyed everything about him. Why? What was there about him? He wasn't terribly tall. He *was* terribly handsome, but a lot of men were terribly handsome, and she didn't turn into a lecherous old lady watching them walk across a room.

"These are amazing, Claudia."

She salivated at the way he said Claud-ya. "They're bridal hats."

She'd drawn ten different sketches. Some had veils, some netting. One had a feathery plume.

Julian studied them, each in turn. "A wedding line. Brilliant."

She was nearly overcome with desire for him.

Looking over the large sketch pad, he didn't quite smile. "I'd love to." As always, he knew. "Especially after watching you create. You have no idea how much I'd love to."

Oh, yes, she did.

"We're already late," he said.

There was an edge about him she'd noticed that last morning in Charleston. "We could be later."

He shook his head.

"What game are you playing?" she asked.

A muscle worked in his cheek. "Tell me something, Claudia. How far would you go to get what you want?"

She rose slowly to her feet. Keeping her gaze as steady as her gait, she said, "You know me, Julian. I go all the way to get what I want."

His eyelids lowered part way. "Do you?"

She felt the first prickles of apprehension, and not in her big toe. "What do you mean?"

"How badly do you want me?"

She leaned closer and lowered her voice provocatively. "I think about you when I wake up in the morning, when I step into the shower, when I have my first sip of coffee. I think of you every time the phone rings, when I take off my clothes at night and crawl into bed alone. There, are you happy?"

"I feel the same."

"Then what's this embargo about?"

"Why, it's about discovery, of course."

She narrowed her eyes at him. "You're discovering that we can both go without if we have to? But we don't have to."

"It hasn't been easy for me, either." Of course, he pronounced it eye-ther.

"So what is it you're waiting for?" She couldn't help touching him.

"You don't know?" he asked.

She felt a warming, a soft mewling and gentle swelling that drew her closer to him. "No, I don't know. What is it that you want?"

"Want?" He touched her breast. "You mean besides your lush body? You're such an innocent, Claudia."

She moaned, and through half-closed eyes she looked at him. "I'm thirty-five and as innocent as a cat burglar with a pillowcase full of the good silver."

He smiled, and she swore he'd never looked more beautiful.

"What do you want, Julian?"

"I want you to marry me, of course."

A Chinese gong went off in her head. Her mouth fell open and her hand fell away from his arm. "What the hell are you talking about?"

"I'm afraid I've decided not to attend the wedding reception with you after all."

It wasn't like Claudia to stare stupidly.

"Why?"

It wasn't like her to ask stupid questions, either. In her defense, he was still massaging her breast. It was affecting her brain.

"I'm only a man, Claudia. I just asked you to marry me. Your response was exactly what I expected but far less than what I'd hoped."

"You can't want to get married. You're practically still a boy."

"Grow up, Claudia. Enjoy your friend's wedding." He sounded angry.

"Julian, you can't be serious."

"Don't you know? I've been serious since day one."

She whimpered when he took his hand from her breast and started for her door. "Where are you going?"

"You sound like a wife already."

"That's not funny."

"I know." His blue eyes narrowed, and she knew he was serious. "Watching you sketch made me realize that I don't want to play games anymore."

"But what we have is perfect as it is."

"What do we have?" he asked.

Did he sound sad?

"Julian."

"That's what I thought. I'll be at Dusty's Pub later if you want to talk. Cheerio."

He walked out of the house. And she watched him.

He drove away. And she let him.

He wanted to marry her? Was he stark, raving mad?

Or was she?

CHAPTER 19

Sara leaned forward, elbows on the table, her back to the small dance floor. The candles burned low; the wedding reception was winding down.

The bride and groom had left for their honeymoon on Carter's motorcycle. Their destination was top secret. Many of the four hundred guests had gone home, too.

Sara, Brooke, and Claudia sat in a semicircle at a small table. Eve had been a beautiful bride. No one was surprised. The surprise had come two months ago when she'd announced she was marrying former bad-boy Carter McCall. By then everyone had assumed she would never marry, which just went to show that nobody ever really knew.

The weather had been hot and breezy, perfect for a summer wedding, the ceremony a mix of tradition and quirkiness. By the time it had started, most of the curls had slipped from Eve's hair, so that the tresses hung like wavy cornsilk to her waist. She'd glided down the aisle behind Brooke and Sophie. Natalie Harper, Eve's sister-in-law and everyone's favorite (and Alcott's only) local attorney played the organ. Saxon McCall, Eve's father-in-law, gave her away. The flowers had been grown in the aunts' garden, and had been arranged by Eve's closest friend, Samantha Bell. Reverend

McCall, one of Carter's brothers had said the prayers and blessed the vows; his other brother served as his best man. The photographer had captured the essence of the day, from the bald-headed ring bearer asleep on his father's shoulder, to the light in the eyes of the bride and groom, to the light glinting off the shiny heads of the McCalls. The cool reserve the junior bridesmaid displayed toward the matron of honor had been captured, too. Brooke wore the look of a deer frozen in the glare of headlights. Although not in the photographs, Claudia wore a similar expression.

Sara tried to ease the poor bouquet out of her friend's grasp.

Holding fast, Claudia continued plucking the petals from the flowers. "Everybody thought it was hilarious when I caught the blasted bouquet. Very funny. I didn't catch it. I put up my hand to protect my face as I was walking by."

Brooke nodded sympathetically. "Eve overestimated the strength with which she had to toss it."

Claudia made a disparaging sound. "Pitchers *toss* baseballs with less force."

Brooke and Sara both smiled.

The wedding meal was long over, the leftover cake drying out the way wedding cake always did late in the reception. The lights had been dimmed over the dance floor where a handful of couples still swayed to the slow music.

"Any luck with Sophie?" Sara asked.

Brooke shook her head.

"At least she's speaking to you again."

"If you consider asking me if she can spend the night at the Callaways and then telling me she wants Ginger and Pete to adopt her speaking to me." Brooke sighed.

"You have to admit the kid's got spunk," Claudia said.

"Why is it that Colin had the affairs, but I'm the bad guy?"

"Because," Claudia said as if Brooke should know the answer, "you're the mother and Colin is a weasel who ducked out of the reception right after dinner rather than face the music."

This time it was Brooke who made the disparaging sound. "I've been honest with Sophie from the start, or at least as honest as I feel is healthy for her. She's known this marriage is over. She was starting to come to terms with it and Colin walked in and usurped everything with three plane tickets to the other side of the country. And he thinks I'm supposed to jump at the chance? He can think again."

"Don't tell us," Sara said quietly. "Tell him."

Brooke and Claudia both looked at her.

Sara ducked her head shyly.

"She's right." Claudia pulverized the daisy petals. "You have to tell Colin in no uncertain terms once and for all."

Unaccustomed to having her opinions valued, Sara smoothed a crease from the pale pink dress she'd initially re-fused. It had been waiting for her when she'd arrived back from her counseling session yesterday, after she'd played the piano.

She'd played the piano!

The note said, "It isn't my color or my size. It's yours. Wear it or use it to clean under your bed. Whatever."

Feeling excited and weightless, she'd held the dress up to her and twirled around the room. The garment was far too pretty to use to clean under any bed. Claudia had known that, of course. Claudia was not an easy woman to say 'no' to. Which brought Sara to the point she was trying to make.

"All three of us agree that Brooke needs to talk to Colin. What about you, Claudia? What are you going to do?"

"About what?" Another daisy bit the dust.

"About Julian." Leaning forward, Sara looked into her friend's brown eyes. "Julian asked you to marry him. He's kind and considerate and smart and accepting and in your own words, fabulous in bed. What in the world are you afraid of?"

"First of all, he didn't ask me, he told me, and who says I'm afraid of anything?"

Brooke and Sara exchanged a look.

Reaching across the table, Sara patted both her friends'

hands. "Everybody is afraid of something." She rose lightly to her feet. "I have to pick up Seth in a few minutes. Good luck to both of you. Goodnight."

Watching her meekly walk away, Claudia said, "Why do you suppose it is that a woman who was beaten and abused is doing better than we are?"

Knowing a rhetorical question when she heard one, Brooke stood, too.

"Are you leaving?" Claudia asked.

Brooke nodded. "I'm going to give Colin a piece of my mind. What will you do?"

Claudia wiggled her toes. Not a twitch to be had anywhere.

Julian wanted to marry her. He couldn't be serious. Getting married was not in her plans, and never had been. And he stinking knew it.

"Claudia?"

She found it difficult to look into the concern in Brooke's blue eyes. "Don't worry about me. I'm fine. Go give Colin hell."

Brooke stared back at her. "I can practically hear the wheels turning in your brain. What are you thinking?"

Standing, too, Claudia said, "I'm thinking about calling Julian's bluff."

Claudia arrived at her destination without a clear plan.

Needing to think, she'd driven around Alcott. That had taken about *five* minutes, reminding her that small towns weren't good places to drive through when you needed a lot of time to think.

She drove to the town square, parked down the street from Dusty's Pub and walked over. She was a little over-dressed for the bar scene in Alcott, New Hampshire. She would have been more comfortable if she'd changed into slacks and low heels, but she wasn't wasting this dress.

It was Saturday night, and Dusty's was doing a good business. Julian was the only person who didn't look up when she sashayed inside. She had no doubt he knew she was there.

He was chalking his cue stick. Russ Tate and Jeremy Sooner said something to him. He still didn't look at her. Fine. She stayed near the front of the room and waited. Nobody was ruining her entrance.

Julian had changed out of his dark suit. It wasn't fair. Men looked good no matter what they wore. At least this man did.

He finally gave in and glanced her way. At last, she started toward the back of the room.

"Hey, Claudia," Jeremy said.

"How you been, Claudia?" Russ asked.

"Jeremy, Russ." She looked at Julian.

Seemingly unconcerned, he blew on the tip of his cue stick, lowered it, and sauntered to the far end of the table. His faded jeans bagged in the seat. He could eat anything he wanted, and still didn't have much in the derrière department, one more thing that wasn't fair.

He bent over the billiards table, the action drawing her gaze to a few other departments. He certainly wasn't lacking any place else.

She stared at her toe.

Nothing.

"Drop something?" Jeremy asked.

It wasn't easy to keep from glaring. "Jeremy, Russ," she said sweetly. "Would you mind giving Julian and me a little privacy?"

"We're playing a game of pool here."

Russ elbowed his friend. "Come on, Jer, I'll buy you a beer."

He'd always been the smarter of the two.

After the Alcott men sauntered away, Claudia said, "We need to talk, Julian."

He finished the shot. The five and seven went in, but the cue ball ended up behind the eight ball, which meant Julian wasn't quite as unaffected by her presence as he wanted her to believe.

"Interesting men, Russ and Jeremy," he said quietly. "I understand you went to the prom with Jeremy and to the moon with Russ."

She rolled her eyes.

"What did you want to talk about? Nice bouquet, by the way."

She placed the dilapidated flowers on the edge of the pool table. "I caught it tonight."

"*You* caught the bouquet?"

"Just lucky I guess." She glanced around. Her arrival had drawn an audience. Glaring at three local fisherman ogling her, she said, "Do you mind?"

"Last I looked it was a free country," one of them said. But they all quit staring openly. Smart men.

Claudia turned her attention back to Julian. "Are you ready to tell me what happened earlier?" she asked.

He took another shot, and put in another ball. "I know why you run from me."

"I don't run from anyone."

He put in another ball and generally acted as if she hadn't spoken. "It's because nobody's ever told you no."

She opened her mouth to refute it.

"You snap your fingers and life falls into place. You learned to read at the age of three, graduated from high school a year early, skipped college entirely and launched a business when you knew darned well that ninety percent of small businesses fail."

"I only skipped college to tick off my father. How was I to know a college degree wouldn't be necessary for the success of Hats?" She might as well have kept quiet for all the attention Julian paid her.

"Hats turned a profit the first year and continues to grow at an amazing rate. Poor, smart, bored little Claudia needs a challenge."

Must his every move remind her of how incredibly attractive he was? "That's what this is about?" she asked a little too loudly to keep this private. "You're trying to challenge me? I should fire you."

"My resignation is on your desk in Charleston."

To her annoyance, she was worried. A vision of Hats headquarters without him flashed through her mind. The place would be dismal. It certainly wouldn't be fun. Although daring and even impetuous at times, Claudia was not a woman who willingly cut off her nose to spite her face. "I refuse to accept your resignation."

He waved as if at a bothersome mosquito. "Fine. It isn't really on your desk anyway."

She all but threw up her hands.

"Are you ready to hear the rest, Claudia, dear?"

She noticed that the other patrons had grown quiet. "By all means, enlighten *us*."

Some of the onlookers smiled.

"Where was I?" Julian asked.

"I was snapping my fingers."

The women at a nearby table chuckled. Julian, however, didn't so much as crack a grin. "As I was saying, you snap your fingers, and I come running. I run your company in your absence. I negotiate deals with customers and outsmart your competitors. I warm your bed and pleasure your body. And whenever your toe gets twitchy—" He made a point of looking all around. "Well, you know what I do for your toes."

"Did he say toes?" Russ asked.

"Who cares about toes?" another man quipped.

Julian continued to stare at Claudia. "When you start to get jumpy, all you have to do is hop a plane. Except you don't want to escape me anymore, and that scares you."

"You're crazy. Delusional. Scared? Me?" But Sara had said something similar earlier. "I'm not afraid of you, Julian."

He stopped pretending to concentrate on the eight ball near the side pocket. "I didn't say you're afraid of me. You're afraid of love."

"Who said anything about love?"

A suggestion of sneakiness showed in his blue eyes. Didn't her mother tell her never to trust a blue-eyed man?

Claudia walked toward him, and was rewarded by the caress of his gaze. The fact that he wanted her made her even more brazen. She didn't stop until she was toe-to-toe with him. Like a sinuous cat, she eased around him, making contact along the way.

He didn't move.

"We have something, Julian." Her voice was sultry and deep. "We have passion. We have respect. And we have fun. When all is said and done, we have freedom." She was whispering now, and the poor patrons had to settle for trying to read her lips. She pouted as she came around the other side of him. "I know you want me, darling." She raked her fingernails down his back.

"Can you see her hand?" somebody grumbled.

Someone on the other side of the room said, "It's on his ass, and there's definite cupping."

"Uh-uh-uh." Julian stepped out of her grasp and out of her reach. "Look but don't touch. Don't make me have to tell you again."

"Would you spank me?"

"After the wedding, I'll spank you if you'd like."

A few of the women fanned themselves with their paper drink napkins.

"What is this ridiculous idea you have about getting married?" Claudia asked.

"There's nothing ridiculous about it. We'll resume our sex life after the wedding. We'll have to make up for some lost time, won't we?"

She swallowed a soft moan. "I'm not marrying you."

Nobody had to rely on lip-reading that time.

"Then I won't be able to lower the zipper down the back of that amazing dress, will I? I won't be able to unfasten your bra, or toy with your panties."

Her eyes closed part way and suddenly her decadent underwear felt constrictive. She felt the burning need to rub against the entire length of him. "Julian." She wasn't above pleading.

"There will be no silk scarves, no scented body oil, no wet kisses. Anywhere."

"If you don't marry him, honey, I will!" Russ Tate's wife yelled, "Sorry Russell."

"This is ridiculous," Claudia said.

"Quite the contrary."

"Quite the contrary," she mimicked. She glanced at the eavesdroppers. "Is it just me or does he sound crazy?"

"Sounds like he's got it all figured out to me," Jeremy Sooner grumbled into his beer.

Claudia glared. "Who the hell asked you?"

Julian cracked his first smile. "Claudia, Claudia, Claudia. You knew when you walked in here that you were going to agree to marry me. You even brought the bouquet."

"I was going to call your bluff."

"I'm not bluffing." His smile was gone, and in its place heat beckoned to her irresistibly.

"You would marry someone who doesn't love you?" she asked.

The crowd gasped.

Score one for Claudia.

"Of course you love me."

"You're saying I love you but don't know it?" she asked.

"I'm saying nothing of the kind."

He put his cue stick down and sat on the edge of the pool table. She'd seen him assume this position in boardrooms and bedrooms.

"You know it," he said. "You just haven't admitted it."

She laughed, but it came out sounding strained.

"You've loved me from the beginning. You don't believe I would have stuck around for three years if I believed for a moment you didn't love me, do you?"

"You guys have been together for three years?" the bartender asked. "That's got to be a record for Claudia."

The bartender was right.

Okay. Claudia was speechless. Not one single smart-aleck retort came to mind.

Speaking of records.

"Do you love him?" somebody asked her.

"Because if you do, you should marry him."

She made a sound deep in her throat and raked both hands down her face. "How should I know? I'm trying to think here and I would really appreciate a little peace and quiet."

"You should settle it over a game of billiards!" somebody called.

Julian straightened from the edge of the pool table, and came toward her with the grace of Baryshnikov himself. That was who she'd wanted to have a love affair with when she was a girl. Later, she'd changed her alliance and had fallen madly in love with Prince Andrew. To this day there was no doubt in her mind that if she had actually met the prince, he never would have married Fergie. Her eyes focused on Julian. There was something about that British accent.

He leaned forward and spoke so close that his lips grazed her earlobe. "What do you say, Claudia? Are you up for a friendly game of pool?"

Something warm grazed her hip. Her blood thickened, but her resolve returned. And she smiled. "By all means." She spoke loud enough for the others to hear. "We'll settle this once and for all. But let's be certain of the terms."

"If I win," he said, "You'll marry me. Tonight."

Her eyebrows rose. Tonight? He wasn't leaving her any leeway. "And if I win," she said, "You'll come to my house where I can have my way with you. Tonight."

"I'd like to be a fly on that wall," somebody said.

"What could he possibly do to her toes?" another patron quizzed.

Claudia held out her hand. He took it, but instead of shaking it, he kissed her palm then placed it over his heart, which was beating steady and strong.

"Oh, my," somebody said.

"Didn't somebody say he was a billiards champion a few years ago?"

"No kidding? Then what's Claudia doing?"

"Maybe she wants to lose. I know I would."

"Claudia doesn't like to lose."

She and Julian stared at each other.

"Name your *pleasure*," she said.

"Later. But we'll play rotation."

Claudia took a coin off a nearby table. Holding it up for everyone to see, she offered it to Julian. "You toss. I call tails."

The patrons smirked.

"I guess that means he's heads," Russell Tate said. "Ow!" He rubbed his arm where his wife's elbow had jabbed him.

Julian flipped the coin. "Tails it is. Perhaps today is your lucky day."

She chose a stick, chalked it, and racked the pool balls.

"She looks like a pro, too," somebody said.

Claudia smiled, for she could have been a pro if she'd wanted to be. She was very good. Good enough to beat Julian on more than one occasion. Her incentive to beat him again was strong. She put in three balls, then missed a difficult shot. The good news was, she hadn't left Julian a good shot, either.

He checked the table from every angle then took his shot.

The stupid three fell in.

His smile was victorious.

She sauntered around the far end of the pool table. Leaning over, she rested on her elbows, offering him a delectable sneak peek, compliments of the little gap at the neckline of her crimson dress.

He peeked. He ogled. And then he put in four more balls. He was taking aim at a fifth when somebody's phone went off. He jerked, and everyone held their breath.

The damn ball still went in.

He put in two more before missing.

Finally, it was Claudia's turn. She chalked her stick again. This was it. She couldn't miss. If she did, and he got another turn, the game would be over and she would be forced to marry him, forced in this day and age, when nobody forced Claudia to do anything she didn't care to do.

She studied the lay of the balls on the table, calculated the angles from every direction. She made two good shots. Out of the corner of her eye, she saw Julian ease around to the far end of the table directly opposite her best shot. He sat on the corner near the pocket, swinging one foot nonchalantly. His shirt pulled taut across his shoulders, his jeans across his thighs.

She put in another.

This was fun. She'd left herself a good shot, too. Still, she concentrated. Easing the stick back, she slid it, testing her angle. It was an easy shot. She couldn't miss. She brought her stick all the way back.

"How's your toe?" he whispered.

The felt tip connected with the cue ball, which slipped right on past the nine without touching it. It bounced off the bumper then stopped near the corner pocket.

She glared at Julian. "You cheater."

"It takes one to know one." He cast a pointed look at her chest, then ran the rest of the table. When he was finished, he blew the end of his cue stick as if it were a smoking gun.

Everyone clapped.

She turned in a half-circle, imploring the onlookers. "What, you're on his side?"

"He won you fair and square," one of the three fishermen pointed out.

"You think I don't know that?" She placed a hand to her forehead.

"We're not even married yet," Julian said. "Don't tell me you already have a headache."

Everybody was a comedian these days.

"What are you going to do, Claudia dear?" he asked. It was almost as if he felt sorry for her.

That rankled.

She turned on him. "Why, I'm going to goddamn marry you, what else?"

He grinned.

It wasn't easy to maintain a good simper when he beamed all that masculine appeal at her. But she gave it a shot.

"Part of your terms was to get married. Correct?"

He folded his arms. "That's correct."

"Tonight," she said.

"That's right."

Smiling sweetly, she said, "But Julian dear, we can't possibly get married tonight. We don't have a marriage license."

He pointed at the piece of paper one of those fishermen was holding up. "Sure we do."

She snatched it out of Jeremy Sooner's hand. "Funny, I don't recall signing this."

He shrugged.

And she whispered, "You forged my name." Damn this burgeoning admiration.

"Don't worry. The signature on the marriage certificate will be authentic."

She faced him, her mouth gaping.

The smile slid from his lips and his arms slid to his sides. "Will you marry me, Claudia? Will you live with me, work with me, fight with me, outsmart me, make love with me? Will you be my wife, my lover, my partner, my friend?"

She stared, mute, as big, fat tears formed in her eyes. How many times had she looked at him in exactly this way, committing the sight of him to memory. How many times had she tried to understand what was going on in the deepest recesses of his mind? How many times had she lusted after him, looked forward to seeing him, to hearing his voice?

A million times. Why?

Her toe finally twitched. She loved him. "Holy shit."

He smiled.

"You're not too young for me."

He shook his head.

"Or too beautiful."

He shrugged.

"You're my equal."

He nodded. And waited.

A tear spilled over. "I love you, Julian Bartholomew." She rushed to him. "Who knew?" She reached for him. "And if you say uh-uh-uh one more time, I'll—"

"You'll what?"

"I'll marry you tonight."

He raised his eyebrows and lowered his chin. On his way to her mouth, he whispered, "Uh-uh-uh."

The audience cheered.

After the kiss, Julian and Claudia started toward the exit.

"Don't forget your bouquet," somebody called.

"Toss it here," Claudia called.

For the second time tonight, she caught the bouquet in self-defense. The last thing she heard as she and Julian left Dusty's Pub was Dusty herself say, "Even when Claudia loses, she wins."

Claudia liked the sound of that.

CHAPTER 20

Brooke went charging up the sidewalk at Stone Cottage, only to stop abruptly on the step. Soft strains of music wafted through the screen. Chopin was her favorite of the classical composers. Colin had given her an entire CD collection for Christmas one year. She didn't like the sound of this.

Just inside the door, she slipped out of her shoes. Dropping them near Sophie's flip-flops and the cat's dish, she noticed a dark jacket hanging over the back of a kitchen chair. A bottle of Château Latour was uncorked on the counter.

"Hello, Brooke."

Colin's deep voice drew her around.

He sat in the shadows in the next room, the cat asleep next to him. His feet were up, his white shirt open at his throat, a small glass empty on the table at his elbow. "You look lovely as always. Would you like a glass of wine?" he asked.

She shook her head.

He rose slowly and smoothly, then stood, waiting for her to enter the room. "I don't want to lose you, Brooke."

"You've already lost me!" She switched on a lamp then blinked against the sudden brightness.

"Where's Sophie?" he asked.

"She's spending the night with the Callaways. You can't stay here tonight, Colin."

"You're angry."

"What you did was unforgivable!" She swung around, her hands clenched into fists.

"I'm going to get help for that. I am sorry, Brooke. You're the only woman I love."

Brooke had fallen for his sincerity and wounded emotions two years ago. "I wasn't talking about the affair. Or should I say affairs." She knew of two. Most likely there had been others. "I was talking about what you did to Sophie today. You got her hopes up, and that was cruel."

"It's cruel to want to hold our family together?"

"I suppose you were thinking about holding our family together when you were holding Deirdre."

A muscle worked in his jaw.

As the music faded in the background, he reached for his empty glass. "I wasn't thinking, period. Deirdre was a mistake. I know that now. I don't miss her, but I miss you more than I can say, more than you'll ever know."

She stepped aside as he neared.

He walked past her, and into the kitchen where he placed his glass on the counter and reached for the wine. This time he poured two, offering one glass to her.

She must have followed him. Standing in the middle of the kitchen, waltz music flowing around her, she shook her head again.

Colin set her glass on the counter next to his. "How can I make it up to you, Brooke?"

She turned away.

"I'm begging you. How?" His hand went to her shoulder, drawing her slowly around.

She wrenched herself away. "You can't make it up. I gave you a second chance. Now I want a divorce."

"What about Sophie? Have you thought about what that would do to her? Let's go to Seattle, just the three of us.

We'll have a wonderful time. We'll take Sophie to the Space Needle and the Pike Place Market. There's a pulse in that city that's catching. It's beautiful this time of year. Sophie will love it, Brooke, and so will you."

She stared at him, infuriated. "I just told you I want a divorce. I don't have the energy or the desire to forgive you, Colin. You've proven that you don't deserve my forgiveness. You don't listen. You don't hear. All you can talk about is the pulse in Seattle?"

Something about that made her look more closely at him. He stood six feet away, tall and lean and too attractive for his own good.

"When have you been to Seattle?"

His eyebrows rose a fraction.

She waited for the lie. And it was as if he knew.

Instead of lying, he took the direct approach. "I flew there two weeks ago."

"For business or pleasure?"

The question hit its mark. Still, he didn't retaliate. "I've been offered a consulting position for a company that is cutting edge."

"I see." She really did see. Everything. The surprise gift of a "family" trip to the West Coast was another ploy, line fifteen or twenty-eight or ninety-one on his hidden and very personal agenda.

"They're offering a decadent salary, Brooke, and an appealing benefit package, profit sharing, more vacation, and flexible hours. You won't have to work at all if you don't want to. We can start over in a place that's exciting and new. It will be the way it used to be when Sophie was little. We'll all be so happy again. It'll be perfect."

It was all so clear suddenly. This was how it would always be with Colin. He would always be looking for that pulse, that excitement, that new beginning, and the pipe-dream of perfection.

"No, Colin."

His eyes narrowed the way they'd narrowed so many times in the past. "You sound like my mother. "No-no, Colin." Will you slap the back of my hand, too?"

There was a time when she would have taken that to heart. She'd been so eager to please him. All it had taken was the slightest criticism and she'd drawn herself in. Colin was very adept at doling out thinly veiled criticism. When he'd insinuated that she'd put on weight, she'd dieted. She was a little surprised he hadn't said anything recently. When he'd mentioned, over and over, that it would save time if she put her shoes and socks on differently, she'd finally done it his way. When he'd insisted it would be too much work for her to decorate their historic house in Society Hill in the manner it *deserved* to be decorated, she'd gone along with his wish to hire the best professional decorator in the city. It *was* beautiful, but the house bore the decorator's personality, not the Valentines'.

"You should have talked to me before buying those tickets, Colin."

"Sophie's my daughter, too," he said.

If Brooke had had her way, they would have had more than one child. She hadn't even had a say in that.

She shook her head. "Everything you do, you do for a reason. *Your reason.* You showed up in Alcott a day early to give you more time to butter me up."

"And you stiffen every time I touch you. It's like buttering a frozen Thanksgiving turkey."

No one could make a few pounds sound like twenty better than Colin. She laughed, but there was no humor in it. She thought about the book she'd once kept on her bedside table. Oh, no, he wasn't going to make her believe their waning sex life had been all her fault.

"There's one thing you keep forgetting. I'm not the one who had an affair."

"Aren't you?"

She spun around, her long blue dress tangling around her

ankles. "What is that supposed to mean?" She'd spoken louder than she'd intended. She could see he didn't like it.

"You and the shrink looked pretty cozy when I arrived yesterday. Sophie tells me you've been seeing a lot of him. Are you in counseling, Brooke?" The words were cutting and dripping with innuendo.

She could feel her face growing hot. She had no reason to blush. Furious with him and with herself, she said, "I haven't even so much as kissed another man, let alone slept with anybody. Can you say the same?"

"Of course. Miss Perfect Hospital Corners."

They squared off.

"I thought perfection was what you wanted!"

"Maybe if you opened your mouth when I kissed you, I wouldn't have to find someone who does!" He was yelling now, too.

"That's right." She took a step toward him. "I drove you to have affairs so I could come here and fall in love with another man."

Brooke's fist went to her mouth, then slowly fell away.

She'd stunned them both.

Colin stood a few feet away, tall and silent, teeth clenched, a muscle working in his jaw. She'd shaken him to the core.

She was shaking, too.

Of course he recovered first. "Well, well, well. Little Miss Perfect Hospital Corners isn't so perfect after all." He grabbed his jacket off the chair and the wine off the counter and left without another word.

The porch light was on at the Callaways.

Ginger opened the door before Brooke could knock. "I know it's terribly late," Brooke said.

"Not if you're a night owl like me. Who needs a doorbell when we have Duke and Rusty? Down boys. Sh. Come on in, Brooke."

"Is Sophie awake?"

"The girls were still talking a little while ago. How are things with you?" Ginger was in her bathrobe. Still dressed, Pete snored softly from his recliner in front of the TV.

Something about the everyday clutter of a house with four girls, two dogs, a sleeping man and the kind, funny woman who was at the center of it all put a lump in Brooke's throat. "Colin knows it's over. I came to take Sophie home. Was she very weepy?"

"Girls this age are all weepy. It's been an emotional day for her, but I think she'll be relieved to see you."

"She's angry with me."

"She's no dummy. She knows enough about life to have figured out what's gone on. She knows you love her, sugar. And don't worry. I have enough daughters already."

Brooke hadn't expected to smile.

"I'll be right back."

Brooke could hear Ginger climbing the stairs. She hadn't handled tonight very well. Colin was angry and Sophie was *weepy* and Brooke felt the strongest desire to fix everything. Her marriage was over. She'd known for two months. Perhaps, subliminally, she'd known for two years.

Colin had done it again. He'd tried to make her feel responsible, as if she were somehow to *blame* for his weaknesses.

One of her professors in college once told the class, "Don't let the world decide who you are."

Brooke had come very close to letting Colin decide who she was.

A sound in the doorway drew her around. Sophie stood slightly apart from Rebecca and Ginger. Her eyes were puffy, her borrowed pajamas a little short for her.

Brooke rushed over and gathered her little girl into her arms. "Let's go home, Sophe."

"Home to Philadelphia?"

"For tonight, let's go home to Stone Cottage." Wrapping

an arm around Sophie's narrow shoulders, she started for the door.

"Mom, I'm wearing pajamas. Did you just come from Aunt Eve's wedding? Are those your slippers?"

Realizing that she must look a mess in her wrinkled bridesmaid dress, falling hairstyle and smeared makeup, Brooke glanced at Ginger.

With a wink, Ginger said, "That's the nice thing about daughters. You always know where you stand in the fashion department and every other department."

It was amazing how good it felt to be understood. "Thanks for everything, Ginger. We'll return Rebecca's pajamas tomorrow," she called over her shoulder.

"Bye, Rebecca," Sophie said.

The redhead waved. Nobody bothered to say goodbye to the big brute of a man who'd slept through the whole thing.

"Men are funny," Sophie said as she ran across the dewy grass.

"Sometimes."

"What Daddy did isn't funny."

"No, it isn't."

"Did he leave?" Sophie asked, her voice suddenly small.

"Alcott?" Brooke started the car. "No."

"How can you be sure?"

Pulling out of the Callaways' driveway, Brooke said, "He wouldn't leave without saying goodbye to you."

"Sometimes I wish he wasn't such a jerk."

Brooke patted Sophie's knee.

"But I still love him, ya know?"

"I know, Sophe. He loves you, too."

Sophe sighed deeply. "I'm sorry I'm a brat sometimes."

Tears stung Brooke's eyes. "You're not a brat. You're human."

"I love you, Mom."

"I love you, too."

The day ended far better than it had begun.

* * *

Fluffy padded after Brooke from room to room, generally getting under her feet and in the way. Bending down to pet her, Brooke said, "It feels strange to be here without Sophie, doesn't it?"

The cat purred contentedly.

"Don't let it bother you too much." She picked up Fluffy and carried her with her through the small house. She'd returned from the airport in Manchester an hour ago. Sophie and Colin were on their way to Kentucky to meet Sophie's horses.

Colin had appeared on her doorstep early this morning, looking more uncertain than she'd ever seen him. They'd finally had that difficult conversation with Sophie. All three of them had cried. It had been a defining moment.

Colin wasn't happy that Brooke couldn't, or as he'd said privately, wouldn't forgive him, but he was beginning to realize that she meant it. Completely unaccustomed to losing, he was going to have to learn to accept this. Although divorces were never fun, theirs wouldn't be ugly.

He'd canceled the trip to Seattle. More than likely, he'd *postponed* it. The blinders were finally off Brooke's eyes.

He'd offered to take Sophie to Disneyland for her birthday. Sophie wanted to go to Archie's horse ranch in Kentucky. That had been the surprise Brooke had planned. She'd produced the tickets she'd hidden under her mattress, and after a long discussion, it was decided that Colin would take Sophie this time, Brooke the next.

They were going to have to learn to share their daughter. It wasn't going to be easy. Watching that plane take off, Brooke had felt bereft.

She and Colin had a lot of decisions to make. Brooke didn't know what the future held, but, turning in a circle in the kitchen at Stone Cottage, she felt certain that she could handle whatever came her way. That serenity must have been apparent, for Colin had looked at her for a long time this morning. Perhaps he'd finally realized what he was losing.

Two months ago Brooke had felt shocked, saddened, humiliated, disappointed and somehow lost. It had been a summer of discovery. Now, at summer's end, she'd found her way back to herself. She'd rekindled old friendships, and formed a new one.

She thought of Mac.

In her mind, she saw him pretending to be interested in learning to cook, when he was more interested in being close to her. She thought of him telling her about his father, and racing her to Breakwater Road. She thought of how honorable it had been of him to resist, and that vein of the uncivilized in him that had made resisting so difficult.

She missed him, missed talking to him and laughing with him and matching wits with him. Colin knew she was in love with Mac.

Perhaps it was time she told Mac.

Surely he would know what was on her mind if she knocked on his door in the middle of a lazy Sunday afternoon wearing a sundress and a come-hither smile. All the better. Now, where were her keys?

Mac opened the door to find Brooke standing on his front stoop, chewing nervously on her lower lip. "Is something wrong?" he asked.

"Yes." The breeze whispered through her hair and fluttered the hem of her pale yellow dress. "Something is very wrong. You see, I'm in love with a man I haven't even kissed." She stopped fidgeting and focused on him. "I don't want to deal with yesterday, Mac, with doubts and regrets, or with tomorrow, with worries and logic."

"What *do* you want?"

The rest of her nerves seemed to melt away. She placed both hands over her heart and, tipping her head slightly, gave him a smile that went straight to his senses. "I want to make love with you."

He opened the door all the way.

CHAPTER 21

Mac closed the door with one hand and reached for Brooke with the other. Finally, she was in his arms. At last, at long last, he was kissing her. It wasn't a tentative first kiss; it was wet and wild and possessive. She opened her mouth, and it wasn't enough. He had her against the wall, taking her gasp of surprise into his own mouth.

He pressed his body to hers, and was seized with sensation, the warm touch of mouths, the erotic dance of tongues, the heat of two bodies seeking, wanting more. Fingers wide, he covered her breast, slowly massaging. She wasn't wearing a bra. What else wasn't she wearing? Desire kicked through him, turning him rough, devouring.

He had to slow this down or he would take her right here. "Brooke."

She turned her head slightly, dragging in a ragged breath. "I understand why you didn't want to do that outside."

So, she was in the mood for a dangerous adventure? He reacted to her sass in the most fundamental of ways, and in other more surprising ways. The frenzy inside him calmed slightly. He'd thought about her a hundred times, worried, wondered, wanted.

"Where's Colin?"

"Gone," she said.

"From the face of the earth?"

He was pretty sure she wanted to smile. "Not quite."

"Pity."

"And he liked you, too."

"You're a terrible liar."

She moaned softly at what he was doing to her breast though the thin fabric of her summer dress. "I told him I want a divorce."

"He couldn't have been happy about losing you. Anything I can do?"

She took a shuddering breath. "I seem to be facing a dilemma."

"I'm good with dilemmas."

"Perhaps in this instance I should be the judge of that."

He stopped what he was doing and stared into her eyes. "I'm listening."

Mac looked so serious. Reaching a hand to his face, Brooke said, "I've been told I'm not very good at this. Perhaps I should stop talking before I ruin everything, but first I was wondering how a woman went about asking a man where she might find his bed."

"You were wondering that, were you?" He took her hand, and then he took her mouth. This time the kiss was tender.

She opened her eyes when it was over, and found him watching her. She remembered the first time he'd looked at her this way, as if he knew something about her that even she didn't know.

They started toward the stairway, passing cardboard boxes along the way. "Are you going someplace, Mac?"

"I boxed up my father's things."

"I see."

"And some of mine."

She thought about the implications. "I meant what I said earlier. I don't want to deal with doubts and regrets and worries and logic," she whispered. "Let's not talk until later."

"Whatever you say."

They walked up the first flight of stairs hand in hand. After a heated kiss at the top, they proceeded up the second flight, arm-in-arm. He couldn't keep his hands off her long enough to make it all the way to his room. He touched her through her clothes, and kissed her, steering her backwards, his hands roaming the entire length of her back, holding her to him, molding, kneading, moving in a dance as old as time.

Vaguely, she was aware of the ocean scent on the breeze, of a big bed and masculine furnishings. Her zipper rasped. And then there was cooler air on her shoulders, her bare breasts, her thighs. Fixing her gaze on his face, she slipped out of her shoes and stepped over her dress which had pooled on the floor. She stood naked before him.

"I love a woman who dresses for success."

The heat in Mac's eyes made her glad she'd gotten up her nerve to travel lightly. He tore his shirttail from his pants. She'd never seen anybody unbutton and then discard a shirt so fast. He unhooked his belt, and unfastened the top closure of his chinos. Bending down, he kissed her mouth, tracing her lower lip with his tongue. Her knees went weak.

Instead of burrowing into his arms, she lowered his zipper, and then his pants. When he reached for the waistband of black, low-riding briefs she settled back to enjoy the show.

"Are you having fun?" His voice dipped so low she could almost feel it skim the tops of her feet.

"I always have fun when I'm with you."

He touched the hollow at the base of her neck, and slowly glided his fingertips down the center of her chest, grazing her breasts, each in turn, with the back of his hand. "I feel the same, Brooke. I love watching your eyes. I love watching you cook." His briefs came off, and he stepped closer, a lot closer, drawing her to him, his arms going around her back.

She arched into him, against him, learning his body as he learned hers. Her head tipped back and she moaned. "What else do you love?" she asked.

"I love watching you laugh."

She moaned again at what he was doing with his fingers and his mouth. Suddenly, she had to do some exploring of her own. She pressed her body to his, breasts to chest, her hands gliding to his waist, his thighs, his butt.

"I love watching you outsmart me," he said.

"It isn't easy."

His chuckle had a lot in common with a groan of pleasure. "I love watching you run. Especially that first time when you wore a flimsy bra."

She should have known he'd noticed.

She found him with her hand, and smiled as he groaned. Sinuous and sure, she eased down his body.

Sometime later, he said, "I love watching you do that."

She was a little too busy to smile.

He didn't give her free rein for long. Before she knew how it had happened, the bed was at her back, and his legs were tangling with hers. He held her hands over her head and worked magic, his lips on hers.

And then he moved his magic elsewhere.

She held on to him with everything she had, and she was still coming apart at the seams. Giving herself up to sensation, she didn't want him to stop, and yet she needed the weight of him on her, and the final connection of him and her, united.

Crying out, she saw him smile. He saw to protection, and she saw to him. Sitting on his lap, she straddled him. He rolled her underneath him so fast she gasped. He was careful with her after that, but not gentle. She wrapped her legs around him, insistent.

"Easy," he crooned.

"I don't want easy. I want everything."

"Be careful what you ask for." Oh, he was wicked.

She was wicked, too, moving, luring him on. It turned out she couldn't take all of him, after all. He started to move, slowly at first, and then faster, their pleasure building, pure and explosive. She'd never been prone to noisy outbursts. She was different with Mac. With him, she was embarrassingly noisy. It only fueled his passion. He shuddered, over and over, taking her in a raw act of possession.

The degree to which she responded shocked her and thrilled him. His heart pounded and hers hammered in her ears. Their response was powerful, galvanizing. It was beautiful. And it took a while to catch their breath.

It was a long time before he moved, easing away, but only slightly. She couldn't even manage that. Moaning aloud, she shuddered, another delayed reaction.

"Whoever told you you aren't good at this was wrong. Perhaps you should consider the source."

She smiled. She couldn't help it. There was something so *Mac* about his attitude. "I love you, Mac."

"Good."

She finally worked up the energy to turn her head. "And?" No more being a doormat.

"I'm thirty-nine years old and I've never been in love before. I love you, Brooke. I've never said that to another woman."

Pressing her hand to his cheek, she said, "I'm thirty-six, and I've never been in love like this. Now, tell me about those packing crates."

He watched her with his extraordinary eyes, analyzing her expression. Whatever he said, she knew it would be the truth.

"I've been offered a position on the International Board of Psychiatric Research."

"That sounds like an honor."

He shrugged.

"Where?"

He kissed her knuckles until she relaxed them. "In France."

"That's wonderful."

"You never have to lie to me Brooke, not even to spare my feelings."

Suddenly, Brooke was aware of the afternoon light and her nakedness. It made her feel shy. "When will you leave?"

"Who says I'm leaving?"

She could only look at him, for she'd automatically assumed he would accept the offer. "What will you do?"

"Whatever it takes to spend the rest of my life with you."

Tears filled her eyes.

"That is, if you'll have me."

Looking into his eyes, a dreamy intimacy passed between them. "First, I have a few questions for you."

"I understand there's the little matter of your divorce, and of course Sophie's well-being."

"Yes. I think Sophie is going to be okay. But that isn't what I'm talking about."

He moved to his side, head propped on one hand. "A test?"

"Don't put words in my mouth." A certain look entered his eyes. "You have a dirty mind, Dr. Elliot."

"It takes one to know one. You were saying?"

She rolled onto her side, too. Resting her head on a pillow, she traced tiny circles on his shoulder. "If I were food, what would I be?"

"Are you hungry?"

"Your answer is important to me."

The pupils of her eyes were dilated, so that only a thin ring of blue encircled them. Mac didn't want to talk about food, not when those delicious stirrings were returning, and he had a beautiful naked woman lying next to him. He and Brooke had both come to Alcott with serious issues. This wasn't about issues. This was about a man and a woman, respect and trust, lust and love.

"If you were food, you would be dessert, definitely dessert."

Still, she didn't smile. "What kind of dessert?"

"Something at once wholesome and completely decadent. Something soft, moist, tasty. Something like ripe, fresh-picked strawberries in sweet, rich cream, drizzled with smooth, melted chocolate."

Her eyebrows rose slightly; he knew she liked his answer. "That's better than being a frozen Thanksgiving turkey."

"What?" he asked.

"Never mind."

Oh, no. She wasn't getting away with that. If it was important for her, it was important for him. "What would I be?" he asked.

She appeared to give that some thought before saying, "Some kind of shish-kabob, I think." She made those figure-eight patterns on his chest. "Something colorful and slightly spicy, a different flavor in every bite, bold, strong, tender and mouth-watering." Those figure-eight patterns inched to his waist. "Are you ready for question number two?"

"Keep going lower and you'll know what I'm ready for."

She swatted him but she didn't smile. "What side of the bed do you sleep on?"

"I sleep in the middle."

"You didn't even hesitate. That means I can sleep on either side and still be close to you."

"There's something else you should know, Brooke."

This time, she was the one listening.

"Elliots don't love easily, but when we love, it's for forever."

"Oh, Mac."

He sucked in a ragged breath, for her hand had moved lower. "Are we done talking now?"

She nodded. But of course she didn't stop talking. "I'm glad I came to Alcott this summer."

"Honey, you aren't the only one."

Their lovemaking started more luxuriantly this time. They'd already discovered their most sensitive places. Lo and behold, they found a few new ones. "Claudia told me I should do this."

"The hat lady?"

She groaned. "She doesn't answer her phone. I wonder where she is."

"She eloped with her Brit."

"Claudia and Julian eloped?" She stopped doing what she'd been doing and looked at him. He, however, didn't stop, and she almost forgot her question.

His answer was a murmur placed gently at her breast. "I was in the crowd when he—" He kissed his way to her waist. "When he won her fair and square in a billiards game."

Brooke cried out as he made yet another discovery. "Oh, Mac, I don't think that move was in the book." She groaned, for this man was a dream come true, the kind of dream she hadn't even known she'd been having until she met him.

He did it again, and it was glorious. It was amazing, really, all of it, their chance encounter, their mutual respect, the feeling that she'd known him forever. Was it chance? Or was the rest of their lives destined to begin at summer's end?

"What book?" he asked.

For a while, she was too busy to comprehend the question. Eventually, she remembered the book she'd once kept on her night stand. "I'll tell you later," she whispered.

She thought she heard him laugh when she told him sooner rather than later. But then sooner and later were relative when a man and a woman who were friends and lovers had the rest of their lives.

EPILOGUE

It was summer again.

Subliminally, Mac was aware of the scent of it, the feel of it, the promise of it, but he was in too big a hurry to give it his full attention. He'd made good time on the drive from his new clinic in Manchester. The right turn onto Marsh Street, the left onto Maple, followed almost immediately by the slight jog onto Captain's Row had become automatic this past year, and yet he always experienced a crescendo of the senses when he crested the top of the hill.

The crescendo he experienced this evening was of a different nature, for one of Sara's students was practicing for tonight's piano recital in the house next door. Mac parked in his own driveway. Grabbing his suit jacket from the seat next to him, he hurried across the sloping lawn.

All three of the former Potters were in the kitchen when he entered. It wasn't uncommon to find them together here. After all, the kitchen was command central for Brooke's catering business, and the rest of the first floor comprised Sara's music academy. Since the venture had been Claudia's brain child, it wasn't surprising that she spent as much time in Alcott these days as she did in Charleston. Since reuniting, the three commiserated often. Tonight, Sara smiled shyly, and

Claudia winked. And Mac knew this was not their usual commiserating.

"What are you three up to?"

Brooke tilted her head slightly, her expression part invitation, part challenge. Although Mac responded to it in the most fundamental of ways, he didn't miss the covert glance his wife cast her friends, and neither did they. Claudia reached for a tray of sweets that Brooke had prepared for Sara's piano students and their families, and Sara hurried after her to light the candelabra atop the baby grand.

Subtle they weren't.

He turned to Brooke. "Okay, what are *you* up to?"

"What makes you think I'm up to anything?" Her eyes were wide and innocent, but her barely there smile begged to differ.

"I know women. And I know you."

She laughed out loud, and he knew that whatever she had up her sleeve was something good. Her hairstyle was new, as was her loose-fitting summer dress. She looked radiant tonight. If they'd been alone, he would have drawn her to him and made her knowing smile part of his own. But there were at least a dozen people in this big old house this evening, and more were arriving this very minute. Any one of them could interrupt.

As if on cue, the door swung open. "Mom, Rebecca says she thinks she's going to puke. Hey, Mac!"

Sophie and her best friend stopped at the counter. "Splash your face with cool water, Rebecca," Brooke said. "And when you're done, take these trays out to the long table okay?"

Rolling her eyes, Rebecca said, "No one takes me seriously." She grabbed one of the large trays of cookies and left in a huff.

Reaching for the other tray, Sophie said, "Ginger told her to picture everyone in the audience in their underwear. I think that's gross, so I'm going to pretend you're all horses." Taking the other tray, she turned, tall for thirteen, and particularly regal looking in her white silk blouse and black skirt.

"Why horses?" Mac asked.

"Because everyone knows horses are very forgiving."

The door swished shut, and Mac said, "You'd never know she had her navel pierced last week."

Brooke felt herself smiling. It never ceased to amaze her how often she and Mac were of the same mind. They finished each other's sentences, anticipated each other's needs. He could discuss nearly anything. But he listened, too. He was so gosh-darned willing to make her happy. She loved to make him happy, too. Not that it was difficult.

In his own words, he was easy. True, he was easy to get into bed, but he was complicated in his own right. That only made him more interesting to her. And it made trying to stay one step ahead of him both challenging and fun. Her divorce from Colin had been final in mid-winter. She and Mac were married in February in a quiet, intimate ceremony. And since it had been Sophie's decision to begin the school year in Alcott, they now all lived in Archie's old house on Captain's Row. Mac had had a small stable built at the back of the property. Now, every morning Sophie's horses stood in the pasture watching the sunrise over the ocean. And Brooke had never imagined that she could be this happy.

Arranging the coffee carafe, sugar and creamer on another tray, she said, "Can you believe Eve and Carter are going to have twins?"

He made one of those sounds men make to let a woman know they were listening.

Adding the ginger ale to the punch, Brooke said, "Claudia said orders are pouring in for her new wedding hats faster than her designers can produce them."

"Mmmmmmm."

"And Tommy McCall's latest test results are back. He's been off chemo for three months, and he's clear."

"That's wonderful, Brooke. It was just as wonderful when you told me this morning before I went to the clinic. You remember this morning, don't you?"

As always, the heat in his voice found its way into her

bloodstream. "Perhaps you should refresh my memory," she said. "Later."

His silence drew her gaze.

He stood near her new industrial, stainless steel, state-of-the-art range, his hands on his hips, his feet planted, green eyes steady and full of challenge. Mac was a patient man. That didn't mean he'd forgotten his earlier question: *What was she up to?*

The answer made her feel giddy. She drew closer without breaking eye contact. Placing a hand on either side of his face, she stretched up on tiptoe and kissed him. He always took it like a man. How had she gotten so lucky?

Sometimes it scared her, being this happy. It was Sara who'd told her that happiness was not something to feel guilty for.

They'd all come far this past year, but Sara had come the farthest. Sadly, Miss Rose had died last fall. Now Sara and Seth lived in the big house with Miss Addie. Claudia and Julian were working on yet another new line of hats, this one for children. And then the little wand in Brooke's home pregnancy test had turned blue.

"Did you tell him?"

Mac was ending the kiss when Claudia burst into the kitchen again. "Tell me what?" he said.

"For God's sake!" Claudia pushed her wavy hair behind her ears. "The suspense is *killing me.*"

Resting her hand on her growing belly, Brooke met Mac's gaze. "Dr. Bradley ordered another ultrasound today."

"Why didn't you call me?" Mac asked.

"I wanted to surprise you."

"Is everything all right?"

"Perfect. I'll show you the printed image later."

Sophie bounded in again. "Sara said to tell you you'd better take your seats."

When she bounded out again, Mac reached for the punch bowl, indicating that the women should precede him. "Is she going to be all legs like Sophie?"

"All legs," Claudia snorted. "You men and your Johnsons."

Mac stopped so quickly the punch sloshed in the bowl. Guiding him to the side table, Brooke helped him lower the bowl to safety. Only then did she place her hand where their child was growing.

"It isn't a girl?" His voice was low, husky.

She shook her head and gave him another smile. Behind them people shuffled and chairs creaked as everyone took their seats. When Brooke and Mac were seated, too, she leaned over and whispered, "You're going to have the opportunity to experience that father-son relationship after all."

Mac was stunned. He'd always pictured himself surrounded by women. He would have been thrilled to give Sophie a half-sister. He would have been comfortable and content raising a daughter.

"Are you happy?" Brooke asked quietly.

A son? He was going to have a son.

Brooke reached for his hand. Tommy McCall was at the baby grand, his feet dangling a foot above the pedals. And Mac caught a glimpse of the future. In it was a boy with his eye color and Brooke's smile and a thread of Archie's temperament.

Mac shook his head to clear it.

He was going to have a son.

Dazedly, he looked at Brooke. Happy? He was terrified. And in awe, and in the center of it all was a new and bottomless peace and joy and wonder.

Tommy finished his piece. The Callaway sisters were up next. And then it was Sophie's turn. No one clapped louder than Mac when she took her bow.

When the last of her students had finished, Sara moved to the center of the room, quietly commending the children. Shyly, she thanked everyone for coming.

"It's not over yet," Claudia called.

Surely, Sara hadn't left anyone out.

Claudia stood. "You haven't played, Sara."

She tried to protest. "Tonight was for the children."

"So please play for them," Claudia insisted.

Awkwardly, Sara cleared her throat.

Claudia didn't budge. And it occurred to Sara that as strong as she'd become this past year, she was still no match for Claudia.

Her students began to chant. "Miz Walsh. Miz Walsh. Miz Walsh."

Heat crept up Sara's neck. Taking back her maiden name had felt bold and scary. It reminded her of how far she'd come. She glanced at Seth, who sat in the third row, all smiles, Miss Addie next to him, looking feeble but proud. Brooke and Mac sat with Sophie, Tommy with Liza and Jack, Claudia with Julian, and so on. And they were all looking at Sara.

She looked to Brooke for help. Brooke only nodded.

Seeing no way out of it, Sara seated herself at the bench. She wet her dry lips, and swallowed nervously. Clasping her shaking hands tightly, she took a deep breath and closed her eyes. Her fingers came down on the keys, deft and agile, light and swift.

Even the youngest spectator stopped fidgeting.

Since Sara had no music to read, she kept her eyes closed and played from memory, and from her heart. Her music flowed through the room, as playful as laughter, as sad as tears, and as honest as life. It carried through the windows, open again, now that summer was finally here, down the sloping lawn, over the horses grazing in the pasture, all the way to the ocean, and back again, enveloping all who heard.

When it was over, there was a moment of complete silence. And then applause erupted. Feeling herself blushing, Sara opened her eyes.

Brooke and Claudia were there, suddenly. "I think they want you to take a bow, Sara," Brooke said.

"God knows you've earned it."

She allowed herself to be drawn to her feet. Reaching for their hands, she said, "We've all earned it."

"But you're the gifted musician," Brooke said.

"I couldn't have done it without you. Now, do you want to argue? Or do you want to get this bow over with so we can eat?"

Brooke and Claudia exchanged a look. Claudia said, "I think we've created a monster."

And together, The Three Potters took a bow.